ESCAPE TO
New Orleans

A Novel from the deMelilla Chronicles

D1412121

STEPHEN ESTOPINAL

LIBROS

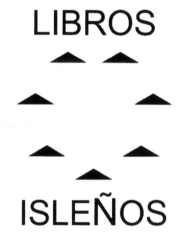

ISLEÑOS

Libros Isleños Publishing

Gonzales, Louisiana 70737

ISBN-10: 1467982113

ISBN-13: 978-1467982115

To the Love of my Life
Marie Elaine Russell

CHAPTER 1

Salvador tightened the mainsheet until the faint flutter that had appeared in the sail faded away. The canvas firmed and once again he shifted his gaze eastward across the boat's bow where the black mass that was Gran Canaria grew out of the sea. His two passengers were huddled in the fishing boat's narrow stem, a canvas scrap their only protection from the incessant sea-spray. It had been a rough crossing from Tenerife and all aboard the plunging *barca* were soaked.

The girl was about sixteen years old and the boy, she said he was her brother, may have been eight. She was dressed in a fancy ladies' gown. The left side of the green lace bodice was stained with blood and with her left hand she held a gory linen cloth to her face. The light from the full moon reflected off the sail and Salvador could clearly see the uninjured side of her face. She was a beauty. Her long, brunette hair cascading over her right shoulder was decorated with a single, tall silver comb to which clung the remnants of a veil.

"I am Mézucasa," the girl had said when she came running along the breakwater toward Salvador where he was securing his boat for the night. "I will pay you to bring my brother and me to Gran Canaria," she told him. "We must leave now." Her request was accompanied by a gold coin, an *escudo*, which she proffered with her free hand.

He knew the name she gave was false for it was not a Christian name. All Spanish well-born ladies carried Christian names, or the priests would not baptize them. Marked by her accent and bearing, Salvador could easily see this girl was well born. Before the Spaniards came, the people of Tenerife called themselves "Guanche." "Mézucasa" meaning "daughter of the moon," was a Guanche name. Salvador had decided it was likely the girl was a daughter of a Guanche mother and a highborn Spanish father. The gold coin she gave him erased his curiosity and he ushered her and her brother aboard.

The nighttime sail to Gran Canaria demanded all of Salvador's experience and seamanship. He guided the lateen-rigged boat close-hauled into a stiff wind, tacking her often as she cut through the roiling sea created as the constant open-ocean rollers curved around Gran Canaria and echoed off her stony coast. If he had allowed the boat to fall under the lee of the tall island during the crossing, they would have been becalmed or worse, beset with swirling and unpredictable back-drafts on a churning sea and he would have had to row.

The crossing done, they coasted between a brace of stone watchtowers bracketing the entrance to a small natural cove wherein several piers jutted out into the calm, protected waters of a port-village. Guards in the towers watched, but did not react to the small sail that passed beneath them. Salvador had sailed to this town many times and his fishing boat was recognized. The port was called *Agaete*, and the town's *Regidore*, a combination of mayor, prosecutor, judge, and militia commander, held jurisdiction over the sea for three miles in every direction from the mouth of the harbor entrance and ten miles inland of the town, nearly to the center of the island.

"We are at Agaete, *señorita*," Salvador said.

The passengers stirred from under their canvas shelter and looked upon the island of Gran Canaria for the first time since boarding. The sky was growing bright with the rising sun, but the pier and town remained dark, shadowed by the great mountain in the center of the island. The boat touched the pier and Salvador held it steady against a piling as the girl first pushed the boy up onto the dock then followed him. She took the boy's hand in her right and hurried toward the town, a small canvas bag slung over one slender shoulder and her left hand holding the handkerchief to her face. She did not say anything to Salvador, nor did she look back as he watched them disappear into an alleyway.

Doña Maria Artiles y Ventomo, *Mézu* to her friends and family, pulled her brother through the narrow lanes of Agaete eastward toward the distant jagged ridgelines backlit by the rising sun. The alley opened onto a trail at the edge of the town. The trail climbed steadily toward the southeast and was bordered by brush, stone debris and outcroppings of volcanic rock. The few people who were about stopped their morning chores and gawked at the blood-stained young girl leading a child toward the high mountains. She did not acknowledge their questions or pause. She needed to get beyond the province of Agaete's *Regidore*. The man was a friend of *Ricohombre* Alguazil Cabitos y Cabrón of Santa Cruz de Tenerife, to whom she had been betrothed and from whom she was now fleeing. She knew if she were captured in Agaete, she would be returned to Tenerife. Ten miles inland and one mile up she would cross into the province of *Don* Raphael Arinaga y Suerios. *Don* Raphael was a friend of her late father and the *Regidore* of a port on the east coast of Gran Canaria called *Gando*. There she would be safe. There she could rest.

The trail was well worn but steep and Mézu was not dressed for such an excursion. Her face throbbed, but the searing pain she had felt when Alguazil Cabitos first struck her had dwindled into a dull ache. Her dancing slippers were coming apart, torn by the rough path, and her footprints in the dusty trail were lightly flecked with blood. Her gown had swept along the dusty road, snagging on brush and rocks beside the narrow trail until she shortened it by tearing a strip from the bottom. The boy had been better dressed for foot travel, but he was young and struggled bravely to keep up. After a few hours of travel, both were exhausted.

They had reached a small plateau on the trail wide enough to accommodate a small traveler's *santuario*. It was little more than an altar festooned with flowers and supporting a statuette of the Blessed Virgin. A small bench faced the altar and an awning supported by four posts covered both. The *santuario* provided shade and a place for the mountain traveler to rest. Someone had placed a small bowl filled with scraps of bread at the feet of the Virgin—an offering. The bread was fresh and Mézu said a prayer of thanks before sharing the bread with her brother, Ignacio.

She decided they both needed a short rest, reasoning a brief respite free of the sharp rocks and brush that bracketed their path would do no harm. They had traveled five miles, maybe more. The trail ran along the bottom of a long draw between two steep volcanic slopes extending up to high ridgelines that towered over them. The sun was nearly overhead and she could see where the trail she had been following continued, its narrow course climbing abruptly up to a point where the two ridgelines met several miles to the southeast. She was certain that the junction of those ridgelines was beyond the *Regidore* of Agaete's control.

Mézu placed the boy on one end of the pew and collapsed at the other. She rummaged through the small canvas bag she carried and removed two hard biscuits and a leather flask. She gave one of the biscuits to her brother and offered him a drink from the flask. He had finished the bread quickly, wordlessly wolfing it down.

"Wet your lips with this wine, Ignacio," she said. "Then after you have eaten, I will give you some more. There is not much left."

Ignacio, who appeared on the verge of tears, sipped a little from the flask and accepted the hard biscuit. He had not cried when his sister appeared in his room, face covered with blood, and ordered him to dress. She brought him to a storeroom where a slave was putting items in a cloth bag. Even then, Ignacio asked nothing, responding obediently to every instruction.

Any other boy would have wailed and demanded to know why, Mézu thought. Either Ignacio was in shock or the still fresh memory of their parents' death had rendered him detached from sudden misfortunes. Concerned with escaping while there was time, Mézu had not properly prepared for their flight from Tenerife. They had a little watered-down wine, some bread and a few biscuits. The one *escudo* she had was spent securing their transport and they had eaten the bread during the passage to Gran Canaria. Her canvas sack now contained four *reals de plata* and seven copper *maravedíes*. She carried no clothes for herself or Ignacio. The trip from Tenerife to Gran Canaria had lasted the remainder of the night. *Had it only been last night?* She thought. They had been able to rest in the boat and she did not want to pause at the *santuario* for long.

Last night, there had been a formal ball to celebrate her betrothal, or more correctly, the betrothal of *Doña* Maria Artiles y Ventomo to the powerful *Ricohombre* Alguazil Cabitos y Cabrón. There were over a hundred guests in attendance, important people from every village on the island of Tenerife. Cabitos' assault had taken place in an antechamber, away from the view of gathered gentry. He had left Mézu sprawled on the floor as he stormed from the room to call one of his guards to arrest her while Cabitos went to the ballroom to explain away *Doña* Maria Artiles' sudden absence. She had escaped the chamber, exiting the main house before the guards arrived. Cabitos was informed, but any search for her was delayed until all the guests had departed for their homes. Once he was free to act, Cabitos would waste little time in finding her and imposing his will on her. She had been presented to all of Tenerife as Cabitos' betrothed by *Don* Artiles years ago before the rich merchant's sudden death. The dowry had been paid. The betrothal was to have been certified, and sanctified, by the Church as a prelude to the ball. Without parents to protect her, *Doña* Maria Artiles —Mézu— was his property.

❧

He watched as the girl came up the steep trail with the young boy in tow. She had been nearly a quarter of a mile away when the contrast of her green gown on the ash-colored trail caught his eye. He was ascending from Mogán, where he had sold several goats, on his way to *El Dorso de la Mano* (the Back of the Hand) and the high trail home when he saw them.

He could see the port town far beyond and below the small pair of figures struggling up from Agaete. Below the two travelers, the trail was empty.

He searched the slopes above the trail and selected a bare place where the rock jutted out ten feet above the path from Agaete. He carried a wooden pole, nearly twenty feet long and tipped by a foot-long iron point. Such poles were used by the goatherds of Gran Canaria to control their flocks and move about the jagged terrain. He jabbed the iron tip of the long pole into the edge of the trail, leaned it toward the steep slope and, hand over hand, ascended to a flat rock above the trail. Once on the rock, he pulled the pole up after him, laid it on the ground and squatted to wait for the distant travelers. As he studied them, he began to realize the travelers he watched were not doing well. Their progress was slow and the girl appeared to have been injured. Her companion was a young boy so tired he could barely walk.

The *santuario* of the Most Blessed Virgin of the Clouds was below him. The roof hid the altar from view, but he could see the short pew. He watched as they entered and collapsed on the bench. When the girl took bread from the altar and gave some to the child, he stood. Placing the point of the long pole on the trail below him, he descended silently, sliding down to a place less than thirty feet from the bench where the two travelers rested. He walked over to the shelter, rested his goatherd's pole on the edge of the awning and paused. Neither occupant of the bench had heard him and they seemed to be sleeping.

She was the most beautiful girl he had ever seen. Angela had been the love of his life until her father had given her in marriage to Manuel Gomez, a pig farmer in Agüimes. He had considered stealing Angela away, but where could he have taken her? Where could they have hidden on the island? Now, a girl resting on a bench, her feet pulled up and tucked under the ragged hem of her tattered green gown, held him. A sensation he had never felt before flowed up from his chest and caused his ears to burn. All memory of Angela Guerra vanished from his mind.

He removed his hat and cleared his throat. Neither occupant of the bench moved. He took a deep breath.

"*Buenos días, señorita,*" he said.

The girl gasped and sat up. She pulled the boy toward her and cowered on the far end of the bench. She held a bloody compress to the left side of her face, but her right eye was wide, light grey in color and it made his heart race.

"Forgive me. I did not mean to startle you, *señorita*," he said. "My name is Diego deMelilla y Tupinar, at your service. Please accept my apologies, but I think you are in need of assistance."

The girl visibly relaxed but she continued to hold the still-sleeping boy close to her side.

"*Señor* deMelilla, it is I who should apologize," she said. "It is not my custom to sleep in public, but we were so exhausted and I was afraid that you might—." She stopped midsentence, seeming to reassess the situation. "My name is Mézucasa. This sleepyhead is my brother, Ignacio. We are from Tenerife."

"Mézucasa, I think you should allow me to see to your injury," Diego said. He perceived her wound was serious and her failure to introduce herself properly troubled him. One normally stated their Christian name, their father's family name and then their mother's family name upon introduction, as Diego had done. Depending upon the situation, an *apodo* (nickname) may also be stated. The beautiful Mézucasa was hiding something.

"I am not seriously hurt," she said.

"I can see otherwise, *señorita*," Diego said. "Please permit me to help." He took the now-empty bowl from the altar and placed it on the ground underneath the bench where Mézu rested. Diego knelt next to the bench, removed the haversack he carried and set next to Mézu. Ignacio, still sleeping, snuggled against his sister, inadvertently making room for Diego to work. He removed a flask from the haversack and filled the bowl with water from the flask. She could smell a sweet hint of rum as he filled the bowl. Rum was often mixed with water to prevent it from turning stale.

"Please, permit me," Diego said as he touched Mézu's hand holding the compress and gently pulled it away from her face. The blood on her hand and the linen handkerchief had turned into a sticky gel. He washed both her hand and handkerchief in the bowl as he studied the wound. The sight sickened him. There were two deep lacerations extending from just above the outside of her left eyebrow across her eye and ending on her cheekbone near her nose. The orb of her left eye had been ruined. The remains of the eye had contracted into the socket, hidden by her eyelid. He had no doubt that she had lost the eye.

"After I clean this linen cloth, I shall fold it into a pad and bandage it to your face, *señorita*," he said. "A linen bandage will not fester as one made of cotton might." It was something his father had told him. That old soldier had been well versed and practiced in the treatment of wounds.

She watched Diego carefully as he cleaned her hand and face. He was a large man, wide in the shoulders and tall. His hands were big, calloused and strong, yet gentle. She examined his face as he leaned close to his work. He might have been eighteen years old. His head was large, wide and with heavy brows. His long brown hair was pulled back and tied behind his head, the color matching his short beard. His eyes were a sparkling, mesmerizing blue.

He wore a cotton shirt and short trousers that ended at his bare knees. Between the knee and ankle he had a kind of lacy, loose fitting sort of stocking that tied below the knee and hung to the tops of his foot wear, a type of shoe Mézu had never seen before. A cape of soft leather, perhaps goat skin, fringed in fur was draped over his shoulders. His black hat, now on the ground next to him, had a flat, wide brim, and a small round dome. Kindness and concern accentuated his weathered face as he tended to her injury. Taken all together, she believed him to be the most wild and beautiful man she had ever seen.

He placed the folded linen to her face and, taking her left hand, positioned it to hold the pad in place.

"Hold this for a moment, *señorita*," he said as he reached into his haversack for something.

She complied, following his every move with her good eye. He withdrew a clean cotton cloth from the bag and, holding opposite corners, flipped the cloth into a band which he tied about her head to hold the pad to her face. He reached into the haversack again and drew out a tightly folded lace cloth.

"A gift I purchased in Mogán," he explained as he released the string and shook the fabric free, revealing it to be a lace shawl. He placed the shawl over her head and dropped it in place.

Her hands were shaking as Mézu removed the silver comb that still clung in her hair and pulled the torn remains of a veil from the high back. She rearranged the comb to hold the shawl in place. It would not do for a grown woman to go about bareheaded. She pulled a corner of the shawl across the left side of her face until it covered the bandage and tucked the end into the comb to hold it in place. She instantly felt more comfortable as if the simple act of covering her head finalized her apparel.

She shook Ignacio awake. The boy stirred and sat up, rubbing his eyes.

"Mézu, who is this man?" Ignacio asked.

"This is *Señor* Diego deMelilla y Tupinar," She said. "He is —."

"I am a friend, Ignacio," Diego interrupted. "Please call me Diego. Your sister is in need of some help, and you as well I think." Diego shifted his eyes to Mézu. "*Señorita* Mézucasa, allow me to bring you to my home where we, my mother and sisters, can provide you with food, drink and rest. Once you have recovered, we can discuss further what is to be done."

Mézu stiffened and looked about, seemingly to suddenly realize her situation. "Do you know *Don* Raphael Arinaga y Suerios, *señor*? I must reach *Don* Raphael's house. He is a friend of my family."

"*Don* Raphael is the *Regidore* of Gando. I know him well. My father served with him in the army," Diego said. "He controls Gando, Agüimes and inland to include my home. He is my *Regidore*."

"How far is it to you home?" she asked. "Are we in his lands now?"

"It may be five miles to my home from here, but it is higher in the mountain and it will take three hours to get there, if you can walk. Here we are in lands governed by the *Regidore* of Agaete. The ridge just east of here marks the beginning of *Don* Raphael's jurisdiction. When we are high enough to see *El Roque Nublo* (The Rock of the Clouds) we will be at the border and near my home."

"Please," Mézu said, struggling to her feet, "let us hurry."

"I am so tired," Ignacio whimpered. It was the first time he had really complained.

"Then you shall ride," Diego said. He showed them where there were holes cut in the bottom of his leather cape. He slipped his arms through the holes and the cape formed a sack on his back. The move revealed a short sword tucked into Diego's belt Mézu had not noticed before.

"I can carry an injured goat or a kid on my back in my cape. Ignacio can ride and sleep on the way, if you wish." Diego lifted Ignacio and swung him onto his back. Mézu lifted the corners of the cape and Diego put his arms through the holes in the tail. The boy rode comfortably, securely held in place, his head over Diego's shoulder.

"Come, *señorita*," Diego said as he collected his haversack and Mézu's canvas bag. "We will climb to the crest yonder. There I will show you where we are bound."

Mézu limped onto the trail and followed the tall stranger. He moved as if the boy weighed nothing. Ignacio look back at his sister, grinning, then he lay his head on Diego's shoulder and closed his eyes. Diego retrieved the long pole and, using it as if it were a simple walking stick, headed up the trail toward the east. He paused frequently to help her along and even suggested she hold onto the edge of his cape if she should tire. Unburdened, Mézu was able to keep up until they reached the crest of the ridgeline.

"There is *El Roque Nublo*," Diego said pointing to a huge rock that seemed to be almost an obelisk. "And there is Teide."

He pointed toward the west where Mézu could see the island of Tenerife and its snowcapped central volcanic mountain of Teide for the first time since coming to Gran Canaria. The island seemed as if it were rising out of a sea of clouds backlit by the setting sun.

"We are above the clouds," she said almost reverently.

"I have often dreamed of climbing Teide," Diego said. "But I have never even been to Tenerife. Surely, you must have ascended Teide, *señorita*."

"No," Mézu said, the wonder and majesty of the view overpowering her. "I have never been this high before."

Diego faced toward the east and whistled a series of notes. The sound was so loud it woke Ignacio and caused Mézu to start. He saw her questioning expression and smiled.

"I am calling my sisters. I tell them to meet us on the trail with milk and cheese. I tell them we have guests." He issued another phrase of whistles and waited.

Mézu could hear an answering series of faint, song-like returns. The sounds were beautiful, delicate and clear in the high air. Diego continued along the ridgeline toward the east with Mézu following, her hand on Ignacio's foot. It felt wonderful to be walking on nearly level ground. It had seemed as if they had been climbing forever.

There were more whistles from the east, closer than before and soon Mézu could see two girls coming toward them. They appeared to be about thirteen years old. They were dressed similarly in the garb of the local mountain peasant women and gave the impression of being twins. Each wore an ankle-length white cotton skirt and a white cotton blouse. A green bodice of heavy woven wool was tightly cinched about each girl's chest. A long cotton veil covered the head of each girl, cascading down their shoulders and back to the waist. Their faces were exposed and their veils held in place by wide-brimmed black hats with flat crowns.

"These are my sisters," Diego said as the girls stopped before them. "Francesca deMelilla y Tupinar," the girl holding a haversack curtsied, "is the elder, by a half-hour. And this is Francina deMelilla y Tupinar," the other girl now curtsied. She was carrying a spear and a stone-tipped mace. "This lady is named Mézucasa and the lad here is Ignacio," Diego said.

The girls paused; expecting more in the way of names. Francesca broke the awkward silence, "It is my pleasure to meet you, *señorita*," she said. "And mine as well," Francina added.

"Please call me Mézu," Mézu replied with a nod to each.

"Here are your *magado* and *sunta* as you instructed, brother," Francina said as she handed first the spear and then the mace to Diego.

"And here is some milk and cheese for your friends, as you asked," Francesca said, giving Mézu the haversack.

Diego knelt so Ignacio could climb down to accept the leather flask of goat's milk Mézu withdrew from the haversack. Francesca cut generous portions of cheese with a knife she produced from a hidden fold in her dress and gave one to Ignacio and the other to Mézu. She cut another portion which she offered to Diego, but he waived it away. Ignacio was the beneficiary of the rejected cheese.

"How did your sisters know to bring these things?" Mézu asked. "This cheese is delicious as is the milk."

"I spoke to them in the whistle-words of the ancient ones," Diego said. "A few in my village have learned to use the language. The people of Gomera know it well. My father's people came from Gomera." Gomera was another of the seven populated islands that formed the Canarian archipelago.

"I have heard of such a thing," Mézu said. "Whistle-words were not used by the Guanche of Tenerife."

"The ancient ones of Gran Canaria were called the *Amazigh*. It was a time when this island was called *Tamarán*," Diego said. "The Amazigh did not use the language of the Guanche." He looked toward the west. The valleys were now in darkness and the sun was nearly below the silhouette of Teide. "Please go with my sisters to my mother's house now. Eat along the way and do not tarry."

"Why do you not come with us?" Mézu asked. She oddly felt as if Diego were an old friend and the sisters he was directing her to follow were strangers.

"I will wait along the trail here for a short time. Perhaps I will catch up with you before you reach my mother's house. Three men have been following us," Diego said. "I think they are *vigilante* from Agaete."

CHAPTER 2

Diego watched his sisters and their guests as they departed for his home. The path they followed went southeast for a mile or more to a wide and relatively flat area called "The Back of the Hand," a high plateau from which several ridgelines stretched out to the sea, like the fingers of a giant hand. From there the way home was one of several trails radiating out from *El Dorso de la Mano*. All trails either ran along the side slope of a ridgeline or descended into the valley between high, rocky rims. No trails this far from the sea crossed a crest from one valley to another. Once a trail was chosen for an intended destination, travelers were committed to that route until they were within a mile of the sea where the steep fingers of ridgelines became flatter, allowing trails between valleys.

However, Diego was skilled in the use of the long goat herder's pole, the *lanza*. The steepest and tallest of ridgelines were no barriers to him. Diego could use the *lanza* to perform *el Salto del Pastor* (the shepherd's leap). He could pole vault across narrow gullies, climb vertical cliff faces and virtually fly down any slope. Spaniards would often say the Canary Islanders, the *Isleños,* could fly.

He stepped off of the trail and moved toward the north where an outcropping hid him in darkness. He leaned his *lanza* against a cliff face, put his right hand through the leather loop on the handle of the *sunta* so the weapon hung at his elbow and slipped the *magado* into a sheath sewn in his cloak. He gathered several fist-sized stones, piled them near his feet and watched the men coming from the west as the last glimmer of day faded away. The first man in line wore the uniform of a village peace officer, what the Spaniards called a *"alguacil"* (catchpole). The other two were slaves. Diego knew they were slaves for they were unarmed. He remembered his father's words. *"When a man wishes to make another a slave, he must first disarm him. An unarmed man can be subdued; an armed man has the means to resist."*

The catchpole drew nearer. Diego could see the man was old, maybe 40 years or more. He was fat and panted breathlessly in the thin air. He carried a halberd. The blade was rust-stained and the long wood shaft was slightly warped. The purpose of the battered weapon was to indicate the old man's office. In skilled hands a halberd could be dangerous, but Diego sensed this halberd was not in skilled hands. The catchpole's uniform was old and worn. Or rather his coat was, for his "uniform" comprised a Spanish militia coat, blue with red facing, covering a simple peasant's cotton shirt, pants and sandals. His hat was a tall, black, flat-topped and narrow-brimmed affair sporting a dull red cockade on the left side. The slaves were younger men similarly garbed but without coats or hats.

"You are far from home, my friend," Diego said, his voice booming out from darkness. Startled, the man placed the halberd in the "guard" position across his body. The two wide-eyed slaves scrambled behind the man as if seeking shelter from a wind.

"Who is there?" the man said, his voice trembling. The man had spent his life in the coastal village and had never been up in the mountains at night. "I am *Cabo* (Corporal) Gomez of the Agaete Civil Guard," he said, drawing himself up slightly.

Diego hurled a rock far to the left of the three huddled on the trail. It clattered loudly and created a small slide of gravel giving the impression of someone coming down to the trail. The three turned as one toward the sound.

"Why does a corporal of the Agaete Civil Guard come to *El Roque Nublo?*" Diego asked. "Agaete has no business here. We think you are thieves come to steal from the men of the high mountain." He threw another stone to the right of the trio. Gomez swiveled his head around, clearly concerned they were being surrounded.

"We are no thieves, I tell you *señor*," Gomez stammered. "We are on official business. We seek criminals who have escaped Tenerife— a woman and a child."

"You say you seek a woman and a child. What woman or child would come here, to the high mountains, at night?" Diego tossed another rock toward *El Roque Nublo*. The noise it made caused Gomes to flinch. "We say it is you who have been stealing from us."

"*Señores*, I say we followed reports of a girl and a young boy leaving Agaete. I swear to you in the name of the Most Blessed Virgin. We saw a man and a woman far ahead of us, headed here. We wanted to question them," Gomez said.

Diego realized that from a distance Mézu, with the shawl covering her head, would have appeared to be a peasant woman and, with Ignacio riding in Diego's folded cape, he would have seemed to be a man carrying a backpack.

"A man and a woman is not the same as a woman and a child. If you are who you claim to be, you are far beyond the lands that answer to Agaete," Diego insisted. "If what you say is true, return to Agaete and tell your master he can send to *Don* Raphael Arinaga, Lord of these lands, and he will search for Tenerife's escapees. I counsel you, *Cabo* Gomez, do not let the rising moon find you here."

Cabo Gomez led the way west. The three must have found the descent easier going for they were soon gone. Diego stepped back out on the trail and hurled another stone in the direction of the fleeing catchpole and his men. He was rewarded with a shout of alarm from far down the trail.

Escaped criminals, Diego thought, *a beautiful, battered girl and a boy?* Not likely. Criminals would not seek refuge at the home of *Don* Raphael Arinaga, a man known to be pious, law-abiding and appointed to his post by close counselors to the King, Charles III of the House of *Borbón*. He picked up the *lanza* and balanced it over one shoulder. The trail ahead was relatively level and he knew it well. The moon was not yet up, but the stars provided enough light for him to walk safely home. When the moon finally rose the trail became well lit and Diego jogged the last half mile home, blissfully anticipating renewed conversations with the beautiful and mysterious Mézu.

ᐧᓄᐧ

Daylight was fading when the women and Ignacio left Diego. Francesca led the way followed by Mézu and Francina. The three took turns carrying Ignacio piggyback. Night fell quickly and Mézu was compelled to hold the tip of Francesca's veil to keep on the trail. When they reached the southeastern edge of *El Dorso de la Mano*, the moon had risen and Mézu had no trouble following the sisters along a trail that pitched steeply down between long ridgelines. She could see the vertical face of a cliff paralleling their line of travel on her left. Occasionally, they passed short paths jutting off from the trail and ending at wooden rectangles affixed to the stone of the cliff. Francesca whistled a phrase and one of the rectangles swung away from the cliff spilling light across the trail followed by a female form holding the door open with one hand and beckoning with the other.

"We are home," Francina said as she put Ignacio down.

"*Hola*, mama," Francesca said as she kissed the woman on both cheeks. Francina stepped around Mézu and greeted her mother as well.

"Mother," Francesca said, gesturing with her left, "this is *señorita* Mézucasa and her brother, Ignacio. They are the travelers Diego met at the *santuario* of the Most Blessed Virgin of the Clouds; Mézucasa, my mother, Yadra Tupinar y Laguna."

Yadra held out her hand to Mézu, drawing her into the light flickering out of the doorway. The old woman's face showed concern as she examined the bloody gown and bandage. "My son did well to send you here, *señorita* Mézucasa," she said. "The Most Blessed Virgin of the Clouds is there for the troubled pilgrim."

"Please call me Mézu, *señora* Tupinar," Mézu said with a curtsy.

"And I am Yadra. Come in. Sit at the table and let me see your injury."

Mézu did as she was told. She removed the shawl that Diego had given her to wear as a veil and presented it to her hostess. "Your son gave me this," Mézu said. "He said it was a gift. I am afraid it has been stained with blood in one corner."

Yadra folded the shawl and placed it with Mézu's silver comb on a small shelf. "My son has carried that gift for several months," she said. "I am pleased he found someone worthy." Yadra collected an iron pot of hot water from an alcove in the wall of the cave. A small oven and fire-pit had been carved into the rock. Mézu could see the smoke from the fire drawn up through a hole in the alcove, evidently a crude chimney. The room was lighted by a single wax candle, its flickering light revealed a few details.

There were several benches or ledges carved out of the rock around the room, containing stores of pots and canvas sacks. A shuttered window and the door they had entered were set in a wall made of plastered stone placed across what must have been a wide entrance to a natural cave. Two passages from the room led deeper into the cliff and she could see curtains or perhaps another wooden door, closing off portions of the cave. The interior dividing walls were plastered stone construction similar to the exterior wall.

The day had been growing quite cool, it was December and they must have been a mile up in the mountain. Walking along the windy trail wearing only an evening gown and a shawl, she had felt cold, but not freezing. It felt good to be out of the wind and the little cooking fire in the stone oven comfortably warmed the interior of the home. Mézu had lived all of her life on Tenerife at sea-level. Never, in all that time, had she ever seen a fire used to heat a house.

"Oh, *mi corazón* (my heart)," Yadra whispered as she removed the bandage Diego had applied and re-cleaned the wound. "Who did such a thing to you?" Yadra had been a soldier's wife and she could recognize that Mézu's injury was the result of a blow.

"It was my fault, *señora*," Mézu mumbled. "I was too outspoken. I permitted my anger to rule my wits."

"No child of God deserves to be so struck," Yadra said, her own anger growing. "Did he use a weapon?"

"No, just the back of his hand," Mézu replied. "He has a large ring, a ring of office. It was *Don* Alguazil Cabitos y Cabrón, *Regidore* of Santa Cruz de Tenerife who struck me. Until last night, I was his betrothed. Now, I would rather enter a convent than marry such a beast."

"Only cowards strike over mere words," Yadra said.

"*Señora*," Mézu spoke softly glancing at Ignacio as he talked with the twins. "If I can reach the lands governed by *Don* Raphael Arinaga y Suerios, I should be safe. He was a friend of my father and my father's family. He will protect me."

"Why cannot your own family protect you?" Yadra asked.

"My parents were killed two years ago when Dutch pirates raided our villa," Mézu said. "I had been promised to Alguazil Cabitos by my father since I was ten, so I and my brother moved to his villa. Last night was our formal betrothal *gala*." *Last night?* She thought. *Had it not yet been one full day?* "He struck me and would have locked me away, but I escaped with my brother."

"We are *Don* Raphael's subjects," Yadra said. "And you are among friends, fear not for that. Now come into my room and we will see that you are properly dressed."

Mézu's gown was a tattered mess. In many places her chemise peaked through the rents and tears in the delicate green fabric. She rose, surprised by how stiff she felt, and followed Yadra past a curtained doorway and into a small bedroom. Yadra carried the candle with her and the flickering flame cast a circle of light sufficient to reveal the entire cell. There was a single chair and a wooden bed frame containing a thin mattress supported by ropes woven into the frame. Pegs had been inserted into holes along the wall on which hung a half-dozen dresses and one colorful skirt. Shelves cut into the wall held other folded garments.

Yadra selected a simple white dress from the wall. From the folded garments she collected a chemise, a veil, and a bodice. From a peg in the corner, she retrieved a small black hat similar to those the sisters wore.

"Here, *señorita*," she said as she gave the garments to Mézu. "I will leave you here to change. I fear we will never repair your gown, but I will do what I can. Please know that you are to consider our home as if it were your home. Now I will see to your brother."

Yadra left the candle and was gone through the curtain as Mézu, stunned by the open and generous reception, could only mumble, "*Muchas gracias, señora* Yadra." She sat on the chair and slowly unlaced her dancing shoes. They were in tatters and fell away as the eyelets were freed of their laces. Her feet were sore and cut in several places. The bleeding had stopped and she looked forward to being able to wash them. The floor of the cave was a clean, smooth stone and felt cool and comfortable beneath her bare feet.

She slipped out of the green gown; it too had been torn to rags. When she removed her chemise, the room seemed suddenly cold against her naked skin. Shivering, she hurriedly donned the clean chemise and dress. The dress had drawstrings about the waist, which she cinched as she smoothed the fabric into an even pattern. The attire accentuated her figure, emphasizing the curves of her hips and breast.

She then added the bodice, which fit her well and provided a modest covering to the dress. She laced it closed and adjusted the sleeves of the dress. She smoothed her hair and held it with one hand until she had covered her head with the veil. She placed the hat squarely on her head to hold the veil in place. She had never worn a broad-brimmed, square crowned black hat before, so she attempted to imitate the dress of the sisters. She picked up the candle and walked back through the curtain into the main room.

Ignacio was already seated at the table where he was finishing a dish made from ground grain meal called "*gofio*" which had been mixed with water, baked into a circular, flat loaf and wrapped around a strip of meat. The glow from the small oven and one additional candle filled the little dining room with a dancing, golden light.

"*Señorita,*" Yadra said as she added a dish to the table, "please, have some *gofio* and meat. I know that a little milk and a few bits of cheese were not enough. You and your brother have traveled far."

Mézu sat and accepted the offering. She noted that the two sisters were busying themselves about the home, moving some blankets to a spot near the door and transferring things from one room to another.

"Please, *señora,*" Mézu said as she tasted a bit of the meat. It was so delicious it caused her to pause a moment. "Please, do not trouble yourself. I am in your debt too much as it is."

"Tish!" Yadra replied. She indicated the bedroom Mézu had used to change clothes. "The room behind you is yours for as long as you wish. We will make a place next to the bed for Ignacio. I will be in that room." She indicated a doorway across from the front door.

There was a sharp "tweet" outside. Yadra turned toward the front door. "You may enter, son. Our guests are eating."

The door swung open and Mézu could see Diego placing his tall herdsman's staff against the exterior wall before he stooped and turned to enter the home. He removed his hat and cape and placed them on a peg near the door. The spear Francina had brought him, they had called it a *magado*, was sheathed in the cape. He hung the mace – the *sunta* – on the same peg by the leather loop on the handle. Then he stood to remove the short sword belted to his waist. His back was to her and she marveled at how his muscles undulated under his cotton shirt as he worked at the buckle. She had forgotten how big the man was. Diego nodded toward his sisters and Ignacio as he approached the table.

"*Señorita*," he said to Mézu as he accepted a *gofio* cake wrapped around strips of meat from his mother, "the men who had been following us have decided to return to Agaete. In the morning we will send word to *Don* Raphael that the children of a friend are here seeking his help." He maneuvered his body onto a chair at the end of the table. "The message would be greatly simplified if we could tell *Don* Raphael who you are."

"You are correct, *señor* deMelilla," Mézu began.

"Diego, please," Diego interrupted.

"*Señor* Diego," Mézu said with a sigh. "I am Maria Artiles y Ventomo. My father was the merchant *Don* Pedro Artiles y Bentura of Santa Cruz de Tenerife."

Yadra gasped and looked at her son. "*Don* Pedro Artiles," she said finally, "was well known to this house, and well loved. I had heard he had been killed three years ago, maybe more."

"You and your brother are welcome here," Diego said. "My father had a long history of service with your father. They both served the King in Melilla against the Moor."

"How wise is the Blessed Virgin," Yadra said, "to send you both to us for protection."

"Your husband was a *compadre* of my father?" Mézu was astonished at the revelation. Her father never spoke of the days when he and *Don*

Raphael had battled the Moors near the Mediterranean fortress city of Melilla. He simply said they all did what had to be done, no more. Now she had found refuge with the family of another from that old conflict.

"Your father, *señorita*," Yadra said quietly, "once owned my husband."

Diego placed a cup of wine before Mézu, "*Señorita* Maria, refresh yourself," he said.

"You are my benefactor, *señor* Diego," Mézu said. "Please call me Mézu."

"Mézu," he started again, "after you are refreshed, please come outside. The village wishes to welcome you. One of the problems with whistle-words is the lack of secrecy. All in the village heard me call my sisters." Diego finished his meal, downing his wine in one gulp. "We will send word to *Don* Raphael in the morning," he said. He went out without his hat or cape. Mézu could see the flicker of a large fire through the doorway as he left.

She could hear many voices outside. Then she heard singing and laughter. Diego's strong voice was distinctive. "*Doña* Maria Artiles y Ventomo and her brother, Ignacio Artiles y Ventomo are our guests. They are the children of *Don* Pedro Artiles and I have pledged to help them."

Mézu had reached the door and was prepared to go out when she heard a voice call out, "please sing for us, Diego. Sing a *décima* for us." She paused at the door and listened as a deep baritone voice filled the night air.

> *"He was bound by a chain*
> *Forced to a distant city*
> *The day was Christmas*
> *The place was a Fortress"*

> *"The city was called Melilla*
> *His back felt the whip*
> *Blood was on his hand*
> *They came, the unbelievers*
> *With a sword he did repel*
> *Then, liberation and home"*

She opened the door and stepped out to see a crowd of two dozen or so men, women and children. Diego turned and extended a hand toward her. "I present *Doña* Maria Artiles y Ventomo," he said with a tilt of his head. Men removed their hats and the women curtsied. "Welcome *Doña* Maria," they said as she went to each in the firelight. Once the greetings were completed, the villagers bade their guest good night and returned to their homes along the cliff face.

Diego and Mézu reentered the house and joined Yadra at the little table. "Ignacio is already asleep at the foot of your bed, Mézu," she said. "My daughters have retired as well. My son is going to watch over his flock tonight." Yadra gave a stern look toward Diego. "Your bedroll is by the door."

Diego frowned and then shrugged his huge shoulders. "Good night, Mézu," he said. He picked up the bedroll, retrieved his hat and cape and was gone.

"Good night, Diego," Mézu called after him. She suddenly wanted to spend more time with Diego.

"What was the meaning of the *décima?*" Mézu asked Yadra after Diego had left.

"It is the story of my husband," Yadra said. "The story of how he won his freedom in battle. Once he was free, he was given the name deMelilla, and returned to the Canary Islands. Now, off to bed with you."

Mézu entered the bedroom. She held the candle over Ignacio and saw that he was sleeping comfortably. She removed her borrowed clothes and climbed into the bed dressed only in the thin chemise. Diego's beautiful singing would not leave her mind. She checked her bandage, closed her good eye and felt relief rushed over her in a wave. Sleep overcame her quickly.

☙

A small, cold, wet hand grasped her arm. Mézu was awake in an instant. The room was totally dark. Her mind cleared and she remembered where she was. "Ignacio, is that you?" she whispered. Salty water dripped onto her face. "Ignacio, talk to me. We are among friends."

"Mézu," the voice was not Ignacio's. "Mézu, do not return to Tenerife."

"Faith?" Mézu tried to sit up, but the little hand held her down. "Faith Glas? How can it be?" Mézu used the English word "Faith" for it was a name; the name of a little girl who had, with her mother, been guests of Alguazil Cabitos a year ago. Faith and Mézu had become good friends during the month they were in Santa Cruz.

"Faith," Mézu began to weep. "I did not know. I could not have known. "

"I have come to warn you, Mézu," Faith's voice filled the darkness. "Now sleep, sister."

༄

A light appeared under the drawn curtain of the bedroom. Mézu sat up, suddenly fully awake. The dream of Faith Glas was fresh in her mind. The house was beginning to stir. She looked over at Ignacio and saw that he was up and gone. She heard his little voice on the other side of the curtain talking with one of the sisters. She swung her feet down and began to stand so she could dress. When her feet struck the stone, she felt water splash and the side of the bed felt wet. She hurriedly dressed in her borrowed clothes and opened the curtain to see Yadra, Ignacio and Diego seated at the table.

"Good morning, Mézu," Diego said. "I trust you slept well."

She wanted to rush over to Diego and embrace him. Instead she said, "Thank you, Diego. I did sleep well."

CHAPTER 3

T he door swung open and Francina peeked in. "Ignacio, have you finished eating? There are some children out here who would like to meet you."

Ignacio nodded and began to rise.

"I see a little milk still in your cup," Yadra chided. "Finish it, then Francina and Francesca will show you around."

"*Sí, señora* Yadra," Ignacio said and he lifted the cup to his lips to down the last of the milk. He turned the cup toward Yadra so she could see it was empty. She gestured him toward the door. "Francina, remember Ignacio has had a hard trip. Do not exhaust him."

Ignacio was out the door in an instant and the sounds of children laughing flowed in from the trail. Yadra looked at Mézu. "Forgive me for not asking your permission, Mézu. If you do not wish your bother to play outside, I will call him back."

"There is no presumption, *señora* Yadra," Mézu said as she found a seat close to Diego. "This is your home and we are the intruders."

Yadra sat across from Mézu, her eyes examining her guest. She reached over and placed the back of her fingers on Mézu's forehead.

"There is no fever," Yadra said. She indicated a stool near the oven next to a steaming iron pot. "Please, remove your veil and hat, *señorita*. Come sit close by the fire so I may clean your wound."

Mézu placed her veil and hat on the table. She hesitated, reluctant to abandon her place next to Diego, but he rose and took her by the elbow to escort her to the stool. Once Mézu was seated, Diego stood behind her and placed a massive, gentle hand on her shoulder.

"My mother is a well-known healer in our village," Diego said. "She has tended many injuries. Tell us if you feel any discomfort."

Yadra murmured gently as she removed the old dressing. "Oh, my heart, tell me if I am hurting you." She cleaned Mézu's forehead and cheek with a warm, damp cloth. Mézu closed her good eye and relaxed as the woman's hands cleaned her face. The gentle rubbing was soothing and reassuring. Absentmindedly, Mézu reached up to her shoulder and placed her hand on Diego's. The man's closeness comforted her in a way she had never felt before.

"Your wounds are healing well, but I am afraid that you have lost the eye," Yadra said. "I have something I think will help,"

Mézu opened her eye to look at the item Yadra held. It was a leather eye-patch. Until that moment, Mézu had not comprehended—had not been prepared for the consequences that resulted from the loss of an eye and what it meant. Now she realized she was to be forever disfigured, forced to wear a leather patch like some war veteran. She wanted to sob, but choked it back. Her free hand went to her mouth and the hand that held Diego's tightened. He squeezed her shoulder in response, pulling her slightly closer to him. She allowed his presence to engulf her for a moment.

"See how the lace is knotted?" Yadra said, hoping to distract Mézu.

The leather strap did not tie. The free ends were interwoven in such a way the patch could be tightened or loosened by sliding a knot along the binding. Yadra took the hand Mézu held to her mouth and placed the eye-patch in it. The leather was soft and pliable. The edges of the patch had been rolled and stitched into a padded border. Mézu placed the patch over her ruined eye, looped the binding over her head and pulled the strap tight. It fit perfectly. She looked up at Yadra. The old woman's eyes were moist and she placed a hand under Mézu's chin.

"Diego made it for you," Yadra said. "Is it comfortable?"

"Yes," Mézu said. "I can hardly feel it, although my face is still tender and sore." She turned her head to look at Diego. "Thank you, Diego. How did you find the time?"

"I had to remain awake as I watched my flock," Diego said with a shrug of his huge shoulders. "It helped me pass the time."

"I have been a burden long enough," Mézu said, shaking the dark mood from her mind. She went to the table and retrieved her veil and hat. *Yadra's veil and hat*, she thought. *My wardrobe consists of borrowed clothes.* "Tell me what I can do to help with the chores. I will not be a lay-about."

"First, come with us to morning Mass," Yadra said, picking up on the forced shift in Mézu's mood, "then we will begin the chores. We have sent word to the port at Gando. The messenger will return before nightfall. Until then, you can help me by sprinkling grain onto the stone while I turn the mill. We must be careful that you do not exhaust yourself. You are still weak."

Mézu knew adding grain to a hand mill while someone else did the hard work of turning the stone was child's work, though she had never done it. She had lived a life of privilege. All of her life had been spent dancing, gossiping, reading, writing, singing, and primping. She had watched servants perform every chore necessary for the maintenance of a household, but performed none herself.

"Come, Mézu," Yadra said, taking her by the hand, "the others are waiting."

Mézu was about to protest that she was without shoes when she noticed that Yadra was barefoot as well. When they walked out to the trail she saw Ignacio, Francina and Francesca waiting for them along with two boys about Ignacio's age. None of the boys wore shoes. Diego had not come with them. Mézu wanted to ask him to come with her, but she did not have a chance to speak to him.

"Hurry, Mama," Francesca said, "Mass is about to start."

As they walked down the trial, Ignacio introduced the two boys, Andrés Tupinar and José "Acero" Tupinar. "*Doña* Yadra is our aunt," Acero said proudly. "We will tell everyone you are coming." The boys raced ahead along a trail that seemed to simply continue downhill to a distant bend without interruption. Suddenly, the boys disappeared to the left into the face of the cliff. A woman appeared on the trail and looked toward Mézu. She gave a small wave and was gone again.

"My sister-in-law, Lucia," Yadra said. "She is the mother of Andrés. We need not hurry any longer, Lucia will see to it that Mass does not start until we are there."

The four women reached the place in the trail where the boys had disappeared. There was a wide plateau back from the trail recessed beneath a high stone ledge, almost a grotto. At the back of the grotto there was a wide stone doorway bracketed by windows in the stone wall. The church had been carved out of the solid rock of the cliff face. A priest stood by the door with Lucia and two other women and motioned everyone inside.

The interior of the church was dark, lighted by a few candles and what sunlight spilled in from the open door and windows. Rows of benches faced an altar rail which ran between the pulpit on one corner and an entrance for a baptismal on the other. All had been carved from stone. The little church was filled to capacity by the three dozen or so women and children of the congregation. Aside from the priest, only two other men were present, ancient and frail.

Mézu had first thought Yadra went barefoot to avoid embarrassing her own shoeless condition. Now she could see fully half of the women and all of the children present were without shoes. The shoes worn by the sisters were of a strange design and did not appear to have rigid soles.

Unlike the Masses Mézu had attended before, this church did not have an area set aside for the wealthy and influential in the front, reserving the rear or side walls for the less affluent. When she had attended Sunday Mass in Santa Cruz, she sat among bejeweled women and men, each examining their neighbors for the newest fashion trend. Coats, dresses, laces, stockings, pantaloons, hats, decorations and buckled shoes of every color and fabric filled the pews until one penitent could not move past another. She had not even noticed those in the rear or standing along the wall.

She was struck by the obvious poverty of the people gathered about her. Dresses were of plain white cotton. Vests or bodices were wool or leather. Veils were plain cotton or linen, though often woven into an intricate lace. Every woman wore a black, square topped hat with a flat brim. Some hats sported a brass buckle or only a ribbon around the crown to adjust the fit. There was no jewelry, no silver combs, no rings or bracelets. Weathered hands, callused from labor fingered rosaries made by knotting cords or polished seeds on a string. Every face that met her glance smiled and nodded a greeting. These folk were as poor as any Mézu had ever heard about. Yet, they were happy, laughing and gracious.

After Mass, Mézu was introduced to two dozen or more women. Fully half were named Maria. Lucia, Yadra's sister-in-law, had been baptized "Maria of the Lights" so the name she used, her *apodo*, was Lucia. Another woman was named "Maria of the Roses" so her *apodo* was Rosa. Mézu explained that her full name was "Maria of the Moon" and therefore her *apodo* was Mézu. None of the women had heard of "Maria of the Moon" as one of the manifestations of the Most Blessed Virgin, but that did not mater. Mézu was from Tenerife and that was explanation enough.

A near mob of squealing children and chattering women crowded the trail during the walk back up to the deMelilla home from the church. Upon arrival at the home, Mézu was invited to sit near the doorway on a low bench of stone as the talk, and offers of assistance, continued for nearly an hour.

"Where is Diego; where did he sleep last night?" Mézu managed to ask during a lull in the conversation that swirled about.

"It is all I can do to convince him to attend Sunday Mass," Yadra explained with a roll of her eyes. "He has gone to tend to his flock and then work in the vegetable garden. We need to prepare for the spring planting."

"Is this not his home as well?" Mézu continued.

"Yes, but when he watches over the flock he sleeps in a small grotto," Yadra gestured for Mézu to come out with her onto the trail. "There, see the wide smooth stone?"

"I can see a stone that looks like a sleeping dog," Mézu said, shading her one eye as she looked up into a seamless blue sky.

"That is it. It is called *El Piedra de Perro*. There is a grotto beneath the dog stone as comfortable as his room here."

"Have I put him out of his own home?" Mézu asked in a soft voice only Yadra could hear.

"It would not do for a young lady of marriageable age to sleep in the same house as a young man who is not a relative," Yadra said.

Mézu looked back up at the stone. It saddened her to think of Diego forced from his own home because of her and her impetuous flight from Tenerife. This afternoon, when the messenger returned, she would arrange a meeting with *Don* Raphael. He would protect her and provide a place for her to stay until she could recover her property from Alguazil Cabitos. Perhaps another night here, she thought, no more. She would leave a few coins to compensate the villagers for their trouble and be gone.

⁓

The messenger returned just before sundown leading two heavily laden burros. He was preceded by a platoon of squealing children racing to alert their parents. The messenger, a stooped old man called Soño, was also the village purchasing agent. People would tell Soño of items they desired to buy and he would make a list, he was one of a half dozen in the village who could write. Bolts of cloth, needles, buckles, salt, pots, pans and other things the villagers could not do without or make themselves comprised the list. When enough orders were collected, Soño would go down to the stores in Agüimes or even as far as Gando. He would spend a day or two finding bargains. The costs of the items were negotiated and paid for before Soño would attempt the day-long trip down to the coast. If he paid less for the item in town, which was often, he pocketed the profit. If he was forced to pay more, a rare event, Soño would suffer a loss.

Mézu had to wait until the villagers had collected their goods before she could speak to Soño. It had been Diego who requested Soño to inform *Don* Raphael that Maria Artiles was seeking refuge, so he and Yadra accompanied Mézu to speak with the old man.

"Diego!" Soño waived the three over to where he was tending his burros. "*Don* Raphael is in Spain, in Cádiz, visiting his cousin, the Grand Duke. His servant told me he should be back in three weeks."

"Did you leave a message?" Diego asked.

Soño looked at Diego and twisted his face into an expression that made Mézu laugh. "Of course I did, Diego," he said. "I wrote it on clean paper, folded it– I had no sealing wax you see– and I addressed it 'to his most excellent Lord'."

"What did your message say, *señor?*" Mézu asked.

"It said

'Most excellent Lord, *Don* Raphael Arinaga y Suerios, *Regidore* of *Gando*: Greetings and may the Most Blessed Virgin watch over your house and your reign. I am pleased to inform you that the daughter of *Don* Pedro Artiles of Santa Cruz de Tenerife is in *Pueblo de Cuevas* (village of caves). She kisses your hand and begs sanctuary. She abides at the home of deMelilla,'

"I gave the letter to the *jefe* himself, *señorita,*" Soño said, bobbing his head. "He will see it placed in *Don* Raphael's hands. I have his word."

"Thank you, *señor* Soño," Mézu said uncertainly. "Did the *jefe* say when *Don* Raphael was to return to Gando?"

"Yes, *Don* Raphael is to return before the end of this month. He will send word for you then, I am certain," Soño said. "*Don* Raphael is a just man."

☙

"I must obtain my own clothes," Mézu said as she guided grains of wheat through a hole in the grindstone. "I have some money. Perhaps I could buy a dress, some shoes and a veil. You have been so kind, but these are your clothes."

"Buy a dress?" Yadra seemed shocked. "We will pay señor Soño to bring us some cotton cloth when next he goes to Agüimes. Together, we will make two dresses for you, and a bodice. Lucia said she will give you a pair of shoes that do not fit her anymore. As for a veil, Diego gave you the shawl. If you feel you must pay something, give Soño a *real* for the cloth. As for the rest, the Most Blessed Virgin has sent you to us. Her love for our service is our reward."

A week had passed since Mézu arrived at the little village of caves. She had recovered enough of her strength to help with the chores. She worked in the garden, helped with the cooking and mended clothes. Yadra had to show Mézu how to perform each of the tasks, but she did not have to do it twice. Mézu learned quickly, worked hard and contributed to the family. Yadra realized she would miss Mézu when the time came for her to depart for Gando. The girl was pleasant, happy and thoughtful. She had become close to Francesca and Francina, almost as if she were their sister.

Mézu did not brood over her disfigurement and, though high born, she treated everyone in the village with respect and consideration. Yadra could see similarities between Mézu and her father, Pedro Artiles. It was obvious she was the man's daughter. Twenty years had passed since Yadra last saw Pedro. She had watched her husband Doramas embrace Pedro when the men parted in the port of Gando.

"Doramas," *Don* Pedro Artiles said, "you are the fiercest warrior in all of Christendom. I give you your freedom and name you Doramas deMelilla. It is fitting you carry the name of that warlike city–for yourself and your children so the world may know here is a warrior. Now go, marry Yadra and live in peace."

Yadra found it hard to believe the young and powerful Pedro she remembered was now gone, killed by Dutch raiders. She saw some of his mannerisms in Mézu–and courage.

"*Señora* Yadra?" Mézu asked as she noticed the woman was lost in thought.

Yadra brought herself back to the present. "I am sorry, *señorita*. I was reflecting on a memory. What were you saying?"

"Could you come with me to talk with Soño? I have some money and would like to buy enough to dress properly."

"Of course," Yadra said. "We can go now. I have to order some things myself."

They stepped out onto the path and turned east, in the direction of Soño's home. The trail ran downhill and would bring them past the church. They could see someone coming up the trail. It was a man dressed in stockings, billowing trousers and a colorful jacket. Even at a distance, the women knew this man was a stranger. As the distance between the travelers closed, Yadra took Mézu's hand and squeezed.

"Say nothing," Yadra whispered.

The man stopped before them and sneered, "I am looking for the deMelilla, uh–house. Direct me to it."

"Who are you, *señor?*" Yadra said, pulling Mézu slightly behind her.

"I am Sebastian Minóso, deputy to *Don* Alguazil Cabitos y Cabrón of Santa Cruz de Tenerife. I am on my Lord's business."

"You are mistaken, *señor,*" Yadra lifted her head. "This is *Pueblo de Cuevas*, on the island of *Gran Canaria. Don* Raphael Arinaga y Suerios is Lord here."

"I know that, fool. *Don* Alguazil and I are guests at the home of *Don* Raphael Arinaga. We await that Lord's return. Even as I was departing for this place, *Don* Raphael's ship was sighted. My Lord has sent me here to find this deMelilla house. We are told *Doña* Maria Artiles is in hiding there. Now direct me to the place."

"DeMelilla is not there," Yadra said. "He has gone to Mogán."

"Did he bring the girl with him?" Minóso sneered.

"Let us go into the church there," Yadra pointed to the open door not twenty paces from where they stood. "We can ask *Padre* Tomás."

Yadra pulled Mézu behind her as she hurried into the church. Minóso sighed and followed the women into the church. *Do these peasants never do anything without asking some fool priest?* He thought.

"*Padre* Tomás," Yadra called as she and Mézu stopped at the communion rail. Women were not permitted beyond the rail. "There is a *hidalgo* (nobleman) here seeking the deMelilla home."

Father Tomás appeared from the doorway behind the pulpit, a puzzled look on his face. He had recognized Yadra's voice. Why would she be here calling to him concerning questions about her own home? He opened a gate in the altar rail and stepped out between the women and Minóso. Father Tomás glared at Minóso's enormous, feathered hat until the man removed it with a smirk.

"What business do you have with deMelilla?" Father Tomás asked.

"I have come to arrest *Doña* Maria Artiles," Minóso fanned his face with the hat. "She is the betrothed of my Lord and has run from her responsibilities. I have been told she hides at the deMelilla house."

"Indeed?" Farther Tomás seemed shocked. "Was her betrothal blessed by the Church? Was the ceremony of binding performed and prayers said?"

"No. She left the day the ties were to be made. But that is none of your business, priest," Minóso was becoming impatient. "She was bound under contract given by her father. Now tell me where she is, for I can tell you know."

"You have no authority here, *señor*," Father Tomás said. "You seek her on a civil matter. Had the ceremony of betrothal been blessed at a Mass I would be bound to help you. Only officers of *Don* Raphael Arinaga can execute a civil arrest here."

"I will go to every door until I find the place," Minóso said, forcing his hat back into place.

Mézu spoke, startling everyone. "I am Maria Artiles," she said. "No need to molest these good people."

"You take me for a fool, girl?" Minóso scoffed. "*Doña* Maria is a fine lady, not a disfigured peasant wench."

"*Doña* Maria has been granted sanctuary by me," Father Tomás said angrily. "Quit this place and return to your Lord if you value your soul. Stay and I will call the villagers to have you beaten to the border of *Pueblo de Cuevas.*"

"Father Tomás is it?" Minóso said. "I will report this to my Lord. You will answer for refusing me."

Minóso rushed from the church. He paused at the trail, seeming to contemplate continuing up to the village. Then he cursed under his breath and turned away from *Pueblo de Cuevas.*

"Mézu," Father Tomás touched her chin, turning her head until she looked into his eyes. "Tell me, as God is our witness here you did not perform the ritual of betrothal before a priest."

"I swear, Father," Mézu said, her eye never wavering from the priest. "I did not betroth myself to anyone in the sight of God."

"Then the only hold they have on you is the contract your father made," the priest said. "You cannot be made to marry the man, but you are his subject and he could force you back to Tenerife. He can keep your dowry and claim payment beyond that. You could be forced into debtor's prison, unless you enter a convent. Even then, he could dictate the terms under which you are cloistered."

Yadra and Mézu left the church and walked home without speaking. When they arrived, they met Francesca, Francina and Ignacio preparing supper. Diego had actually gone to Mogán and was not expected back until after dark. If he were very late, he would stay at the dog stone and come home in the morning. Yadra related the events at the church to the family gathered around the table and led them in prayer to the Blessed Virgin, petitioning her for direction.

"No mention was made of Ignacio," Mézu said. "Could he stay here with you? There is nothing but danger and abuse for him on Tenerife."

"He is already a son to me," Yadra said. "And you are as a daughter. God will not take you from us. We will find a way for you both to stay."

"I wish Diego were here," Mézu said as she placed her head into her hands. She sighed heavily, but did not weep.

CHAPTER 4

It was near midnight when Diego crossed the plateau above the village. He had gone to Mogán to sell two she goats. His herd needed to be culled, for the dry weather had reduced forage and he wanted the money. Mézu needed a pair of proper shoes, not some worn-out hand-me-downs. The small amount of coins Mézu had, he thought it may have amounted to a few *cuarto*, had been spent buying material to make clothes for herself and Ignacio. Diego knew she would resist accepting the shoes, but he would insist.

Mézu filled his thoughts when they were apart and overpowered his senses when he was in her company. She was highborn, no doubt, and she was a strong, capable woman. Yet he was determined to court Mézu. He dared to believe he could prove himself worthy of such a woman.

Diego's father often said that the difference between lords and peasants was a matter of attitude. Doramas took care to insure Diego's combat skills included protection from intimidation. The old man had fought in many campaigns against the Moor and Christians too, English and French heretics. He had won his freedom because of his skill as a soldier and his daring in a fight.

"Great lords dress in fancy clothes," Doramas would say, "but cut them and they will bleed. You are as fine a man as any lord, my son. Stand aside for none."

Leaving the plateau, Diego did not take the trail down toward his home. Believing it much too late to wake the household, he went directly to his place under the dog stone. The moon was up and full, nearly directly overhead as he approached the cave that had become his temporary home. He turned a corner and came into full view of the entrance to the grotto. There, he stopped in surprise. There was a light at the opening.

Not a candle nor a lamp, but a small round ball of bluish-white light. He could see around and through the light, which dimmed and brightened in a regular pulse. Nothing supported the light, nothing burned. It cast a faint glow on the ground and against the cliff face. There were no shadows, just the light. Then it began to move.

At first, Diego thought the light was coming to him, but it veered and went directly south, over the edge of the cliff above the village. The vertical smooth stone cliff was without handholds and could not be climbed or descended, even by an *Isleño*. Diego rushed to the precipice and looked down to the trail that snaked through the village a hundred feet or more below. The light moved along the trail and then disappeared.

Diego wondered what it was that he had beheld, not knowing what to believe. He had heard stories of *luces de fantasma* (ghost lights) since childhood. He had scoffed at those who claimed to have seen such a thing, now his head spun. He rubbed his eyes and returned to the grotto beneath the dog stone.

During the weeks he spent in this substitute housing he had made a few improvements. There was a bed of straw and several blankets as protection from the cold night air. He placed his haversack and cape, the *magado* still in its sheath, near the bed. Stripping off all his clothes, he slipped under the blankets and placed his short sword next to him. He was exhausted but could not sleep. *What was that light? What did it portend?* Finally he felt himself drift to sleep.

⁓

Instantly, Diego was awake. He detected movement just beyond the entrance to the grotto. He could hear footsteps. They were faint, but clear. Then a figure moved into the moonlight. It was a woman. She had a sheet draped over her head and shoulders hiding all her features except for a pair of bare feet. She paused at the entrance and pulled back the sheet. It was Mézu!

Diego raised himself to one elbow and began to speak. Mézu rushed to him and placed her fingers on his lips. She let the sheet fall to reveal she was dressed in only a chemise. The sight of her beautiful form in the moonlight made Diego gasp.

Her hand still on his lips, she pulled back his blanket and slipped in next to him. Then she pulled him close, removed her hand from his mouth and kissed him. He felt her warm, smooth skin against his.

"Shh," she said when their lips parted.

⁓

Diego woke with a start. The moon had set and Mézu was gone. How could she have left without waking him? The ghost light – Mézu – he began to wonder if he had dreamt it all. When he threw back the blanket he caught her scent and drew it in. It had been no dream. Why had she gone? He dressed hurriedly and stepped out onto the trail. To the east the sky was beginning to lighten. It would be full daylight very soon.

He descended the trail to his home only to find it vacant. The fire in the oven was smoldering and the remains of a breakfast were on the table. There were no signs of a problem, still he felt strangely alarmed as he walked briskly down the trail.

He arrived at the church as morning Mass was just concluding. He looked in through the open door and saw Mézu standing with the rest of his family. Relief poured over him and he entered the church. The villagers in attendance were not leaving. Father Tomás stood in the cramped aisle talking to Yadra and Mézu. Their expressions indicated the conversation was somber and serious, though he could not yet hear what was being said.

"Here is Diego!" Father Tomás said.

The women turned to face Diego. He looked into Mézu's eye, but he could not read her face. His sisters were standing a little to the side, Francina holding Ignacio's hand. A sense of dread filled him again.

"What is the matter, Father?" Diego said as he moved into the circle next to Mézu. He felt her take his arm. He had been afraid that last night had been a mistake, an aberration. The simple, hidden touch of Mézu's hand on his arm filled him with relief. Love was the only explanation.

"We have been given word that Mézu will be sent for," Father Tomás said. "She is to be arrested by Cabitos' men and brought to Gando."

"How can that be?" Diego asked. "*Don* Raphael is lord here. He would not arrest the daughter of Pedro Artiles."

"*Doña* Maria Artiles is not of this place," Father Tomás explained. "She is a citizen of Santa Cruz de Tenerife and subject to the rule of Cabitos. *Don* Raphael will not violate the law, even for a friend."

Mézu looked up at Diego. "Fear not for me," she said. "I shall go to a convent. Even Cabitos cannot prevent me from committing to Christ."

"Once you are in his control he may do anything he pleases," Diego said. "He could prevent you from going into a convent by accusing you of heresy. He could have you put to the question."

"But he cannot force me to marry him," Mézu said. She looked at Diego and suddenly he understood. Because she was no longer a virgin the contract with her father had been irrevocably broken. Cabitos would be forced to reject her as his bride.

"There is another way," Diego said. He looked at Mézu as he spoke to Father Tomás. "Father, Mézu could marry me, if she would have me."

"Yes," Father Tomás said, his expression brightening. "If Mézu is your wife, she will no longer be a citizen of Santa Cruz. Your people will become her people. She would, by canon law, be a citizen of *Pueblo de Cuevas*."

"I will not force Diego to marry me to save my life," Mézu said.

"Will you marry me to save my life?" Diego asked. "If men come to take you, I will fight to keep you here. If you go, I will pursue you or die."

"Look at me," Mézu said, unmindful of the several witnesses to their conversation. "How could you marry such a disfigured woman? You deserve better."

"There is no better woman for me," Diego said. "God has sent you to me and I love you."

Mézu paused for a long time, studying Diego's face. "Then I will marry you," Mézu said. She was startled by sounds of approval from the people in the church behind her. All could hear what was being said.

Yadra embraced Mézu kissing her on both cheeks. Diego's sisters embraced as well and called her "sister."

"There is one problem," Father Tomás said. "We must wait two weeks before the ceremony can be performed."

"I have known others who have married without delay," Yadra said. "If we wait, Cabitos' men will take her."

"Those marriages were hurried because the women were with child," Father Tomás whispered.

"Then say Mézu is with child," Diego suggested.

"That is something I cannot just assert to dodge the law," Father Tomás replied.

"Then I say I am with child," Mézu interrupted. "Who could deny it?"

"Will you pledge to me that you are?" Father Tomás asked. "Can you swear to it here, in God's Holy Church?"

"I will confess to you now that I may very well be," Mézu replied and held Diego's arm closer to her side.

༄

It was near midnight when the last of the wedding guests left the deMelilla home. The celebration was as impromptu as the wedding had been. When it was announced that Diego and Mézu were to be married then and there, villagers who had attended the morning Mass stayed for the wedding ceremony. Most sent for their husbands, as the morning Mass was predominately attended by the women of the village.

After the wedding, the villagers rushed home to gather wine, cakes and other treats before congregating at Yadra's home. A reception line developed with everyone congratulating the newlyweds. The villagers passed Diego, Mézu and Yadra as they entered the house, hugging and kissing each in turn in a seemingly endless stream of genuinely happy faces. Singing and laughing, people overflowed the cave onto the trail. Men built a large bonfire so the celebration could continue late into the night.

When most of the celebrants had relocated outside, Diego led Mézu deeper into the cave to his room. She had never been this far back into the cave though she knew more rooms existed.

"We will live here for a short while," Diego explained. The small oil lamp Diego carried showed a spacious room with a large bed. Pegs and shelves carved from the rock walls held clothes and other items. He looked at Mézu, the flickering light played across his face. He cleared his throat before continuing. "A week ago, I paid *Don* Raphael's clerk in Agüimes a fee for the little meadow around the dog stone. I will build a house, a strong house of stone."

"Where will you build the house?" Mézu asked, surprised by the revelation. She did not think Diego had been planning for his own home. *Where did he get the money?* He has done more than plan, he has acted, yet he had never spoken of it to her.

"I think it will do well to build the house against the grotto under the dog stone," Diego said. "It will reduce the number of walls I must raise and it will make for a strong house." He paused, studying her face. "I know I should have told this to you before, but I had no hope that you would even consider me as anything more than a friend. I could not tell you how I have grown to love you." The he looked away. "I have done you no favors, Maria Artiles. The life we have up here is hard. You will have to work the soil, grind *gofio*, and when you sleep it will be on straw mattresses on rope woven frames."

"How could you not know, Diego deMelilla?" Mézu pushed the lamp he held between them aside and pressed her soft body into him. "Your mother could tell, your sisters could see it, all of *Pueblo de Cuevas* knew I loved you. I loved you from the time I saw you at the *santuario* of the Most Blessed Virgin of the Clouds. I could not hope you would–." He stopped her words with a kiss.

༄

Mézu lay next to Diego in his room. The revelers had all gone. The house was quiet. She lifted his muscular arm and rolled into his embrace.

"Are you awake?" She asked quietly.

He nodded his head then gathered her hair with his free hand and held it to his face, drawing in her scent.

"Two years ago," She began, "there was an Englishman – actually a Scotsman I think. There is a difference. His name was George Glas." She paused for a moment and when Diego did not respond she continued. "He had attempted to establish an English port on the coast of Africa. The Grand Duke Rivero in Cádiz, *Don* Raphael's cousin, was concerned the English would use the port as a base against the Canary Islands so he had Glas arrested and brought to Santa Cruz de Tenerife. While Glas was in prison his wife and daughter came to Santa Cruz to be near him while they petitioned the Crown to release him. They stayed at Cabitos' estate and I became friends with the daughter, Faith Glas."

Mézu repositioned herself until she could see Diego's face in the dim light from the lamp near the bed. Diego had placed a small stone on the lip of the lamp until the flame it produced was tiny.

"George Glas was released by the Crown. He, his wife and Faith sailed from Santa Cruz bound for England on an English ship, the *Earl of Sandwich*. Alguazil Cabitos had spies in the English crew. The crew was told Glas had a great treasure hidden in his luggage. Before the ship reached England, the crew attempted a mutiny. They killed the ship's captain and George Glas. His wife and my friend, Faith, were thrown overboard by Cabitos' spies before honest men in the crew regained control. This was in November of 1765."

"Over a year later, I was told of the murders and Cabitos' involvement. It was on the night I was to become betrothed to Cabitos in the eyes of God – betrothed to a heartless murderer. I confronted Cabitos and when he laughed at me – when he called me a silly fool, I said I would tell the world he was a killer of children. That was when he struck me. That was the night I crossed to Gran Canaria. The next day, I met you."

There was more that she did not tell Diego, could not tell him for fear he would think her mad. She could not explain how it was Faith Glas, dripping with sea water, who came to her room that December night of 1766, the night before her betrothal was to be solemnized, and told of the horrors aboard the *Earl of Sandwich*. Mézu knew Cabitos had instigated the murders because a ghost had told her. Neither could she tell how Faith had come into her room the night before her wedding to Diego.

"Go to your man, my sister," Faith had said, sea water still dripping from her hair. "If you do not go to him tonight where he sleeps even now in the grotto beneath the dog stone, you will never see him again."

It was because of the ghost of a murdered girl that Mézu came to Diego that night in January of 1767.

℘

There was a pounding on the door. Diego opened to see several men standing on the path that led to his door. He recognized two as *Don* Raphael's soldiers, bayonets fixed to their muskets. The other two were strangers. One was dressed as a monk. The other wore fancy clothes in the latest fashion topped by a hat alive with feathers.

"*Buenos días, señores*," Diego said. "You need not pound on my door."

"Enough, fool," the man in the foppish hat snarled. "I am Sebastian Minóso, deputy to *Don* Alguazil Cabitos y Cabrón of Santa Cruz de Tenerife. I know that Maria Artiles is here and I have a warrant for her arrest." The man offered a parchment, confident that Diego could not read.

To Minóso's amazement, Diego took the document and read it.

"It says here *Don* Alguazil has ordered this lady's arrest for breach of contract," Diego said as he tossed the paper back to Minóso. "The warrant is of no authority here. *Don* Raphael is lord of this place." He could see *Don* Raphael's men stiffen with pride. They were uncomfortable with allowing these foreigners from Tenerife to order people about.

"Maria Artiles is a citizen of Santa Cruz and a subject of *Don* Alguazil," Minóso snarled. "Now turn her over or I will take her."

"You have been misinformed, *señor*," Diego said calmly. "Maria Artiles y Ventomo is my lawfully wedded wife and a citizen of this place. Your warrant is worthless."

"Stand aside," Minóso ordered and he stepped toward the open door.

Diego's hand shot out striking Minóso in the center of his chest. The man stopped as if he had struck a stone wall.

"Come against me, *señor*," Diego whispered, "and I will ruin your pretty bonnet by crushing it and the skull beneath."

"How dare you, insolent fool?" Minóso said. He turned toward *Don* Raphael's men. "Do your duty. Arrest this fool and pull him aside."

The soldiers did not move, clearly resenting Minóso. Finally one said, "Our orders were to assist in the arrest of a woman of Tenerife. Clearly, none is here."

"Right," the other said. "We need to return to our lord and ask if he desires a citizen of this village to be taken."

"Fools," Minóso was scarlet with rage. "The man lies."

"Send this monk to the church you passed on the way. Have him ask the priest. He performed the ceremony three days ago." Diego said. "He will tell you that Maria Artiles y Ventomo was married to Diego deMelilla y Tupinar in the sight of God and this entire village. Father Tomás recorded our marriage in the great book at the church in Agüimes." He looked at Minóso, "Call me a liar again and I will cut your heart out."

Minóso stepped back. "Will you cowards do nothing?" he said to the soldiers. When they did not answer, he turned to see the men were already walking down toward the church along with the monk. Minóso turned pale.

"Who is it, my husband?" Mézu said as she joined Diego at the door. He raised his elbow slightly until she could snuggle against his side.

"You!" Minóso yelled, pointing an accusing finger.

"Yes," Mézu said. "It is I, the disfigured peasant wench."

Diego's face darkened and he reached inside the doorway. When he brought his hand out again he was gripping the stone mace called a *sunta*. The sight of the *sunta* and Diego's black expression sent Minóso running down the trail to catch up with the others. His hat fell into the dust behind him and he made no effort to retrieve it.

"*Don* Raphael may summon us, but not before he has confirmed what those men will tell him about our marriage," Diego said. "The next summons will be from him and we must be prepared to answer it."

೧

The summons did come two days later. It did not come in the form of a written warrant for arrest. Instead, Father Tomás brought word that *Don* Raphael was holding general court in Agüimes. General courts were conducted from time to time. Civil suits, criminal trials and religious inquisitions were all held on the same day, usually a Wednesday. Accused, plaintiffs and witnesses alike, when addressing the court, would stand within a square formed by four twenty-foot long timbers laid out, one to a side and centered before a great platform. *Don* Raphael and other lords and ladies would be seated on the platform, as if at the theater to hear arguments and pronounce judgments.

Diego and Mézu began the long walk down to Agüimes before dawn on the day they were to appear in the *cuatro maderas* (four timbers). By the time the sun had risen they had been joined by nearly everyone from the village. They crowded into the narrow streets of the town forcing travelers to stand in doorways to let them pass. Diego led the way with Mézu holding his left elbow and walking slightly behind him, as was the custom for married couples. Diego wore his cape over his cotton shirt and short trousers with woolen gaiters over heavy shoes. The *magado* rode in its sheath and the *sunta* was tucked in his belt. He wore his short sword as well.

Mézu wore a simple cotton blouse under a leather vest and a pleated skirt of alternating red, blue and white stripes. Her veil was the one Diego had given her on the day they met and was held in place by a wide-brimmed black hat with a flat crown, sporting a brass buckle in front. She had a fine pair of shoes made of cow's leather, though she preferred the soft leather slippers Diego had made for her.

When they reached the court the people of the village formed around the side of the timbers opposite the platform. After a wait of no more than an hour, a man walked out from behind a curtain on the platform and announced, *"Don* Geronimo Cuebelo de Morina and *Doña* Maria Antonia de Morina." A lord and his wife entered onto the platform and took their seats near the back. This was repeated for this lord and that, until the benches on the platform were nearly filled.

Then the herald announced, *"Don* Alguazil Cabitos y Cabrón of Santa Cruz de Tenerife and *Doña* Melchora Cabral."

Diego watched as a thin, dark, tall man in a powdered wig, dressed in silks, ribbons and comically pointed shoes with polished brass buckles walked to the front of the platform. A rapier in a fine scabbard was at his left side and a sheathed dagger at this right. He was about twenty-five years old and accompanied by a woman in a blue gown cut so low it appeared as if her breasts rode on a tray. Diego's eyes narrowed with hate. There was the man who had struck out Mézu's eye and now sought to take her from him.

"Who is the woman?" Diego asked of Mézu through clenched teeth.

"One of his mistresses," she replied. "He has several, all well paid."

"Barón Raphael Arinaga y Suerios, *Regidore* of Gando and Agüimes and *Baróness* Sevestiana Morales y Denente," the herald boomed.

Don Raphael and his wife proceeded to the front of the platform. He was a muscular man and, though forty-five years old, clearly vigorous and active. His wife was about ten years the man's junior, stunningly beautiful and dressed in blue. Her gown was covered in sequins and she wore a long, silk veil supported by a silver comb. The veil was pulled away from her face and cascaded down both shoulders. After the baron and baroness took their places, there were only two seats left on the platform.

"Grand Duke Rivero y Zerpas de Cádiz and Duchess Maria Collado y Villavicencio de Cádiz," the herald bellowed. The Grand Duke was only slightly older than *Don* Raphael, but portly and shorter. He had returned with *Don* Raphael from Cádiz for a visit. The trials today were to be a demonstration of *Don* Raphael's reign.

The herald stepped to the front of the platform. "Now *Barón* Raphael Arinaga, Lord of Gando and Agüimes, says to all who have come to seek justice – stand before *Barón* Arinaga and be heard."

"I beg to be heard," Cabitos announced as he stood.

"Come within the *cuatro maderas*, *señor*, and be heard," said the herald.

Cabitos walked to the rear of the platform and descended steps that were hidden behind some curtains. He stepped into the square of timbers, faced the platform and, with a sweep of his plumed hat, bowed. He straightened to his full height and addressed the platform. His voice was high pitched, almost feminine.

"Grand Duke Rivero," he nodded at the Grand Duke who retuned the gesture. "And *Barón* Arinaga," he continued with another courtly nod, "I come to beg for justice. I have been defrauded, a contract has been broken and the miscreant refuses to recognize my authority over her. Return to me she who is, by solemn contract, betrothed to me."

"Do you, *señor* Cabitos," *Don* Raphael rose to speak, "intend to marry this woman?"

"No, my Lord," Cabitos fanned his face with his hat, "She has lain with another. I intend to have her imprisoned for her violation of betrothal and then sent to a convent for the rest of her life. She has insulted me beyond repair."

"Name this woman to the court," *Don* Raphael said.

"Her name is Maria Artiles y Ventomo," Cabitos sneered and then turned to face Mézu and Diego.

Don Raphael leaned to whisper in his wife's ear. *Baróness* Sevestiana Morales placed her fan before her lips and the two conversed intently for more than a minute. Finally, when the Grand Duke moved to join the discussion, *Don* Raphael called the herald over, whispered a few instructions and the herald moved to the center of the platform.

"Maria Artiles y Ventomo," the herald ordered. "Come now into the square."

Cabitos moved toward one side of the square, his face painted with a gloating smile.

CHAPTER 5

*D*on Raphael looked at the crowd of peasants that had gathered on the far side of the timber square. All the men, except for one, stood with their hats in their hands and their heads bowed. The women were dressed in long dresses, full length veils, leather or wool vests and black hats, obviously poor peasants from the mountains. The man who had not removed his hat, a large man, stepped forward into the square. A woman with a leather patch covering her left eye stepped forward with him. The man removed his hat and, with a sweep of his left arm protectively moved the woman until she was slightly behind him. *Don* Raphael did not recognize either person, though the man reminded him of someone.

"The herald has called for Maria Artiles," *Don* Raphael said, glaring down at the man. "Who are you?"

"I am Diego deMelilla y Tupinar, my lord," the man said. "Maria Artiles y Ventomo is my lawfully wedded wife. Send for the church records, my Lord. We are enrolled as required by the law."

"Diego deMelilla!" *Don* Raphael exclaimed. "Are you related to Doramas deMelilla?"

"I am, my *Barón*, the son of Doramas."

Don Raphael turned and went to his wife, gesturing for the Grand Duke and *Don* Geronimo Cuebelo to joint them. The four talked, this time loudly enough for some to hear. "Can this be true?" *Don* Raphael was incredulous. "First the daughter of *Don* Pedro Artiles, a peer and a man to whom I am greatly in debt for his service against the Moor, is brought before us on charges of infidelity. Now we discover she claims to be married to the son of Doramas deMelilla, the greatest warrior I have ever known and the man who personally rescued the *Baróness* Sevestiana Morales and saved my life. I see the hand of God at work here. *Don* Geronimo, send for the book of marriages, please. And ask the Bishop to come, if he is there."

Don Geronimo hurried off the platform. The church was less than a block away. He would arrive at the church to find Father Tomás and Bishop Plazencia patiently waiting, marriage book at hand, having anticipated being summoned to the square.

"Question Cabitos further," the Grand Duke said. "Ask for proof. If she has broken a betrothal blessed by the Church, her crime must be punished, daughter of a friend or not."

Don Raphael returned to the front of the platform. "Show us the record of the betrothal ceremony, *señor* Cabitos," he said.

Cabitos' expression changed. "*Barón*, I have not explained the situation well. The betrothal was a contract I entered into with *Don* Pedro Artiles before his death. The formal act of betrothal before the altar of God was to have been performed the day this woman fled my jurisdiction."

"*Señor* Cabitos," the Grand Duke intervened. "Then you are entitled to keep the dowry. The law grants no other relief."

"When she fled she took with her a jewel of great value stolen from me, Most Excellent Lord," Cabitos said. "That jewel alone is worth more than the token dowry. The marriage, if these – people – continue to pretend there was one, was in haste and not according to the custom."

"Cabitos lies, Most Excellent Lord," Diego said, addressing the Grand Duke. "Maria Artiles arrived at *Pueblo de Cuevas* with less than two *pesos* in her possession. She had been wounded by a cowardly villain and it was only by the grace of God she has survived. I tell all here – the cowardly villain that struck out the eye of Maria Artiles was Alguazil Cabitos."

The collection of nobles on the platform gasped. A man, obviously a peasant, had accused a peer of cowardice and a crime, but worse, he had used the name of a *Ricohombre* without deference. Many on the platform believed commoners had grown insolent. Since the English uprising nearly a hundred years ago, when Protestant heretics had beheaded their king, the peasants across Europe have grown bolder. They had even begun to address one another as *"señor* and *señora"* when such titles should be reserved for nobles. Now here stood a goatherd openly disrespectful of a titled Lord.

"I demand this man be silenced!" Cabitos shouted. "I will not be accused or insulted by a peasant – a herder of goats from a village of caves."

Don Raphael stepped to the rail across the front of the platform. Mindful of the need to regain control of the inquiry, he looked over to Mézu. "Maria Artiles. Are you the daughter of *Don* Pedro Artiles y Fuentez de Roche?"

Mézu stepped forward and answered in a strong voice, "I am, *Don* Raphael." Even in this formal setting she had the right to address the Baron as *Don* Raphael instead of *Barón* Arinaga because her father's rank, therefore her rank, was the equal of a Baron.

"*Doña* Maria," *Don* Raphael continued. "Were you betrothed of *señor* Cabitos before the altar of God?"

"No, *Don* Raphael,"

"Did you take a jewel of any value from the house of *señor* Cabitos?"

"No, *Don* Raphael."

"Was it *señor* Cabitos who struck out your eye?"

"Yes, *Don* Raphael."

"*Barón* Arinaga," Cabitos scoffed, "how could you even listen to the lies from these peasants?"

"*Señor* Cabitos," *Don* Raphael spoke slowly, deliberately. "*Don* Pedro Artiles, this lady's father, was *cristanos viejos* (old Christian, meaning his lineage could be traced back to service under King Ferdinand and Queen Isabella) and a lord greatly respected by all who knew him."

"True," Cabitos said. "I knew him well. But his daughter did not inherit the man's honor. Her mother was, after all, Guanche – a corrupting influence, I do not doubt."

Don Raphael's face darkened and his wife hid her face behind her fan.

"I should advise you, *señor*," the Grand Duke interjected. "*Don* Raphael's mother was also a Guanche."

Cabitos was silent. Yet, if he could appeal to canon law, he might yet win his case. "My apologies, *Barón* Raphael Arinaga – my passions in being betrayed and robbed have overcome my decorum. Please forgive me."

Don Geronimo appeared at the platform with Bishop Plazencia and Father Tomás. He escorted the Bishop and the marriage book to the front.

"Bishop Plazencia," *Don* Raphael continued to glare at Cabitos. "Does the name Maria Artiles y Ventomo appear in the marriage book?"

"My lord," Plazencia turned toward the square and spoke in a voice intended to carry to the crowd, "it is recorded here that Maria Artiles y Ventomo was married to Diego deMelilla y Tupinar on the twenty-third day of January in the year of Our Lord 1767. Father Tomás performed the rites. He is here if you wish to question him."

"Tell me further, Bishop," *Don* Raphael continued, "if the marriage had been in haste, without the customary waiting period, is it invalid."

"No, my lord," Plazencia laughed, "Only if one of the parties were already married would this union be invalid."

"You have your answer concerning the marriage, *Señor* Cabitos," *Don* Raphael said.

"There remains the theft, *Barón*," Cabitos turned to face the peasants gathered beyond the square, "I insist the jewel, a diamond, be returned to me. If it is not returned, you are compelled to send Maria Artiles in chains to Tenerife."

Diego took Maria by the elbow and walked with her back to where Yadra and his sisters stood. "Please stand with mother, Mézu," he said. "Trust in me." He returned to the center of the square. "*Barón* Raphael

Arinaga," he said, "the man Cabitos is a liar and a coward. Let the question be put to the test."

"I will not stand for this," Cabitos shouted. "I demand satisfaction. I would chastise this peasant, but one does not duel with commoners."

"*Señor* Cabitos," Bishop Plazencia announced, "the question has been presented. This will not simply be a duel between men; it will be a test before God. Victory will be granted to the honest man."

"No!" Mézu called out. "Please, my husband, do not do this." She knew of Cabitos' reputation with the rapier and dagger.

"It has been decided," *Don* Raphael said, holding up his arms. "God has sent these men into the square and they shall test the question with the weapons they have with them."

This pleased Cabitos. He was carrying a rapier and a dagger and he considered himself among the best in the use of these two weapons, having won numerous duels against skilled opponents. His confidence was bolstered when he saw that Diego appeared to be armed with only a short sword and a staff he carried on his back. Cabitos walked to the southern edge of the square and removed his cape and hat. He drew his rapier with his right hand and removed the belt holding the scabbard, tossing it aside so that he would not be encumbered by it. He pulled his dagger from his belt with his left and turned to salute the platform. "Let this be to the death," he said. "I am ready, *Barón*."

Diego walked to the north side of the square and withdrew the *magado* from its sheath in his cape. He removed the cape and tossed it to the ground. Though he did not show it, Cabitos was disconcerted when he realized Diego had been carrying a lance in the sheath on his back, not a staff. The weapon looked well-worn and sported a long, narrow steel blade ending in a needle-like point. Diego pulled another weapon from his belt that had been hidden by his cape. It was a stone-tipped mace. He put his right arm through a leather loop on the handle of the *sunta* so it would hang at his elbow. A slight drop of the hand would allow the handle of the *sunta* to fall into his palm, ready to be used. He discarded the short sword for it was no match for a rapier. He gripped the *magado* with both hands. His right hand was about a foot from the butt and his left about two feet above his right. He took a deep breath and said, "I am ready, *Barón*."

"Begin," *Don* Raphael said.

Cabitos rushed forward, the thin blade of the rapier pointed directly at Diego's face and nearly invisible to him. Diego parried the point and, when Cabitos flicked the blade in a small circle to avoid the parry, Diego brought the point of the *magado* up slightly, stopping the rapier and, slapping the point aside, reposting quickly. Cabitos avoided the repost and fell back, circling the rapier to catch the shaft of the *magado* if Diego were to continue forward.

Both weapons were designed to stab, not slash or cut. The rapier was quicker, lighter but the *magado* was of a greater length. Diego's exceptional strength enabled him to react as quickly with the heavier weapon as if it were a rapier. Unlike the flexible blade of the rapier, parries with the wooden shafted *magado* were solid, unyielding, no matter how vigorous Cabitos' attempts at engagement and thrust.

Cabitos began to circle toward Diego's right hoping to gain an advantage by trapping the butt of the *magado* against Diego's side. Cabitos feigned to his left then spun to his right. He attempted to get past the razor sharp head of the *magado*, but Diego, deftly stepping aside, struck Cabitos on the temple with the shaft just below the steel tip. Had Cabitos been a few inches further away, his throat would have been cut. Cabitos began to feel fear. *No man with a spear can defeat a rapier and dagger*, he thought. He stepped back to wipe his brow and stole a look at the platform. *Don* Raphael was smiling.

Each attack by Cabitos was met with a parry and a lighting quick repost. Cabitos began to panic. In desperation he stooped low, then rose and, leading with his dagger, pushed up on the *magado* and slipped past the tip and lunged with the rapier. Diego reacted quickly, but Cabitos had inadvertently rotated the blade of the rapier until the cutting edges were vertical. The edges of a rapier are held horizontally so the flat blade will slip between the opponent's ribs. Because the rapier had been turned until the edges were vertical, the blade whipped around Diego's parry and caught the billowing front of Diego's shirt.

Diego had twisted away and it should have been enough to avoid the thrust but, redirected by the shirt, the rapier' tip deflected and plunged into Diego's side, the blade scraping across his ribs. Cabitos felt the rapier cut into Diego's flesh and lunged forward until the hilt struck. All he need do now was stab with his dagger and Diego would be dead.

When the hilt stuck his side Diego grabbed it with his left hand and held it against him. Instead of stepping back, Diego stepped forward, twisted to his right and, using only his right hand, brought the tip of the *magado* to Cabitos' chest. This prevented Cabitos from stabbing with the dagger and, because Diego held the hilt, Cabitos had to release the rapier or be stabbed to death. Cabitos jumped back and retreated to the far edge of the square, dagger at the ready, to watch Diego. Cabitos had driven the rapier through the man. The hilt was against Diego's side and blood flowed down his shirt to stain his trousers. Cabitos need only wait until shock and the loss of blood brought the big man down.

Diego straightened up and shifted the *magado* to his left hand. He stabbed the butt of the *magado* on the ground to support himself. Diego wavered a little and grasped the rapier with his right hand. He slowly drew it out of his side as if he were drawing it from a scabbard, looked at Cabitos and laughed. Diego hefted the *magado* with his left hand, tucked the shaft under his arm and leveled it at Cabitos. He held the rapier in his right and pointed it at Cabitos. Diego gave a great shout and rushed at the stunned man.

The sight of Diego pulling a rapier from his side had unnerved Cabitos and the sudden rush completely panicked him. He dropped the dagger and stumbled out of the square, crawling on his hands and knees to the edge of the platform to escape. Diego stopped at the timber marking the limit of the square and watched Cabitos disappear behind the curtains that decorated the platform. He returned to the center of the square and faced the shocked royalty on the platform.

"Maria Artiles is my wife. She came to me with nothing belonging to another. Is there any man here who disputes this?" Diego shouted.

"The question has been put to the test," Bishop Plazencia decreed. "*Señor* Cabitos has been found to have lied."

The people of the village rushed into the square. Mézu immediately examined Diego's wound, tears streaming down her right cheek.

"The blade simply scraped along my ribs, wife," Diego said. "It will heal."

"The blood is bright, not dark," Yadra observed. "The bleeding is even now beginning to abate. Let us get him home and attend to it."

"Not yet," Diego said. He gave the rapier to Mézu and walked over to where Cabitos had dropped his dagger and picked it up as well. He returned to Mézu. "Here," he said, "this dagger is for you. Wear it in your belt. Never go without it. I will instruct you in its use."

"Silence," the herald's voice quieted the people. "Hear the *Barón* Arinaga."

Don Raphael held up his arms until all were looking at him. "*Doña* Maria Artiles y Ventomo, wife of Diego deMelilla y Tupinar, you are free to go."

The crowd resumed their celebration of Diego's victory and Mézu's exoneration. Villagers surrounded the couple in a congratulatory mob laughing, shouting people.

Cabitos climbed the steps at the rear of the platform and inched toward *Don* Raphael. The herald alerted *Don* Raphael to Cabitos' appearance. Others on the platform pretended not to see Cabitos, for the man had embarrassed them all.

"What do you have to say for yourself, Cabitos?" *Don* Raphael whispered when he reached Cabitos. The significance of the absence of "*señor*" or "*Don*" in the Baron's address was not lost on Cabitos.

"*Barón*," Cabitos had found his voice. "I humbly submit to the verdict of this court. Who could have stood against a madman? But, I beg you. Please have the rapier returned to me. It has been in my family for a hundred years."

"Then, you should have not released it," *Don* Raphael said.

"My lord, Please. Do not allow my temporary weakness to take such an heirloom from my family," Cabitos bowed.

Don Raphael turned his back on Cabitos and walked to the edge of the platform. Diego and Mézu were still in the square amidst their celebrating friends. Again the herald called for silence. "Diego deMelilla," *Don* Raphael began. "Alguazil Cabitos y Cabrón of Santa Cruz de Tenerife begs that the rapier be returned to him, for the sake of his family. What say you, deMelilla?" *Don* Raphael was clearly amused.

"The weapon is not mine, my *Barón*," Diego said. "I gave it to my wife."

"*Doña* Maria," *Don* Raphael turned toward Mézu, "What say you? Will you return the weapon?"

"*Don* Raphael, I am responsible to my family to use our valuables wisely," Mézu said.

Don Raphael knew it was the custom in *Pueblo de Cuevas* that the women of the household controlled the finances. The men were too occupied with other matters to be distracted by what little money any of them had. "Would you sell it to Cabitos?" he asked.

"No, *Don* Raphael."

"Will you sell it to me?"

"Yes, *Don* Raphael," she said with a curtsy.

"And if I should then sell it to Cabitos?"

"*Don* Raphael," Mézu smiled, "If I should sell it to you, then it is yours to do with as you see fit."

"How much, then?"

"I have heard Cabitos brag that this rapier was worth a thousand *escudos*," Mézu said. "I am certain that was a lie. I think one hundred *escudos* would do."

She had quoted a price that was fair for the blade. It was made of excellent Toledo steel and had a jewel in the pummel that was alone worth that sum.

"Done!" *Don* Raphael said.

"Husband," Mézu said. "We have now enough to build our house. May we go now and tend to your wound?"

Diego looked up at the platform. They could not go without permission. *Don* Raphael waved them away. "Go Diego deMelilla," he said. "I can see that your father has taught you well."

∽

Melchora Cabral sipped at the cup of wine. She looked across the lip of the goblet with her dark, sparkling eyes. "Come, my dear," she said. "We shall soon be home and this whole affair behind us."

"Behind us?" Cabitos roared. "It will never be behind me." He leapt from the cot causing Melchora to spill the dark wine on her breasts.

"Do take care, my love," she chided. "This is excellent wine."

Cabitos grunted and walked to the bank of windows across the rear of the ship. They were returning to Tenerife and Cabitos had put the captain out of his cabin. The windows offered a beautiful view of the wake of the ship and the wine-dark sea that rolled beneath.

"Banned," he muttered. "I have been banned from Gran Canaria and Cádiz."

"What of it, my dear?" Melchora asked, always the pragmatist. "You still rule Santa Cruz de Tenerife and you have taken all of that woman's inheritance."

"I have it now," Cabitos placed a supporting hand against a window frame. He was a little drunk. "If the Grand Duke or even Arinaga were to decide it, they could go to the King and I would find myself in Mexico swatting little flies."

"I will swat them for you," she lied.

"*Mierda,*" Cabitos said.

CHAPTER 6

"You there," the clerk shouted from the edge of a doorway. "The King has an offer to make to you." A wide desk was spread across the entrance to a pub. It had been recessed from the open doorway enough to provide a path for the customers to come and go. The pine surface of the desk was littered with papers, three ledger books and two small leather sacks that clearly bulged with coins.

Diego looked around him. Everyone seemed to be scurrying along the stone-paved road. The sun was directly overhead and beat against the stone walls of the continuous row of shops, warehouses, and pubs that lined the west side of the road. The east side of the road was bordered by docks, slips and piers that jutted out into the harbor of Gando. A few awnings had been spread to keep the July heat from windows and doors. Wagons, carts, and sleds laden with every manner of goods were being pulled along the road by an assortment of horses, mules, oxen and men. He dared not stop in the middle of the road amongst such traffic, so Diego stepped to the doorway.

"How is it you claim to speak in the name of the King?" Diego asked.

The clerk, sensing he had a possible recruit, hurried around the desk and walked up to Diego, a ledger book in his hand.

"The King has declared an army regiment be raised for the New World. It will be the Fixed Infantry Regiment of Louisiana," the clerk said as he leafed through the ledger until he reached a page with the words "18 July 1778" written across the top. "You will be paid forty-five *reals* when you sign and another forty-five when the ship arrives at Louisiana. Until then, you will be paid eight *reals* a day until you board the ship. Think of it, a silver *real de a ocho* each day you must wait."

Diego laughed, "I am a married man with a family. I am not free to join the army."

"Even better!" the clerk exclaimed. "The King wants settlers. Men with families will be given a house, two horses and supplies when they reach Louisiana."

Diego shook his head, "No, friend. I have just sold several goats to ships' captains so the crews may have fresh milk at sea." He started to walk away.

"Wait, friend." The clerk could see his signing bonus evaporating. Diego was very tall, nearly six foot, and muscular. The top bonus, forty-five *reals*, was awarded to the man who could sign a recruit over five feet-three inches tall. "The first ship sails on the twenty-sixth of this month. There will be other ships throughout the year. Talk to your wife. Talk to your children. Land, rich farmland, free from drought, can be yours along with a house, tools and two – two horses. Think of it, man, and then come see me. I will be here until December. Ask for Someruelos."

Diego stepped back into the stream of commerce flowing along the dock front and was instantly carried along until he reached a side street where he extricated himself. The side street led up and away from the waterfront, ascending a steep, narrow stone road between solid walls made of blocks cut from volcanic stone. A gutter, laden with foul wastes, traversed the center of the narrow road forcing Diego to walk near a wall. It had not rained for over two months and only the steepness of the grade and urine from chamber pots moved the contents of the gutter down toward the sea.

Wooden doorways were set into the walls at random locations as were shuttered windows. Higher along the wall, balconies made of the dark Canary Island pine jutted out over the road. Diaphanous curtains in the upper open doorways blew out across the intricately patterned rails of the balconies or were sucked into the building's interior by the breeze that rushed inland from the sea. Diego knew that each door along the road was an entrance to a wide patio filled with a garden and surrounded by a high veranda encircling a courtyard. Windows and doors populated the wall-side of the gallery, opening into the upper rooms of each home. The balconies with their open doors allowed a cooling sea-breeze to flow through the upper rooms across the verandas and down onto the gardens.

The homes and shops of the town folk of Gando were no different than those of Agüimes, the next town Diego would travel through on his way home. Gando, Agüimes and the many other towns scattered along the coast of Gran Canaria with their plastered stone walls, red roofs and balconies could have been mistaken for villages on the Mediterranean coast of Spain or Italy or Greece. He climbed the steep roads between volcanic block walls beneath baked tile roofs of Gando and out into a narrow, winding trail through terraced fields, palm trees and farm buildings. Two miles inland and still climbing slightly, he crossed into Agüimes. The last building he passed on his way out of the village was a distillery that produced wine and *arrack*, a rum-like spirit, from *guarapo*, the sap of palm trees.

The trail Diego walked became steeper and bordered not by walls but cliffs of jumbled stone or volcanic flows frozen into distorted layers. The few plateaus he passed were crowded with palms, each neatly trimmed to facilitate access to the crown where the sap was collected. Seven more miles of mild grade and a half mile of a steep climb were all that separated him from his home above the *Pueblo de Cuevas*. He was without his long herder's staff for he had led the female goats down to the docks on a string. Lacking the *lanza*, he was confined to the well-traveled trail. Otherwise, he would have ascended the side grade to the less circuitous ridgeline and reduced the three hour trip remaining to two.

Diego could see a small cluster of travelers coming down toward him. Another problem with being confined to the common trail was the likelihood of meeting others. Travelers, particularly those from the same village, were expected to stop and chat. Diego did not want any delays on this trip. This was the first time he had been away from home since Mézu had miscarried. The lost baby would have been their third and it had happened early in the term, but still Mézu grieved the loss. Pedro, their son, was now ten years old and big enough to help with the chores while little Maria was seven. Both children were healthy, bright and delightful. Little Maria in particular sensed her mother's sadness and, with some success, did all she could to comfort Mézu.

Ignacio was now a man of eighteen and had taken up residence in the village of caves. He had married in June and was beginning to learn the trade of a leather worker, apprentice to his father-in-law who had no sons. Although the house Diego had built was only slightly removed from the village, it was the only dwelling on the small meadow. They were not quite isolated, but their family had shrunk to Mézu, the children and him and no near neighbors. Diego wanted to be home.

"*Hola*, Diego," someone called out from the cluster of traveler's coming down the trail. Diego recognized Father Tomás' voice and knew he was in for an extended conversation.

"Good evening, Father," Diego responded. "Are you going to Agüimes now? It is late and you will have to come back in the dark if there is to be a morning Mass."

Father Tomás stopped and uncharacteristically urged the villagers with him to continue on. As the others passed out of hearing he took Diego by an elbow and lowered his voce. "*Don* Raphael is quite ill," he said. "The Baroness has been conducting the day-to-day affairs, but it cannot last. There will be a High Mass to petition the Lord God to grant the *Don* a return to health and every priest in the district will be there, but I fear he will not live much longer."

"I must take my leave of you, Father," Diego said.

"I understand, Diego," Father Tomás shouted toward Diego, who was now running up the trail.

ⲟⲟ

Mézu was grinding grain at the stone bench Diego had made near the front of their house. She looked up to see Diego walking briskly toward her. She smiled and straightened up from her labors. The sight of Diego always comforted Mézu. Perhaps it was his confident demeanor and handsome, rugged face. He was strong, competent and a good provider. Maybe it was because a serene feeling of safety filled her when she was with him. More likely, she thought, it was the fact that he loved her so deeply. All in the village could see it, knew it. Why he did was a mystery to her. *Mézu*, she said to herself, *enough with grieving. Your family needs you, Diego needs you.*

"How was your trip into Gando?" Mézu asked in a way of greeting. "Did you get a good price?"

Diego reached out and pulled Mézu to him. He removed her hat and kissed her forehead. "Yes, a very good price," he said. Then he held her closer, wrapping his powerful arms gently around her.

"What is the matter?" Mézu knew something was wrong.

"*Don* Raphael is very ill," he said. "He may die."

Don Raphael had barred Cabitos from the district and prevented any acts of revenge against Diego or Mézu. There had been attempts, but *Don* Raphael's network of informants had alerted the Baron and he was able to thwart every effort by Cabitos until an edict issued by the Grand Duke arrived at Santa Cruz de Tenerife. "Alguazil Cabitos y Cabrón will be removed as *Regidore* and deposed of all his possessions should harm befall Diego deMelilla or Maria Artiles," the dispatch said. "Should Diego or Maria so much as suffer an accident, this penalty will be imposed." That was ten years ago and they had lived in peace ever since.

"The Grand Duke is now in Mexico. Should *Don* Raphael die, only the Baroness will be able to restrain Cabitos," Diego said. "Soon, the

King will appoint another as *Regidore* at Gando and even the Baroness will not be able to help."

"Cabitos must have forgotten us by now, husband," Mézu said. "It has been ten years. We have children." Even as she said it, she knew it was not so. The humiliation Cabitos suffered had nearly driven the man mad. For over a year, he would instigate quarrels over trivial and often imaginary slights until men were reluctant to be in his presence. The duels he fought usually ended at first blood, but two had ended in death. After he married *Doña* Beatris Solier de Malaga, a rich widow from Spain, he had grown less combative. Yet would the death of *Don* Raphael cause the vengeful Cabitos to act?

"I will have friends in Agaete and Mogán watch for people coming from Tenerife," Diego said. "Cabitos dare not act until a new lord is appointed. The Baroness will inform the new *Regidore* and perhaps our protection will be renewed. If not, we must be ready to act."

"What action could we take?" Mézu asked. "He may send many against us, or accuse us of heresy, even instigate an *auto da fé* as he did against Melchora Cabral when he grew tired of her." Melchora Cabral was pulled before a Court of Inquisition because Cabitos wanted to rid himself of her, and she knew too much of his private affairs to be sent away. She was put to the question, confessed almost immediately, repented convincingly and sentenced to life in a convent where she had to learn to write with her left hand. The questioning had ruined her right.

"Then we must leave this place if we lose the protection of the *Regidore*," Diego said. He tried to sound as if such a move was a simple thing. "The King has asked for settlers for Louisiana. Once away from the Canary Islands, we would be subjects of the Viceroy of Mexico."

"I learned today that Domingo Antonio and Francesca Mauricio are even now waiting to leave for Louisiana on the *Sacremento*," Mézu said. "Also Juan Gonzales and Andrea Ruiz left for Gando yesterday. They will go on the *Sacremento* too, I think. The drought has driven many down to the towns."

"Juan and Andrea!" Diego exclaimed. "They have eight children." The folk Mézu mentioned were of the poorest in *Pueblo de Cuevas*. The drought would have driven them to starvation had not their neighbors provided food and drink.

"Nine," Mézu corrected. "How can we leave this house? Our farm and your flock, it is not much, but it is all we have."

"That is the advantage to being poor, dear wife," Diego laughed. "We can flee with all we own and not be heavily burdened." His smile faded. "Keep a canvas haversack filled with dried meats and biscuits by the door along with two skins of wine. Pedro and Maria will stay near the house. Be ready to leave at a moment's notice until we know who will be *Regidore.*"

"Put those thoughts aside. It is time for supper, my husband," Mézu said and she led Diego by the hand to their house. "Call Pedro," she said when she opened the door. "He is about somewhere adventuring. Maria is in the house, preparing our table."

Diego turned toward the west and whistled a series of shrill notes and waited. A distant answering call assured him that Pedro had heard his father and was on his way home. He followed Mézu into their house, ducking as he entered. Little Maria had set the table with wooden bowls and spoons. Maria was stirring the contents of a cast iron pot and looked back at her father. She had the same haunting grey eyes of her mother. The pot was suspended over a fire and the house was filled with the smell of vegetable stew.

"The pot is too heavy for me, Papa," Maria said as she swung the iron bar holding the pot away from the fire.

Diego lifted the pot then carried it to each place and waited as Maria ladled a serving into each bowl. Mézu passed her fingers through the child's hair as she was being served and kissed her cheek when the girl proudly looked up at her. A scuffle at the door announced Pedro's arrival. The noise was caused by the boy leaning his miniature *lanza* against the house next to his father's. Once they were all seated, Mézu recited the blessing, crossed herself and looked at her family. Everyone was watching her expectantly.

"I am feeling much better," she laughed. "Eat before your meal grows cold."

The children brightened. Their mother's sadness had worried them, but now she seemed to be herself again. Mézu reached across the small table to squeeze Diego's hand, his touch reassuring her that all would be well.

⁖

Don Raphael suffered for three months before he died. The Baroness was able to arrange her affairs, for she planned to return to Cádiz to live with her son and daughter-in-law. The King had not yet appointed a new *Regidore* and who that would be had not been decided by the last week of November. Diego had sold much of his flock, converting his assets to coin and he busied himself with chores around the house, not wanting to go down to the towns until more was known. He was spreading plaster on a wall where it met the cliff face when he saw a young boy running toward him.

"Are you Diego deMelilla?" the boy asked when he reached the house. Diego did not recognize him, but he looked as if he were from Agaete, for he came from the west, wore long trousers and shoes. None of the boys from Mogán, the only other town of significance to the west, could have afforded shoes.

"I am," Diego said. He put his bucket of plaster down and wiped his hands on his shirt.

"My father says to tell you that eight men came by boat to Agaete. One was a lord and one had a musket. My father thinks they are from Tenerife."

"What is your name?" Diego looked westward. It was early morning, which meant the boy had run from Agaete in the dark.

"Gabriel Gil, señor," the boy said.

Diego laughed at the irony of Gabriel bringing such a message. He knew who the boy was now. Miguel Gil was a craftsman in Agaete who had made a fine pair of boots, worth several *escudos*, for Cabitos on Tenerife. When he sent the boots to Cabitos, the man cheated him by claiming the boots were inferior, though he wore them often, and refused to pay. The opportunity for revenge and a few coins were enough to enlist Gil as a spy in Agaete.

"Gabriel, I thank you," he said. "Come with me." Diego brought Gabriel to the door and opened it. Mézu looked up from her mixing bowl. "This is Gabriel Gil from Agaete," Diego said. "He has traveled hard. Give him some refreshment and then send him to Ignacio's place to rest."

Diego strapped on his short sword and tucked the *sunta* in his belt. He donned his cape, the *magado* in its sheath, but left his hat on its hook by the door. "I will be back in a little while. I need to go west as far as the *santuario* of the Most Blessed Virgin of the Clouds." As he spoke he looked toward Mézu and noticed she was slipping a narrow dagger, the one taken from Cabitos, into her belt. She returned his gaze, her grey eye and expression was one of determination and defiance, not fear.

"I will send Pedro up onto the dog stone," she said. Pedro could communicate using the whistle words, Mézu could not. Diego had not told Mézu that Gabriel carried a message, but she knew. "We will be ready," she said as she kissed him at the door.

Diego took his long *lanza* from its place next to the door. There were no goats to shepherd, but there may be a need to move across the steep slopes that bracketed the trail to Agaete. He heard the door close behind him as he jogged across the relatively flat plateau toward the west. There was a place on the way to the *santuario* where the trail narrowed called *punto de cuchillo* (knife point). Two men could not walk abreast for a distance of a dozen feet or so and the trail turned sharply around the stone cliff providing cover and concealment from people coming from the west. On the north side, a solid stone cliff rose nearly vertically for ten feet where it became a precipitous slope of broken stones for another twenty feet to the ridge line. On the south, the solid smooth stone slope continued for a hundred feet before ending in jagged stone rubble.

Diego reached *punto de cuchillo* without encountering anyone coming from the west. Gabriel has reached him in time. He stopped at the corner of the sharp turn and listened. He could not hear anything so he moved further along until he could see the trail for a half-mile west. The trail ran along the edge of the slope before pitching down to the bottom of the draw. Eight men were coming up in single file. One was dressed in courtier's garb. He wore a fancy, feathered wide-brimmed blue hat, tight stockings, blossomed trousers, a bejeweled jacket and carried a musket. Diego recognized him at once. It was Cabitos' lackey, *Don* Sebastian Minóso.

Three men dressed in simple white jackets over cotton shirts and trousers preceded Minóso. Minóso and the three in the lead carried sheathed rapiers on their right sides and, no doubt, daggers at their left. Four unarmed men trailed the rest. They carried what appeared to be chains and staffs, perhaps yokes.

Diego took a breath and stepped out into the open. "Minóso," he yelled, "run back to the crawler or die here." Cabitos had been given the pejorative name "the crawler" by his enemies because of his undignified escape from the square.

The eight men halted in astonishment. Minóso said something to the first three who unsheathed their rapiers and began to sprint toward Diego. The rest followed at a trot. This was to be a *carrera de cerdo* (pig race). It was how pigs were caught along the narrow trails. A few boys would sprint after the pig causing it to run as fast as it could. Both pursuers and pursued would quickly tire, but the rest of the party, jogging at a comfortable pace would soon catch up and one or two fresh boys would race forward, forcing the pig into a dead run while the rest of the party resumed a comfortable jog. Soon, the pig would fall exhausted and would be easily caught. There was only one way to defeat the strategy.

Diego watched as the three men ran full tilt toward him. He stepped back out of sight and leaned his *lanza* against the smooth stone cliff. He chose several large stones from the rubble at the edge of the trail and stacked them near his feet. He picked up a large one as he heard the pounding of feet coming toward the turn. Timing it carefully, he threw the heavy jagged stone at the turn in the trail just as the lead man turned the corner. The stone struck the man's face with a sickening sound.

The man pitched over the edge of the trail without uttering a sound. The second man looked in astonishment at his companion spinning down to the canyon floor and was struck on the side of the head by a second stone. He wheeled away, dropped the dagger from his left hand and grabbed his face. He pushed the third man back and fell to his knees. The third man had enough wit to dance backward and dodge the third stone.

"Get him!" Minóso yelled.

"He is around the turn, *Don* Sebastian," the man shouted as he ran several yards back toward Minóso. "Bring the musket. He cannot run away without being seen!"

Diego moved around the corner enough to see the third man scurrying toward Minóso who was now about twenty yards from the turn. The injured man followed, swinging his rapier behind him in a comical attempt to protect his back. Diego threw another rock that thumped against the man's back and elicited a girlish squeal.

Diego returned to the far side of the turn listening to Minóso yelling at his men in an attempt to restore order. He placed his *lanza* against the smooth vertical wall of the cliff and climbed the twenty-foot shaft to a ledge. He paused and, hearing continuing chaos among the pursuers, climbed another twenty feet to the crest of the ridge in two quick placements of the *lanza*. He carefully laid the *lanza* on the crest and selected a large, jagged rock which he lifted above his head with both hands. He walked across the crest to a point above the trail west of the turn.

Diego could see down to the trail without obstruction. Minóso's wide-brimmed hat was moving below him. The end of a musket protruded from under the hat and two men, rapiers swinging before them, moved with Minóso. The three were huddled so closely together it appeared as if a feathered blue disk had sprouted blades and a musket.

Diego threw the stone down at the cluster. Without waiting to see the results of his throw, he reached down and grabbed two fist-sized stones. He returned to the edge of the cliff just as a musket discharged. Smoke billowed across the scene below him and the air was filled with the clatter of steel on stone and screams. He could see two men falling to the canyon floor. One was Minóso. He threw the rock at the remaining armed man who had dropped his rapier and was running west after the men who had been carrying the chains and yokes. He threw another stone high toward the retreating men. They were now well down the trail and it clattered behind them at their heels. They managed to increase their flight. Diego had remembered how his father told of the conquest of Gran Canaria and how the people had driven the Spanish off by throwing stones down on them from the high cliffs.

Diego recovered his *lanza* and ran toward the east and his home. When he was close enough to be heard, he alerted Pedro. They would have to gather what they could and leave. Cabitos would be sending others to *Pueblo de Cuevas*. "We go to Agüimes!" he whistled. "We must go now!" Pedro's answer came. "Yes, Papa. I hear you. I hear you."

Diego reached his home to find Mézu and the children prepared to go. He placed his *lanza* against the wall and instructed Pedro to do the same with his. "We will not need these where we are going," Diego said.

"Must we go now?" Mézu asked. "It will be full dark before we reach Agüimes."

Diego, not wanting to seem as alarmed as he felt, calmly and quietly described what had happened earlier on the trail to the *santuario* of the Most Blessed Virgin of the Clouds and his confrontation with Minóso.

Diego picked up Maria and signaled Pedro to lead the way. "I am sorry, but we must go now," he said. "Your brother knows we have given him all that we leave behind – house, flock, garden, everything. We must go now and hope that others have not been sent by way of Gando." They started down the narrow trail away from the only home Diego and the children had ever known.

CHAPTER 7

"Pedro," Diego whispered. "Take that trail to the left. It cuts back uphill. Follow it carefully, for it is rarely used. We will be right behind you."
It was night, but the moon had risen, full and bright.

"That is not the way to Agüimes, father," Pedro replied, even as he obeyed. Mézu followed Pedro without comment. Little Maria rode on Diego's back, sleeping in the fold of his cape. *I remember carrying Ignacio this way ten years ago*, Diego thought. *How could it have been ten years?*

"We are not going to Agüimes, Pedro." Diego said. "Your aunts and your grandmother live there and their houses will be watched." Francesca and Francina had married brothers, Juan "Perno" Viera and José "Clavo" Viera. The Viera family owned a furniture shop where much of the best furniture on Gran Canaria was made. Yadra lived with the Viera family where she helped with the business and raised grandchildren. Perno and Clavo's mother had died leaving the Viera household without women until Diego's sisters and mother had moved in.

Diego moved closer to Mézu and lowered his voice. Pedro could probably hear them, but the unused trail they had taken required the boy's full attention in the moonlight. "If Cabitos acted in haste when he sent men from Agaete, any men sent to Agüimes would not yet have arrived. If he had planned before he acted, men could be in Agüimes watching the Viera house – watching for us on the chance we escaped Minóso. All in *Pueblo de Cuevas* heard me whistle to Pedro we were going to Agüimes. Let them search for us there. We are going to Gando. Our protection here is gone and we must leave the islands."

The trail switched back and forth as they climbed the ridge away from the valley road to Agüimes. They crested the ridge and joined a well-worn track that turned east. The sea was clearly visible in the moonlight until they descended into another valley. There were few farms or houses along this route, for this valley was narrow and the sides lacked plateaus of any size. The few residences they did pass were dark and, surprisingly, no dogs barked nor goats bleated. The moon was hidden by the sides of the canyon, forcing them to move more slowly in the darkness, guided by Pedro's sharp eyes and the starlight.

The stars were beginning to fade in the east as the sky lightened slightly. Pedro stopped and looked back to Diego who nodded and signaled for Mézu to take Maria. Diego moved in a crouch until he was next to Pedro.

"I heard horses and men talking, but now it is quiet," Pedro reported.

"Where do you think they were?"

"That way," Pedro pointed south in the direction of Agüimes.

"Go to your mother and wait there," Diego said. Pedro moved away silently. *Ten years old and already he moves like a soldier*, Diego thought and he moved further along the trail to the east until he could see where it intersected the coastal road. Across the road lay the southern end of Gando and the dock-side road. Traffic was beginning to move through the town as merchants, dock workers and sailors began another day. Diego returned to his family. Maria was awake now, but sleepy.

"This is a well-traveled path," Diego said. "We will wait until some of the farmers and vendors come down to the market and we will mix in with them. We will go to the road along the docks and follow it north."

"What will we do after that?" Mézu asked.

"We are going to meet a man named Someruelos," Diego said. "I hope we are not too late."

Pedro looked inland and whispered, "Someone is coming, Papa."

Diego moved his family to the side of the trail and waited. The shuffle of feet grew nearer and figures could be seen coming toward them. The light was better now and Diego could make out two men moving with switches. He picked Maria up again and pushed his family into the brush slightly as a herd of pigs appeared along the trail. Two pig farmers were bringing their animals to market. Diego could see several women, some carrying children, and a few men behind the farmers. He let the pigs and the farmers pass, and, signaling Mézu and Pedro to follow him, joined the group of villagers as they crossed the road to Gando. He looked up and down the coastal road as they crossed but saw nothing of the riders Pedro had heard.

They moved with the villagers to the port road and then north. Eventually the traffic became one of drayage mixed in with the pedestrians. Sleds, carts, wagons, burdened men intermingled with villagers and vendors moving along and across the port road in a confused turbulent flow. The combination pub and recruiting station Diego had visited a few months ago was just ahead. Diego pulled his family into a recess formed by two walls that were not flush. He could see Someruelos talking to two men, courtiers by the look of their livery. The men walked to the edge of the pier where a group of people was gathered. They appeared to be three or four families huddled together with bundles at their feet waiting for something.

The courtiers spoke to each man and women in the group. They exchanged a few more words with Someruelos and left going north along the port road. Someruelos made a gesture toward the departing pair. He spoke with the families for a moment and returned to the pub. Diego waited until the courtiers were lost in the crowd before he and his family reentered the traffic going north. They soon reached the pub and Diego pulled his family to the desk. Someruelos looked up and recognition flashed across his face. Diego believed the recognition was not from his visit months ago.

"Remember me, friend?" Diego said.

"Yes, I do. You are the tall man who was not interested in joining the army," Someruelos replied.

"I have reconsidered," Diego said. He saw Someruelos glance north where the courtiers had disappeared. "I am told that you will receive a reward of forty-five *reals* if I sign. Those men who just left will rob you of that reward."

"I am in the service of the King," Someruelos said. "Those – gentlemen – think I am their servant to do their bidding." He looked at Diego. "You seem to be a man of good character. Are you a butcher?"

Diego shook his head.

"Good. I cannot recruit butchers. Neither may I enlist executioners nor gypsies nor mulattoes," Someruelos said, still looking north.

"I am none of those things," Diego said. "What must I do to sign?"

"Tell me your name and the name of your woman."

"This is my wife."

"Pardon, please," Someruelos continued. "I will enter your names and the names of your children in this ledger which will go with the recruits to Louisiana. I will copy the names to this second ledger," he indicated another book, "which will go to Cádiz. I will add your height to the second ledger, for it is the record from which I am paid. I will place only the names of the adults in this third ledger which is to go to the *Regidore* so he may be apprised of how many have left his realm in the service of His Most Catholic Majesty."

"I remember you said I would receive forty-five *reals* when I sign," Diego said. Someruelos nodded, "And *eight reals* a day while you wait. That will not apply if you enlist today for you will join those fine people yonder." He indicated the cluster of families at the edge of the pier. "You would leave today."

"If I enlist today, we would depart today?"

"After a representative of the church confirms the recruits are of good character and of this parish, all will be carried to a schooner in the bay and brought to His Majesty's Ship of War; the *San Juan Nepomuceno* – a ship of seventy-four guns." Someruelos' attitude indicated that was an important fact, but Diego was ignorant of ships.

Diego withdrew for a moment to consult with Mézu. "If I sign today, we leave today," he said, more to himself than to Mézu for she had heard the full exchange. "I think Cabitos has sent some of his courtiers to find us, not soldiers or catchpoles, because he seeks us without warrant and does not have the sanction of the Baroness or the new *Regidore*. He is attempting to use the confusion created by *Don* Raphael's death to murder us or take us back to Tenerife. The men that we saw talking with Someruelos must have been in Cabitos' hire. They described us; you saw the man's expression when we approached him."

"Then we cannot simply walk away," Mézu said. "He will report us." She touched Diego's arm. "Look who comes toward us now."

Diego turned in the direction she indicated and saw Father Tomás walk up to Someruelos. "Father Tomás is the church's representative," Diego exclaimed. He left Mézu with the children and went back to Someruelos.

"Diego!" Father Tomás exclaimed and slapped Diego on the shoulder. He leaned in to whisper, "I thought you and Mézu had been taken. Cabitos' men are everywhere. The new *Regidore* is *Don* Josef Aguilar y Cabitos, the son of Cabitos' eldest sister. Come take sanctuary in the church while there is time."

Diego guided Farther Tomás over to Someruelos. "Here is the priest who will vouch for us," Diego said. "But there is another matter, and let this priest be a witness. Those men who you were speaking with moments before I arrived were looking for me, were they not."

"They were looking for your wife," Someruelos admitted, "if she be your wife."

"She is this man's wife," Father Tomás said.

"Then I make this offer to you," Diego continued. "Enter our names in the ledger to be carried to Louisiana and the Ledger bound for Cádiz, but omit us from the church book."

Father Tomás looked disapprovingly at Diego for a moment, and then it began to dawn on him. "Someruelos will be paid according to the book sent to Cádiz and you, Diego, will be enlisted in the army according to the book that travels with you to Louisiana. Only the book that stays here will be examined by *Don* Josef Aguilar, and there will be no mention of you."

"What remains," Diego said, "is a question of trust. When I sign, I will leave my forty-five *reals* here for you, *señor* Someruelos – a *douceur* (gift) – if we do not appear in the church book. Pledge before this priest that you will not report us and also refrain from entering us in the church book. A simple thing and you shall have doubled you recruiting reward."

Someruelos smiled as he opened the Louisiana ledger, "*señor*, your name please." There were three columns on the page. The first was labeled "*Gente de Armas*", the second "*Niños de Pecho*" and the last "*Total de Personas.*" The ledger had several pages that had been filled out and it carried a running total for each page.

Someruelos entered the information Diego dictated at the bottom of the page. Under the column "Men at Arms" he wrote:

1 ..... Diego de Melilla
Maria Artiles, wife
Pedro, son of 10 years
Maria, daughter of 7 years

Nothing was entered under "Small Children" for that was reserved for children under one year old. Under "Total Persons" Someruelos entered "P...4". Diego and his family were the last entry and Someruelos added up the count from the roster. There were fifty-three men at arms. Counting men, women and children there were two hundred two people, nineteen of them children under the age of one, destined to be passengers aboard the *San Juan Nepomuceno*, bound for Louisiana.

Diego looked at the four families gathered at the dock. "Where are the rest of the people?" he asked.

"They are already aboard the *San Juan*," Someruelos said.

Diego looked out into the harbor. There were some two-masted ships lashed to the pier each with streams of stevedores moving on and off. Other ships of about the same size were anchored nearby amid a brood of smaller barges and skiffs loading or unloading cargo. A boat with a single mast was approaching the dock.

"Where is the *San Juan?*" Diego asked. None of the ships in the harbor or those tied to the pier seemed large enough to hold two hundred two passengers.

"She is not here in Gando," Someruelos said. "The caravel coming yonder will bring all of you to the *San Juan.*" He pointed to a small ship with a triangular sail weaving its way through the anchorage.

The single-masted little boat banged alongside the dock and two sailors jumped out, holding the ends of ropes to steady the little sloop. They did not tie to the dock, but simply held the caravel close to the pier while the five families climbed down into the open boat. Diego handed down the few possessions each family had and was the last passenger aboard. He had never been aboard a boat in his life, not even a small skiff. The sensation of unsteadiness when he stepped aboard was almost overpowering. He joined Mézu and the children under a small platform in the stern. Above them a sailor held a long lever attached to the rudder and shouted commands to the crewmen. None of the words made sense to Diego. Though entirely in Spanish, there were words sprinkled throughout the commands Diego had never heard before.

The sailors jumped aboard and, using long poles, pushed away from the dock. The caravel listed to one side, causing Diego to grip a brace supporting the platform above. He could feel the boat moving forward, gaining speed amid slapping canvas and shouting sailors. One sailor moved among the passengers and directed them to shift positions toward the high side of the tilted deck. Soon there was a steady gurgle of water beneath the bow and an occasional splash of sea water sprayed across the huddled families. Most, like Diego, had never been to sea.

Once, a spray of water from the bow reached Diego, wetting his hair slightly. He tasted the water and was startled. He had been told the sea as salty, but he had never tasted it before. Mézu looked at him in mild amusement.

"I remember my first taste of sea water," she said. "It is not unpleasant, but I am told to drink it will make one sick." She said this more for the children, who were also fascinated by the sea and the movement of the deck beneath them, than for Diego.

The caravel passed through some jetties and into the open sea. The pitch and roll of the boat increased until even the sailors had to move carefully, holding to rails or stays as they moved. Diego stood, still with the platform brace locked in his hand, and looked across the downwind rail of the caravel. It appeared to him that a little more tilt and the edge of the deck would be below the water. Indeed, now and again the foaming sea would splash onto the deck and drain away.

He forced his eyes away from the deck and looked at the island of his birth. He watched the port town of Gando pass toward the north. Another cluster of houses could be seen further up the mountain side. He had never seen Gran Canaria from this perspective and it took him a moment to recognize the second cluster of houses. It was the town of Agüimes. Mézu joined him, her presence comforted him. The sea was not a stranger to her. When she was a child, Mézu had often joined her father sailing a small skiff about the harbor of Santa Cruz. Diego looked for the Rock of the Clouds, but he could not see beyond the ridgeline immediately above Agüimes.

The sea to the south, the direction they were sailing, seemed empty save for another small ship coming north. The ship also tipped sharply to one side as it tacked toward them. Diego could see it had two masts supporting several triangular sails as she came on, canvas billowing tightly and white foam churning beneath the bow.

"It that the *San Juan?*" he asked.

The sailor at the tiller laughed, "That little thing? No. If I am not mistaken, she is the *Pegasus, Don* Alguazil Cabitos' caravel. I am told he is come to Gando to see his nephew installed as *Regidore.*"

Diego felt Mézu pull closer to him and put her head against his arm, hiding her left eye.

"We must pass beneath him," the helmsman said. "We cannot steal the great man's air." The man steered to pass between the *Pegasus* and the distant shore of Gran Canaria. The constant wind was from the east and this maneuver ensured they would pass downwind, so the sail of their little boat would not intercept the wind – "steal air" – before it reached the other ship. They also could see well into the *Pegasus* as she passed for she was heeled and on a close tack. Several well-dressed men, clearly not sailors, crowded the bow. They gestured toward Gando and animatedly conversed with each other. Diego thought he saw Cabitos, but he could not be certain.

"Where is the *San Juan*?" he asked after the *Pegasus* was well past.

"She is berthed at Santa Cruz de Tenerife," the helmsman said. "She will weigh anchor as soon as this lot is aboard."

Diego looked at Mézu and laughed. Had he known his enlistment included a trip to the island of Tenerife, he would never have come. Now, as he and Mézu fled toward Tenerife with their children, their sworn enemy has passed them at sea and bound for the port they had just quit. They would be aboard a ship bound for the New World before dawn tomorrow, no longer subjects of the island lords.

Mézu looked up at Diego, her grey eye sparkling. "Remember what *Don* Raphael said so many years ago when you went against Cabitos?"

"I did not hear him say anything of note," Diego said with a shrug.

Mézu smiled, "When he conferred with the Baroness I heard him say, 'I see the hand of God at work here.'"

CHAPTER 8

D iego straightened from the rail. He had never been so sick in his life. Another wave of nausea swept in and he attempted to heave again, but noting issued forth but a single strand of spittle.

"Is Papa going to die?" Maria asked in a hushed whisper.

"No, baby," Mézu said. "It is simply seasickness. He will feel better when he has become used to the motion of the ship."

"I would welcome death," Diego said, having overheard his daughter's concern. "The sailors laugh and call me *terrateniente*. I confess – I am meant for the land." He groaned again and made another attempt to bring up something with no success. He cautiously returned to sit next to Mézu and the children. He was exhausted and closed his eyes. They had been at sea for six hours as they circled the southern side of Gran Canaria and he had heaved for four of those six. Now the caravel was headed northwest directly toward Santa Cruz. This last stretch would take another five hours, if the wind held and it always held, so they would arrive at the *San Juan Nepomuceno* around eight at night, just before moon rise. He had begun to hope the nausea was beginning to abate.

"They tell me the *San Juan* will wait for us and, as we are the last to muster, she will depart immediately for Louisiana." Diego took a deep breath. *Perhaps I will live*, he thought. *If the men I met yesterday had returned to Agaete, they could have sent word to Tenerife but that message should have missed Cabitos. More likely, it was known to them that Cabitos was bound for Gando. In that case, a message by land would have to circle around the north side of Gran Canaria for there is no coast road across the south. That message would have reached Gando about the same time as Cabitos.*

"Do you think Someruelos will keep his word?" Mézu asked.

"I think he will. Father Tomás will see to it. If not, it will not matter. Once we are aboard the *San Juan* we will be beyond Cabitos' authority. Cabitos will think us still on Gran Canaria and it will take several days searching before he will be convinced we are not. Tenerife should be safe for us for several days. Even so, we must not go ashore there."

The caravel was on a starboard tack, the favorable tack for the lateen-rigged ship, and she raced along. The helmsman revised his estimate of their arrival to seven o'clock. "The lights of Santa Cruz and the ships in the harbor will be enough to make out the *San Juan*," he said confidently. "You will see. She cannot be missed."

Diego and Mézu watched the high white peak of Teide on Tenerife grow over the port bow of the caravel and the jagged mass of Gran Canaria fade to the starboard. Diego looked for *El Roque Nublo*, but the high seaside cliffs of Gran Canaria were too close and blocked his view. Daylight was fading and he despaired of ever seeing the Rock of the Clouds again.

The sun had fallen behind the snow-covered peak of Teide, creating a prolonged twilight as the coast of Tenerife slipped closer. Mézu gripped Diego's arm tighter. "I think I recognize those buildings," she said, indicating a cluster of white-walled, red-roofed buildings nearly invisible in the fading light. "It is a place called *Las Caletillas*. My father owned a vineyard near there. We are but one hour away from Santa Cruz." Diego heard a slight catch in Mézu's voice as she spoke and he put his arm around her.

෫ᴥ෧

The little caravel approached the massive side of the *San Juan Nepomuceno* from the lee side. The huge ship loomed above the deck where the deMelilla family and their companions gathered their meager belongings. Lines had been tossed to the caravel and she was being hauled toward a rope netting that hung from the side of the ship. Once the caravel was near the ship, canvas bags filled with wood chips were hung between the vessels to cushion them as there was a slight sea running, even though they were behind a breakwater. They were so close to the side of the ship that the bow, stern and deck rail of the tall ship was hidden from view by its massive, curved wooden side. Two parallel rows of small doors populated the side, the ends of the rows disappearing from view around the curve of the hull. Diego learned later these doors were called gun ports.

Rope netting had been lowered from the hidden deck above to the caravel. A lower gun port near the netting swung up and was held open by a brace. A sailor appeared at the door. "Pass up your baggage," the man said. The open port was only four or five feet above the deck of the caravel so it was a simple matter to hand up the canvas sacks containing bundles of clothes and other items belonging to the passengers. An official-looking canvas bag sealed with a brass band beaten around a red cord was handed through the gun port as well. This bag contained correspondence for *Don* Domingo Morera, captain of the *San Juan* and included the roster of recruits for the army.

"Women next," the sailor said. Small children were handed to their fathers and the wives of the recruits were directed to climb only a few rungs of the rope netting to gain access to the gun port. The huge cannon, capable of firing a thirty-six pound solid steel shot, had been pulled far back from the port so the opening was sufficient. The women crawled into the port one at a time with ease if not poise.

"*Niños*," the sailor announced. The single baby was passed up to his anxious mother followed by the rest of the children. Pedro, proudly in charge of his father's *magado*, and another young teen were the last to go into the ship through the gun port before it was closed. Only the men, all new army recruits, remained aboard the caravel.

"Up you go, men," the helmsman of the caravel said as he gestured toward the rope netting.

Diego was first to attempt the climb for he did not like being separated from his family and was eager to board the ship. He looked up to see the netting disappear around the curve, the tumblehome, of the ship. Climbing was a simple matter for him and he started up with ease. He passed the first row of gun ports and the side of the ship transformed into a steady slope. He could see faces peering down at him as he ascended. There was an opening in the ship's rail and Diego vaulted through to find himself surrounded by uniforms of an incredible variety.

"Over here, *tonto*," one of the uniformed men shouted, indicating with the short wooden rod he carried. He directed Diego to a place on the deck at the end of a line of men, some in uniforms and others in civilian dress. A white line had been marked in chalk on the deck and Diego was directed to stand next to a man and place the toes of his boots on the line. He began to ask about his family but the uniformed man shouted for him to remain silent. Another "*tonto*" from the caravel appeared on deck and was pushed into line next to Diego. He stole a glance along the line of men next to him.

Some of the recruits had been members of the local militia in their villages. They wore the varying uniforms, or portions of uniforms. These men had experienced some military training and were at least familiar with the basic commands. Some may have even had combat experience repelling pirate raids. Diego had been trained by his father in hand-to-hand combat with the *magado*, *sunta*, short sword and walking staff but he was ignorant of rank-and-file soldiering.

The last of the new recruits was shouted into place. Sailors and officers of the ship began a chorus of shouts and orders. The rope netting was pulled aboard and the gap in the railing closed with another more closely woven rope netting drawn taunt between wooden cleats. The sounds of straining men and the steady clank of a pawl indicated that the anchor cable was being pulled up short.

"My name is *Cabo* Josef Herrera," announced the uniformed man who had forced each recruit into place. "*Cabo* is my rank. See this," Herrera touched the blue epaulet on his left shoulder. "This means I am a corporal. When you address me '*Cabo*' will be the first word out of your mouths. Do you understand?"

"*Sí, cabo*," the experienced men in the ranks said. Diego and the other *tontos* said nothing. Herrera rushed up to Diego and looked up at the much taller man. "Could you not hear me?" he shouted.

Diego, startled, said, "I could hear you."

"What did I say would be the first word out of your mouth, *tonto?*" The man's face was red and he seemed to be on the verge of madness.

"*Cabo*, I could hear you," Diego said.

"Then why did you not answer me?"

"I did not know I was expected to do so."

The man screwed his face up into a snarl. "The answer to my question is; '*Cabo*, I did not know I was expected to do so.' Now you try it."

"*Cabo*, I did not know I was expected to do so." Diego said.

Herrera returned to his place before the formation. Sailors rushed about, but never between Herrera and the formation. Men had gone aloft, canvas was being spread, and sailors on deck pulled at ropes amid shouts and curses. The deck tilted slightly as the *San Juan Nepomuceno* gained speed. She took a starboard tack bound for the northern tip of Tenerife. Once around that wind-whipped point, they would be bound for Louisiana.

Herrera shouted, "*Atennnn – CIÓN.*" The men with some military experience stood straight and looked forward in silence. Diego imitated their actions. The *tontos* that did not were treated to another tirade by Herrera. Herrera walked to the first ten men in the first rank and touched each on the shoulder as he walked along. With each tap he said, "first squad." He returned to the center and shouted, "first squad, one step forward – MARCH!" Diego, who had been included in that group stepped forward along with nine others.

"You *tontos!*" Screamed Herrera. "You must move as one. The first step you take is to be with the left foot. Who knows which foot is the left?" Some of the men looked at one another. Fortunately, left and right were concepts Diego's father had incorporated into his training.

"*Cabo,*" Diego said, "I know which is left and which is right."

"Amazing!" Herrera shouted feigning joy. "I have found an *Isleños* who knows his left from his right! Private Releva, report to me."

A man in a complete and new-looking uniform trotted up to Herrera. "Releva," Herrera spoke without turning his eyes from the line of ten men, "you are in charge of the first squad. Take them below and see that their families, if they have any, are assigned places. Then I want you to instruct these *tontos*. In the morning I want them to know how and where to fall in and stand at attention. I want them to learn their left from their right. I want them to know how to step forward on command. And I want them to know the ranks of private, *Cabo* (corporal), sergeant, first sergeant, sub-lieutenant, lieutenant, captain and colonel and how to properly address them. Now take them below."

"Yes, *Cabo,*" Releva said. He turned to the first squad and said, "First squad, follow me."

Herrera covered his eyes with his hands and shook his head as the First Squad followed Releva to an opening in the deck and down into the ship. "Mother of God," he said, "Give me strength."

૭৩

Releva brought the men down two decks to the lowest gun deck and then forward to where the families of the most recent recruits were being settled. The gun deck had been divided up in to smaller spaces by hanging canvas curtains or, in some cases, walls of planking. He moved the men to an open space behind the curtained areas where he released them to find their people with instructions to report to him at that place when they heard the call "First Squad."

Diego gave a short whistle and heard Pedro's answer from somewhere forward amidst a forest of canvas hangings and hammocks. He was, through trial and error, able to ascertain isle from room and made his way to the space reserved for the deMelilla family. It was against the hull of the ship and forward of the most forward thirty-six pounder of the port battery. If battle stations were called, the people had to remove the canvas hangings and collect themselves and their baggage to designated areas so the great guns could be worked. The deck above them was where the sailors were temporarily billeted to make room for the families. A squad of Marines had been billeted in a center area of the third gun deck, their presence intended to enforce order.

"She is named 'Serpent's Sting' Pedro said in way of greeting Diego. He patted the side of the huge cannon that formed one boundary of their cubicle as he continued, "The gun captain said we may open the gun ports in hot weather."

Diego kissed his children and then held Mézu close. "I fear it will be a hard journey," he said.

"We will manage, my husband," Mézu said. "It is close, but I am told we are allowed above decks when the weather permits. There is plentiful water but no wine. We will be provided food twice a day and each temporary room has been provided with hammocks and a chamber pot." She laughed aloud. "What more could one ask for?" Then her face darkened. "I heard a sailor tell one of the wives that the trip could take half a year."

The *San Juan Nepomuceno* had weighed anchor at Santa Cruz de Tenerife on the ninth of December, 1778 and she would not arrive at New Orleans until the fourth of April, 1779.

৵৹

The ship fell into a routine within a few days. Herrera drilled the recruits on the main deck. There were enough present for duty each day to form a *pelotón* (platoon) of five squads. After each drill, which introduced new maneuvers and commands each time, Releva would retire with the first squad to review new commands and practice old ones. Ranks, military courtesy, forms of address and other nuances were introduced and ingrained one at a time. Diego learned so quickly that Releva would require him to lead the squad drill from time to time.

While the men drilled, the wives worked at mending clothes, washing, cooking and tending to the children. Every day large sections of the canvas-walled quarters were raised until a large open space was created. Here the children played and Mézu organized a school. She was one of only five wives on the ship who could read. A small collection of slates and chalks had been obtained so the children were kept busy with learning their letters and their numbers, in many cases along with their mothers.

After they had been at sea for a month, Herrera surprised the morning formation with an announcement. "Platoon, Lieutenant Leyba has informed me that he considers your training to have advanced enough that you should be considered soldiers," he said. Lieutenant Leyba was the only army officer on the ship. Herrera had pointed him out once to the platoon from among a crown of gentlemen on the quarter deck. "The lieutenant is most generous," he added. "You will now draw uniforms by squads." Until that moment, all drill had been performed with the men dressed as they came, some shoeless, some without hats and some without coats.

"First Squad," Releva ordered. First squad snapped to attention. "To the Right – FACE!" Each man pivoted in place to face to the right. "At the Quick – MARCH!" The squad moved off briskly, giving all the appearance of a trained unit. Releva halted them at an open hatch leading to a storage area below the quarter deck. There he directed one man at a time to advance to a desk where a clerk gave him a bundle which contained: one pair of shoes, two blue trousers, two blue shirts, a white waistcoat, one pair of knee-high white gaiters, a black leather belt, a white uniform coat, and a cotton haversack. The clerk had each man sign for the equipment and plopped a bicorn on his head. The hat had a red bow-like cockade on the left side. After the men had drawn their uniforms, Releva sent them below to dress. He followed them down to supervise the change into uniforms.

The men formed up in the erstwhile play area. The families of the first squad gathered about to marvel at the transformation that had occurred. They wore white coats with blue facing, blue cuffs and silver buttons. Their shirts were blue as were their trousers. They all wore shoes, some for the first time in their lives. White gaiters covered the shoes until just the toes and soles could be seen. The gaiters, buttoned on the outside of the leg, rose above the knee where a black leather strap secured it in place. A white haversack was suspended at their left hip by a white leather strap that crossed from the right shoulder. The bicorn hats were squared away on each head, the red cockades identical in size and form.

"Platoon, fall in!" came a shout from topside. The first squad double-timed to the stairs, up onto the deck and into their familiar position. The other members of the platoon were in full uniform as well. Herrera called the platoon to attention, performed an about-face and stood at attention himself. An officer, wearing the same white and blue uniform as the platoon, stepped up to face Herrera. Diego knew the man was an officer, a lieutenant, for he wore a gold epaulet on his right shoulder. This must be the mysterious Lieutenant Leyba.

"Sir," Herrera said with a smart salute, "the platoon is formed and all are present for duty or accounted for."

Leyba returned the salute. "Thank you, *Cabo*," he said. "Please take your post."

Herrera stepped back one step, saluted, faced to his right and marched to the right end of the First Squad where he positioned himself next to Releva.

"Gentlemen," Leyba said in a deep booming voice that could be heard by the sailors in the tops. The ship's hands not busy with some function had gathered to see what an army platoon should look like. "My name is Lieutenant Fernando Leyba y Padróna. *Cabo* Herrera has informed me that this platoon has earned the right to be considered soldiers of His Most Catholic Majesty, Charles the Third, King of Spain and the Indies. I have observed your training and I concur. I declare this platoon to be the third platoon, first company of *El Regimiento Fijo de Infanteria de la Luisiana*."

Diego sensed the ranks stiffen with pride, as did he. He could see their families gathered near the forecastle, watching the ceremony.

"*Cabo* Herrera," Leyba shouted, "To the front and center."

Herrera marched briskly to his former position facing the lieutenant, saluted and stood at attention. "*Cabo* Herrera," Leyba continued, "you are hereby promoted to the rank of *sargento* (sergeant) with all the privileges and responsibilities of such an office. Henceforth you shall be the platoon sergeant of the third platoon, first company of the Fixed Infantry Regiment of Louisiana." He stepped forward and buttoned a blue epaulet to Herrera's right shoulder. When he stepped back Herrera saluted and said, "Thank you, sir."

"You are further instructed, sergeant," Leyba continued, "to recommend five candidates for corporal from this platoon to serve as squad corporals. You will now have the men draw weapons and continue with their training."

Herrera saluted again. Leyba returned the salute and withdrew to the quarter deck. Sergeant Herrera faced the platoon. "You heard the lieutenant. We are to draw weapons by squads. First squad, draw weapons from the quartermaster now." Until this moment, the platoon had been training with cannon ramrods as substitutes for muskets.

Releva commanded his squad to face to the left and marched them to the quartermaster's port. They were issued a musket, an empty cartridge box, a bayonet and a flint kit. Once they were armed, Releva moved them to an open area of the bottom gun deck and had them form a circle for instructions on the cleaning, care, maintenance and the manual of arms. Unlike the sailors, who had their weapons locked away until needed, soldiers were expected to keep their weapons with them at all times.

CHAPTER 9

"Lock!" shouted Sergeant Herrera. This was the first time Diego had ever loaded his musket. During the second month at sea, the platoon had learned nomenclature, maintenance, repair, setting flint, cleaning, fixing bayonet and dozens of formations and movements. They had practiced loading the weapon using imaginary cartridges. They had dry-fired unloaded muskets and watched sparks dance around on empty pans.

Now the platoon stood at the side rail, all squads in a line and facing the wind. They had been issued a dozen paper cartridges. Paper was rolled around a wood dowel of the same caliber as the weapon. One end of the paper was twisted before the roll was removed from the dowel. A lead ball was dropped into the roll followed by a measured powder charge. The powder end was twisted into a seal forming a finger-sized container of shot and powder.

A block of wood with two dozen holes sized to receive the cartridges was set within a leather pouch fitted with a flap or cover. This cartridge box was slung by a wide leather belt across each soldier's shoulder and adjusted so that it rode on the right hip. With their cartridge boxes on the right and their haversacks on the left, each man bore the familiar traversing pattern of belts across his chest.

Diego turned his body slightly to the right and brought the lock of the musket to his chest with the muzzle pointed toward the "enemy." All fifty men in the line moved as one. They had practiced this drill for weeks. He pulled the hammer of his musket back until it clicked into the half-cocked position. Using his thumb, he pushed the frizzen forward into the open position, glanced down to insure the pan was empty and waited. As with all commands to formed men, the orders were broken up into two groups. The first group, call preparatory commands told the soldier what to expect and the second, the command of execution told him to do it. Commands of execution were barked out sharply so as to be heard even in battle.

"Handle – CARTRIDGE."

Diego and every other man in the platoon, moving as one, slapped his cartridge box with his right hand, lifted the leather flap, removed one paper cartridge by pinching it between thumb and forefinger and placed it next to his chin.

"Prime – LOCK."

Diego brought the powder end of the cartridge to his mouth and tore the end off with his teeth. He tasted powder for the first time, a gritty, sooty almost salty taste. He poured a small amount of powder from the cartridge, enough to fill the pan. He closed the pan, looked forward and waited.

"Cast – ABOUT."

Diego released his right hand from the musket and brought the barrel up, placed the butt on the deck near his left foot. The weapon was canted slightly until the lock was pointed at his right foot and he held the torn end of the cartridge next to the muzzle.

"LOAD."

Diego poured the remainder of the powder into the barrel of the musket and stuffed the lead ball in after the powder, still wrapped in the paper.

"Withdraw – RAM."

The scraping sound of fifty steel ramrods being withdrawn from their cradles filled the air. The move was performed by the right hand alone. Diego heard the clatter of a dropped ramrod to his left and the instant cursing of Herrera. He reversed the steel shaft in his hand, touched the cup of the ramrod to the muzzle and waited.

"Ram – CARTRIDGE."

Diego forced the ramrod down the barrel. He felt it contact the paper-wrapped ball about halfway to the breach and drove it all the way down until it was compressed against the powder charge. Giving it a few taps, he removed the ramrod and placed the trailing end into the guides under the musket. He slid it down until just the cup was above the muzzle.

"Return – RAM."

He gave the cup a slap and it snapped into place. He lifted the musket and placed it at shoulder arms and waited. Herrera paused until every man had shouldered his weapon. If they had done everything correctly, all fifty men had a loaded and primed musket on his left shoulder.

"Make – READY."

Diego brought the musket from his shoulder with its barrel tilted up slightly yet pointed toward the "enemy" and pulled the hammer to the rear until it locked at full cock.

"PRESENT"

He brought the stock into his shoulder and leveled the weapon toward the imaginary "enemy."

"FIRE!"

Diego pulled the trigger. He was rewarded with a jolt to his shoulder and a loud report. It was only the second time in his life that he had heard a musket fired, only there were fifty firing all at once. The smoke billowed back into his face and the smell of it caused the image of Minóso to come into his mind. He saw the man spinning down through space toward the floor of the canyon.

"Recover."

Diego lowered the musket and positioned it so that the lock was at his chest.

"Handle – CARTRIDGE."

The sequence began again. They fired all of the cartridges they had drawn from the quartermaster. After three rounds of firing, misfires had begun to occur. Herrera ran from one to the next instructing each on the cause of the misfire. Some men tried to load their weapon even thought it had not fired, their actions had been so trained into them they were acting without thinking. Herrera, assisted by three acting corporals, was up and down the line dealing with each problem. Eventually, all cartridges had been fired or spilled onto the deck.

The platoon was dismissed into squads for weapons cleaning, repair and to discuss the firing drill. Men who had experienced misfires were counseled, loudly and firmly, to correct what had gone wrong. Diego looked at his squad mates. Each one had powder-blacken faces, particularly at the corner of the mouth, caused by residue from tearing the cartridges open with their teeth.

Once the muskets were cleaned they were placed in a wooden rack attached to the forward bulkhead of the gun deck. They were secured in place with a wooden bar to prevent them from dislodging in a rough sea. The men kept the rest of the accoutrements with them to be cleaned and stored near their sleeping hammocks. Two of the squad who were veterans of the disciplined militia had produced short swords from their baggage and added them to their armaments.

The defense of towns and villages along the coast of the Canary Islands was provided by regular Spanish army units supplemented by uniformed militia units made up of townsmen. These were called "disciplined" militia because they received the more regular and extensive training than the general militia. These units were often experienced in combat having had to defend their towns against pirate raids or other incursions. The Canary Islands, located at the eastern end of the trade winds, was the best jumping off point for expeditions to the new world.

Diego was not a militia veteran. But his father had trained him extensively in the use of personal weapons. After Herrera approved short swords or daggers as acceptable additions to the issued weaponry of the squad members, Diego decided to include his own battered short sword. He returned to his family's sleeping area next to *Serpent's Sting* and using the cannon's carriage as a seat, began to polish the worn leather of his short sword's belt and scabbard. He watched Mézu and the children as he worked. The women on the lower gun deck had organized games for the children, helped in the preparation of food and performed chores in support of the gun deck.

Diego marveled at how well Mézu and the children were adapting to life at sea. The chores of everyday life were modified but little. Their living area was being maintained in a neat and orderly fashion. Household items had to be stored away when not in use. Clothes, bedding and utensils, when not in use, were locked away in a chest or lashed to pegs on the bulkhead. Just as the great gun on which Diego now sat, everything had to be secured to prevent it's being tossed about should the sea rise, a storm hit, or a sea battle develop.

"What are you doing, Mézu?" Diego could see that she was sewing, but he could not determine what she was working on.

"I am making a shot sack for *Serpent's Sting*," she said. "First I cut three circles of canvas." She showed him a large portion of old sail folded next to the bulkhead. "I have cut the circles the same size as the bore of the cannon and have sewn them together, one on top of the other, to make a thick pad." She showed him the pad she had just finished. "I then place the pad in the center of a larger circle of canvas and set four four-pound balls at the edges of the pad to hold it in place." She reached into a barrel next to the cannon and withdrew a solid iron four-pound ball and placed it on the pad. This she repeated until four balls were arranged on the pad. The four iron balls covered the pad to its edges. "Then I fold the edges up to form a sack and add stiches to keep it in place." Mézu worked quickly with the heavy needle and thread. She wore a leather heel pad and a wooden driver to assist her in pushing the needle through the layers of stiff canvas. "Two more layers of four-pound balls are added before I sew the top of the sack closed."

He watched as she finished the sack she was working on. "The gun captain says the sack is loaded into the cannon as if it were a solid shot. When it is fired, the sack is rent open and the balls scatter out to sweep the enemy away," Mézu said as she pulled the ends of the sack upright.

She started to cut another set of circular pads and glanced toward a barrel of four-pound shot that seemed to be as full as before. "One more, then I will be done for the night," she said.

While she worked, Diego stepped out into the open deck between rows of canvas-walled chambers. He noticed a naval officer moving along the line of curtains. He would stop here and there to chat with unseen people in their enclosures. As he approached Diego he neared one of the lamps suspended from the overhead. Diego recognized him. He was *Barón* del la Paz, the first-subaltern and third in command. The officer was about twenty-five years of age. His face was deeply pock-marked and one lip pulled away to reveal a tooth. He wore a powdered wig and a blue waistcoat embellished with brass buttons. His shoes had great buckles and the nails in the heavy soles clicked as he walked. Diego nodded as the officer passed, but the man did not deign to acknowledge Diego's presence.

Del la Paz must have just started the evening watch. His habits were as predictable as sunset. All of the sailors and many of the passengers knew the man's habits out of self-preservation. It is always wise to know where your officers are. Unless the weather was violent, del la Paz would walk the upper deck, the middle gun deck and then the lower gun deck checking on crewmen of the watch. He would then exit one of the forward hatchways that opened to small platforms on each side of the base of the bowsprit. If the ship was running with the wind starboard of the beam, he would exit the port hatchway. If running at a port tack or reach, he would choose the starboard hatch. He would go to the rail and look up at the fore watch perched near the first yard to insure the man was watching the sea ahead and then do the same for the man in the crow's nest.

The small platforms on either side of the base of the bow sprit were called the "heads." This was the forward-most part of the ship that was not mast, sail or yard. Unless they were beating into the wind, it was also down-wind from the rest of the ship. This is where sailors came to answer the call of nature and also where the passengers emptied their chamber pots. After checking on the watch, del la Paz would step up on the gunnel, grasp a stay to steady himself, unbutton his trousers and relieve himself. Then he would return to the quarter deck. It mattered not if he had the morning watch or the dog watch, his routine was unchanged.

Toward the end of the second month at sea the ship was moving comfortably in a following sea running on a port-side reach. Many of the passengers had abandoned their hammocks for make-shift beds of baggage and rolled canvas. It was a pleasant, if temporary, relief to be able to stretch out. The hammocks were best when the ship was rolling about, but one was required to sleep on one's back, folded at an uncomfortable angle.

Diego had finished his maintenance chores and lay next to Mézu, another activity for which hammocks were unsuitable. The children, more flexible and adaptable than their parents, were asleep in their hammocks swinging only a foot above the deck. Diego had noticed that Mézu seemed troubled by something and, now that the children were asleep, he welcomed the chance for private conversation.

"Husband," Mézu said just as Diego was going to speak. "What do you know of the officer they call the *primo* subaltern?"

"The first subaltern is third in command on this ship," Diego said. "The Captain, *Don* Domingo Morera, commands the ship. After him is Lieutenant Reyes and then *Barón* del la Paz, the first subaltern."

"How is it a baron is only third in command?" She asked.

"His family purchased his commission, I would guess. He is young. Perhaps he is not experienced at sea. Why do you ask?"

"De la Paz has made a – lewd demand of one of the women passengers," Mézu said in a whisper so soft that Diego could barely hear her. "Isabella Campo, the daughter of Miguel Campo, was threatened." Isabella Campo was, perhaps, fifteen years old and very pretty. The family had come from the island of Gomera. "She and her mother are terrified," she continued. "They cannot tell Miguel for fear he will act in anger. The *Barón* has told them if the daughter does not submit he will see that the father is charged with a crime."

Diego did not know what to say. He was relieved that such a threat had not been made against Mézu. What if it had? What could he do? If he complained to the captain it would be the word of a baron against that of a private soldier. On Gomera, the people were bullied and abused, treated as if they were the property of the descendants of Betancour, the lord who seized the island, not as subjects of the King of Spain. Living in this condition, they were terrified of royalty and often forced to reach "accommodations."

"What has he demanded?" Diego asked, more to give himself time to think than seek a response. He knew the answer.

"She will be sent for tomorrow night. Del la Paz will go off watch at four in the morning. He will send for Isabella and she is to go to his cabin, the one he shares with the Lieutenant Reyes. Reyes will be on watch. What should we do?" Mézu asked.

"There is nothing we can do," Diego replied. "The girl must go when she is sent for. It could mean her father's life." Mézu turned away, visibly dissatisfied with Diego's answer.

Diego was equally unhappy about his answer and could not sleep. He tossed about until midnight. Giving up on sleep, he rose quietly so Mézu would not awaken and walked to the curtain that separated their sleeping area from the rest of the gun deck. He parted the curtain and looked aft toward the enclosure for the Campo family. His mind was racing. Tomorrow night it would be Isabella. Who would it be next? Had del la Paz molested the passengers on the second gun deck and had now worked his way down to the lower gun deck?

There were only two lanterns providing light for the gun deck swinging from hooks in the beams overhead. Diego saw Isabella Campo in the faint, flickering light. She was standing in the center of the gun deck, her head down. A man was speaking to her, his back to Diego. He could not hear what was being said, but it caused Isabella to nod her head. The man gestured for Isabella to return to her family quarters. Once the girl was past the canvas curtain, the man turned around. Just as Diego has suspected, it was *Barón* del la Paz.

Del la Paz began walking forward and Diego stepped back behind the curtain. He could hear del la Paz walk past. The ship was on a port-reach so the man would be going to the starboard head. Diego waited until del la Paz was well past him before looking out of the curtain again in time to see him ascend to the starboard head.

Diego stepped back and took a deep breath. He looked at Mézu, beautiful and asleep. He moved silently, for his feet were bare, to the barrel beside *Serpent's Sting* and removed a four-pound shot. He slipped out through the crease where the curtain of their enclosure butted against the side of the ship. He moved along the hull toward the hatchway to the port head checking aft as he went. The fire watch was slumped against the aft-bulkhead. The two lanterns swinging between the fire watch and Diego blinded the man to anything moving in the forward part of the gun deck. Diego moved slowly without swinging his arms, lest the fire watch catch a glimpse of movement, and went up the steps out onto the port head.

A storm was stirring off to the starboard. Lightning flashed silently and the air felt cold. There were no lamps on the bow or foredeck lest the watch be blinded. The moon was not to be seen, nor were there stars. Some light from further aft reflected off of the sails and Diego could see enough to distinguish spars, stays and yardarms. The sails had been reefed for running at night and the yards were set for a port reach, canting the sails until the port head was hidden from the fore watch.

Diego looked across the top of the base of the bowsprit. He could see the top of a bicorn hat, del la Paz's hat. Diego moved until he could see del la Paz's forehead and waited. He hefted the shot in his hand. It reminded him of the stones on Gran Canaria. Then del la Paz seemed to rise and move forward. He had stepped up onto the gunnel. Lightning flickered, clearly revealing the man's face. There was no doubt, it was del la Paz. Diego hurled the four-pound solid iron shot as hard as he could.

CHAPTER 10

iego stepped down onto the lower gun deck. He could see the length of the ship between the lines of canvas enclosures. The two lanterns swung on their chains as the ship began to respond to the increasing sea. Thunder rumbled and he could hear the splatter of rain behind him. The man on fire watch was sitting against the aft bulkhead. Diego was certain the man still could not see him because of the lamps between them. He stepped to his right, lest a flash of lightning silhouette him in the hatchway and walked along the bulkhead until he reached the canvas enclosure assigned to his family.

Mézu was asleep on the makeshift bed. The ship's increased motion would not disturb the children in their hammocks but it would soon awaken Mézu. Diego hurriedly tied their hammocks to the iron rings set in the overhead beams for that purpose. He picked Mézu up, causing her to stir without fully awakening. She sleepily recognized what he was doing and snuggled her face into his neck as he placed her in the hammock.

"Go back to sleep, wife," he whispered. "It is but a little past midnight."

"Is there a storm coming?" she asked. "I thought I heard thunder."

"It is a small shower, nothing for this ship." He kissed her and laughed to himself. Two months ago he had never been on a boat, now he found himself assessing the threat of a storm at sea. He climbed into his own hammock, his ears straining to hear beyond the regular creaks and groans of the ship. He listened for shouts of alarm. He closed his eyes. The image of del la Paz's lightning-lit profile filled his mind. There was no way he could have missed. If he had missed with the shot, del la Paz could not have seen him. He fell asleep, rocked by the ship's motion.

ᚊ

Diego was awakened by a staccato series of drumbeats followed by an extended roll sounded from the center of the gun deck. Reveille for the army and army families was the same every day. The distinctive drum beat of "first call" provided a warning to all that morning formation would be in one quarter of an hour. Many were up and about before first call, but Diego had slept soundly. He rolled out of his hammock to see Mézu helping the children dress.

"You slept well, husband," she said. She braced herself against a bulkhead as the ship rolled to the starboard and then settled stern-first as a following sea passed beneath them. The ship surged ahead again and Mézu finished dressing the children. "I fear we will not be allowed topside today," she said. Rough seas or foul weather would condemn the passengers to the gun decks. Top side would be chaotic with sailors rushing about on a rain and sea soaked deck to this sheet or that downhaul, answering the demands of an angry sea. It would not do to have women and children underfoot.

Diego slipped on his trousers and tucked in his shirt. "I will take this out," he said and he picked up the chamber pot. It contained enough to warrant a trip to the head. "I will not send you out in this weather." Emptying chamber pots was usually women's work on the ship, but during times of rough seas or storms men often performed the chore. Diego had to make his way along the gun deck with one hand against the overhead and the chamber pot in the other. Mézu was not tall enough to firmly press against the planking above and it would have been a struggle for her to reach the head without spilling the contents of the chamber pot.

Fighting to keep his balance on the rolling deck, Diego reached the steps to the starboard head just as Releva was coming down.

"Good morning deMelilla," Releva said. "It is wet out. If it is not rain blowing down from the forecastle, it is the sea foaming up from below." Releva, Diego's squad leader, had been promoted to *cabo* and addressed everyone in his squad by their surname.

"Will we be sent to the pumps today, corporal?" Diego asked. Rough seas would often open seams on the great ship. Manning the pumps required no training in seamanship, so the captain would send soldiers down to help the sailors. It was back-breaking work deep in the bowels of the ship. Those manning the pumps were often knee-deep in bilge water.

"I think it likely," Releva replied. "The *pulpos* are in a panicked state." Soldiers would often refer to a sailor as a "*pulpo*" (octopus). Releva leaned closer to Diego as if what he said was a secret. "It seems that they lost someone last night."

"Lost?" Diego said. "How can you lose someone on a ship?"

"How indeed?" Releva laughed. "The man is not lost on this ship. He is lost in the sea. What is more, the man lost was the commander of the watch. You know him, that Mallorcan scum, the subaltern."

"Subaltern *Barón* del la Paz?" Diego asked.

"Yes," Releva hissed. "And the world is a better place without him."

"He never did me harm," Diego said as Releva continued on his way down to the gun deck.

Diego stepped through the hatchway to the head. Rainwater blew across the top of the deck above spraying out toward the gunnel. Streams of water poured from scuppers to the left and the right of the hatchway. The water landing on the canted foredeck drained toward the scuppers on the lee side while the gale-like wind blew across the flooded deck sending water to cascade over the forward edge of the deck and down onto the head. At the same time, the ship plowed ahead into mountainous seas sending saltwater up onto the little open platforms beside the base of the bowsprit. The rainwater was not uncomfortably cold. Contrastingly, the sea water was chilling.

Happy that he did not need to visit the port head, which was on the lee side and must have been thoroughly deluged, Diego braced himself and stepped out onto the head and to the gunnel. Rainwater blew onto his back seemingly undiminished by the acres of sail and ship upwind of his perch. He poured the contents of the chamber pot over the gunnel making certain to keep the lip of the pot in contact with the top of the gunnel. It would not do to give the swirling wind an opportunity to bring a sample of the contents back aboard.

The ship dove into the back of a wave and foaming sea water soaked him. He turned to one of the streams from a scupper and rinsed out the pot. While he tended to this chore, he carefully examined the area. Everything appeared to be in order. He did not see blood or parts of clothing or broken rails or splintered wood.

He grabbed a stay anchor to brace himself and peered over the edge of the gunnel. The sea was billows of white foam jumping from the bow. He could see a fluke of an anchor disappear into the sea and emerge again from the foam. The anchor had been lashed so firmly in place it had been made a part of the hull. He waited for the ship to climb a crest before he worked his way to the stairs and back down to the lower gun deck.

The gun deck had been transformed from a narrow alley between canvas curtains to an open area. Each family had removed and stowed the canvas dividers in preparation for the morning formation. Diego returned the chamber pot to the wooden crib that kept it from rolling about. He decided not to change clothes until he knew what his duties would be. If he were assigned to the bilge to labor at the pumps, he might as well remain in wet clothes.

"Thank you, husband," Mézu said. "I do not think I could have managed that chore today."

"It is wet out," Diego said. "At least the chamber pot is well rinsed."

The drummer appeared at the foot of the stairs and began the roll and tap pattern signaling assembly. Normally, assembly was held topside and the entire platoon would form up on Sergeant Herrera. When conditions dictated, a squad or squads might fall in separately at the direction of their squad leaders. The lower gun deck housed two squads and the second gun deck housed the other three. Today the army was to form up by decks.

Releva stood at attention near the center of the gun deck with his head tilted slightly because of the low overhead and one hand pressed against the planking above to steady himself. Acting Corporal López, the other squad leader and junior to Releva, moved to a position that would place him on the right of the formed squads. The men knew to form up in a rank facing their leader beginning at López and his squad and then Releva's men.

"Steady yourselves," Releva barked as the men moved to their positions. The order meant that they were allowed to modify the position of "attention" by pressing one hand against the overhead. The drummer ceased and vanished up the stairway to perform the same call to the second gun deck.

"*Atennn –CIÓN*," Releva barked. Nineteen men stood in tight formation forming a straight line covering less than sixty of the one hundred twenty feet of the lower gun deck. The starboard battery was at their heels. The wives and children were interwoven among the port battery, silently waiting to see what the orders for the day would be. Releva performed an about face and waited.

Captain *Don* Domingo Morera y de Málaga descended to the aft stair and positioned himself in front of Releva. Morera did not brace himself by putting a hand to the overhead, but set his feet wide and moved in harmony with the ship. He held his hat under one arm. Three sailors and two young ensigns had followed him down the stairs with a folding chair, a ledger, a small wooden box and a table. The sailors unfolded the table and set it to Morera's right. One of the ensigns placed a ledger on the table, adjusted the chair and sat down. A sailor placed the wooden box on the table. The ensign open the box, a portable writing kit containing ink, quills and a tiny knife.

"Sir," Releva said as he saluted. "First and second squads, third platoon are present. There are none absent, sir."

"Take your place, Corporal," Morera said. Releva marched to the right end of the formation.

"Now hear this," Morera said in a booming voice conditioned by years of shouting orders. "A naval officer is missing. Does anyone here not know subaltern del la Paz by sight?"

The ensign seated at the table had been trimming the tip of one of the quills as Morera spoke. He dipped the quill into the ink and wrote a line in the ledger. Morera glanced at the scrivener and the man nodded.

"I will come to each of you and ask you some questions," Morera said. "Do not lie to me, for I cannot be fooled." He walked to Releva who had posted himself at the far right of the rank. "What is your name and rank?"

"José Releva, Captain," Releva swallowed almost audibly. "Corporal Releva, sir," he added. The quill could be heard scratching on the ledger.

"Corporal Releva, did you see subaltern del la Paz at any time last night?"

"No, Captain. I did not see the *Barón*."

Morera looked at Releva until the man swallowed again, then he moved to the next man, López. He asked the same questions of López and received the same answer and moved to the next man.

"What is your name and rank?"

"Private Diego deMelilla, Captain."

"Private deMelilla, did you see subaltern del la Paz at any time last night?"

"Yes, Captain."

The quill stopped momentarily and resumed scratching more furiously than ever.

"What was the time when you saw *Barón* del la Paz, Private?"

"It must have been just after midnight, Captain. I think I heard the watch bell."

"Where were you when you saw the *Barón*?"

"I was at the opening to my shelter, Captain. It is just forward of the foremost port gun, sir, the one the sailors call *Serpent's Sting*."

"What was the *Barón* doing when you saw him?" Morera's eyes fixed on Diego's most intently.

"He was in conversation with a girl, Captain."

"Report to my cabin, deMelilla," Morera said. "We will speak further later."

Diego hesitated and Morera shouted, "Now, this instant. Report to my cabin and tell the guard you are to stand by my cabin door until I return. Now Go!"

Diego stepped forward one step, saluted and trotted to the aft stairs. He could see Mézu over the captain's shoulder. She had one hand to her mouth. He turned aft, trotted to the steps and went up without a backward glance.

Morera continued with his interrogation of the men in the ranks. Each man denied having seen the *Barón* the previous night. When he finished with the men, he turned to the families that were scattered about the port battery.

"Which woman here had words with the *Barón* this past night?" Morera's voice was calm, but loud. None of the women moved. "Come now!" he said somewhat more sternly, "who here had words with del la Paz?"

Isabella Campo raised a shaking hand.

"You, child," Morera said. "Come here." Isabella walked from behind her mother where she had taken refuge and continued to the captain, her steps were so small the instep of one foot did not go beyond the toe of the other.

"What is your name, child?" Morera was attempting to speak gently, but he only managed to transform a shout to a growl.

"Isabella Campo, Lord Captain," Isabella said with a curtsy. She had never addressed a lord before in her life. She felt as if she might swoon.

"What was it the *Barón* said to you, Isabella?" Morera had finally managed to produce a conversational tone.

"He said the same thing to me as he had said the night before, Lord Captain."

"Captain is enough, child. There is no need to use 'Lord,'" Morera said. "What was it that he had said to you the night before?"

"I am ashamed to speak it before these people, Lord Captain."

"Nonsense," Morera was beginning to lose his patience. "You have all been locked in this ship in close proximity for months. Do not tell me there are secrets. Out with it."

"He told me, Lord – he would send for me after his watch was over. I was to go to his cabin and lay with him. It was my turn to be his bride for the night."

"What!" Morera shouted. "Do not write that down, fool," he gestured at the ensign at the table and the man's busy quill stopped. *I had been warned the man was a libertine, but this was a child! How long has this been going on?* Morera stomach churned. *Under my nose! The man's cabin is just below mine.* There was no question that this terrified girl was telling the truth. What began as an inquiry into an accidental death was now becoming a murder investigation with – how many suspects? Fathers and husbands of the women on his ship numbered forty. Everyone waited as Morera, lost in thought, stood looking at Isabella.

He shook his head and said, "Is that your mother?" He pointed at the woman who had been shielding Isabella.

"Yes, Lord Captain."

"You and your mother are to go to my cabin and wait for me. This officer will escort you." Morera took the ensign not seated at the table by the elbow and pushed him aft toward the steps leading up. He waived at the other ensign. "Put that away. We no longer have need of it," he said. The ensign pushed a cork into the ink well, put it and the quills into the writing kit and closed it with an audible "pop." He stood, positioned the kit under one arm and shuffled the ledger under the other as the sailors folded the chair and table. Ensign and sailors left the lower gun deck with their burdens leaving the captain standing in silence facing the families of the first and second squad.

Morera turned around and faced the rank of soldiers. He examined their faces. *Did they know their women were being–?* He looked for signs of hatred or anger. What he saw was as a line of expressionless soldiers staring straight ahead.

❦

Diego ran up to the steps to the second gun deck, circled around the base of a mast and continued up another set of stairs to the open main deck. He ran aft to another set of steps and up to a raised portion of deck just forward of the quarterdeck. The door to the captain's cabin was set under the quarterdeck. He entered and descended to a narrow hall that ran the breadth of the stern. The door to the captain's cabin was set against the aft side of the dimly-lit passageway and guarded by two Marine sentries.

A sailor Diego recognized as last night's fire watch stood against the opposite bulkhead under a line of louvered skylights. The sailor began to speak when one of the sentries hissed, "*silencio.*" Diego was directed to stand against the bulkhead next to the sailor. He peered through the louver slats to see the feet of people moving about on the mizzen deck. He watched as two women, Campo's wife and daughter, accompanied by an ensign, ascended to the mizzen deck from the main deck. They stepped onto the mizzen deck so he could only see their feet as they made to starboard and the stairs he had descended moments before.

A shaft of light shot through the end of the passageway as the ladies and their escort entered. The ensign preceded the women to the captain's door and opened it for them.

"The captain says these women are to wait within," the ensign said to the guards. "Have these men been allowed to converse?"

"No, *Señior*," one of the guards said. "They have not spoken a single word to each other, as the captain has commanded."

"Good, see that they do not." The ensign went into the captain's cabin and closed the door behind him.

Again, a shaft of light cut across the starboard end of the passageway and three sailors struggled down the steps with the folding table, chair and writing kit. They were followed by the ensign-turned-scribe who had recorded the interrogation on the gun deck. One of the sentries opened the cabin door and stepped back to admit sailors, equipment and scribe. The door was closed again by someone within the captain's cabin. Diego looked at the erstwhile fire watch and the man shrugged.

"Do not speak or even sign to each other," said one of the Marines in Portuguese-accented Spanish. "Stare at the bulkhead opposite you and remain still."

The seas had moderated considerably after the sun had risen and now the ship pitched gently, listing slightly on a starboard tack. The creak of rigging and the unwavering list told Diego the ship was making good time. The passageway was growing stuffy and a trickle of sweat made its way down the small of his back. There were sounds of hurrying feet on the mizzen deck behind him, but Diego did not turn to see. He could tell by the pace of the feet and shouts that Captain Morera was crossing the deck.

The door at the starboard end of the passageway banged open and several officers stepped down into the hallway and began to make their way toward the captain's cabin. Diego could see Lieutenant Reyes in the lead, followed by a Marine officer, Lieutenant Leyba and Captain Morera. The Marine sentry on the starboard side of the cabin door stepped into the center of the passageway, backed up to clear the doorway and shouted, "Captain on deck."

The sentries stomped the deck and came to attention. Someone within the cabin, alerted by the sentry's shout, opened the cabin door and the officers filed in. The door was closed again and the sentries returned to their posts. Sounds of scuffling and voices could be heard from within, but Diego could not understand what was being said. He watched the Marine, the one with the Portuguese accent, as a river of sweat escaped the man's shako and trickled down to his collar.

The door opened and Isabella Campo came out followed by her mother and the ensign. The women were both weeping and mopping their faces with handkerchiefs. Isabella caught Diego's eye and he thought he could see a faint smile wash across her face as she was herded past him to the starboard. They ascended the steps up to the mizzen deck amid the swish of dresses and sobs. The passageway was again silent, more so after the commotion surrounding the women.

"Nuñez!" The shout from within the cabin caused the sailor standing next to Diego to jump. "In you go, Nuñez," said one of the sentries. The man who had stood fire watch walked into the captain's cabin as if he were facing certain death. The door slammed shut and there was another round of shuffling feet and muffled voices.

Nuñez had not been in the cabin more than ten minutes when the door opened again. Diego could see Nuñez's back as the man stood at attention. "Return to your duties," a voice commanded from somewhere in the cabin. Nuñez mumbled, "Yes, sir. Thank you, sir." The man turned around and exited the captain's cabin at a near run.

"DeMelilla!" Diego did not recognize the voice that called him. It was not Captain Morera nor was it Lieutenant Leyba. He stooped to enter the cabin and, once in, he was forced to remain hunched by the low beams and decking above. Morera was seated at a desk with the wide and open stern windows behind him. Sergeant Herrera stood in a far corner almost hidden by the others in the room. He was looking intently at Diego who nodded slightly before turning toward Morera and fixing his stare over the officer's head. Diego could see the straight, unwavering line of the ship's wake trailing across a sea so blue it seemed to glitter. A skylight was open above the captain's desk and the sea breeze flowed in through the windows and out of the skylight. The change in temperature from the stuffy passageway to the nearly cool cabin was striking.

"Well?" Morera growled.

Diego straightened as much as he could and saluted. "Private Diego deMelilla reporting as ordered, sir."

"Private, you indicated to me earlier that you had witnessed *Barón* del la Paz speaking with a girl about midnight last night, is that right?"

"Yes, sir."

Morera paused and when Diego did not elaborate further he said, "Where were you when you observed this conversation?"

"I was standing at the opening to my family quarters, sir."

"And where is that? Be specific, private."

"It was at the foremost, port gun station on the lower gun deck, sir. My quarters are near the thirty-six pounder named 'Serpent's Sting,' sir."

"What was the time?"

"I think it just after midnight, sir." Diego noticed the folding table in a corner of the cabin. The ensign was scribbling furiously.

"Did you know the girl?"

"Yes, sir."

"Well, who was it?"

"Isabella Campo, sir. The girl and her mother were here a few moments ago."

"And what did you hear del la Paz and Isabella Campo say?"

"I could not hear them, sir."

"Who else did you see at that time?"

"There was only the fire watch, the man named Nuñez, sir. I did not know his name at the time, sir. I was in the passageway with him just now, when he was called in here, sir."

"How long was their conversation?"

"I do not know, sir. They were already speaking when I saw them. The *Barón* finished speaking only a few moments after I saw them."

Morera was growing aggravated at Diego's persistence in answering only the question asked. "And what happened next, private."

"Sir, the *Barón* sent Isabella back into her enclosure and started walking forward."

Again, Morera paused hoping Diego would continue. Then he said, "Then?"

"I stepped back into my enclosure, sir."

"Continue."

"I heard *Barón* del la Paz walk past my enclosure, sir." Diego said.

"Did you see where he went?"

"No, sir."

"Did he go up to the head?"

"I don't know, sir," Diego said. "He must have, sir. I did not hear him come back by my quarters."

"What did you do after the *Barón* passed your quarters?"

"I rigged hammocks for my wife and me, sir. We had been sleeping on the deck but the sea was getting up and I hung the hammocks, sir."

"And then?"

"I placed my wife in her hammock and them I climbed into mine, sir. We slept until the morning, sir."

"You said you did not hear del la Paz return from the head, is that right?"

"Yes, sir."

"Did you think that curious?"

"I did not think on it at all, sir."

"Did you see or hear anyone else after del la Paz passed your enclosure?"

"No, sir."

"When was the last time you were at the head?"

"Just before morning formation, sir. I emptied our chamber pot off the starboard head, sir."

"You did? Is that not women's work?"

"Usually, sir. But the sea was up and I thought it best I do it, sir."

Morera looked at the other officers in the room and asked if any had questions of their own. Each man shook his head as the question was put to him.

"Return to your duties, Private deMelilla," Morera said.

"Yes, sir." Diego saluted and left. He walked past the sentries into the passageway and had turned to the starboard when he heard the door slam behind him. He had been expecting to be called back. If Nuñez had seen him last night when he crept to the port head and if the man had reported that fact to Captain Morera, Diego was doomed. It felt as if a spear were aimed at his back as he made his way to the stairs. When he stepped up onto the mizzen deck, he let out a long breath.

◌

Releva and López had organized a bayonet drill for the squads and were prepared to begin when Diego came down from his interview with the captain. Today they were to begin a new exercise. Instead of shadow drills with bayonets against an imaginary foe, they were to substitute cannon rams for bayonet-tipped muskets and spar each other. The families had gathered around to watch, as they often did. Silence descended when Diego came into view.

"Well," Releva said. "Welcome. Get a ram and take your place."

Two squads faced each other, rams in the "guard" position with the sheepskin-wrapped "sponge" end pointed at their opponents. They worked on "thrust" and "parry" on command until the men were exhausted. Shadow drills were nothing like this workout. Parries were not made against the air, but against a determined thrust of a heavy shaft. Diego, more as a reflex than a willful decision, added a quick riposte to his parry. He stopped his ram just inches from his opponent's chest.

"Stop!" Releva shouted. He walked over to Diego and faced him. "Left the Captain's cabin feeling playful?"

"No, corporal."

"What was the meaning of that last move?" Releva asked.

"It was a simple riposte, corporal." Diego said. "It seemed like the natural thing to do."

"Not everything can be found in the manual, corporal." Sergeant Herrera spoke from the rear of the crowd of observers. Herrera and Lieutenant Leyba were the only seasoned combat veterans in the platoon. Those that had been in the uniformed militia had never fought in ranks against an equally armed foe. Pirates ran away when confronted by any disciplined force.

Herrera came out of the crowd and stopped next to Releva and spoke to Diego. "DeMelilla, is it not?"

"Yes sergeant," Diego answered.

"Where were you taught bayonet skills, private?"

"I have never used a bayonet, sergeant," Diego admitted. "I have been trained in the use of the *magado*. I think the bayonet can be used as if it were a *magado* and to good effect."

"No doubt," Herrera said. "Give me a ram, and we will see."

One of the soldiers offered his ram to Herrera, who accepted it and waved Diego over to the center of the gun deck. Soldiers and their families instinctively formed a circle around Diego and Herrera. Diego had trouble standing up straight, the gun deck offered no headroom, rendering several maneuvers impossible. It would be simple and straightforward.

Herrera began defensively with short thrusts and strong parries. Diego made a thrust which Herrera parried to his right and then answered with a lighting fast riposte. Diego just managed to fend off the riposte and he stepped back. Herrera was very good. Two more passes failed to produce a hit.

Herrera lunged and was parried and, expecting a riposte, came to the guard position and swept his ram to the right where Diego's riposte should have come. Instead of a direct thrust, Diego circled his riposte under Herrera's parry and punched the sergeant hard in the stomach. The man sat down with an "umph!"

"Well done, private," Herrera managed to say as he sat on the deck. "I hereby appoint you bayonet instructor for the platoon. See me later and we will make a schedule for you."

Diego helped Herrera to his feet. "I did not intend to harm you, sergeant," he said. "Are you alright?"

Herrera turned to Releva. "Carry on. You will not be finished today until each of you has gone against deMelilla here."

The rest of the day was consumed in the most vigorous bayonet drill the decks of the *San Juan* had ever seen. Drill done, the exhausted men stood for the last formation and were dismissed for supper. There were only two meals a day, breakfast and supper. Soldiers and families gathered about the center of the gun deck. Some lounged on cannon carriages, sat on water pails or the deck. For some reason, all seemed to gather about Diego. Mézu touched Diego's hand. "It is late, my husband. I must put these little one to bed." She began to herd Pedro and Maria toward their station. "The seas are calm tonight," she said. "I think I will not use the hammock."

Diego was about to follow her when Private Campo approached him. "I must tell you now," the man looked about then returned his eyes to Diego, "I owe you more than I could ever repay." He placed a hand on Diego's shoulder. "Thank you, Diego deMelilla y Tupinar."

Campo stepped back and his wife rushed up to Diego, tears in her eyes, and embraced him. "Thank you," she mumbled.

When she released Diego, Isabella Campo came forward and took Diego's hand. "Thank you, *Don* Diego deMelilla." She said and she kissed his hand.

Diego returned to his enclave in a stunned silence, not knowing what to make of it all. It was as if they had known. He lowered the canvas curtains, lacing the corners together. He looked into the swinging hammocks of each child and saw that they were well asleep.

Mézu had created a bed of folded canvas and sacks against the bulkhead. She smiled at Diego and pulled the sheet back for him.

CHAPTER 11

The night of the thirtieth of March came and they had been at sea for nearly four months, never setting foot on land. They had passed south of the islands of Hispaniola and Cuba without landing, the tall mountains of each clearly visible to the north as they followed the westerly track of the trade winds. The islands appeared to hover above the seas, their shorelines far over the horizon. There were no sick aboard and their crossing was blessed with frequent rains, so there was no need for fresh water. No need to stop at Santo Domingo or Bahia de Santiago or back track to Havana. No, the orders were to make for the Mississippi straight away. Cuba slipped away to the east and Morera ordered the helm down until they were sailing north by west on a starboard tack.

As soon as the stars began to appear on the evening of March thirtieth, Captain Morera dangled the sextant before his eye and announced, "The latitude is near. We must be alert." He ordered sail reduced that night until the *San Juan* was practically running on bare poles. Near on to dawn, the lookout high in the *carajo* (crow's nest) called down, "deck there; a light, port three points off the bow." There was no moon, for it had set, and the sea appeared as black as pitch.

"Get a bucket and fetch me some sea water," Morera ordered. A sailor obeyed and when the bucket was presented to him, Morera dipped in his hand and tasted the contents. "Leadsman to the chains!" he shouted and sailors rushed about until two were perched on the anchor chains, port and starboard, tossing sounding leads.

"Ten fathoms and mud!" one of the leadsman called out. He had not only measured the depth, but had examined a sample of the bottom trapped in a recess in the sounding weight.

"Away anchor," Morera shouted.

The clatter of the anchor chains woke the entire ship. It had been four months since the anchors had been dogged into the bow. Now the *San Juan Nepomuceno* swung at anchor in a gently rolling sea. She settled down with her bow pointed toward the brightening sky, mounting each gentle swell that passed beneath her. Every person on board, down to the youngest child, was aware that something had changed.

There was no need to roll "first call." Sailors and passengers alike crowded onto the deck to greet the morning sun.

"Look at the sea!" someone exclaimed. Everyone rushed to the rail and looked down to see a muddy light-brown ocean. All of their lives the sea had been blue-green near shore or a deep sparkling blue when far from land. They had been far from land for the better part of half a year.

"The great river is near," said one of the sailors. "That is why the captain tasted the sea last night. What you see is the muddy river water floating atop the sea. When we set sail, watch our wake and you will see the true color of the ocean billow up from under our keel."

"Deck there; sail to the north-northeast," called a voice from the *carajo* atop the tallest mast.

"That will be the pilot boat, bringing us a guide," said the sailor.

Passengers were sent below where they would not be under foot, but the captain ordered all the gun ports opened, so they could see and enjoy the air. It was a warm last day of March.

Diego watched through the gun port, his arm across *Serpent's Sting* as the pilot boat ranged alongside of the *San Juan*. Mézu looked out over his shoulder while the children lay under the gun's muzzle, intent upon what was occurring. Diego marveled that someone would venture this far from land in such a tiny boat. He looked north-west, for land was to be found in that direction, or so the sailors claimed. He saw nothing, perhaps a small smudge on the horizon, but no tall mountains or jagged cliffs he had come to expect with a landfall.

One man, probably the pilot, carefully timed his leap to the ladder. When his little boat was on the crest of a long roller, he expertly transferred himself to the ladder and disappeared over the gunnel. The little pilot boat sheared away the instant the man's foot left its deck and turned north-northwest running well on a starboard beam reach. Shouts and footfalls echoed from top side and soon the clank of a pawl in the forward capstan told all they would be underway again. The *San Juan Nepomuceno* drifted sternward for a few moments until the captain ordered the helm hard to starboard. Her head began to fall to the port until she was nearly abeam of the wind. Then the captain ordered canvas unfurled and sheets drawn in. The sails filled with a satisfying "pop" and the ship surged ahead. The helm came up a few more points and soon the *San Juan* was racing along after the disappearing pilot boat on her own starboard tack.

"I can see land," someone shouted from an upper deck. Diego strained his eyes and slowly a long, flat green line grew out of the brown sea. Then several buildings could be seen standing on stilts among tall grasses and stunted trees.

"Those buildings are on *Isla Reina Católica*," a voice advised from several guns away. It was Nuñez, one of the sailors assigned to the lower gun deck. "There are a few buildings where pilots sometimes stay and a light-house on the island, but people do not live there year-round. In the late summer and early fall, the season of the hurricanes, everyone goes to Belize, further up the river."

"Where is the river?" someone shouted.

"We are in the river now," Nuñez replied. "Go to the starboard side and look. See those tall grasses and trees? That is the other bank."

Diego studied the bank opposite *Serpent's Sting*. Trees had replaced the tall reeds and the wooden buildings had fallen astern. He estimated that the bank was about three hundred yards away. He crossed over to the starboard side to see a solid wall of trees along a bank that was at least three hundred yards away. He had never imagined a river could be so wide. There were no rivers on Gran Canaria. A few small, stony creeks radiated down between certain ridgelines, but they were dry most of the year. Now he was on a river large enough to carry a great ship.

"Once," Mézu said. "When I was perhaps seven, my father brought us to Seville. We traveled up a river, but it was not nearly as large as this."

The wind held steadily from the east, so the *San Juan* ran easily on a starboard beam reach all day. Sailors were busy adjusting yard arms and sheets as they piloted slight bends in the river, yet they never once were compelled to tack or wear ship. The brown water raced past the hull as if she were making twelve knots, but the land did not seem to keep pace, slipping by at half that speed.

Another stand of buildings appeared clustered among the trees. It was the settlement of Belize, someone said. A pasture had been cleared and Diego could see cattle grazing on little ridges of grass hemmed in by walls of trees. Nothing could be seen beyond the trees. No hills, no towns, nothing. The passengers had to content themselves with watching the scenery pass through the gun ports, for the decks were too busy with sailors scrambling to adjust the rigging and keep the *San Juan* in the center of the river.

Soon they reached a place in the river the sailors called the "Head of the Passes." Here, to Diego's amazement, the river widened. Their heading was more northerly and now Diego watched a setting sun over a forested bank more than eight hundred yards away. He walked to the starboard side and saw an identical line of trees. They were cast in a golden hue and easily eight hundred yards or more distant to the starboard. As he watched through a starboard gun port, another cluster of wooden buildings and a palisade appeared on the bank. He could see figures walking along the bank. With a great river to their front and forests all about, the little place seemed forlorn and lost; the men, almost apparitions.

"Fort *Mardi Gras*."

Diego was startled to see that Nuñez had joined him.

"What does it mean; '*Mardi Gras?*'" Diego asked.

"It is French for 'Fat Tuesday,'" Nuñez explained. "Most places in Louisiana carry French or Indian names. This fort is on a small pass in the river that was discovered on the day before Ash Wednesday. So the French built that pathetic little wooden stockade and gave it the proud name Fort *Mardi Gras*. I think we will not man that fort much longer."

"I hope I am never posted to such a place," Diego said.

"You could do worse," Nuñez said and drifted away.

They ran at night until the moon set, about three hours before dawn, when Morera had lines run to the trees and furled the sails. It would have done no good to anchor, for the river was both deep and swift. The helm had to be manned all night to insure the *San Juan* remained in midstream. When the sun rose, the sails were unfurled, the ship regained her speed and the lines brought in from the trees. For two days and much of two nights after passing Fort *Mardi Gras*, they sailed between banks lined with trees and nothing else. Once they overtook a merchantman and, after some maneuvering, passed her on her lee side. Small boats, dugouts called "pirogues" and skiffs, some with lateen sails and crewed by red, black or sun-browned men began to populate the river.

On the third day, settlements began to appear. Small houses and cultivated fields appeared more frequently along the banks. Cattle, crops and freshly plowed fields, all bordered in the rear by tall trees passed along either river bank. Nothing could be seen beyond the screen of forests behind the farmland. No distant mountains or towns or anything marked the horizon. All that could be seen was green and alive. It had rained on the second day; a rain harder than Diego had ever experienced. From the looks of the lush green forests on either bank, Diego surmised that drought was a rare thing in this part of the new world.

Although the river twisted about, they generally followed a north-northwesterly course until noon of the third day. They rounded a bend and ran north-northeast for eight miles or so before reaching a place called "English Turn." Here the river curved sharply east, then south and then twisted around until the heading upstream was west. Diego was told that the city of New Orleans lay at the end of that western run. The seamanship and river knowledge required to bring the *San Juan* through the twisted bends of the English Turn was daunting.

Nuñez joined Diego at the gun port. Passengers were still restricted to below decks and out from underfoot of the scrambling sailors.

"That tumble of timbers there," Nuñez said as he pointed upriver where the west bank cut across the bow of the ship, "is Fort *Santo Leon*."

The "fort" was a timber stockade without watch towers or defensive corner redoubts to protect against infantry. It was a fort in name only. Diego looked at the pathetic jumble of broken palisades. There had been several "forts" along the river. None seemed formidable, yet ships fighting the current were forced to pass any given point slowly and provided any assemblage of cannon ample opportunity to do harm. Fort *Santo Leon* had the added advantage of being situated in a sharp turn and facing downstream. A ship coming upriver would have to sail directly into cannon fire without benefit of being able to return a broadside.

"Across the river," Nuñez continued, "is Fort *Santa Maria*."

Both men crossed the lower gun deck, Diego stooping to avoid hitting his head on the low beams. "I think there is not a gun mounted there anymore," Nuñez said. "Behind the fort there is a quarantine hospital and a pilot's station. We will be getting a new pilot before we try to run English Turn."

Dilapidated as they were, Diego could see the two forts presented a formidable problem.

Santo Leon would fire down the length of an approaching ship while *Santa Maria* raked the decks, preventing the ship's crew from working the rigging. No ship could make the tight turn without adjusting yards, sails and spars. Diego remembered his father's words, "The only way to take a shore battery is from the land." Neither fort was prepared for a land assault.

The men watched as the pilot boat came downstream from Fort *Santa Maria* and swung alongside. This time there was no swift discharge of a single man. There were shouts from the upper decks, sails were shortened, sheets adjusted and the *San Juan* slowed until she was barely making headway against the current.

Sergeant Herrera appeared on the gun deck. "First squad, on me," he shouted.

Releva hurried the men of the first squad into place and assumed his position on the right end of the line of ten men.

"First squad is to collect all of their people and property. Leave nothing behind," Herrera ordered. "Releva, find which gun port opens above the boat alongside and have your people report there. You will board the pilot boat with the first squad, their weapons, gear, dependents and property. When you arrive at Fort *Santa Maria*, report to the commanding officer for orders."

"We are not going to New Orleans?" someone asked.

"Not today," Herrera said and he strode away.

"Gonzales," Releva barked. "Find the gun port that is centered over the pilot boat. The rest of you people, fall out and gather your things. I want four men to go down into the boat first to help the women and children down. Baggage after the women, then weapons and the rest of the men last."

Gonzales jogged back, "That port," he pointed toward one of the cannon, "opens onto the deck of the pilot boat. There is not a drop of three feet to her deck."

The transfer was rushed, but orderly. Releva was relieved they did not have to send women and children down a ladder suspended over the river. In less than fifteen minutes, eleven fully armed soldiers, six women, nine children, one infant and twelve bundles of clothes, pots and supplies were passed through a gun port and onto the deck of the pilot boat.

Releva was the last to leave the *San Juan*. The little pilot boat was crowded with people and gear. The women huddled near the center of the deck holding their children close. The sudden change from the immense, protective and enclosed *San Juan Nepomuceno* to the open, small lateen-rigged pilot boat was unnerving. The sky was a bright blue, but the deck of the pilot boat was in the shadow of the warship. None from the *San Juan* had left the ship since December of 1778 and it was now the fourth of April, 1779.

Diego moved to where Mézu and the children had gathered their two small cloth sacks of good. He instinctively positioned himself to her right so she would not have to swivel her head to see him.

"Did not the wives warn of this move?" he asked. Diego had always joked that the wives knew more of what was on the morning schedule than did Sergeant Herrera.

"Lucia Enrique was emptying a chamber pot when she heard one of the sailors call to the officer of the deck," Mézu said with a triumphant smile. "She heard him report there was a signal from the fort saying a message was being sent by boat. We all knew something was going to happen. We did not know what."

Calls from the deck of the ship intensified as the air was filled with the sound of sails being filled, sheets being tightened and yards being cranked around. The pilot boat was pushed away from the *San Juan* by her crew of four and it quickly fell astern of the ship. Once clear of the *San Juan*, bright sunlight flooded the open deck causing many to shade their eyes. The sailors hoisted the lateen sail and sheeted it into a close haul to a starboard wind.

The little boat jumped ahead and for a moment Diego thought they would catch up with the *San Juan*, but the larger ship continued to increase in speed while the pilot boat did not. The steersman put the helm down until they were headed for the low dock that jutted out from the bank below Fort *Santa Maria*. Releva was talking to an army officer. Diego had never seen the officer before, so he assumed the man had arrived with the pilot boat and the orders that were sending them ashore.

The pilot boat sailed to within a few feet of the dock when the main sheet was loosed and the sail luffed. They touched the dock without the slightest bump, aided by hands on the dock. The sailors jumped onto the dock and lashed the boat's moorings fore and aft.

"Everyone ashore," Releva shouted, "same order as we boarded."

The dock seemed to sway under Diego's feet and he wondered at how such an unsteady pier could stand. He watched as Mézu and the children made their way off the dock, staggering as if they were drunk. Releva directed his group to a building that was attached to the fort and told them to wait there before he disappeared into the fort. Diego had never seen a fort like *Santa Maria*. Forts on Gran Canaria were massive and made of stone quarried from the volcanic rock. *Santa Maria* was made of timber and earth. There were no stones, no bricks, just sticks, cast iron hinges and mud.

Diego made his way to where Mézu had gathered their children and goods. Pedro and Maria were running about in small circles, falling to the ground and laughing before leaping to their feet again and repeating the process.

Mézu held out her hand to steady Diego. "Mariners call the condition 'sea legs' when the land seems to move," she said. "It will soon pass."

Releva came out of the fort. "First squad, be prepared to fall in on my command in full uniform, muskets, bayonets, cartridge boxes, haversacks and short swords, if you have them. Women and children, into the fort; *Señora* Pérez will show you to your quarters and where to stow your things."

After a few moments of scrambling, the families of the soldiers went into the fort and the men of first squad readied themselves for whatever was to follow. Two men, each pushing a wheelbarrow filled with small bundles came out of the fort and positioned themselves to the left and right of the trail that lead inland from the fort.

Releva stood with his back to the fort, the river on his left. "First Squad, fall in!"

The men formed a single line, centered on and facing Releva. Diego was on the right end of the formation.

"Column of twos to the right – FACE," shouted Releva.

Diego faced to his right as did the third, fifth, seventh and ninth man in the file. The man who had been on Diego's left, the second man in the file, stepped one pace forward, faced right and stepped another pace forward, stopping next to Diego. Every even numbered man in the file did the same, so in an instant a single line of ten men was transformed into two columns of five men each, facing away from the river.

"Sling – ARMS!"

The men adjusted the slings on their muskets and placed them, muzzle up, on their left shoulders.

"You will advance to the quartermaster's men," Releva said indicating the men at the wheelbarrows, "and draw three packets of cartridges. Each packet contains two dozen cartridges. Place two of the packets in your haversacks and fill your cartridge boxes from the third."

The men did as they were told. They opened the tightly wrapped paper packets of twenty-four cartridges and placed each cartridge, bullet end down, into the holes drilled into a wooden block secured at the bottom of the leather box. The process had broken ranks so the men reformed the squad into a column of two without command.

"Tighten slings!" Releva ordered. Muskets were removed from shoulders and the slings drawn taunt.

"Fix – BAYONETS!" The men pulled their bayonets from the leather holsters at their sides and fitted them on the muzzles.

"Shoulder – ARMS!"

The men placed the muskets on their left shoulders, the trigger guard resting against the end of the collarbone.

"At the quick – MARCH!"

The first squad marched down a slight slope onto a muddy, rutted road. Diego could see a wheat field, green with new shoots and a plot of dark green garlic. The ruts in the road were filled with water and the trees seemed to shimmer in the bright sunlight. They were marching through a fantastically rich land, feeling and looking like soldiers and headed – they knew not where.

CHAPTER 12

They had traveled southeasterly, with the river on their left, along a road that was a mud trail through dead indigo stalks that had escaped the harvest in August. New shoots of the plant were working their way up between the debris of old vines and stubble created by the winter's die-back. The sky was a deep blue and the air was heavy with the scent of new growth.

Oh, Mézu, Diego thought. *We will never be hungry again!* Gran Canaria was a place where fresh water could sometimes be scarce and crops could fail. The wheat fields in Agüimes were small and on scattered terraces, the largest of which was smaller than the field he had seen behind Fort *Santa Maria*. In the volcanic Canary Islands arable land had to be created from rock-strewn slopes. The famous wheat fields of Agüimes had taken a hundred years to create. When famines struck, whole villages would suffer. Mothers starved so their children could eat. Young men joined the Spanish army or navy so there would be one less mouth to feed. But here, Diego saw farmlands or wooded forests with no sign of rocks or sand. Everywhere the soil was a rich black or dark brown and to his left was a river of water sufficient to irrigate the planet.

This was the first time in four months that Diego had walked so far in a straight line. They had come about five miles at the quick march and he could tell others in the squad were becoming a little winded. The road began to curve toward the north. The squad rounded the bend in the road and Diego could see people coming south toward them. There must have been thirty people, mostly women and children and a few old men. They had bundles on their backs and some were leading animals such as goats or pigs. The mob of people parted and stepped to the side of the road to allow the soldiers to pass. Many called out in French while gesturing toward the north. The children and some of the women were crying.

Releva halted the squad and began to talk with one of the old men who had shouted out in Spanish instead of French. Releva was the squad commander and as such his normal station was at the rear and left of the left column. Diego's position in the squad was the first man in the right column. Because of the distance from the conversation and the turmoil of crying children and other shouting in French, Diego could hear none of the conversation between Releva and the old man. While he waited he examined the frightened people near him.

The women wore dresses of the same general pattern. The hems were to the ground and the upper part of the dresses ended in a high collar that was buttoned tightly around their necks. Some of the dresses were blue or green with ruffles at the shoulder with long sleeves. All of the women wore bonnets tied tightly under their chins, the long visors hiding their faces from all except whom they faced directly. Some wore boots and others seemed to be barefoot.

Releva finished his conversation and the crowd began to move toward the south.

"Squad!" Releva shouted, "In quickest time. Lock and Load!"

"*Mierda*," Diego heard someone say behind him. This was not a drill.

Diego removed the musket from his shoulder and placed the butt against his hip. He pulled the hammer to half cock and opened the frizzen. He gave the trigger a pull to be certain the hammer was at half cock and was not going to fall while he was loading the weapon. He reached around with his right hand and fumbled open the leather flap to his cartridge box. He grabbed a cartridge by its twisted tip and brought it to his mouth. Pinching the cartridge just above the powder, he bit off the twisted paper. His mind raced through the twelve steps to loading a musket as he worked.

He sprinkled a little powder from the cartridge into the pan and pulled the frizzen down, locking the powder in the pan. He could hear the men behind him clicking their pans closed as well. He grasped the musket at the fore-grip and dropped the butt to the ground near his left foot. He poured the remainder of the powder in the cartridge down the barrel and pushed the ball, still wrapped in paper after it. He withdrew the ramrod from the recess under the barrel, inverted it and placed the cup into the barrel. He rammed the charge to the bottom, the bayonet hampering the process only a little, and bounced the rod twice before withdrawing it and returning it to the recess. He placed the loaded weapon on his left shoulder and came to the position of attention.

"At the quick – MARCH!"

The squad resumed its march to the north. The few people they encountered on the road now were running south. Soon Diego could only see one man coming toward them. He was stumbling and holding his arm across his body. He stepped off the road, wading through knee-high weeds, and stopped when the Squad drew abreast of him. He looked beaten, out of breath and terrified.

"You are too few!" the man shouted in heavily French-accented Spanish and resumed his flight south.

They traveled another half-mile without encountering anyone until they came to a small, seemingly deserted village on the bank of a bayou that flowed out of the Mississippi River. The bayou was only a hundred feet or so wide, but it flowed with a strong current to the east.

Diego could see a large barge moored on the opposite bank next to a dock crowed with men. Many of the men were pointing to the east and shouting in French.

Releva halted the squad a dozen paced from the bank of the bayou, cupped his hands to his face and shouted, "Use Spanish!"

"To your east," one of the men shouted. "They are to your east just beyond the mule barn! Run!"

Releva ordered, "Right – FACE." A squad in a column of two became two ranks of five men each facing toward the east.

"At standard time – MARCH."

Diego could see them now, a cluster of maybe two score men, armed with cane knives and wooden clubs. Two had firearms of some kind. The mob had been pulling a rowboat toward the water, but stopped when they saw the ten soldiers arrayed across the trail along the bank of the bayou. The squad moved at the slower "lock-step" pace of close order drill, each man's shoulder touching his neighbor. The sun was low in the western sky and Diego recognized that it would be in the enemy's eyes, if these men were the "enemy."

"Guard – BAYONET."

Diego removed his musket from his shoulder, placed the butt against his hip and pointed the bayonet forward at eye-level. Out of the corner of his eye he could see the tip of the bayonet of the man behind him extend over his shoulder. They moved forward until the first building of the village was next to the front rank. There was less than a yard between the end of the rank and the wall of the building. The sharp drop to the bayou was two paces to Diego's left.

"Squad – HALT!"

The mob began to move toward them, shouting at the Spaniards, the people on the opposite bank of the Bayou and each other in an unrecognizable babble. Some were reluctant to advance, others urged their fellows on and a few pushed the men in front forward. Diego could not understand the words that were being shouted. It might have been French, but he did not think so. Most of the men in the mob were black. All were dressed in rags.

"Front rank – KNEEL."

Somewhere in the mass of screaming men a decision was reached. The two men armed with what appeared to be fowling pieces discharged their weapons toward the squad and the mob rushed toward them filling the narrow road between buildings and bayou. Diego heard a whirling sound as his hat was snatched from his head.

"Make – READY!"

Diego pulled the hammer back to full cock.

"PRESENT!"

Diego leveled his musket at the mass of men charging up the street.

"*DISPARAR* (Fire)!"

Diego pulled the trigger and the musket bucked against his shoulder.

The mob staggered as men were thrown back upon those behind. They had been packed so tightly together on the narrow trail that every one of the ten balls sent their way struck somebody. Some balls passed through men in the front to hit those in rear.

"Lock and Load – Present when Ready!" Diego and the front rank stood – the musket had to be loaded from the standing position. He hurried through the loading process keeping one eye on the mob, fearing they may surge forward again before he could reload. Instead of rushing forward, the mob pulled the dead and wounded back to the end of the street and regrouped. They moved forward once more just as Diego knelt and presented his musket. After what seemed like minutes, Diego perceived the barrel of a musket appear over his shoulder. The man behind him had finally reloaded.

"FIRE!"

Again the musket kicked against Diego's shoulder and men coming toward him were thrown back in a spray of blood. This time the mob did not halt, they continued on, screaming.

"Front Rank, Defend – BAYONET!"

Diego jumped to his feet and prepared to engage the enemy with his bayonet.

"Second Rank, Lock and Load! Present when ready!"

A coal black man, eyes wide and screaming incoherently came at Diego. The man wielded a small hatchet, but before he could get close enough to strike, Diego stabbed him in the throat with the bayonet. The man dropped his weapon and staggered toward the bayou, forcing one of his companions off the small bluff with him and into the swirling water. Temporarily without an opponent opposite him, Diego stabbed another attacker in the side as the man attempted to pull a musket away from the soldier to his right. A muzzle appeared over Diego's shoulder and he heard Releva's hoarse voice command "Fire."

Orange flame poured onto the mob and once more they stopped, unable to proceed because of the dead mounded before them. This time, as the mob pulled back Releva ordered, "Advance – BAYONET."

The squad picked its way over the dead and dying, reforming on the move as they passed the tangle of bodies. Diego glanced to his right to keep his proper position and saw his squad moving forward with him, bayonets dripping gore. White uniforms soaked in blood and faces blackened by powder from the cartridges, they advanced in perfect formation. They were a frightening sight.

Another man came at Diego with a pitchfork pointed straight ahead. Diego parried the fork and riposted, driving his bayonet into the man's stomach. The man fell screaming and clutched the shaft of the bayonet. Diego kicked the man in the chest to withdraw the bayonet and stepped over him, keeping in rank.

The enemy now numbered fewer than twenty men, most of whom were unarmed. The majority of the mob had been killed, wounded or simply run away. Confronted by the determined advance of the Spaniards, the mass of angry men became a terrified herd bent upon escape. Those who were armed dropped their weapons and fled beside the unarmed. None attempted to surrender and they scattered into the brush beyond the little village.

"Halt! Lock and Load, shoulder your musket when ready!"

Diego reloaded, never taking his eyes away from the brush where the survivors had escaped. There was some more shouting from behind him and Diego twisted his head to see the barge that had been moored on the opposite bank of the little bayou was being pulled across loaded with mounted men and several leashed dogs.

"The militia," Releva said. "Now that the heavy work is done, the local militia will round up the stragglers."

"Who were these people?" Gonzales asked.

"Slaves from the indigo plantation," Releva said. "They were going to try to make it to the lakes to the east. If they could cross the lakes they would be in English territory."

"They were poorly led," Gonzales said.

"They were desperate," Diego said. Diego noticed a soldier from the squad leaning against the building at the western end of the village. The man was holding his hand, his head on his chest.

"Who is that, corporal?" Diego asked, nodding toward the soldier.

"It is Nezer," Releva said. "He had the ends of two fingers on his left hand cut off. Otherwise, we have had no casualties."

The barge landed and the dogs were released. Releva directed the squad to stand against the buildings as the howling dogs raced by followed by a dozen mounted men with *escopetas*, the short muskets favored by mounted men, and sabers.

"Is this what we are here for, corporal?" Diego asked. "Have we been brought from Gran Canaria to put down slave revolts?"

"You are here, deMelilla," Releva said, "to kill the king's enemies."

෫ා

Andrés de Almonester y Roxas, Secretary of War for the province of Louisiana walked into the office of Bernardo de Gálvez y Gallardo, Governor Colonel of Louisiana.

"You were correct, my Colonel," Almonester said. "The attempt was made disguised as a slave revolt."

"And were any of the conspirators captured?" Gálvez asked.

"No, my Colonel," Almonester said as he lowered himself into a chair. "Two of the twenty-three killed may not have been slaves. It is hard to tell. All of the people who were captured proved to be slaves fresh from Africa."

"Were any of our people killed?"

"No, my Colonel. One was wounded, that is all," Almonester examined his fingernails. "Leyba sent but a single squad from the *San Juan*," Almonester said, "ten men against nearly forty. How they did it, I cannot tell."

"Hurumph!" Gálvez grunted. "They accomplished it because they are Spaniards."

"In truth, my Colonel," Almonester replied, "they were almost entirely *Isleños*. The remainder of the recruits on the *San Juan* disembarked here, along with their families."

"We do not know," Gálvez continued, "if we have thwarted the attempt to intercept the Americans or not." The English colonial revolutionaries were being called the "Americans" by the people in Louisiana because the Declaration of Independence bore the heading the "United States of America." Gálvez stood and paced the width of the room behind his desk. "*Señor* Pollock must be allowed to bring his – goods north."

Oliver Pollock was an American revolutionary and a spy. He was working to bring gunpowder, muskets, medicine and other war materials north on the Mississippi River to the Ohio and on to Fort Pitt and the American forces battling the English. Gálvez had been informed that a slave revolt would be instigated in Louisiana by the English. During the resulting confusion Pollock would be killed and his several long boats filled with war supplies would be stolen. Gálvez believed Leyba had not realized the importance of defeating the uprising. If he had, he would have sent more than a single squad when word of the revolt reached him. Still, the revolt was put down and, so it seems, the spies were killed. This was not the first time foreign agents had stirred rebellion. It seemed as if the entire world were ripe for rebellion.

"We have yet much to do, my friend," Gálvez said. "Inform Lieutenant Leyba we will require some of his men – more than a mere squad, to be sure."

Gálvez followed Almonester to the door and waited as the man exited. Gálvez's clerk stood when the men entered the outer office. Almonester waited as the clerk hurriedly opened the door to the hall and, with a final nod to Gálvez, left. The clerk closed the door and turned around to see that Gálvez had not returned to his office, so the man waited expectantly."

"Renaldo, please send for Captain Jacinto Panis. Have him come here at once."

"*Sí, Gobernador*," Renaldo said with a bow.

"They are coming back!"

Mézu heard the call from the road below the fort. She gathered her children and rushed to the edge of the road where she was joined by the other families. Far up the road she could see the column of men, two abreast. The sun was beginning to set and its red light painted the soldiers as they marched south. She could see Diego, hatless and in his usual position in the front of the right column. She was beginning to wonder why Diego was hatless when she began to realize the white uniforms were not cast red by the setting sun. It was something else. As they drew closer, she could see that the men were haggard, dirty and covered in blood.

Some of the women wailed and others pulled their children closer. Mézu could hear the women around her counting the number of men and murmuring the names of their loved ones when they were recognized. The squad was halted on the street and faced toward the fort. Releva posted himself center front and ordered, "Salute – ARMS!"

Diego removed his musket from his shoulder and held it vertically before his body, the muzzle straight into the air and the hammer just inches from his stomach.

"Empty – PANS!"

Diego lifted the frizzen and dusted the powder out of the pan with his fingers. He then held the hammer with his thumb, pulled the trigger and lowered the hammer.

"Sheath – BAYONETS!"

Diego lowered his musket, grasped the bayonet, twisted it to pass the lug, removed it from the barrel and sheathed it.

"Order – ARMS!"

Diego placed the butt of the musket on the ground next to his right foot and held it vertically against his right side.

"When you are dismissed, withdraw the charge from your piece before you enter the fort or greet your people. The armorer will come around with a screw if you should have any problems. Clean your weapons and keep your cartridges dry. Tomorrow we will march to New Orleans."

Diego caught Mézu's eye and smiled. Seeing the anguish on her face, he mouthed, "I am not hurt. Stay there." He walked to a log that had been placed along the path to the fort and, inverting his musket, tapped the muzzle on the log. Paper and a lead ball appeared at the end of the barrel after only a few bounces. He pulled the ball and paper free and poured the excess powder onto the ground. He tucked the ball in a pocket, walked up to Mézu and took her hand.

"Mother of God," Mézu said. "What has happened?"

"The army has not tarried in providing us with work," Diego said. "Did you see how things are growing here? And there is fresh water everywhere. Our farm will flourish."

"Diego," she whispered. "You marched away five hours ago and return looking as if you have been to hell."

"Some were sent that way," Diego said. "I do not know why or even who they were. Maybe we will learn more tonight, but now I have to clean my musket, bayonet and this uniform."

∾

The women and children spent the night in the crude barracks that ran along one wall of Fort *Santa Maria*. The men bivouacked in bedrolls in the courtyard. The fort had three ancient cannons that pointed toward the river. Diego held a candle close to the breech of one to read the inscription. It was in French and all he could understand was the date: 1672. The thing was over a hundred years old.

Releva detailed a guard rotation, three men in shifts of two hours. He posted the men to watch inland for he believed there would be no threat from the river. In the morning, a wagon drawn by a mule was brought to the fort's gate. Baggage and small children were loaded onto the wagon and the squad formed up in the road where they had been dismissed the evening before. Most had changed into their spare uniforms for there had been no opportunity to wash clothes.

Releva had the squad move forward in tactical formation. Two men were posted as advanced guard and sent well ahead on the road beyond the sight of the wagon. Two more men were placed several yards ahead and well to the left and the right of the road but where they could see the advanced guard and the wagon. The women and older children followed the wagon and the remainder of the squad marched along either flank of the civilians. All of the soldiers had fixed bayonets.

In about an hour they reached the bayou that had been the scene of the fight the night before. There were no signs of the battle. Villagers were about and when the Spaniards arrived, they were cheered by a dozen farmers and boatmen. The wagon was worked onto the barge and ferried across the narrow bayou. Diego learned that the bayou was named *Terre Aux Boeufs* which meant "land of the oxen" in the local tongue.

It required two more crossings before the small caravan could be assembled on the north bank and the trek to New Orleans could be resumed. They rested at noon near a small stream leading away from the river. It was called Bayou *Pecheur*. Mézu, who could speak a little French she had learned in her youth, said it meant "Fisherman's Bayou." The men were allowed to eat with their families and when the march resumed, Releva had them parade in formation. They were near the city now and he no longer felt the need to guard against ambush.

The first thing that Diego noticed about New Orleans was the smell. The road was bordered by ditches filled with stagnant water. Once, the squad had to halt when a man leading an ox sled from the city stopped near the edge of the road, blocking the way. He paid no mind to the soldiers as he uncovered a barrel that had been lashed to the sled and tipped the contents into the ditch. He did the same with the two other barrels, turned the sled around and pulled to the side of the road to allow the caravan to pass. Everyone hurried past the sled for the contents of the barrels had been dipped from outhouses or collected from chamber pots throughout the city.

It was nearing dusk when they arrived at a redoubt called Fort Saint Charles which marked the downriver corner of the city. A barracks was attached to the fort which was to be the temporary home of the settlers. The rest of the passengers from the *San Juan* were there, giving the squad's arrival the feeling of a homecoming. That night one of the men produced a *bordonúa* and played with skill while Diego's deep baritone voice filled long barracks and the children laughed and danced. At last, they had arrived in New Orleans.

CHAPTER 13

"A tennnn – CIÓN," Sergeant Herrera bellowed in his "parade ground" voice. The third platoon had been assembled in the street under the shadows of the guns of Fort St. Charles. City folk stopped their morning chores to watch the soldiers in their white uniforms and gleaming muskets. Sergeant Herrera examined the ranks from his position at the center front of the formation. He barked a command or two and the men adjusted accordingly. Satisfied, he faced about, assumed the position of attention and waited. The many sloopes, boats and barges that plied up and down the river did not seem to distract him at all. He turned his head over his right shoulder and commanded, "Parade – REST." The sound of fifty men changing to the position of parade rest sounded as if one great beast had stamped a hoof. Then they waited.

A carriage pulled up on the street upriver of the formation. Two officers and a man in civilian dress climbed out followed by a clerk who rushed to recover something from the boot of the carriage. Diego recognized one of the officers as Lieutenant Leyba. He had never seen the other officer, the civilian or the clerk before. The group from the carriage stood near the road and talked together for a minute before Leyba broke away and strode toward Sergeant Herrera.

"*Atennnn – CIÓN*," Herrera shouted when it was clear to him that Leyba was going to take command of the formation.

"Sir, third platoon of the Fixed Infantry Regiment of Louisiana is present," Herrera held his salute.

"Thank you, sergeant," Leyba said, returning the salute. "Take your post."

Herrera marched to the front right corner of the formation and dressed on the first rank.

"Stand at ease," Leyba ordered and the entire formation relaxed and fixed their eyes on Leyba. "*Señor* Langois is the contractor who has built the settlement cottages in *Concepcón*." Leyba gestured toward the civilian. "*Señor* Coron –" Leyba indicated the clerk who was setting up a small field table on which the man placed a ledger. "– will read off the names of the families who are to be granted cottages in *Concepcón*, a place not fifteen miles from here."

The settlers had been promised they would be provided a small plot of land, farm tools and a cottage. There had been some rumors that the families would be garrisoned together and the men marched off to some battle, a rumor given validity by the action near Fort *Santa Maria*.

The information they were now receiving relieved many wives.

"*Señor* Langois will post himself at that vessel," Leyba pointed to a single-masted river sloop. "When your name is called, fall out to gather your family and goods. Report to *Señor* Langois before you board."

Langois walked slowly upriver and stopped by a gangway that stretched from the bank on the river to the deck of the low, wide sloop.

"You may begin, Coron," Leyba said.

Coron cleared his throat, "Campo, Miguel!"

Campo came to attention, shouldered his musket and stepped out of the formation. Before he had cleared the front rank, Coron said, "Nieves,

Bernardo." Another soldier left the formation. By the time Coron was finished only fifteen *soldados* (private soldiers), Diego and Sergeant Herrera remained in the formation.

"Close ranks!" Leyba said. The men moved up and to the right as their location required until there were two ranks of eight men each with Herrera posted on the right of the front rank.

"You are now assigned to the Cabildo," Leyba indicated the other officer. "This officer is Captain Jacinto Panis." Leyba pronounced the name "pa-Ná." He is your commanding officer and will instruct you as to your duties." Leyba saluted Panis, "Your unit," he said and strode over to the line of settlers lined up to board the sloop.

"Sergeant Herrera," Panis ordered. "Front and center."

Diego watched as Herrera conferred with Panis. Panis was of medium build and appeared to be a *peninsulare* (a native of mainland Spain). The man did not wear a wig and had black hair pulled into a tight queue that hung behind his gold-trimmed bicorn, a black pointed mustache and a goatee. He wore the tropical Spanish uniform of white coat, blouse, trousers and gaiters. Only the coat's facing and cuffs were *Borbón* blue. He had a confidant air that was not pretentious. Diego also noticed that of all the men remaining only he had children. The other men were either unmarried or accompanied by a wife alone.

Their conference completed, Herrera turned and shouted, "*Soldado* deMelilla."

Diego, startled by the unexpected pronouncement, hesitated and then hurried to Herrera where he stopped at attention.

"This is Private de Melilla, Captain," Herrera said.

"Thank you, sergeant," Panis said in a strong Castilian accent. "Take charge of your men."

"Yes, sir." Herrera saluted and returned to the remaining soldiers. Diego could hear Herrera behind him as the sergeant gave the orders marching the men back to the barracks area behind the mud and timber redoubt so proudly named "Fort Saint Charles."

"Stand easy, deMelilla," Panis said in a conversational tone. "My name is Captain Jacinto Panis. I am told that you were in the skirmish on *Terre Aux Boeufs* yesterday." Panis waited until Diego responded with, "yes, sir."

"Captain Leyba tells me that you conducted yourself with valor and you are known to be highly skilled in the use of the bayonet and short sword."

"I did no more than any other man, sir."

"Truly?" Panis smirked. "DeMelilla, I have been assigned a task by the governor that will require the assistance of a man skilled and experienced in the use of weapons. Corporal Releva has recommended you in the highest terms." Panis paused again, but Diego said nothing. Panis continued, "When we are finished here, go collect your family and see that they are settled in the quarters we have set aside for the wives of the Saint Charles Guard. Sergeant Herrera will show you the room." Panis examined Diego for a moment. "Have you ever fired a rifle?"

"No, sir," Diego knew the difference between a rifle and a musket and that it took special care to properly load a rifle. It was something he had been told about, but never performed.

"No matter," Panis shrugged, "What are your preferred weapons?"

"The *magado*, sir," Diego said, "the *sunta* and the short sword, sir." Diego noticed the officer's quizzical expression. "The *magado* is a kind of lance, sir and the *sunta* is a mace, sir."

"Ah, yes," Panis said, "the traditional weapons of the *Isleños*. Fine. Tonight I will send a man to your apartment. His name is Pesaofe Dardar. He will have some supplies for you and further instruction. Tomorrow, we will depart. We may be gone for two months, or more, so prepare your family accordingly."

"Yes, sir," Diego said, his mind racing. *Separated from Mézu and the children for two months!* He had never spent more than one night away from Mézu since they were married twelve years ago.

"You are dismissed, private," Panis said. "Tend to your family."

Diego snapped his heels and saluted by touching his left hand to the bayonet stud of the musket by his side. He faced about, lifted the butt of the musket until it cleared the ground by about six inches into the position known as "trail arms" and jogged away from the river to find Mézu.

He found Sergeant Herrera first and was directed to return his musket, and bayonet to the armory. His cartridge box and spare cartridges were to be returned to the powder magazine. When asked about his short sword Herrera told him to keep it with him. "You may have cause to need it," Herrera said.

"Where am I going?" Diego asked.

"That, I do not know. You have been assigned to Panis by Captain Leyba," Herrera shrugged. "Beyond that, who knows?"

Diego found the quarters that had been assigned to him and his family. It consisted of two rooms that had been built into the back wall of the redoubt. The structure was entirely made of rough-cut planks with a sloping roof that jutted out from under the long fire-step behind the outer walls. Each room had its own doorway and a shuttered window that opened to the courtyard and they were connected by a passage in the common wall between them. There were thirty such rooms along the fort's landside and upriver walls. The rooms abutting the other walls were for officers, armory, storage and powder. Diego could see the rear of the raised gun platforms from the door of his quarters, but not the guns themselves.

Mézu had already arranged their meager possessions in the two rooms. One room had two rope-net beds and mattresses filled with moss. The walls were lined with pegs on which she had hung articles of clothing. One peg held the *sunta* suspended by the leather wrist loop. His *magado* rested against the same peg. The other room contained a crude table and two chairs. The children would have to sleep on mattresses lain on the floor. Mézu had hung a blanket across the passage to serve as a door. The ceiling was as low as the overhead had been on the *San Juan* and Diego could not stand to his full height in either room.

Diego looked at Mézu with an apologetic expression on his face. "We will obtain better housing once all of the settler cabins have been completed," he said. "There were not enough cabins finished for everyone, so the larger families were given priority."

"We are here, my husband," Mézu said. "I do not think even the *Ricohombre* of Santa Cruz de Tenerife can reach us here."

"I am to depart tomorrow with a captain," Diego said. "He says I will be gone for two months."

"Where are you going?"

"I have not been told where we are bound."

"Who is this captain?"

"Jacinto Panis," Diego shrugged. "I saw him for the first time today. There will not be many of us. Only three, I think. The captain, me and a man named Dardar."

"Do not worry about us, my husband," Mézu said as she kissed Diego. "There are ten young wives quartered here with us. Pedro and Maria will have ten mothers. We will be safe."

The sun was beginning to set and the courtyard was filled with a reddish-orange glow. Mézu had opened the shutters and doors to cool the rooms while the family joined the others around the oven to eat and talk. When darkness fell, lamps were lit and hung next to the doorways so people could retire if they desired. The watch and duties of the garrison had been determined so some soldiers drew weapons and posted themselves at the gate or on the gun platforms, others finished their meals at the common table or brought food and drink to their quarters. Diego had not been on the duty roster.

The meal was a stew of fresh vegetables and ham. It was delicious and the first fresh food they had eaten since leaving Gran Canaria. There was wine and ale to drink as well as water drawn from a cistern. There had been frequent rains for the last few days and the water from the cistern was cool and sweet. Pedro and Maria filled themselves with stew and each was allowed to drink a small cup of wine. A few mosquitoes began to pester the group and Diego herded his family into their quarters. Mézu put the children to bed and latched the door to the courtyard. She hung a fine netting that had been supplied with the bedding over the window and left it open.

A small candle-keep hung in the corner. The candle within provided a flickering yellow light to the room. Mézu had hung a blanket across one corner of the room near the passage into the room where the children were now sleeping. This formed a small triangular space providing some privacy for the chamber pot.

Diego examined the wide frame for the single bed. He checked the ropes woven across between the plain wooden planks of the bed frame. The frame was too short for him, but then all bed frames were too short for Diego. Deciding the ropes had been drawn sufficiently taunt, he lifted the mattress and noticed that it was newly made and freshly stuffed. Unlike the mattresses he had used in Gran Canaria, this one was filled with black, twisted fibers and was surprisingly light.

"It is dried moss," Mézu said. "The laundry woman told me about it. A grey moss gross from the trees hereabout, the French call it, "*Barbe du*

Espagnol." She tugged at Diego's beard. He had trimmed it into a goatee their first night aboard the San Juan after Sergeant Herrera had informed him that full beards were against regulations. His moustache, on the other hand, was wide, full and waxed into points that extended beyond his cheeks, conforming to an unofficial regulation.

"What does '*Barbe du Espagnol*' mean? If I say it slowly, it sounds like 'Spaniard's beard.'" Diego replied as he pulled Mézu closer. They had the little room all to themselves and both were enjoying the palpable increase of tension.

"That is what it means. It is not a difficult language to learn once you adjust to the pronunciations. We are going to live here now and everyone speaks French, my husband." Mézu began to twirl one of the waxed tips of Diego's moustache. "You will have to learn the language. I am told that the Governor Gálvez has even taken a French wife, a *criolla*. They say she is beautiful."

"That is what Spaniards do," Diego said. "Go to foreign lands and marry the most beautiful women they can find."

Their growing moment of intimacy was interrupted by a call from the courtyard. "DeMelilla!" The voice called, "I am looking for Private deMelilla!"

Diego looked at Mézu, sighed and kissed her lips. He reluctantly released her. His embrace had lifter her off her feet and as he eased her down she remained balanced on her toes until he turned to go to the door. Diego pulled the unlatched door open and stepped out. He heard Mézu come to the doorway behind him.

"Here!" Diego shouted.

A small shape in the courtyard turned toward Diego. The man held an oil lamp before him as he walked briskly up to Diego. He was average height, maybe five foot-two inches tall, his dark hair flowed from beneath a wide-brimmed hat that hid most of his features. He wore a large canvas coat with overlapping folds like miniature capes across his shoulders and around his arms. The folds were fringed with unwoven threads as if the cloth were unraveling along the edges. His legs were wrapped in cloth held in place by leather lacing, creating make-shift gaiters from the tops of his shoes to his knees. Only the collar of a cotton shirt and a short length of cotton trousers were visible behind the over-sized coat and gaiters; neither had been dyed but both were now the color of tea. He placed a large bundle he had been carrying on the ground when he reached Diego and shifted the lantern to his left hand.

"I am Pesaofe Dardar," the man said, extending his hand. "My friends call me 'T'Chien.' Are you Private Diego deMelilla?"

Diego took the hand. The man's grip was strong, though Diego's hand engulfed the other. The hand was calloused and leathery from a lifetime of hard work.

"I am," Diego said, glancing down at the bundle that now lay at his feet. He could see the barrel of a musket protruding from the canvas sack. It was not polished steel like every other musket Diego had seen. This barrel was thick, dark brown and had a small raised fragment of iron fixed onto the tip about the size of half a copper coin.

"Good. *Don* Jacinto Panis has sent these things to you," T'Chien said as he pointed to the canvas bundle. The man's accent was one that Diego had never heard. It was not a French accent. T'Chien removed his hat revealing his face for the first time. He had a weathered face with high, almost Oriental cheekbones, no beard or mustache and a beak-like nose. His eyes were large, round and set far apart and dark. "*Don* Jacinto says I am to tell you about what we shall be doing," T'Chien continued. "Can we go into your quarters?"

"Yes, of course," Diego said. He stepped aside and directed T'Chien toward the doorway where Mézu was standing.

"Here is my wife, Maria Artiles," Diego said when they reached the door. "This is Pesaofe Dardar. Captain Jacinto Panis has sent him here with some things I am going to need."

Mézu curtsied. "It is my pleasure to make your acquaintance, *Señor* Pesaofe Dardar."

"Madam, my friends call me T'Chien. Most Spaniards find 'Pesaofe' difficult to pronounce. The French find it impossible, so they call me T'Chien – Little Dog."

"T'Chien, you must call me Mézu." She stepped back into the room. "Please come in. The children are asleep in the other room."

Mézu led T'Chien to one of the chairs at the table and Diego took the other. He placed the bundle on the table and T'Chien began to untie the opening.

"We have some wine, T'Chien," Mézu said, "and some fresh bread. Would you care for some, we have plenty."

"No, *Señora* Mézu," T'Chien said. "Thank you, but I have just come from dinner."

"If you should change your mind, it is here," she said as she placed some cups and a jug on the table. "I think I hear the children stirring," she said. "Please excuse me," and she stepped past the curtained doorway into the next room.

"I have a rifle for you here," T'Chien said as he pulled the heavy barrel from the bag and handed it to Diego. "Here is the stock and the lock." The weapon had been dissembled and T'Chien placed the wooden stock and the trigger and hammer mechanism, the lock, on the table.

Diego noticed that the wall of the barrel was much thicker than a musket and the interior of the barrel had grooves that spiraled down from the mouth. The closed end of the barrel had a single hooked claw, just as did every musket, which would be inserted into a matching slot in the back of the lock. He fingered the slanted piece of iron fixed to the end of the barrel.

"That is the 'front sight blade,'" T'Chien explained. "And this," he touched another half-coin size bit of iron fixed across the barrel four or five inches forward of the closed end, "is the rear sight." The rear sight had a notch cut in the center. The barrel was not round, but hexagonal with a flat iron strip attached to the side opposite the sights. The strip had iron loops on it and a notch cut through it opposite the rear sight. "Watch as I assemble the rifle. It is the same as a musket." T'Chien placed the lock mechanism in the stock and inserted a screw through a brass-encircled hole in the side of the stock and into a threaded hole in the lock. He turned the screw by hand until he could not grip it anymore and tightened it down using a copper coin.

T'Chien placed the hooked end of the barrel into the recess in the lock and pushed the barrel down into the long slot of the stock. He threaded a wide, flat brass pin through another hole in the forearm of the stock. The hole in the forearm was aligned with the slot under the barrel so the brass pin locked the barrel into the stock. He then slipped the ramrod down the loops under the barrel and snapped it into place and gave the rifle to Diego.

The ramrod was wooden, not steel, and it had a brass cup on the end. The rifle was much shorter than Diego's musket, but nearly as heavy. It did not have a bayonet locking stud. The powder pan, frizzen, hammer and flint were half the size of a musket. Even if it had been equipped with a bayonet, the rifle's short length would make it ineffective in a close fight.

"I might as well use a club in a close fight," Diego said, clearly unimpressed by the little rifle when he mentally compared it to the tall, heavy and bayonet-tipped musket.

"If you are in a close fight, it is too late for the rifle," T'Chien said. "Then it is swords, knives or tomahawks." T'Chien placed his hand on the hatchet tucked into his belt. He pulled a bundle of heavy canvas from the bag and unrolled it across the table to reveal a coat identical to the one T'Chien wore, except that it was clean and probably new.

"This is a hunting frock," he said. "My woman has rubbed it thoroughly with bee's wax to keep the water out," T'Chien said. "You will not need your uniform. Your shoes, trousers and shirts will be fine, but no coat or uniform hat. Here is a hat for you." He tossed a folded leather skull cap to Diego. "You should wear your gaiters to keep briars and ticks out of your shoes."

T'Chien stood and gestured at the remaining items in the bag. "There is a possible bag in there. Wear it instead of a cartridge box. It has flints, powder and rifle balls in it. Bring your haversack and a bedroll. We will be gone for at least two months but we will be on foot. Do not bring more than you need."

"What about food, water?" Diego asked.

"Bring enough food and water for three days. More will be provided along the way," T'Chien made his way to the door. Mézu came from the neighbor room and stood next to Diego as T'Chien ducked out of the apartment and turned to face them.

"We will come for you at first light, Diego. Good night, *Señora* Mézu." T'Chien gave a little nod toward Mézu.

"Good night, *Señor* T'Chien," she said.

Mézu put her arm around Diego's and squeezed. "Come to bed, my husband," she said.

CHAPTER 14

D iego stood with Mézu at the doorway of their quarters watching the morning formation of the duty soldiers. Maria held her mother's hand and Pedro leaned against the wall trying to appear unconcerned. Light was just beginning to filter over the wooden palisade of Fort Saint Charles and the open gate facing the city was alive with people involved in supplying the post. Only a score of soldiers were garrisoned at the fort. The walls and cannon platform could accommodate nearly a thousand men, but this was a police garrison, not a frontier post. Disciplined militia throughout the city would rally to the fort if the city were threatened by a large force. The daily routine of the soldiers stationed here included peace-keeping patrols and the unbearable tedium of maintaining a wooden, earth-filled palisade in nearly tropical conditions. As portions of the French-built wooden walls rotted away, the Spanish replaced them with locally produced brick.

Don Jacinto Panis and T'Chien appeared in the gate following several women carrying bundles of laundry. Diego did not recognize Panis immediately, for the man was in the same dirty woodsman garb as T'Chien and he had shaved off his goatee and moustache. T'Chien pointed toward Diego and both men worked their way around the formation of soldiers and the scurrying civilians.

"Good morning, deMelilla," Panis said. "Good morning, *señora*." He nodded toward Mézu. She curtsied and said, "Good morning *señores*."

"Mézu, this is Captain *Don* Jacinto Panis," Diego said although he was certain she knew it. "These are our children, Pedro and Maria." He indicated the sullen Pedro and little Maria who pressed against Mézu.

"I fear, *señora*," Panis said, "we will require your husband for several weeks. Has he told you what we are about?"

"He has not, Captain," she said.

Panis examined Diego and nodded approvingly. Diego had the rifle slung over his right shoulder, the curved shoulder plate just visible next to his head. The frock, which had no buttons, was held closed by a wide leather belt. He had the *sunta* tucked in the belt on his right and a short sword hung on the left. The narrow brim of the leather cap was turned up. A bulging haversack was positioned on his left and the possible bag on the right, their straps crossing at Diego's chest. He had a bedroll across his shoulders secured by leather cords tucked into the front of the cross straps. Diego held the *magado* as if it were a walking staff, the brass knob of the butt next to his foot.

"A good start, private," Panis said. "You must, however, shave off your goatee and moustache. They proclaim you to be a soldier of Spain more than any uniform."

"Yes, sir," Diego said. He held out the *magado* to Pedro who hurried to take it. As he turned to re-enter the building he began to unbutton his haversack.

"If you have a shaving kit," Panis called after him, "leave it here." Then the captain turned to Mézu. "He will be hard to recognize when we return, *señora*," Panis said.

"Will he be covered in blood?" Maria asked from behind her mother's apron.

"The last time Diego marched away he returned covered in blood and grime," Mézu said. "It frightened the children."

"It frightened Maria," Pedro said. He added *"señor"* after a slight pause.

"How old are you, Pedro?" Panis asked.

"I will be eleven this December, *señor.*"

"Nearly a man," Panis said with a smile. He would have identified Pedro as Diego's son without an introduction. The boy was nearly as tall as his mother. His hair was blond, but it was the sparkling blue eyes that marked him as Diego's offspring.

Diego came out of the doorway wiping his face with a rag. He had to stoop to fit under the lintel and when he straightened Mézu saw her husband without a beard for the first time in her life. She suddenly had a sensation that she would never see Diego again. The premonition was so strong that it forced a tear to her eye. She stood on her toes, placed her free hand around his neck and pulled him to her. She kissed his lips then whispered, *"Vaya con Dios."*

Diego sensed the mood change in the normally stoic Mézu and it puzzled him. The last time he had seen her frightened was the day he fought Cabitos a dozen years ago. He looked into her grey, tearful eye and touched her cheek. "I will return," he said. "Doubt it not." He squatted to kiss little Maria. "Be good for your mother, baby girl," he said.

"Good bye, Papa," Maria said.

He stood and accepted his *magado* from Pedro. "You must be the man of the house for a while. Be careful and carry your responsibilities with honor."

"God loves and protects the careful man," Pedro said quoting a phrase his father had often used.

"A wise observation, young man," Panis said. "We must take our leave now."

The three men walked through the west gate, only Diego pausing to look back and give a final wave to his family. After Diego disappeared, Mézu lifted her apron to her eye and wept. She went into the apartment sobbing with little Maria holding a fold of Mézu's dress. Pedro folded his arms and stared west. He heard Maria's voice through the window beside him.

"Momma," she said, "why are you crying? Papa will come home — will he not?"

⁊

Diego followed Panis and T'Chien through the streets of New Orleans. After leaving the fort they walked upstream for several blocks before turning north. Most of the buildings were made of unpainted wood. T'Chien said the cypress lumber was resistant to rot and did not need to be painted. The few brick buildings Diego saw were newer and in the Spanish style. France treated New Orleans as if it were a wilderness trading post, even when indigo plantations began to prosper. Spain had controlled Louisiana for well over a decade now. She actively recruited settlers and administered local government with the intention of transforming the collection of hovels she had inherited from France into a city.

Even by European standards, New Orleans was a filthy place. The men walked along planks placed along a narrow strip of mud between the buildings and the sewerage-filled ditches that paralleled the roads. The roadways were paved in manure, pocked with muddy holes and scarred by sludge-filled ruts. They had to cross narrow, single-plank bridges at every cross-street. The ditches were lined with wood at these crossings so the planks would not work their way down into the banks. Once away from the river the warehouses and government buildings gave way to residential houses jammed together so tightly a man would have difficulty walking between them. *A fire would level this entire city*, Diego thought.

They passed the last row of houses and the timber walkway ended. They walked along the edge of a road crowded with wagons and ox sleds. Diego could see a forest of masts over the traffic on the road.

"Those masts you see are schooners in Bayou Saint John," T'Chien said. Those were the first words spoken by any of the three since leaving the fort.

"After we board our schooner I will explain to you both what we are to do," Panis said.

The bayou had a well-worn path along the bank where teams of mules pulled barges and schooners along the narrow waterway to and from Lake Pontchartrain. They passed a few vessels that were being unloaded and one that was taking on some cargo. Panis turned abruptly onto a plank that led up to the low deck of a schooner with a pair of masts. He directed his companions toward the bow and instructed them to find a place among bundles of blankets stored there. Panis went to the stern where several men were gathered. There was a brief conversation and then the sailors broke apart. Some went to the fore and others to the aft mooring lines. Two others went to the gangway and the captain hollered something in French toward a man holding a team of two mules.

The teamster stopped his mules where the forward mooring line was wrapped around a tree. The line was doubled around the tree. An end was tied to a cleat on the schooner, the line run out around the tree and then back to the deck cleat. The sailor at the fore line cast one end of the line free and the teamster pulled it ashore and freed it from the tree. He coiled the excess line until he had enough to throw back to the sailor who secured it once more on the cleat. The teamster put the line over a large iron hook on the end of the beam slung between the hitches.

The man at the tiller, Diego assumed it was the schooner's captain, shouted a series of orders and the plank was hauled aboard, the mule team started and several sailors manned long poles to fend the schooner away from the bank until they had gained enough way for steerage. The sailors busied themselves with storing lines, securing cargo and other chores.

Panis joined Diego and T'Chien in the bow. "This is what we are about," he said quietly and checking that none of the sailors could hear him. "We are going to scout British forts at Mobile and Pensacola. I traveled to these ports last year, but now there is a great tension between Spain and Britain, I must return as an English tradesman. We will travel overland into the Floridas, find the rivers that flow past these places and go down to the British positions."

All of the land east of Lake Pontchartrain to the Atlantic Ocean and south of the thirty-first parallel was known as "The Floridas." West Florida was the land between the Mississippi and the Apalachicola Rivers and south of 32 degrees 22 minutes Latitude. East Florida extended from the Apalachicola to the Atlantic and south of 31 degrees Latitude. North of these latitudes was the colony of Georgia.

"This schooner will bring us across Lake Pontchartrain to a river called the Tchefuncta. We will be smugglers bringing iron pots, pans, knives and other tools up the Tchefuncta. We will sell some at a few British settlements near the mouth of the river then go inland under the pretense of selling to the natives. Once we are beyond British eyes, we will strike east overland."

"It will be hard for me to pass as a smuggler," Diego said. "I cannot speak a word of English."

"Do not worry," Panis said. "Few people in West Florida beyond the isolated British trading posts can speak English. Most of the people we encounter inland will speak Choctaw or something like it. In those cases, T'Chien will be our interpreter. If we meet English speakers, I will do all the talking. I will use the name 'Jack Ford.' Do not address me by rank or title. Even when we are alone, address me as 'Mister Ford.' I will use Diego and T'Chien. Is that clear, Diego?"

"*Sí, Meester* Ford." Diego said.

"T'Chien?"

"Yes, Mister Ford." T'Chien said. "I can use a little the English." He said in that language.

"Good," Panis said. "Now get some rest. It will be a long time before we can rest again once we cross the lake."

The mule team reached the mouth of the bayou and the teamster waited until there was slack in the line, pulled it free of the hook and tossed it aside. A sailor pulled the line aboard while his shipmates raised sails and trimmed lines. Diego was stunned at the size of the lake. It was more of an inland sea. The north shore was over the horizon and the strong east wind had generated a respectable sea. The schooner heeled to her starboard as the sails were set for a full beam reach. The westward rolling chop slapped the windward side of the hull occasionally sending a spray of brackish water across the deck.

T'Chien huddled with Diego in the bow on the lee side where they were less frequently doused with spray and presented a lesson in the proper loading of a rifle and how he should arrange his kit.

T'Chien dug into Diego's possible bag. "I put all you will need in this bag, but it will be up to you to keep it stocked." He pulled out a brass cylinder with a leather string attached to an eye on one end and a thin brass tube protruding from the other.

"This is your priming horn," T'Chien said. "You open it like this." He unscrewed the end with the tube. "The powder you put in here should be fine. Look." He sprinkled a little of the contents of the cylinder into Diego's hand. The grains were the size of beach sand, much finer than the powder Diego had used in the muskets. T'Chien screwed the cylinder closed again.

"Now watch." He pressed the end of the tube in Diego's palm. The tube slid into the cylinder and when T'Chien withdrew it a small mound of powder was left behind. "That is for the rifle's pan. With rifles, the pan is primed last, not first like your battle musket." T'Chien tied the leather string around the strap of the possible bag so the priming horn was suspended at Diego's stomach. "Keep your horn here."

He pulled a cotton handkerchief-sized cloth from the possible bag. "This is your ball rag. I will show you what that is for in a moment." He tucked a corner of the cloth under the leather string holding the priming horn and let it drape down.

"Here are your cartridges," T'Chien said as he pulled several paper casings from the bag, each about the size of a man's little finger. "These are paper-wrapped common powder. I put a dozen in your bag. There is a pocket sewn in the bag for cartridges. The balls are in another pocket, here." He put the cartridges back and fumbled a little in the bag before he pulled the ball out. It was slightly smaller than a musket ball.

"This is a fifty-four caliber ball. Your rifle is an English trade rifle, a fine weapon and very common in the Floridas," he said. "Oh, your loading knife!" T'Chien dug in the bag again and produced a small knife on a leather string. It had a curved blade about the size of a thumbnail and he tied it on the strap of the possible bag next to the powder horn and ball rag.

T'Chien stepped back and examined Diego for a moment. "Well, at least you are beginning to look like a woodsman, now for a lesson in loading and shooting. Cast-about your rifle."

Diego recognized the command and, supposing it meant the same action as in the case of a musket, he placed the butt against the outside of his left toe with the hammer facing his leg.

"Get a cartridge," T'Chien said. "Nobody is going to be telling you what to do. You load at your own pace. Now, tear the end of the cartridge, put the powder down the barrel and toss the paper away." Diego did as he was told.

"Now, put a corner of your ball rag over the muzzle like so." T'Chien covered the rifle's muzzle with a corner of the cloth. "Get a ball, put it over the barrel and push down until the cloth folds up like the pedals of a flower." Diego found a ball and pushed it into the barrel.

"Further," T'Chien snapped.

Diego pushed until the top of the ball was level with the mouth of the barrel.

"Now, cut away the excess rag," T'Chien said. He collected the excess cloth with the fingertips of one hand and sawed it free from that trapped under and around the ball.

"Draw your ramrod and ram the ball home."

Diego pulled the ramrod free, twirled it around and placed the brass cup on the ball. He pushed, but the ball did not move.

"Not like a musket, is it?" T'Chien said. "Grasp the rod a few inches above the ball and pull down hard." Diego did so and the ball moved a few inches.

"Again, but do not try to do more than half a foot at a time, lest the ramrod break. There is a mark on the ramrod, a ring scratched around it. See?" T'Chien showed Diego a slight groove cut around the ramrod just below another brass fitting. "When that mark is even with the muzzle, ball and charge are properly seated."

Diego seated the ball and withdrew the ramrod. He slid the ramrod into place beneath the barrel.

"Good. Now prime your pan."

Diego placed the rifle in the musket-priming position, with the barrel pointed slightly downward and to the left and the lock mechanism at his solar plexus. He placed the hammer at half-cock, tested the trigger, opened the frizzen and put the tip of the priming horn in the powder pan, pressed and released. Powder poured from the tube until it filled the little pan. He slapped the frizzen closed.

"Now you are ready to fire the weapon," T'Chien said. "Now, *punteria*."

"Aim?" Diego asked. "What does that mean?"

T'Chien laughed. "Musketeers are never taught to aim are they?" The lesson that followed had Diego's head swimming. When it was done, T'Chien pointed at some sea birds that were riding the choppy waters. "Use what I taught you and take aim at the flock of birds. Shoot when you think it best."

Diego pulled the hammer to full cock and took aim, carefully aligning the front sight blade with the notch in the rear sight. He pulled the trigger and a spout of water shot up halfway between the flock and the ship.

"Not bad," T'Chien said. "Reload and try again."

Diego's second try was close enough to start the gulls into flight. When he lowered the rifle he noticed a dark green line across the horizon.

They were approaching the north shore of Lake Pontchartrain. "Reload and try again," T'Chien said.

"Well, T'Chien," Panis said. Diego had been concentrating on his lesson and aiming so much that he did not notice when Panis had joined them. "How is our rifleman?"

"He is doing well, Mister Ford," T'Chien said. "Very well indeed. Before very long, he will be as adept as any man."

T'Chien's response reminded Diego of Panis' alias. He had forgotten. *This scouting business challenges the mind*, Diego thought. *And our lives depend upon getting it right.* Physical challenges, duels and even combat did not create the feeling of inadequacy Diego was experiencing trying to adapt to a new weapon and new country. Soon, he would be surrounded by strange languages and immersed in territory controlled by a potential enemy.

The schooner slid into an opening in the cypress trees that lined the shore of the lake. They had entered another river. There were no haul trails along this shore, only a flooded forest of cypress trees. The captain ordered long oars, called sweeps, to be brought out. Sailors and passengers alike hauled on the sweeps and the schooner inched forward against a mild current. Diego did not believe one could find as much fresh water anywhere in the world as he had experienced in Louisiana. In the Canary Islands fresh water was a rare commodity stored in stone cisterns or hollows in some caves. The land was dry and the sea was wet. Louisiana seemed not to know if it were land or sea.

The cypress trees along the banks of the Tchefuncta gave way to brush-crowded land. Soon the bank was transformed into a proper shoreline forest with scrub oaks and then pine trees. They were about three miles from Lake Pontchartrain when a trading post drifted into view. A man from the shore hailed them in English and Diego's heart sank. *Oh, Mézu*, he thought. *What has your favorite goatherd gotten into now?*

CHAPTER 15

The trading post was a series of buildings gathered about in an irregular cluster stretching back from the pier at the river's bank. A dozen huts flanked or stood behind the main building. Each was constructed by leaning tall poles against each other to form an inverted "V." Thirty or more pairs of poles were lashed together creating a long, narrow single-room shelter. The walls were also the roofs and plastered with dried mud and shingled with palmetto fronds. The ends of the shelters were enclosed by blankets or crude palisades of saplings. Diego watched as two naked children, both about two or three years old and painted with red mud, exited one of the huts and ran to the edge of the river pointing at the schooner and jabbered incoherently.

Trees and posts formed the square framework of the central building of the trading post. Two live pine trees formed opposing corners of the main structure. Heavy posts had been added every ten feet or so along the thirty foot length of each wall reducing the span of the floor beams. Horizontal poles were lashed to the corner posts and trees about two feet above the ground to form floor beams. Poles and planks were spread across the floor beams and covered with blankets. The roof was of woven palmetto fronds and the sides were of canvas. Today was warm and clear so the sides had been rolled up and reefed. Crates, barrels and other goods were on display in no discernible pattern around the floor. Panis jumped from the bow of the schooner onto the swaying pier as the sailors secured lines about pilings.

A man emerged from the interior of the main building and stepped down onto wood planking that had been strewn along the path to the pier to form a crude walkway. He was short, wide and dressed in sailor's slops and a filthy cotton shirt. He wore buckled shoes without stockings and a wide-brimmed straw hat that folded over his ears. His full beard showed no signs of care and his long hair splayed from beneath the hat in tangled strings. Mud had been forced from beneath the planks covering the wood with a slippery, red-brown layer, and the man struggled to keep his feet as he descended to the pier.

"Wait here," T'Chien said as he left Diego in the stern and wove his way forward to join Panis at the dock.

Diego could not hear what was being said and he watched as the three men gesticulated wildly. The man in the straw hat turned, shouted something toward the trading post and resumed his animated conversation. A woman came from one of the huts carrying a rolled and bound deerskin. She was dressed in a blue cotton dress that was ragged and muddy from her ankles to the ground. Her bonnet had been white at one time.

Straw Hat took the deerskin, removed its bindings and, with the woman's assistance, spread it out for inspection. Fingers were added to their gestures as quantities had become the focus of the discussion. Panis waved one of the sailors onto the pier and spoke with the man, and sent him back onto the schooner. The sailor rummaged through the goods in the deck cargo. He selected a cast iron pot, an iron fire tripod, several knives and a hatchet. He put the knives and hatchet in the pot and folded the tripod. He balanced the tripod over one shoulder and, picking the pot up by its handle, brought the goods to Panis. This generated more discussion.

An agreement was reached and sailors began carrying some of the deck cargo to the pier. Straw Hat would examine each delivery, direct the sailor to place it aside and send him up to the trading post. The woman and another young boy would help the sailor balance a bundle of deer-skins on his back and send him back to the schooner. The captain directed the storage of each bale of skins until the foredeck was mounded high. Canvas was thrown over the pile and lashed down.

Panis and T'Chien returned to Diego in the stern. "We are going ashore here," Panis said. "Gather our things and follow me to the dock. Diego, do not talk to anyone."

Panis and T'Chien had decided what would be needed for the expedition before they had departed New Orleans. Bedrolls, pans, cups, canteens, dried food, grain and a host of other items were packed into three backpacks or stuffed into haversacks. Diego used his *magado* as a walking staff and carried his rifle slung and unloaded on his left shoulder. He also carried the spare canteens and a Dutch oven lashed over his backpack. *Now I know why I was chosen for this trip*, he thought. *They needed a big man to serve as a pack mule.*

Panis wore a compact backpack and, carrying a loaded rifle at the ready, led the way ashore. Diego followed, almost hidden by his burdens. T'Chien, wearing a backpack and carrying a rifle, came last. The little caravan moved up the slope and through the village along a well-worn trail. People came to the edge of the trail to gawk at the strangers. Diego was struck by the variety of faces. Many had features and complexions similar to T'Chien, but just as many appeared to be European, their skin weathered into a coppery-brown hue. Still others displayed traces of Africa in their aspects. Their clothing was just as diverse. A man with European features stood next to his family dressed in a beaded deerskin shirt and leather stockings while the next man, clearly an Indian, wore a fringed hunting frock, felt hat and gaiters nearly identical to Diego's garb.

"These are mostly Choctaw," T'Chien said. "The villages we will encounter first as we move north will be Choctaw. When we move east we will meet the Mobile, kin to the Muscogee, sometimes called Creek. In truth, there is little difference between the tribes or the villages. They war constantly, yet intermingle freely and accept refugees into their families."

They left the village along a wide trail that was nearly a road except it lacked any signs of horse or wagon traffic. The way had been worn smooth by innumerable footsteps. Little commerce traveled overland for it had to be carried on men's backs or by *travois,* sleds made of long poles on which goods were lashed and pulled along by hand. Diego wondered why they had left the river so soon for he saw many dugouts and skiffs at the landing.

"Why did we not obtain a boat?" he asked. "There were several streams leading inland."

"Rivers are full of travelers and there are many villages along their banks," T'Chien said. "We go north keeping away from the rivers because we do not wish to be seen. We will go north for three days, then east for several weeks."

Three days north then weeks to the east! Diego could not comprehend the vastness of the land. Three days walking would be enough to cross Gran Canaria twice. Now they were walking at a strong pace along a narrow trail through pine forests and they would continue in one direction for weeks! It had been a cool morning when they left New Orleans, but now sweat began to stream down the faces of the travelers even as the sun began to set.

They began to encounter hills and the trail no longer ran straight but snaked around along round hill tops. The path occasionally dipped down into a creek bottom where they would wade through shallow, black water before climbing to another knoll. Now that they were far from any major waterway or villages the trail grew faint. Diego hoped that Panis or T'Chien knew where they were going for he was lost. He doubted he could even find his way back to the landing they had left only a few hours ago.

"We make camp here," Panis said indicating an open area among tall pines. "Ground your pack and wait here," he said to Diego. He nodded to T'Chien who dropped his pack and bedroll then jogged off to the south parallel to the trail they had just traveled. Panis grounded his gear, except for his weapons, and trotted off north leaving Diego alone. Free of his burdens, Diego walked west until he could barely see the grounded gear in the fading light and waited. He could not explain why, but it did not seem wise to simply squat among the bedrolls and wait. The thought of building a fire never crossed his mind.

Diego fished a strip of jerky from his haversack and slowly ate it, pausing at times to listen to the forest around him. A cat-sized animal with a bushy, striped tail the length of its body came from the east toward the grounded gear. When it neared the packs it sniffed them and, seemingly alarmed, it scurried back into the brush.

The light was fading quickly. Soon it would be full dark and the moon was not due up for several hours. Diego heard movement from the east. Perhaps the strange animal was returning and he concentrated in that direction until the form of T'Chien materialized at the edge of the cluster of packs. T'Chien put his hand on the short sword at his side, crouched and looked about. Diego stood and moved to the campsite without speaking. T'Chien relaxed and then nodded his approval of Diego's actions.

"Here comes Mister Ford," T'Chien said in a near whisper when Diego reached him. "How far did you scout to the west?"

"I was not out of sight of the bedrolls," Diego replied.

"If you had gone a hundred *varas* (yards) further, you would have met Mister Ford coming back to the camp. Now that there are three of us, we will change the scouting pattern." Panis and T'Chien had been scouting the trail and brush to guard against an enemy approaching the camp during the last moments of light. T'Chien was impressed that Diego had instinctively moved out of the camp and he later told Panis – Mister Ford – of the *Isleño*'s trail sense. "The man already thinks like a warrior," T'Chien told Panis, "in a month he will be as cunning a woodsman as there is in West Florida."

"Bedrolls only, no lean-to," Panis said as he reached the men. "We eat now, no fire. I will take the first watch. The moon will rise in two hours and T'Chien will take the watch, two hours, then it will be Diego until first light." It was mid-April and the half-moon would be just past her zenith at first light. The sky was so clear simple starlight provided just enough light to make camp. While they ate, Diego asked about the animal he had seen. "Ah," T'Chien said, "a *shawi*. Good eating, but they will pillage a camp for food if given a chance. Kill the next one you see, if you can, and we might risk a fire to roast it."

☙

Dawn was announced by an increase in the wind that moved the tree tops. The moonlit shades of grey coloring the forest bed and sleeping men began to gain some color. The half-moon was visible through the dancing branches, but the sky behind the moon had lost its deep black tint. It was a cool morning which produced heavy dew covering ferns, brush and even some of the gear. Diego walked over to where T'Chien slept and gave the man's foot a tap with his boot. T'Chien's eyes opened, fluttered a moment before he whispered, "I am awake, rouse Mister Ford."

"I am up," said a voice from a roll of blankets. "Cold breakfast of biscuits and we will be on the trail as soon as we can load up. We will make twenty miles today, God willing."

It was twenty miles of hard travel. Panis had them skirt two small villages along a wide creek known as the *Bogue Chitto* before he had them cross and push north again. When they were within an hour of camping for the night a storm swept across them with driving rain and violent lightning. *I have been in Louisiana for less than a month*, Diego thought. *And that is the fifth rainfall in that time.* The least of those storms had been heavier than any Diego could remember in his life before leaving Gran Canaria. Panis directed them to camp halfway down a steep slope in a bushy area of scrub oaks instead of a hilltop surrounded by tall pines.

A blast of light and noise stunned them as they grounded their packs. A pine tree not two hundred yards up the hill had been struck by a bolt. Pieces of bark rained down on the men and a fire erupted at the base of the tree but was soon extinguished by the torrential rain.

"Does it always storm so here?" Diego asked.

T'Chien gave a chuckle. "Not always. The spring and early summer often have storms such as we see now. The fall is usually dry and the winters wet with drizzling rain that last several days."

"Good for the crops," Diego said.

"There can be droughts," Panis said. "It is rare but many suffer when one sets in."

Their security patrols were not as wide ranging as they would have been because the rain obscured vision and once darkness fell it would be pitch black except for the occasional flicker of lightning from the now receding storm. Panis swept ahead and circled around to come back into the camp from the left. T'Chien back-tracked a few hundred paces and circled around back to camp from the right. Diego went left up the hill toward the still smoldering pine before turning south for several hundred paces. He turned left again until he cut across their back trail. He could see where T'Chien had circled east. Diego followed the freshly trampled earth back to the camp. When he reached the camp there was not a quarter-hour of light left and T'Chien was rigging a lean-to under a large scrub oak.

The canvas awning smelled of bee's wax, which had been impregnated into the weave to repel water. The men ate in silence as another burst of rain passed over the camp. Diego wondered if every meal taken on this trip would be cold salted meat and rock-hard biscuits.

"Tomorrow," Panis said as if he could read Diego's thoughts, "we will enter a large village on the *Rio Perla*. There we will rest for a night while I confer with the head man there. We will sleep in the community hut and eat whatever is offered. Before we move east we will buy cooked meats and cornflower cakes. When we cross the river we will be entering lands of the Creek. Most of the Creek favor the English, a few do not. We must increase our caution."

Night watch duties were the same, but it was nearly impossible to tell the time for it rained the entire night and the camp site was engulfed in darkness. Diego struggled to stay awake listening to the water falling from the trees and thinking about Mézu. Were the children well? Maria would eagerly help her mother, but Pedro was at a rebellious age and required a firm hand. Did these same storms strike New Orleans? He had heard people comment the best time to be in the city was after two days of heavy rain had washed all of the streets clean of filth.

Gradually the rains stopped and the wind ceased to whip the tree tops but the skies remained blanketed with clouds. Diego moved out from under the brush he had used to shelter himself when he began to distinguish patterns in the clouds and looked toward the lean-to. A man on watch would never post himself too near the camp. Every time he glanced toward the shelter he could see more detail, so he decided the dawn was near and he roused his companions.

They shook as much water as they could from their gear and donned their packs. This time the trail was a slippery hazard at every attempt to descend a slope or climb out of a creek bottom. The streams they crossed were full and muddy, none was deep enough to bar passage though twice they had to build rafts for the pack and weapons and swim across. This was Diego's first exposure to swimming but he managed with some instruction from T'Chien.

"You live in Louisiana now," T'Chien had chided. "You will be called upon to swim many times."

They trudged along trails that seemed to Diego to have been more frequently travelled than the faint traces they had followed thus far. Panis signaled a halt and, with a gesture for Diego and T'Chien to wait, trotted up the path which now twisted toward the east.

"We are near a Choctaw town, a *tamaha*, on the *Rio Perla*," T'Chien said. "Soon we will encounter the farms that encircle their town. The town center is a fortified palisade built around a central meeting house. Many houses are inside the palisade, but most are without. I think over five hundred people live there. It is at a place where the Black Creek, the *Bogue Lusa*, enters the *Rio Perla*."

Diego and T'Chien had moved off of the trail with all of their gear until they were hidden in the thick brush. Diego could just see the opening where the trail snaked by their hiding place. Panis appeared on the trail ahead walking toward where he had left the men. Diego gave a gentle whistle and Panis studied the brush until he saw his men. He waived them out onto the trail while glancing toward the east.

"The town leader is friendly to the Spanish, but a few in the town favor the British. Most of the people here dislike the British because they are allies of the Creek," he said as Diego and T'Chien stepped onto the trail. "We will stay in the town for a few days as I gather what information I can about the British. T'Chien, while we bide here, see if you can school Diego on enough Choctaw to pass. Do not attempt to teach him English, his Spanish accent will give him away. I do not think the British will be able to discern if a man speaks Choctaw with a Spanish accent."

Panis and T'Chien, who had been carrying their rifles at the ready thus far on the expedition, slung their arms and preceded Diego toward the east. The pine trees gave way to fields of corn and other grains. Small huts, like the ones at the Tchefuncta landing, sat in the common corner of four fields. The fields were not square, nor were the crop rows straight and regular, but these were farms. Diego had always heard the Americas, aside from European colonies, were populated by savages. But the fields and roads here were as fine as any in Gran Canaria and, not lacking water or good soil, the crops were more robust. The trail they had been walking became a packed road of dirt.

They passed a steep gully that was serving as the town's rubbish tip. Garbage and human waste had been thrown down the slick mud into the tangle of brush at the bottom. The recent rains had filled the lower levels with muddy water in which floated bits of rotten carcasses. They passed through a stand of trees and the town spread out before them. Diego counted over seventy-five huts along the road into the palisade. The fortification did not have loop holes nor were there bastions at the corners, but the wooden walls were well maintained.

A large building dominated the center of the fortification. It was constructed with tall corner poles covered by a palmetto roof and had a raised floor. The walls were woven saplings and plastered with mud mixed with straw. Unlike New Orleans, the town's dirt streets were not covered in manure or the discarded contents of chamber pots. A man wearing a tall felt hat, frayed waist coat, loincloth and leather leggings stood in the doorway. He was tall with dark hair, a long nose, hazel eyes and tanned skin the color of strong tea.

Panis nodded to the man and then, indicating Diego and T'Chien with a sweep of his arm, said in Spanish. "Gentlemen, I give you King José Candelas. He is a good Catholic and *jefe* here. These are my *compadres*, T'Chien and Diego." Diego was startled at the Spanish name, but bowed slightly when his name was mentioned.

Panis explained later that Candelas was the chief in the town because he had married well. Property ownership and ruling authority among these people was controlled by high-born women and only exercised through their sons and husbands.

"King Candelas has agreed to allow us to stay in his town," Panis bowed thanks to Candelas as he spoke. "I have paid the King a silver coin and we will be given the use of a house. We must provide our own meals."

King Candelas was evidently more comfortable speaking Choctaw than Spanish for he spoke at length to Panis in that language. When the conversation was done, he indicated Panis should enter the building.

"T'Chien," Panis said as he handed his backpack to Diego, "Candelas' son will come out and bring you to our house. Wait for me there." He followed the king inside.

A young man of twelve or so, dressed in a beaded deerskin jacket over a cotton shirt and trousers, came out. He said something to Diego who shrugged.

"He says to follow him," T'Chien translated.

The boy walked toward the only gate in the palisade, looking back occasionally to reassure himself that the men were following. They turned south and passed about a dozen huts when the boy stopped and pointed at one that lacked a front or rear. He said a few more words to T'Chien and left.

"Looks as if we are to finish work on this hut if we are to stay here," T'Chien said.

Diego dropped his pack and stooped low to enter the hut. The interior was more spacious than Diego anticipated. He stacked his oversized pack against one wall and Panis' pack against the other. T'Chien placed his things against the opposite wall.

"What now?" Diego asked.

"One of us must stay here at all times while the other collects the materials we need to close this place up," T'Chien said. He untied the ax Diego had lashed onto his backpack. "I will go first," he said as he hefted the ax over one shoulder and ducked out of the hut.

Diego busied himself with clearing away the fire pit and overhead smoke vent in the center of the hut. There was little fuel in the hut, so a fire had to wait. He glanced up to see two small faces looking at him from one end of the hut. The children, girls, were about eight or so. One was fair with black eyes, black hair and a wide Irish face while the other was brown with black hair and light brown eyes. They spoke to him, but he shrugged. They looked at each other and spoke to him again. This time he growled and the girls squealed. They ran away laughing.

The incident caused Diego to think of his children and Mézu. He had never been so isolated from his family before and he ached for them. How long would he be gone? They had traveled far already and yet T'Chien said they were not yet half-way to their destination. Panis no longer seemed to be in a hurry. How big could this land be? If he left now, which way should he go? He reached onto his haversack and fingered the little cloth pouch that held a lock of Mézu's hair.

CHAPTER 16

The town on the banks of the *Rio Perla* was named *Tamahabogue* and became a base camp for the first phase of their expedition. Diego had remained in the town for over a month learning the Choctaw language while Panis and T'Chien scouted east and south learning about the British occupied forts and trading posts. The two men would disappear for days at a time. When they returned they would consult with King Candelas, rest a few days and strike out on another scouting foray.

Diego's language lessons were in a variation of Choctaw known as "trade-talk" in which words and signs were combined to convey a message. The instructions were provided by young Candelas and the two half-sisters he had encountered on his first day in town. The fair-skinned girl was called Tohbic and the other Shohhala. The names meant "White Bean" and "Little One." Unlike Candelas, the parents of the girls did not use the European tradition of first name, family name. These were their childhood names. When the girls married they would be given adult names.

The girls decided they would rename Diego. One day when King Candelas and his son were talking with Diego, Tohbic and Shohhala approached them.

"Shohhala has had a dream," Tohbic announced. "Tell them, sister."

Shohhala looked into Diego's eyes. Her expression was somber and as serious. "You were in a very high place," she told him. "The land was tall and steep. You carried a long pole and you would use it to fly from one high place to another."

"The spirits had decided," Tohbic said. "You will be known as 'Hika Nitah' to the people."

King Candelas translated into Spanish for Diego, "It means Oso Volador (Flying Bear)."

"'Hiko Nito' sounds better," Diego said, touching the end of Shohhala's nose with a forefinger. "'Hika Nitah' is a girl's name."

"That does not mean anything in the language," Tohbic said. "Your name is Hika Nitah!"

"I am Flying Bear!" Diego said in his Spanish accented Choctaw.

"Flying Bear!" the girls exclaimed and they ran around him touching him and then pulling away as he pretended to try to catch them.

❧

Diego commissioned King Candelas' wife, Ruth, to fashion leather leggings and a beaded deerskin jacket for him. The hip to ankle leggings provided protection for his cotton trousers from the brambles and briars that infested the woodlands. The deerskin protected his trousers and fared better than did his old knee-high cloth gaiters. After only a week of limited intrusions into the forests around the town Diego's cotton gaiters were in shreds. The deerskin jacket was lighter and more water proof than his hunter's frock. Diego also improved his marksmanship and woodcraft. He was not yet a frontiersman but, to anyone but a native, he could pass as one.

Each time Panis and T'Chien returned from their forays to the east Diego was required to converse with them in Choctaw until, at the end of a month Panis announced it was time to relocate into Creek country.

"Whatever you have learned, it must be enough for now," Panis said. "We need to move nearer the British forts at Mobile Bay and Pensacola. It is time for us to study those places." Rumors of war between Spain and Britain had been circulating throughout the Floridas. Diego had heard it among the Choctaw and even in New Orleans gossip was rampant that war would be declared soon. The British colonies on the Atlantic coast were in revolt and the ale-house generals all agreed France and Spain would side with the rebels. Panis had never explained why they were surreptitiously traveling about British territory, but Diego knew they were to be spies when he stepped aboard the schooner on Bayou *San Juan*. And, if war had been declared, captured spies were executed.

"We will go to a small village between the Perdido and Escambia Rivers called *Chaha Aiasha* (High Dwelling)," Panis continued. "It is within one, maybe two day's travel of either fort. We will make our reconnaissance and then return to New Orleans." He looked at Diego. "We will have you home before August, Diego."

I have not spent a week with my Mézu since we stepped off the San Juan, Diego thought, *and I have been in the new world for two months!* He had been transformed from a soldier to a woodsman and he wondered if Mézu would even recognize him.

The next morning King Candelas and his son escorted the three men through the palisade gate and to the eastern edge of the town. The road east was well traveled and, although there were several rivers and two marshy flood plains to cross, Panis anticipated reaching *Chaha Aiasha* in five days. They would be in Creek dominated lands, but that could not be helped. Panis spoke English with a Bristol accent and the Creeks were allies of the British so they anticipated being able to move freely. Ruth Candelas crossed herself as the three disappeared on the road headed east.

⁊

Unlike their initial trip inland from Lake Pontchartrain, Diego's burdens were now more or less equal to the others. They carried a bedroll, backpack, haversack, rifle and possible bag. Panis had a rapier in a scabbard on his left hip, T'Chien had a tomahawk tucked into his belt and Diego carried a short sword in a scabbard along with his customary *sunta*, tucked into his belt and his *magado*. Panis and T'Chien carried their rifles loaded and at the ready while Diego carried his rifle slung over one shoulder and used the *magado* as a walking staff.

They traveled quickly along a good road and were ferried across the *Rio Perla* in a single large dug-out by Choctaw farmers within a quarter hour of leaving *Tamahabogue*. Once past the river, the road continued through a wooded, mosquito infested bottomland for over a mile before climbing out of the cypress and gum trees onto rolling pine-covered hills. Leaving the road only once to skirt a village, they traveled without a break for the rest of the day without meeting another person on the trail.

The heat was terrible, for it was now late June, and the humidity was nearly overwhelming. Fortunately, they frequently forded shallow, sandy creeks and did not lack for water. Sweat poured down the faces of the men, sandflies pestered them in the pine forests and mosquitos swarmed them in bottom lands. T'Chien stopped at the first creek ford to smear every inch of exposed skin with thick red clay he pulled from a cliff-like bank. They continued through a pine forest and down to another trickle of a stream where his companions imitated the act.

Panis called a halt next to a meandering stream of tannin-stained water and white sand shoals after nearly ten hours of travel. They must have covered thirty miles or more. They moved north of the trail a dozen yards or so to find a tree-sheltered hollow to spread their bedrolls. Without a word of instruction, the men grounded their packs then each quietly left the site by different routes and circled it a hundred yards out as a security screen. The men returned to the camp site silently and by different routes. They spread their bedrolls and enjoyed a moment of rest to eat a meal of salted pork and cornflower cakes.

"What is the name of the stream?" Diego asked as he tilted his head toward the east.

"It is the *Nashobabok* (Wolf River), I think. I have not been this far from the coast before." Panis said. "If you were to travel down that river for–," Panis pause to think, "– forty miles or so, you will reach the Gulf of Mexico. All the streams we have crossed or will cross flow to the gulf. If you should become isolated or lost, that is the easiest way to go. Find flowing water and go downstream. Eventually you will come to a stream or river that will bring you to the gulf. Then go west to New Orleans. However, every stream will eventually pass through a Creek village or town, so it is no way to go if you wish to escape notice."

The thick tree canopy would shelter them against dew so they did not spread a lean-to. Panis took the first watch and T'Chien would have the second. This meant that Diego had a full four hours of uninterrupted sleep coming and he wasted no time in spreading his bedroll. He pulled off his shoes, leather leggings and deerskin jacket. His cotton trousers and shirt were soaking in sweat and the slight night breeze felt wonderfully cool as he lay upon the bedroll to sleep.

☙

She was sitting on a driftwood trunk that had been beached on the white sand of a creek. The soft moonlit sand tightened into a firm ribbon tracing the edge of a deep, black pool. She wore a green gown that seemed to sparkle. A tall silver comb in her hair supported a long veil that covered her shoulders. Her back was to him, but he knew who it was.

"Mézu?" Diego whispered. "What are you doing here?"

He began to walk toward her, his feet crunching in the soft sand. She did not turn. *She did not hear me*, he thought and he attempted to talk to her again but he could make no sound. When he reached the log she had moved to the end farthest from him.

He could see her profile now. Mézu was staring at something across the creek.

"Mézu," he said again. "Why are you here?"

She did not look at him but pointed across the pool. Diego looked where Mézu had indicated and saw a young girl standing next to the black water. She wore a white gown. Diego thought she must have been swimming for even at this distance he could tell she was soaking wet, her hair was matted to her head and rivulets of water dripped onto the sand.

"Who is she?" Diego asked but when he turned to her, Mézu was gone. He looked back toward the girl across the stream and she had vanished as well.

⁓

Diego opened his eyes just as T'Chien stooped under the tree canopy to rouse him for his turn at guard.

"You do not sleep very soundly," T'Chien whispered. "I am certain I made no sound coming for you."

Diego struggled to his feet and pulled on his leggings, shoes and jacket. His cotton clothes had almost dried during the relatively cool night. He looked at T'Chien, "Quiet night?" The dream had shaken Diego and he reached into his haversack for the pouch containing the lock of Mézu's hair. He removed it from the haversack, freed the leather sting attached to the cloth pouch and placed it over his head. The pouch hung at his chest and he tucked it inside of his shirt. He had dreamt of Mézu often since leaving New Orleans but in previous dreams she had been happy, attentive and loving.

"There is an animal nosing about in the brush," T'Chien said. "What it is, I cannot tell – a *shawi* (raccoon), perhaps." T'Chien nodded toward

Diego's chest. "A leather pouch is much better," he said. Then he pulled a pouch from his shirt and showed it to Diego. "See? Cotton will rot, but this is tanned leather. The north people call this a *náwoti*. This is my *náwoti*."

Diego armed himself with the *magado* and ducked out of the campsite. He walked a few paces uphill where he could post himself against a big pine. The campsite was to his back and the wide tree trunk cast a shadow that shielded him from the light of the setting moon. He was invisible against the tree yet he could see a wide area.

He listened as the night sounds began to resume after the disturbance he and T'Chien had created in changing their watch. A raccoon ambled out on the brush and came to Diego's feet before, alerted by scent, it hissed and scurried away. A shadow moved out of a tree to his left and a huge owl silently flew within a foot of Diego's head. He felt the wind from the bird's wing against his face, but he heard nothing.

He concentrated his attention toward the road which lay out of sight to the south, but there were no sounds, no motion, nothing. Thoughts of Mézu and the children filled his mind and he could not shake the foreboding sensation that engulfed him. Panis had promised they would return by mid-July. If, for some reason that departure were delayed, Diego swore he would find a stream and go down to the gulf. The moon set and the forest was lit by starlight. Shadows were deeper and the night sounds amplified.

❧

Diego had been able to see a few stars through patches in the canopy but they began to wink out as dawn approached. Diego returned to the campsite and stooped under the branches. "First light," he said, "I will take a turn about the camp." Panis and T'Chien were hidden in darkness but he heard them respond.

Diego walked west for a hundred yards and edged up to the road. Satisfied nothing was moving on the road, he went north a hundred yards, then east to the bank of the river. The dark stream ran against the near-vertical west bank and a wide, white sand shoal spread out from the east bluff into the flowing, tea-colored water. He moved south to the trail and returned to the camp.

He had seen nothing worth reporting so he said nothing as he donned his pack and bedroll. They filed back onto the trail and resumed a brisk march east. They forded the river and stopped momentarily to renew their coating of mud. They continued east with a silent, brisk, distance-consuming walk. The trail widened as they entered a tall pine forest and Panis changed the pace into a wolf-trot. Diego felt as if he could continue at this pace for a full day. The sea voyage had softened him. One does not walk very far aboard a ship, but this trip had renewed his endurance.

Panis put a hand up and they halted. He pointed downhill from the trail where the brush was thickest and signaled "go." The three men slipped down the slope and hid in the brush. They had concealed themselves for less than a minute when Diego heard voices coming from the east. Men were coming along the trail. Diego did not dare watch the travelers pass, nor did his companions. It was enough to hear them pass. To look was to risk discovery. They remained hidden for twenty minutes after the last of the people on the trail passed above them.

"I counted twenty men and two mules," T'Chien said as they clustered below the trail.

"Traders, no doubt," Panis said. "The mules were loaded down with pots and pans. We must be getting close to a village. We cannot go around every village if we are to make the Pascagoula River before dark." Twenty was too many for a simple trading party but Panis said nothing.

They regained the trail and struck out east again. After only a few miles they came upon a cluster of fields and a few huts. The people they saw working in the fields paid them no heed as they passed. When they reached the village no one stopped them, though two stout men closely watched their progress until they were beyond the village.

"Why did they not stop us?" Diego asked when they were safely beyond the village.

"They had no suspicions. They assumed we would have been stopped by the trading party that had just left the village," Panis said. "The people on the road were speaking Creek, proper Creek, not trade-talk. We are going to have to stop and chat at the next village if we are to escape suspicion. My Creek is heavily accented, English accent, so we will be accepted. If we meet any British soldiers, it may be a different story."

They entered only one village before they reached the Pascagoula River. Panis talked with a few of the elders while Diego entertained a crowd of children who were fascinated with the *magado* he carried. He showed them how it could be sheathed in a leather channel sewn across the back of his jacket and withdrawn in an instant. When they moved on the children followed them to the edge of the village where they stopped and watched the three men stride out of sight.

There was an English trading post on the Pascagoula but the proprietor, Bill Sneed, was not there. The Englishman's Creek wife and their two grown sons managed the post in Sneed's absence. The men enjoyed a meal of roasted veal and whiskey. A barge that served as a warehouse for bundles of hides was moored at the riverbank and they were offered lodging on the barge. Panis declined, telling Mrs. Sneed that he intended to make several more miles before dark and he requested they be ferried across the river. Once across, Panis led them east until they climbed out of the river's flood plain and were well out of sight of the trading post. He turned south for a mile before he called a halt for the night near a small stream that flowed west into the Pascagoula.

When Diego returned to the campsite from his routine perimeter sweep he found Panis sitting at the campsite with T'Chien and a stranger. A dugout was pulled up onto the bank of the stream. Evidentially, the stranger had arrived by water.

"Diego," Panis said in Spanish, "This is Bill Sneed. He is a friend of Oliver Pollock."

Diego shrugged. Being a friend of Oliver Pollock meant nothing to him.

"Of course," Panis said, realizing that while Pollack was well known in Gálvez's headquarters, Diego knew nothing of the man. "*Señor* Sneed is our friend as well."

Sneed nodded a greeting that Diego returned.

"Gentlemen," Panis said, directing his speech to T'Chien and Diego, "I need pickets. Please tend to it."

T'Chien rose and indicating he would post himself upstream on the little creek, he directed Diego north. Sneed did not stir and Diego had the impression the man did not understand a word that had been said.

Panis and Sneed returned to their conversation as Diego found a suitable picket location.

When darkness fell, Diego returned to the campsite to find Sneed and the dugout gone. T'Chien was spreading the bedrolls and Panis was busy collecting kindling into a pyramid shape. He added a few larger pieces of dried driftwood and struck a spark from a tinderbox. "I think we can chance a fire," he said. "It will be nice to have a cup of tea, do you not agree?" Panis pushed an iron pot hanger into the ground next to the fire and rotated the hooked end over the flame. He suspended a small tin bucket of water from the hook and positioned it over the fire to boil. He produced a block of tea from his haversack and began to shave the edge with a knife, directing the shavings into the bucket.

Diego had never had tea before. Coffee was the beverage of choice in New Orleans and was widely enjoyed in the Canary Islands. Diego accepted a steaming cup from Panis and tasted it. He drank it out of politeness but would have preferred coffee.

"Sneed tells me that the British expect war with Spain to be declared very soon," Panis said as he sipped his cup. "The British have already made formal protests to His Most Catholic Majesty, complaining that Gálvez has been aiding the American rebels and working against British interests. All true, of course. The British have been fostering slave uprisings and financing renegade raids into Louisiana. A formal state of war has not been officially declared, but it exists. We are going to gather as much information as we can about British intent and capabilities. Once we have mapped any improvements to the forts at Mobile and Pensacola and determined troop strength, we will return here and travel down the Pascagoula River to the Gulf of Mexico. There will be a coastal schooner waiting for us in the river's bay to bring us to New Orleans."

That last bit of news provided relief to Diego. He did not relish the prospect of having to travel over the same route back to Lake Pontchartrain.

"Tomorrow," Panis said, "we will move to *Chaha Aiasha*. That will take three days to get there. Just crossing the wide marsh between the Mobile and Tensaw Rivers will take a full day. From *Chaha Aiasha* we will begin our observations of the British at Mobile. It will require all three of us to do a proper job of it."

Before going to sleep, Diego rigged some fine netting he had purchased at Sneed's post over his bedroll by propping it up on twigs. The thin netting was only enough to cover his face and chest. He watched as mosquitos swarmed and bumped the netting. After killing the insects that had managed to get in, Diego struggled to go to sleep. He was exhausted, but his dream of Mézu the night before haunted him. He touched the pouch under his shirt. My *náwoti*, he thought and finally fell asleep wondering what dreams awaited him.

CHAPTER 17

Chaha Aiasha may have meant "High Dwelling," but, having lived in the mountains of Gran Canaria, Diego's understanding of a high place was different from that of the Creek. The village was located on a wide hill forming a watershed that fell away sharply on all sides. The nearby streams flowed either to the Perdido River or the Escambia and *Chaha Aiasha* was located in the center of the only level and arable land for many miles. Pensacola was a day's travel to the south and Mobile Bay was two days west.

Less than a score of farms spread around the small village. Panis presented himself as an English trader looking for a location for a new trading post. He convinced the local *jefe*, Cholah, to provide him the use of a hut by giving the man two leather sacks of black powder.

"We go to Mobile Bay tomorrow," Panis announced as they stowed their gear in the hut. "We will not need bedrolls, and bring four days rations."

T'Chien looked at Diego when he heard Panis' orders and shrugged. No bedrolls meant no sleep or quarters had been arranged. It meant no sleep.

On the morning of the second day they reached the east shore of a wide bay. On that shore, about a mile north of their location, was a small military compound. It was no more than a strong house. The main fort was on the northwest corner of the bay, nearly twenty miles from the gulf and surrounded by a growing settlement. Originally begun as a French fortification, the British had renamed it Fort Charlotte. The settlement was still known by the name of the Indian tribe the French encountered at that site in 1702 – Mobile.

Panis bartered with a fisherman for the loan of a dugout. The dugout was large and easily accommodated the three men. T'Chien and Diego paddled while Panis navigated. They crossed the bay to the town, dodging the boat traffic that populated the bay.

"That little strong house on the east shore is nothing," Panis explained. "It is the fort at the town of Mobile we must inspect. When we land, I will walk through the market and you two must stay close to me as my servants. Speak as little as possible. If you must talk, use only Choctaw."

Mobile was an impressive town. Diego reckoned there must have been over two hundred houses and public buildings built in European design, not very different from New Orleans. The wooden walls of the houses were of milled planks, not logs, and some even had glass in the windows. Most of the people on the street were dressed in western clothes. Those men, who were not sailors or soldiers, wore waistcoats, tall boots and tall hats. Slaves and laborers wore cotton trousers and loose-fitting shirts in the European style. The women wore long dresses, elbow-length gloves and bonnets that shielded their faces from any profile view. The streets were compacted manure over dirt and the ditches beside the roadways were filled with sewerage.

The fort did not have a moat. In the place of a moat, there was a tall wooden palisade made of whole logs sharpened to points and set to encircle the fort twenty feet or so outside of the brick fortifications. Each corner of the main fort sported a diamond-shaped bastion designed to provide enfilade fire on an enemy assaulting the walls. The gate of the wooden palisade opened onto an area facing the main entrance to the brick fortification. Anyone entering the space between the palisade and the wall of the fort would be subjected to flanking fire from the cannons mounted on the high bastions or men firing through loopholes in the brick. British soldiers flanked the gate through the palisade as well as the entrance to the fort. Sentries were posted atop the battlements as well. There were several buildings within the fort, but only the roofs could be seen from the streets of the town.

Panis walked from one vendor's stall to another making a show of selecting the choicest smoked meats or freshest vegetables. One of the stalls had several small kegs of gun powder and sheets of lead. Panis bought one of each and gave them to Diego to carry. T'Chien bargained for a roll of tanned deerskin and strips of rawhide, finally buying half of what he had chosen when he started the negotiations. Diego carried the things Panis had purchased and absorbed all he could of the port.

Several coastal schooners and a flotilla of dugouts crowded the pier and shoreline. Smaller sloops and a double-ended dingy rigged with a single mast sailed about the bay. There were no large ships in the bay or at the pier. When Diego commented on the lack of large ships, Panis explained that merchantmen were reluctant to sail the gulf during the months of July, August and September fearing the great storms, the hurricanes that often appeared during those months. Small coastal vessels could scurry to shelter in any little bay or cove when the signs of a hurricane developed but larger vessels may be too far from a port to escape being trapped against a lee shore.

When they returned to *Chaha Aiasha*, Panis spent a full day in the hut drawing sketches of the defenses of Mobile. He drew in pencil instead of ink so moisture would not ruin the sketches. This was dangerous for, if capture threatened, the sketches would be difficult to destroy and damning. Panis had a large leather pouch, much like an oversized haversack, with a leather flap that could be tightly closed to protect the contents from rain. After each entry was completed, he put the sketches in the pouch and hid it in the weave of the hut's interior wall.

"Tomorrow we visit Pensacola," Panis announced when he finished hiding the pouch. "Two days of observations and then we make for the Pascagoula and then home."

They could not post a guard, as they did on the trail for it would raise suspicions. Why would a trader seeking a location for his post need to mount a guard? So they trusted to the village dogs, which always issued a chorus of barks when any strangers were about, to prevent surprise.

While Panis had been sketching, T'Chien was busy working the deerskin leathers he had purchased. Diego watched as T'Chien worked and recognized the product of the man's efforts before he had completed his task. It was a leather pouch about the size of a child's fist. T'Chien stitched small blue glass beads on one side of the pouch in an unusual pattern and ran a leather loop through holes in the edge of the pouch. He passed the leather loop through a wooden bead and pulled it tight, closing the pouch.

"Look, Diego," T'Chien said, holding the pouch in the palm of his hand and touching the bead pattern. "This is the sign of the bear." He offered the pouch to Diego. "Here, now you have a proper *náwoti*. The people (meaning the Choctaw) will know it is your *náwoti* because of the sign of the bear."

Diego could only mutter *"Yakoke."* (Thank you). He knew if he refused the gift, it would be an insult. T'Chien nodded and left the hut so Diego could transfer the contents of his cloth pouch to the leather one in privacy. What a man carried in his *náwoti* was a very private thing. Diego only had a lock of Mézu's hair within the pouch, for the present.

Panis left the hut as the predawn light washed away all the constellations except the morning star. Diego and T'Chien began to load the backpacks with the items they considered necessary for the trip to the fort at Pensacola. They did not intend to be gone from *Chaha Aiasha* for more than two days so they did not pack bedrolls or much in the way of supplies.

Panis threw open the door to the hut and leaned in. "A change of plans, gentlemen. News has come from London. It is suspected that Spain has allied with France and the American rebels. War will be declared between Spain and Britain very soon, perhaps this month."

Plans had changed dramatically. Now that a virtual state of war existed, the British garrison would be more active. They would not go into town masquerading as tradesman and they would not return to *Chaha Aiasha*. They would go down the Perdido River, which meant they had to acquire a dugout, cutting the travel time, and approach the town from the landside. After they finished their reconnaissance of Pensacola, they would return to the boat and go west along the coast, cross Mobile Bay at night and find their schooner in Pascagoula Bay. Instead of two weeks to reach the schooner, they would make the trip in three days.

They left several items in the hut, things that would only serve to slow them down such as iron pots, the fire tripod, and bedrolls. Panis slung the leather map case over his shoulder then added his haversack and possible bag. They automatically assumed the same order of travel they had become accustomed to – Panis leading, Diego second and T'Chien trailing. When they reached the edge of the village, Cholah, the *jefe*, stopped them and questioned Panis.

"We are going west," he said. Cholah said he could see they were taking the road west. Displaying anger as he spoke the man said, "It is not enough to know you go west. Tell me where you are bound."

"We are going to Mobile," Panis told him. "If there is war, Britain may gain territory to the west. There will be opportunities."

The answer seemed to satisfy and the three filed west. Once they were out of sight of the Cholah, Panis began a wolf trot. In five miles they encountered a small stream flowing to the southwest. Instead of fording the stream, they found a trail going downstream along the bank and followed it for another five miles to a cluster of trapper's huts. There were several dugouts moored in the stream or pulled up on the bank. Five hard-looking men were gathered about a cooking fire. Panis greeted them in Creek and the men visibly relaxed when Panis began to bargain for the largest of the moored boats. If they were to go west following the coast of the Gulf of Mexico, they would need something that could tolerate the open sea. Diego and T'Chien loaded the boat and positioned themselves while Panis finished the negotiations. It cost Panis the last British guinea he had, but the Creek had added two paddles and a large water-skin to the deal. Again, Panis commanded from the bow while T'Chien and Diego paddled.

"Cholah will probably send word to Pensacola about us," Panis speculated. "If we hurry, we will be scouting the main fort before his messenger can reach the town. With any luck, we will be done and on our way to New Orleans before the British can send an officer to *Chaha Aiasha*."

After five miles of rowing down the serpentine stream they encountered the Perdido River. Wider than most streams, somewhat sluggish, and bordered by cypress swamps the Perdido began to expand into a long, lake-like waterway spotted with islands. When they emerged into a bay, Panis directed them south and across a three-mile stretch of open water to a creek that flowed into the bay from the south. He guided them into this creek and after two miles the creek shrank into no more than a trickle. There may have been an hour of sunlight left.

Panis consulted his compass. "Pensacola is only four miles southwest of here. We will camp here and set out in the morning. Tomorrow, we will leave our packs here with the boat."

They slept in the boat, which was large enough to accommodate them. Each man rigged course netting over his face and hands as a protection from the mosquitoes which began to swarm at dusk. In the morning, Panis decided that each man need only carry his possible bag, which held powder, shot and spare flints, his haversack, canteen and his personal weapons. They struck out toward the southwest and in less than an hour they could hear the sounds of hammers, and the air smelled of the sea. They began to move up a slight rise when Panis signaled a halt. Signaling for the men to stay low, he waved them forward. Diego used the shade and trunk of a scrub oak for concealment as he looked west to the town of Pensacola.

Panis explained that the fortification and town of Pensacola that lay before them housed the British headquarters but the defenses of the bay had been divided into several smaller redoubts placed on islands beside the narrow inlet through the barrier islands between the bay and the open gulf. These redoubts could also provide supporting fire against efforts to take the main fortification, Fort George.

Fort George was situated on the western shore of Pensacola Bay where the bay curved sharply east so the fort faced to the south. From this location, high on a hill, the fort had a commanding view of the entrance to the bay and the gulf beyond the barrier islands. The fort had a different design than the fort at Mobile. The brick walls of the fort were about eighteen feet high and speckled with loopholes ten feet above the ground and crowned with battlements. Instead of bastions at the corners of a square, the fort was built in the shape of a large star, enabling one wall to provide enfilade fire along the length of its neighbors. It also had a long, rectangular appendage fortification that ran north, away from the star-shaped battery back toward the town. Barracks, magazines and other support buildings were located in this auxiliary wing of the stronghold. Like the fort at Mobile, it had no moat and depended upon an encircling wooden palisade to delay any attempt at an escalade against the fort.

"Diego," Panis whispered, "go west a hundred yards and post yourself where you can see the northern palisade. Memorize as much detail as you can and return here in one hour. T'Chien, move southeast until you can see the details of the redoubt on the west side of the inlet. Watch for boats. I am going closer to the fort. Meet me here in one hour."

Diego moved west as he was directed and found a location under a bush that allowed him to see most of the town north of the fort. He estimated it had taken him twenty minutes or so to move into position. Moving slowly, he separated the overhanging foliage that concealed him and examined the fort.

The buildings of the town stopped abruptly five hundred yards or so from the palisade. He noticed that the wooden palisade had not been completed along much of the north side, the side farthest from the bay. The star points of the fort lacked bastions on the north side as well, but each had a raised wooden watch tower, though he could not see any sentries on the towers.

He was preparing to withdraw when he heard shouts of alarm from within the fort. Men appeared on the bastions along one wall and two climbed up into the watch tower on the western tip of a star point. They were all pointing toward the bay and shouting.

Someone has been spotted! Diego thought and he shrank back into the brush. He knew he could not run immediately without being seen so he dropped to a crouch and began to duck-walk toward the thicker cover of a tree line. The noise of a gate being thrown open caused him to look back over his shoulder to see ten men armed with muskets rush out of the fort and head directly at him. He ran for the trees. He heard shouts behind him. Only one man was shouting. He did not need to understand the words, he knew what was happening. *A sergeant was shouting orders!*

He turned to glimpse at his pursuers. He saw that the men had stopped in a line and they had leveled their muskets. He had begun to turn away again when something hit the back of his head.

CHAPTER 18

She would not turn and face him. "Mézu, why are you here?" Diego asked. He knew it was Mézu. The high, silver comb supported a veil that dropped down her back into a point near her hips. She wore a green dress with a worn and ragged hemline. They were on the fire-step of a brick battlement, he did not know where, and Mézu was staring toward the sea. The wall they occupied was far above the sea, a castle on a cliff's edge. The wind began to mount and it swept her lace veil back until only the silver comb kept it from being taken away. He could see the darkened edges of the intricately patterned lace where it had been stained with blood, her blood.

"Mézu," he pleaded, "Look at me. Answer me."

She began to turn toward him when she was distracted by something and looked over the parapet. He could see her profile, her grey eye fixed on something below.

Diego moved until he was at the embrasure nearest Mézu. Gripping the stone wall top, he leaned forward and, taking his eyes from Mézu, looked down.

Don Sebastian Minóso stared up at Diego. The man was splayed face up, his arms and legs spread wide, his hair pushed vertically about his face as he fell. *Don* Sebastian's eyes were wide, uncomprehending and his mouth formed a puckered, painted oval. The wall beneath Diego spun about the plummeting Sebastian until the man was gone, lost into the void below. A feathered hat with a crushed crown floated across Diego's vision.

"He was going to –" Diego began as he straightened from the embrasure and moved back to the center of the fire step. He stopped in mid-sentence because Mézu was no longer standing on the battlement to his left. He looked to his right and saw a man's profile a few paces away. It was *Barón* del la Paz! It began to rain and Diego could feel the water being driven against the side of his head. The violent wind pushed against his cheek until it felt as if it were a solid.

An iron ball appeared, spinning toward Paz and the rain. The ball filled Diego's view until he could see every detail of its pitted surface as it rushed toward Paz. The ball ceased spinning and Diego stared at the black pitch-stained sphere until it began to turn brown. Dizziness and nausea overcame Diego forcing him to close his eyes. He tried to call for Mézu but could not.

℮৲

Diego heard a moaning sound and his eyes fluttered open to see a boot inches from his face. He blinked and tried to make sense of what he was seeing. He was prone on a muddy trail with his left cheek pressed against the wet soil. The moaning sound he heard had come from him. The boot disappeared, splashing the bloody mud before his face into his eyes. He struggled to wipe the mud away, but his left arm was trapped beneath his body and his right responded spasmodically, slapping a limp hand against his forehead. Someone rolled him onto his back.

"Oooo ahh, auh auh," a voice said.

Diego thought it might be English, but he had no knowledge of the language and his head was swimming. He doubled up, rolled to one side and vomited. A hand roughly pulled him onto his back again. He looked up at his tormentors. A circle of cocked hats bordered his vision against a background of green tree canopy. The leafy ceiling was spinning in one direction and the ring of hats in the other.

"¿Quién eres?" The voice had changed to Spanish.

Diego caught himself before he answered. He was beginning to remember. Spain and Britain were plunging toward war and he was a spy. His fluency in Spanish, *Isleños* accented Spanish, could mark him as a soldier or sailor of His Most Catholic Majesty and doom him. He looked up and said, "Why am I hurt?" in Choctaw.

There were more voices and shouts behind him. He tried to sit up but the movement caused the world to spin. He rolled onto his stomach and managed to get his knees under him. None offered assistance as he rocked into a kneeling position. The back of his head was burning as if it were on fire. He ran his hand over his scalp, forcing his fingers through a sticky mass in his hair. He felt a loose flap of skin and a stinging groove cut across the back of his head. When he looked at his hand he was not surprised to see it covered with blood.

"You shot me." Diego said in Choctaw.

He managed to look around. The men that encircled him were wearing red coats with yellow facings. The soldier immediately in front of Diego wore a ragged, red sash with a yellow stripe diagonally across the left shoulder of his coat to his right waist – a sergeant. All the men wore tricorns, some with red cockades. All were armed with muskets except for the sergeant, who carried a halberd. Diego could see his own weapons arranged in a neat row on the ground beyond the sergeant. He must have been stripped of them while he lay unconscious. The sergeant looked beyond Diego, motioned for someone to come to him and said something in English. Diego turned to see a barefoot man wearing a fringed, leather jerkin decorated with beads, a cloth cap and stained cotton trousers. The sergeant spoke to the man and pointed at Diego.

"What name?" the man said in a language that might have been Choctaw.

"I am *Hika Nitah*," Diego said.

"What people?"

"I am from a far place," Diego's mind was racing through the possibilities. His trader's level of Choctaw was not going to fool anyone versed in the language. "I am of the *Amazigh*, on the western sea." The *Amazigh* was the name the native people of Gran Canaria called themselves before the Spanish came. Diego's grandmother had taught him a few words in that almost forgotten tongue. The western sea was an ideal location for his fictitious home for it was so distant and mysterious. No one in Europe knew the people, the land or how far away it lay. He wanted to say he was from an island, but he didn't know the Choctaw word for "island." It was barely plausible, but it was the only deception he could think of.

The man spoke to the sergeant who nodded and directed some of his men to pull Diego to his feet. The sergeant led the way back through the northern gate of the fort. Two soldiers supported Diego by his arms and dragged him along while others collected his weapons and accouterments. After several paces, Diego was able to gain his feet and, shaking his arms free, walked on his own surrounded by a close guard. It was not until he began to walk on his own that he noticed his shoes were gone and he did not remember seeing them with his other gear.

They walked past the star-shaped portion of the battlements to an elongated, walled section of the fort trailing away from the bay. The walls were over twenty feet high and crowned with embrasures. Loop holes were cut in the brick at regular intervals and placed eighteen feet above the ground, clear evidence of a fire-step behind the wall. The brick-work appeared to be new and the wooden palisade along this part of the fort had not even been begun. If an attempt to take this fort was made, an attack from the land would be preferred to an assault from the beach even if warships could provide supporting cannon fire.

They entered the fort and Diego could see that a fire-step did encircle the entire wall. Stairs at the corners of the walls provided access to a walkway over a dozen feet above the ground. Unlike Fort Saint Charles in New Orleans where the roofs of buildings served as fire-steps for the walls, buildings within the fort were separated from the wall by about twenty feet. Most of the structures were wooden with wood-shingled roofs. Two of the buildings were brick and one was three stories high with a watchtower centered on the roof. Diego's captors directed him to this building, which faced south and was centered on the parade grounds of the fort. Flags bracketed the single-tread step up to the porch. Diego surmised they were before the fort's headquarters.

They stepped onto the porch, which ran the length of the building. Diego tried to estimate the time of the day by judging the length of shadow cast by the awning of the porch. He guessed it to be ten or so in the morning. If so, he had lain unconscious on the muddy trail for nearly two hours. His guards stopped him at a set of open double doors while the sergeant continued into the building. Diego could see a desk against an interior wall and next to a closed door. The man behind the desk, a thin young man wearing a powdered wig and clearly a clerk, listened as the sergeant spoke to him. The clerk glared across the room and out the open doorway at Diego as the sergeant, who alternately gestured toward Diego and the door next to the desk, spoke in English.

The clerk stood, still looking at Diego as if he were a monster, went to the door next to the desk and rapped once. A voice sounded within and the clerk went into the room, closing the door behind him. The clerk reappeared after what seemed to be only seconds and said something to the sergeant before resuming his seat behind the desk where he shuffled papers to and fro. The sergeant opened the office door and held it while he barked orders at the men escorting Diego. His weapons were carried into the office and arranged on the floor. Diego was pulled into the building, past the sneering clerk and forced into the office where he was placed before a powdered wig.

The wig looked up and Diego saw a British officer – he must have been an officer for gold braid decorated the cuffs of his red coat. The officer closed the book he had been reading and spoke to Diego in English which sounded like "Ooo ah ah ooo" to him. Diego looked blankly at the man.

"*Qui es-tu?*" The officer said. French! The phrase reminded Diego of Mézu and he struggled to remain expressionless.

Then the officer said in perfect Castilian Spanish, "These men are going to take you into the courtyard and shoot you." Diego forced himself to remain expressionless, hoping some flicker of recognition did not betray him. If he was to be executed, he was certain no amount of pleading would change that verdict.

The man who had spoken to Diego in Choctaw was ushered into the room, ostensibly to serve as a translator. Two other officers crowded into the room after the translator. This interrogation was going to go very slowly, for Diego's command of Choctaw was limited. He realized this was an advantage for it provided time for him to fabricate a believable story.

"This man is General Campbell," the translator said. "He wants to know your name."

"I am called *Hika Nitah* by the people," Diego replied.

There was some more conversation with the General. The translator turned to Diego and said, "The General says the name sounds like a woman's name. Where are you from?"

Diego repeated the story about being from the western sea. "It is a place with the sea all around it," he added. This was translated to the General who presented another phrase to the translator.

"Name this place."

"Tamarán," Diego said, remembering the ancient native name for Gran Canaria.

"Why were you near the fort?"

"I was coming to the town."

"Why?"

"I wanted to trade."

"You have nothing to trade."

"Was going to hunt, bring meat."

The translator instructed Diego to remove his deer leather jerkin and, noticing the string, pulled the small leather pouch from beneath Diego's shirt. Diego grabbed the man's wrist and squeezed it until the man flinched with pain. He let go of the pouch and Diego replaced it beneath his shirt. This created an extended conversation between the General and the translator.

"The General says you may keep your medicine pouch."

The interrogation went on clumsily for over an hour. The General, clearly frustrated at the ineffectiveness of questioning a man in a language the subject clearly did not command, dismissed him.

The soldiers escorted Diego to the blacksmith's shop where his shackles had been prepared. The smith produced eight flat iron bands. Each had been hammered into a crescent shape and joined into four pairs by a hinge on one end and flattened flanges on the other pierced with matching holes. A length of chain, less than two feet long, ran between the hinges of one pair while a length of chain about three feet long bound another pair. The soldier held Diego's arm while the smith closed a cuff about his wrist, inserted a small plug of iron into the holes and, holding the cuff on his anvil, struck it with a hammer until the ends of the plug mushroomed, locking the cuff to his wrist. This was repeated until hands and feet were shackled.

Diego's hands were bound with the shorter chain and his feet with longer chains. The chains permitted little movement of his hands and the links between his ankles forced him to shuffle his feet as he attempted to walk. They pushed him along to a small, brick building next to the headquarters. There was no porch and the front wall had an iron door with a single barred window – a jail. The laughing soldiers shoved Diego into the building and locked the door.

Diego looked around his prison. The floor was paved with brick and the walls were without windows so the only light that filtered into the place came through the iron bars in the door. The rafters of the steeply pitched roof were bare and were anchored to the top of the walls by iron brackets mortared into the brickwork. There was no furniture of any kind in the room. Except for a single chamber pot in one corner, the room was absolutely bare. Diego went around the room examining every detail. He reached up toward the top of the wall. If he jumped, he was certain he could grasp the top of the wall. The room was featureless save for an odd line of soil running from the floor to the rafters in one corner.

Diego felt the wound in the back of his head. He could not feel any bone chips or other indications of a severe injury. He must have been turning when the musket ball struck and it grazed his skull creating a scalp wound that had bled furiously but was not life-threatening. The dizzy spells had stopped and his head throbbed, but otherwise his escape from death had been a near miracle. A full squad of infantry had fired their muskets at him from less than sixty yards away and did no more injury than knock away a narrow patch of scalp.

ಎಲ

General John Campbell leaned back in his chair. He was a slight man with a narrow hawk-like face. Tiny, close set eyes were separated by a prominent nose over a thin-lipped mouth and receding chin. General Campbell considered his posting at Pensacola to be a punishment for failing to provide financial support to a certain political clique. The three other men in the General's office, witnesses to the farce of an interrogation, had remained in the room when the man called Flying Bear was removed to be shackled and confined. They were Colonel David Hutchens, commander of the 16th Regiment of Foot, Major Archibald Mitchell of the Maryland Loyalist Battalion and the native translator, John Bankenson.

"Gentlemen, what do you make of our guest?" Campbell asked.

"Clearly a stranger to this place," Bankenson said. "His Choctaw is very bad."

"We could all determine that, Mister Bankenson," Campbell said. "We know what he is not. The question is 'what is he.'"

"The Choctaw are divided in their opinions," Mitchell said. "Some support the Spaniards, many favor our side and most hate us both. The Creek and Choctaw both resent the Georgia colonists because of encroachments onto their lands, so I doubt he is a rebel spy, and the French have been absent from the Floridas for decades. What remains is a Spanish spy."

"He was wearing a medicine pouch – a *náwoti*," Bankenson interrupted. "It is a practice common among native people everywhere. Each man keeps tokens or special magical things in a pouch he carries with him at all times."

"That eliminates the possibility he is a Spanish soldier," Hutchens snorted. "Those papist bastards would be racked for heresy or burned at the stake if they were ever caught wearing anything on a necklace other than scapulars blessed by the bleeding Pope."

"I am not so certain," Campbell said. "I think he toys with us. Let us subject him to a few days hard labor on reduced rations and have another go at him when he is weakened."

Major Mitchell tarried behind as the men took their leave of the General. He waited until the others had cleared the room. "General, a moment sir," he said quietly. "I have a man in my battalion who speaks Spanish perfectly."

ᘯ

The next morning the sergeant opened Diego's cell and pulled him, hands and feet shackled with chains, into the glaring morning light. A handful of bread was thrust into one hand and a cup of water into the other. The sergeant used gestures to direct Diego to eat and drink. When he was finished the cup was taken away and the sergeant herded Diego toward the back of the headquarters by poking him with the tip of the halberd. He was forced to a freight wagon near the northern wall of the fort. The bed of the wagon was stacked high with sacks of goods and other supplies for the fort. Hands and feet still shackled, he was made to unload the wagon and carry the supplies across the courtyard to a depot on the opposite side of the fort.

After he had emptied the wagon, he was prodded over to the blacksmith's shop where long poles used to push barges across the shallow bay were being fitted with iron cup-shaped ends called "shoes" that would prevent the poles from being imbedded in the muddy water bottoms. Each pole was sixteen feet long and he was forced to carry them from the blacksmith's shop and load them on the wagon. He was required to carry them one at a time to increase the number of trips needed to fill the wagon.

The day was spent in make-work toil without a pause. Once he was made to dig a large hole in the packed dirt, then immediately refill the hole. Diego was given water, but no food. At the end of the day he was given a half-loaf of stale bread and a cup of water. When he finished drinking, the cup was taken away and he was pushed into the prison for the night.

Backing into a corner, Diego slid down the wall into a sitting position. He had selected this corner of the prison as "his place." He was barefoot and dressed only in cotton trousers and shirt. His shoes, jerkin and leather leggings had been confiscated along with his weapons, accouterments and haversack.

They had allowed him to keep his *náwoti*. He pulled it from beneath his shirt and felt the form of the lock of hair beneath the soft deerskin. His body ached from the exertions forced on him during the day though the headaches had stopped, yet hard labor seemed to have a medicinal benefit to the wound in the back of his head, for it seemed to be healing without infection. He considered performing another inspection of his cell, rejected the thought and fell into a deep sleep.

At the conclusion of his second day of hard labor, Diego was thrust into his prison to find another shackled prisoner dressed in sailor's slops. The man was leaning against the far wall when the door was opened and he had to step aside as Diego was pushed into the room. Diego heard the iron bar locking the door trust home. He glanced at the newcomer, went to his corner and squatted. He was exhausted and only wanted to lie on the brick floor and sleep.

"My name is José Gomes," the new cellmate said in Spanish. "Who are you?"

Diego inspected the new man without acknowledging any understanding of what Gomes had said. The man was old, approximately the same age as Diego, maybe thirty. He had closely cropped hair and had been clean shaven at one time, for only shadowy stubble appeared on his cheeks and chin. His eyes were wide-set, their color could not be determined in the glim light of the prison. The man was average in height, five and a half feet tall, appeared to be well nourished, tanned and weatherworn, but his legs below the knee-length bottom of the slops were pale, contrasting with the smooth brown color of his hands and face.

"I was captured when my sloop, the *Concordia* was forced onto one of the little islands along the coast," Gomes said. He had walked over to Diego and was offering his hand.

"*Ia apa lokfi,*" Diego said as he stood, still leaning against his corner, to look down at Gomes. The phrase was one of the many insulting, foul phrases young Candelas had taught Diego. "Curse words and foul phrases first; later, trade talk," the boy had said. Gomes did not react to the phrase, but continued to grin and offer his hand. Diego took the hand, gave it one vigorous jerk up and down and released the man's hand.

"How long have you been here?" Gomes continued in Spanish.

Diego said nothing.

Gomes placed a hand against his own chest and said slowly, "José Gomes." He pointed at Diego and said, "Your name?"

Diego mimicked the hand to the chest gesture and said, "*Hika Nitah.*"

"*Hika Nitah?*" Gomes said. "Sounds like a girl's name." Then he laughed.

Diego put his hand on Gomes' chest and said, "Osay Go Mez." He pushed, sending Gomes several steps backwards.

"Yes, that is my name," Gomes said, noticing that the malevolent stare Diego gave him did not convey any desire to gain an acquaintance.

Gomes continued his attempts to communicate for over an hour. Diego worked to ignore the man. *Soft hands and white legs,* Diego thought, *this man was no sailor.* Finally, Diego put a hand over Gomes' mouth and forced him into the opposite corner, making him sit. Diego removed his hand and as Gomes began to protest, he again clapped his hand over Gomes' mouth, glared down and shook his head slowly from side to side. He released his hand for a second time and Gomes remained silent. Diego nodded his head, returned to his place, sat down with his back to the corner, placed his arms across his knees and went to sleep.

CHAPTER 19

Diego suddenly awoke in the silent darkness of his prison and raised his head from his arms. The faint lamp light that drifted in through the single barred window flickered across the floor and splashed just enough illumination in the room for him to see he was alone. The man who had called himself José Gomes was not in the opposite corner where Diego had deposited him before going to sleep. Somehow the guards must have unlocked the door, pulled it open on protesting hinges and extracted Gomes without waking Diego.

A noise in another corner drew his attention. The room had been vacant moments before but now he could vaguely see a slight, familiar form. The lamplight drifted toward the figure to his right filling the corner with an orange glow to reveal Mézu. She was wearing an iridescent green gown, the toes of delicate dancing shoes peaked out from beneath the lacy hem. The tall silver comb in her hair supported a veil which was drawn across her face so that Diego could only see her beautiful gray eyes. He could see both of her eyes! She swept the veil aside and Diego could see his lovely Mézu's face unscarred, perfect, smooth and young.

"Mézu," he murmured as he scrambled to his feet. "How can you be here?"

She smiled as she looked into his eyes, filling him with a surge of joy and love. He desperately wanted to move toward her, but his shackled feet seemed immobile and he whimpered in frustration as he tried to move. Mézu pointed to the top of the brick wall where the roof rafters rested on the masonry and began to drift upward, following the direction her slender hand indicated.

"Please stay," Diego shouted. "Mézu! Maria Artiles y Ventomo; my wife, please do not go!"

⁓

The hinges of the iron door squealed as it was slowly forced open. Diego's head shot up and his eyes blinked as daylight filled the room. The realization that he had been dreaming sent a wave of depression through him and he felt his eyes welling with tears. He had never seen Mézu unscarred, her face undamaged.

José Gomes stood and made his way toward the door blinking vigorously as he adjusted to the glare of the morning light. Diego wondered if the dream had caused him to call out in his sleep. Gomes could have heard his plea to Mézu and would know that Diego spoke Spanish. If Gomes had heard Diego, he did not reveal it as he shuffled to the guard who pulled him out into the courtyard.

The sergeant stepped into the doorway and gestured to Diego to come out. His legs were shaking and, by momentarily bracing against the wall, Diego stood and shuffled to the door. He was given a half loaf of bread and a cup of water. He devoured the bread, for he was famished and drank the water without removing the cup from his lips. He was turned over to a private who directed him across the courtyard to the blacksmith's shop.

Diego had hoped the visit to the smith's shop was to have his shackles knocked off, but that was not to be. A long lever protruded from the side of the shop and the private gestured for Diego to push down on the wooden pole. He complied and heard a rush of air from within the shop accompanied by shouts from the unseen smith. The private gestured for Diego to pull up and push down again. The private moved into the shade, sat on a keg, placed his musket across his lap and went to sleep. It seemed today was to be spent working the smith's bellows.

Because the work did not require much attention, Diego was able to examine his surroundings in greater detail while he labored. He could see the alley between the back of the prison and the wall of the fort, a distance of thirty feet or so. He could see the corner of the headquarters building, the alley behind it and the wagon filled with the barge poles he had loaded the day before. An officer stepped out from the rear of the headquarters, closed the door he had just exited and hurried away. Each tower on the ramparts he could see had two or more guards who appeared alert, scanning the land beyond the fort's walls and within systematically. He tried to identify blind spots, but saw none.

The air was uncharacteristically cool for July and it smelled full of water. The sky was speckled with clouds that raced by going east to west. Diego remembered one of the sailors on the *San Juan Nepomuceno* mentioning the trade winds and how they blew from east to west along the northern gulf coast with dependable regularity, perhaps it was just a blustery day and, never having experienced a July on the Mexican Gulf Coast, he dismissed it.

A young girl, perhaps ten or eleven, covered in soot came out of the smith's shop, looked around and seeing the sleeping soldier, walked up to Diego and gave him a handful of jerked meat.

"Father says," she said in Choctaw, "if you grow too tired to work, I must do it. I do not like."

Diego marveled at the gift for only an instant before stuffing some of it in his mouth, the remainder he hid under his hands as he worked the billows. He chewed vigorously on the tough meat and his jaws ached.

"Are you the one called Flying Bear?"

Diego nodded, swallowed and looked about before stuffing another strip of jerky into his mouth. "Oka," he mumbled and the girl went into the shop and returned with a cup of water. The forge must have heated sufficiently, for the sounds of a smith's hammer echoed from the open doorway. He drank holding the cup with one hand while working the lever with the other, the remaining strips of jerky hidden under his palm. A voice came from the shop and the girl took the empty cup back into the building.

Diego finished eating and fell into a smooth rhythm working the billows. He saw the sergeant coming across the parade grounds toward him and, glancing back at the still sleeping private, he kicked some dirt onto the man's pants leg. The private startled awake and glared at Diego who tossed his head in the direction of the sergeant. The man jumped to his feet just as the sergeant turned the corner of the shop shouting orders at the private, who trotted past Diego, glancing back with an expression of genuine gratitude on his face.

The sergeant prodded Diego into the shop where he was directed to pick up a small barrel of ax heads. The sergeant could not hide his surprise when Diego hefted the heavy barrel up to his shoulder and then waited for further instruction. Employing a small quirt as a prod, the sergeant directed Diego out of the smith's shop and toward the back of the headquarters to the wagon load of barge poles. He placed the keg of ax heads in the rear of the wagon and was directed to lash it down with rope that was coiled as part of the wagon's load.

The sergeant responded to a call from someone standing in the doorway at the rear of the headquarters building. It must have been an officer, for the sergeant stood ramrod-straight, his hands behind his back and the arch of his right foot against his left heel. Instructions were given in the "Ooo ah" sounding English, and Diego recognized some of the answer the sergeant gave. "Sir, yes sir, Ooo ah ah Ooo." The officer stepped back into the entrance and closed the rough-hewn pine door. The sergeant, a worried expression on his pock-marked face, stepped back from the wagon to get a better view of the sky.

The wind had been increasing during the day and now the sky, which was once speckled with racing, white clouds had turned black. The sergeant pushed Diego toward the cell. When they arrived Diego was pushed inside and the door was locked. A loaf of bread covered with ants and a mug of water lay on the floor. Diego brushed away the ants and ate the bread. The wind began to howl through the bars and it was growing darker, though it could not have been much after four in the afternoon.

Diego took the opportunity to study his surroundings while the light lasted. He went to the corner Mézu had occupied in his dream. There was a small mound where the wall met the floor. He thought it was dirt but when he touched it he could not tell what it was. A trail of dirt climbed the corner to the rafter. He wasn't certain, but he thought he could see the rafter move. He stared at it for several moments and when there was a particularly strung gust of wind, the odd dirt-like material drifted down from the rafter as it definitely shifted.

The cell door rattled and Diego thought the sergeant was returning, but it was just the wind. Rain began to blow through the bars and a strange moaning sound filled the air. He went to the door and forced his face against the bars. The rain stung his face as he attempted to see as much of the courtyard as the bars would allow. Occasionally, a soldier would hurry by carrying planks or rope. The wind would make the man stagger and once a gust ripped a plank from a man's grip causing him to scramble on his hands and knees to retrieve it. The sky grew darker until the scenery outside of the cell window had an odd ashen hue. He did not see a guard posted at the iron door and, as the hour grew late, he could not see anyone moving about.

Diego went to the corner where the rafter continued to shift until it seemed as if it were bouncing. He crouched and jumped as high as he could, his fingers barely touched the top of the wall. He stepped back a step or two and made a rush at the wall, leaping as high as he could and managed to grip the top of the wall under the edge of the roof decking. He pulled up and managed to get his other hand on the top of the wall. He shifted his hands one at a time until he hung at the corner next to the rafter.

The shackles on his wrists would only allow his hands to be separated by two feet, but when he placed his right hand next to the rafter, he was able to pull himself up until he could grab at the rafter with his left and it crumbled under his grip. The wood was rotten and riddled with holes. The light, the little that there was in the dank cell, was fading but enough remained for him to see strange white ants rain down with the crumbling bits of timber. He could see the gray rain-filled space behind the prison through the hole he was breaking in the roof. He pulled up forcing his head against the roof decking and it gave way until he was able to worm his chin and elbows onto the top of the wall.

He stopped and looked around. Rain was coming down in torrents, the wind absolutely roared, and he could only see a dozen feet or so through the sheets of water. No one moved within his limited field of view. He risked moving up onto the top of the wall, struggling into a prone position crammed between the roof decking and the top of the wall. He could see more of the alley between the prison and the fortress walls. He saw no one. Guards on the bastions or guard towers, if there were any in this weather, could not have seen the ground at the foot of the battlements in the storm.

Diego swung his feet down, momentarily hung from the wall, and dropped to the ground. He stood with his back against the wall and remained still, the rain from the roof of the prison pouring past his face as he swiveled his head about looking for danger, and seeing none. The wagon was only a vague shadow to his left. He looked to his right. The alley was obscured by rain and growing darkness. He could not see the blacksmith's shop he knew was only thirty feet away.

Diego lowered himself to his knees and crawled across the open space between the prison and the wall of the fortification, then stood and walked along with one hand touching the brickwork, making his way to the wagon. Standing between the wagon and the fortress wall, he looked at the back of the headquarters. There was only one door, three windows on the first floor, and four windows on the second floor; all of the windows were shuttered. The left window on the second floor showed orange lamp-light leaking between the iron-hinged shutters and the window frame.

Diego felt his way to the rear of the wagon and found the keg of ax heads. The ax heads were single-bladed with a sharp cutting edge opposite a blunt maul face. He pulled two heads from the keg and squatted behind the wagon. Because shackles restricted his hand movement, he placed one ax head sharp-side up between his feet with the maul face on the brick apron of the fortress wall and placed the cutting edge between the flanged edges of the left handcuff where it had been riveted closed. He lifted the second ax head with his right hand until the shackle stopped him and struck the cuff with its maul surface, driving it down onto the blade beneath. The flanges of the cuff spread, popped off the rivets and fell away. His hands were free! It took only moments to free his other hand and knock the shackles from his feet.

Still nothing moved, no one could be seen, no shouts of alarm, if any shouts could be heard above the roaring wind. He crossed the alley to the back of the headquarters. The wind was blocked by the tall building, but it remained deafening. He needed weapons and supplies and the only place he knew where such things were was in this building. No light showed between the cracks of the door, nor any of the shuttered windows on the first floor. He felt the door and found it had been barred from the outside. Diego removed the bar and, trying the latch, opened the door. He stepped in and closed the door to utter darkness.

The latch held and, though the door rattled a little, it did not threaten to fly open. He felt around the entrance and found a lamp hanging on a hook by the door. The bottom of the lamp had a small covered recess which held a flint kit. Working by feel, Diego opened the kit and took out a hooked iron scrap, a piece of flint, a small scrap of charcloth and a pinch of jute from the kit. He put the jute in his left hand and pushed the charcloth into the middle of the dry fibers. He held the piece of flint between his fingers and thumb, so it was suspended above his palm, and struck it a glancing blow with the scrap of iron. A sprinkle of sparks rained down onto the charcloth and one caught, making a red, glowing ring in the black cloth. Diego gently blew onto the cloth until the jute burst into flame.

He opened the glass door to the lamp and lit the wick before the jute could burn out. Diego adjusted the height of the wick until it cast a tiny circle of light around his feet. Holding the lamp before him he examined his surroundings. He was in a hallway which continued into the darkness of the building. He listened but the howling wind and driving rain would likely drown all other sounds except, perhaps, a gunshot. He walked up the hall to where it ended in the large foyer where he had been brought when he was first captured. The room was empty.

He went to the door to the General's office and put his ear against the wood. He could not hear any sounds. He took a deep breath, opened the door, went in and closed it behind him. His *magado, sunta* and jerkin were on the floor next to the desk. His rifle, sword, shoes, haversack and possible bag were not in the room. He looked in a closet and found nothing but three empty wineskins and a leather case much like the one Panis had used to keep his sketches. Fearing for a moment Panis had been captured as well Diego pulled the case from the closet and put it on the desk. He was relieved to see it had several words in English stamped into the leather. Deciding the pouch could serve as a haversack, he put the empty wineskins in the bag. He noticed a sealed and folded leather document binder tucked in a pocket of the case, but did not remove it.

A silver tray and cover sat on one corner of the desk and, when he lifted the cover, discovered a small quarter wheel of cheese. He ate the cheese as he searched the room for more food but found nothing else, so he put on his jerkin, slipped the *magado* into its sheath on his back, slung the *sunta* from his arm, finished the cheese and left the room carrying the lamp before him. When he arrived at the back door, Diego replaced the lamp on its hook by the door, snuffed it out and waited in the dark for several minutes. Diego opened the door and looked left and right – he could see only a few feet in the gloom – and stepped through the door, barring it behind him.

He was unshackled, out of the prison and armed, but he had not escaped. The fortress walls still held him captive. There were certain to be guards at the gates or huddled on the battlements, even in this storm. They may not be in the towers, but the gates were bracketed by stone guard shelters. He had not seen any sally gates or other entrances to the fort. Then he looked up at the fire step fourteen feet above his head and remembered the push poles!

He felt his way to the wagon where the poles were stacked on the bed. He pulled one out and stood it against the wall. It was two feet short of the walkway. He clambered up onto the wagon and, bracing the pole on the driver's bench, he touched it to the wall again. It reached a foot above the edge of the fire step! Gathering up a coil of rope from the wagon bed, he ascended the pole with practiced ease and rolled onto the fire step. He looked both ways along the fire step and could not see the ends or the guard towers. The wind seemed as if it would blow him over the wall as he pulled the push pole up onto the walkway and laid it down parallel to the battlements. He looped the rope around the pole and tossed both ends through an embrasure. Easing himself feet first through the embrasure, he held onto the doubled rope and pulled the pole against the battlements. He lowered himself to the ground and pulled on one strand of the rope until it passed free of the pole above and fell onto his head. When his escape was discovered, there would be no evidence on how he got free of the fortress.

The wall blocked much of the wind and rain until he had crept several dozen yards towards the wooded area west of the post. Once under foliage it was nearly impossible to see where he was going. Fearing he may simply wander around in circles, he found a trickle of water running away from the fort and followed it until it joined another torrent. After hours of stumbling and feeling his way along in the dark he noticed that the violent winds were subsiding, rain was no longer a continuous deluge and the sky was turning gray. Dawn was near and the storm was passing. He stopped next to a torrent to fill the wineskins and moved through the woods and out onto a debris strewn beach. He trotted west, the churning muddy gulf to his left, and, certain his escape must have been discovered by now, he wondered how long he could remain free.

CHAPTER 20

D iego looked back over his shoulder as he trotted west carrying the *magado* in his right hand and the *sunta* slung on his right elbow. The sun was brightening the horizon and a fortress was silhouetted against the sky. It must have been one of the outer redoubts that straddled the entrance to Pensacola Bay. Nothing moved on the watchtowers but he increased his pace, wanting to be beyond sight of the fort. He ran along the shore where the wave wash kept the sand wet and firm. An entangled debris line was several yards inland from the beach near the crest of a line of sand dunes.

Concerned he might be seen, he turned inland through a break in the line of dunes only to be halted by a lagoon. The lagoon was wide and it seemed to follow the beach, forming a continuous barrier between the strip of sandy beach and the sheltering trees to the north. Mounds of flotsam covered the area between the south edge of the lagoon and the crown of the dunes along the beach. Were he to attempt to flee west on the north side of the dunes he would have to crawl over logs, stumps, and tangled vines. Having no choice, he returned to the seashore, glanced eastward at the apparently vacant tower, now nearly a half-mile away, and ran west.

After a few minutes of running, the shore curved slightly and nothing could be seen to the west except sand, sea and a sky filled with the orange globe of the rising sun. He wondered how long it would be before his escape was discovered. Had the storm damaged the small coastal sloops in the bay? Diego was convinced the fort's experienced trackers had left in pursuit of Panis and T'Chien. Did the storm aid in their escape or were they even now being brought back in chains? How many were left to pursue him? Would they assume he headed inland? He had no answers to those questions, so he just ran, settling into a wolf run – alternating between a brisk walk for several minutes and then running at a trot until fatigue forced him to walk again.

In about an hour he came to a place where the sand dunes gave way to a dense bramble of scrubby trees and twisted vines. The sky was free of clouds and the wind was gentle but steady from the east. In a few hours, it would be unmercifully hot. He worked his way up a slope and, using the *magado* to pry his way into the brush for concealment, discovered thorny vines covered with blackberries. He ate as many as he could find before he continued moving west within the tree line.

The wooded areas clung to sandy hills covered with a thin veneer of decayed leaves and soil. Diego had never seen such dense foliage before in his life. He attempted to work his way inland by crawling along animal trails that tunneled under brambles and scrubby brush. He finally decided that he could never make much progress inland and worked his way back toward the gulf.

The wooded patch ended and he found himself on the sandy beach again. This time however, the beach stretched to the west as a thin ribbon of sand dividing a river flowing west on its north side and the gulf on the south. Here he ran on packed sand along the river bank, hidden from the gulf by the line of sand dunes.

He followed the river bank for three hours when the river suddenly twisted to the south, flowing into the Gulf of Mexico. The river was pulling logs and storm debris with it as it rushed through the narrow cut that connected it to the sea. He could see the beach resume to the west only a few hundred feet across the violently flowing river. The storm-generated current abruptly dissipated as it flowed out into the gulf, depositing a line of debris which slowly arched to the west, spreading into a fan of bobbing logs, clumps of grass and whole trees that drifted parallel to the beach.

Diego waded into the rushing water and picked a large log that was being swept into the gulf. He hugged the log and propelled it into the flow by kicking his feet. He was swept to sea for a few terrifying moments, then the current slackened and he was able to make headway toward the west. He was well west of the mouth of the river when he was finally able to kick his log toward the beach. His feet touched the bottom when he was several yards from the beach and he released his impromptu raft and waded ashore.

The sun was directly overhead and broiling. He drained one of the wineskins, looked back toward the east, saw nothing and headed west along the beach.

꩜

General Campbell opened the windows on his second floor bedroom, unhooked the shutters and spread them until they latched on the shutter keeps. The sun filled the eastern sky over the top of the battlements. He looked into the courtyard below as a few soldiers began to venture from the guard houses and barracks. He was always amazed at how clear and calm it was after a storm. No doubt, it had been a hurricane. He could hear the Sergeant Major alerting the garrison to be ready to stand inspection in a half hour.

Campbell went down to the first floor and found his clerk and two other enlisted men going from window to window unbarring the shutters and checking for damage.

"No damage in this building that I could find, sir," the clerk reported.

"Send for my brigade commanders, Finch," Campbell said. "There is to be a commander's call in one hour. Include Admiral Parker. Do you know where he can be found?"

"Yes, sir," Finch said, "right away, sir." Finch sent the two enlisted men to inform the appropriate officers.

Campbell strode to the large front doors and, tossing the locking bar aside, walked out onto the wide porch. There were leaves and bits of branches strewn across the porch and on the parade grounds. The buildings within the fort showed no signs of damage.

"Just a little one that time," he said to nobody. *Good thing I called the people in from the redoubts on the islands*, he thought. *First order of business will be to re-populate those forts. One could never tell what the Dons might try; might sneak in behind a storm; would not put it past them.*

The General could see Colonel David Hutchens, who was normally billeted in the headquarter building, returning from his inspection of the town, with Major Archibald Mitchell, who had a house in the town, following close behind. Admiral Parker was expected soon. He had three ships in the bay and they were reported to have weathered the storm without damage. The General waited on the porch until both officers had reported.

"Colonel," Campbell was not known to waste time, "Re-man the positions on Santa Rosa Island and the west battery." He had decided that it would be better to build redoubts on the approaches to Fort George rather than have isolated batteries on the sandy islands bracketing the entrance to Pensacola Bay. Until those new posts were completed, he would continue to man the redoubts. "Major, organize work parties to resume completion of the picket around this post. Later, Colonel Hutchens and I will designate the locations for additional redoubts on Gage Hill. I intend to abandon the batteries across the pass; too easily cut off."

Campbell watched the officers depart to carry out his commands and then reentered the headquarters. "Finch!"

The clerk, who had not seen Campbell come in, nearly knocked his chair over in his haste to come to attention.

"Finch, Admiral Parker is to see me the instant he is ashore. Post a man at the pier to make certain he is informed."

"Yes, sir," Finch said as he opened Campbell's office door for him and stepped back.

Campbell paused at the doorway. "And send for that translator Bankenson."

"Sir," Finch stammered, "Bankenson headed inland three days ago, sir. He and the native trackers, sir, are pursuing those other spies; the ones believed to have been with Flying Bear, sir."

"Damn!" Campbell had forgotten that. He was undermanned as it was and now two dozen of his native allies were blundering around somewhere between here and Mobile looking for ghosts. He stormed into his office and slammed the door.

"Finch, get in here!" Campbell yelled less than a minute after entering his office.

Finch rolled his eyes, straightened his wig and entered the General's office. "Yes, sir?" he said.

"Finch," Campbell, who was digging in his closet, called out over his shoulder, "did you remove the dispatch case?"

"No, sir," Finch said, "it was on your desk yesterday, sir. I have not been in here since, sir."

"It is not here now, Finch," Campbell began pulling out desk drawers, though none were large enough to hold the leather dispatch case.

"Pardon me, General."

Campbell whirled around to see Admiral Parker standing in the doorway to his office.

"Sir Peter!" Campbell straightened up. He grabbed Finch by the elbow. "Get Sergeant Wheat and bring him here," he said through clenched teeth, giving Finch a shove to hurry him away.

"Problems, General?" Parker asked.

"Oh, nothing really, Sir Peter," Campbell said. "Just setting things right after the storm; a hurricane, was it not."

"Just so," Parker said, a bemused smile on his face.

"How soon can you send a sloop to Mobile, Admiral?"

"You need only say the word, General. All our vessels passed the storm undamaged."

"Good. Good," Campbell returned to his desk. "I shall have several dispatches prepared within the hour. I would be obliged if you could send a sloop to bring them to Mobile."

"Of course, General," Parker said. His voice was much calmer than Campbell's. "I shall send the Sparrow. With this wind she will arrive at Mobile before dark this very day."

"Good. Good," Campbell began scribbling away. "I shall send a packet of orders to the pier. Do be so kind as to have the Sparrow come to the pier straight away."

"I will take my leave, sir." Parker said with a bow, "and see to it."

Parker nearly ran into Finch and a red-faced sergeant as he stepped out onto the porch.

"Begging your pardon, my lord," the sergeant said, doffing his hat, "urgent business, sir." The man pushed by Parker urged on by Finch.

Army, Parker thought, *always thrashing about*. He stepped down from the porch, squared his hat on his head and looked up approvingly at a blue sky.

∽

Campbell was seated behind his desk when Sergeant Wheat centered himself on the desk, held a salute, placed his right instep behind his left heel, left hand on his trouser seam, head back and announced, "Sergeant Wheat, 16th Foot, reporting as ordered, sir." He dropped his salute in return to the General's nod. He expected to hear "Stand easy" but the General did not release him, so he held his position of "attention."

"Guard report, sergeant."

"Sir, all guard posts reported a severe storm for the duration of the night, sir." *What could the General be in such a fuss about?* Wheat thought, *there was not so much as a shutter shaken loose during the entire storm.*

"Any reports of people coming or going?"

"No, sir," Wheat's brow wrinkled. "Not a gate was opened, sir. None came in nor went out since sundown yesterday, sir. The posts on the walls saw nothing out of the ordinary, sir, save for the storm, sir."

"Finch!" Campbell yelled past Wheat, who was still locked at attention. "Get two soldiers and bring our guest, Mister Flying Bear, here immediately."

"Sir!" Finch called from the outer office.

"We will see, Sergeant Wheat," Campbell said. "Now that he has been on bread, water and hard labor, I will warrant you, we need to add but a few cane strokes and we will have Flying Bear speaking Spanish like a true dago. He did not trick me, Sergeant. Bankenson said the man's Choctaw was delivered with a Spanish accent."

Without releasing Wheat from attention, Campbell began rummaging around the room again and muttering something about a missing pouch. Exasperated, he snapped at Wheat, "What about this building, sergeant. Did your sentries see anyone prowling about this building?"

"The rain, sir," Wheat swallowed, "when the rain was really coming down, sir, this building could not be seen at all from the guardhouses, sir." He wanted to say the headquarters had several officers billeted on the second floor, much closer and in a position to detect an intruder than a poor private huddled in a guard house but held his tongue.

"Probably sleeping," Campbell growled, "sleeping or drunk."

Finch burst into the room, his face a portrait of confusion and fear. He snapped to attention next to the ridged sergeant.

"Well, Finch," Campbell shouted, "What is it man? Where is our Spaniard?"

"Gone, sir," Finch almost whispered.

"What? For God's sake, speak up man,"

"He is gone, sir," Finch repeated. "The blockhouse was empty, sir. Locked and empty. No sign of the man, sir."

Campbell burst out an incoherent string of obscenities. Finally, falling silent he sat down. "How is that possible? Treason! He had to have been released by an accomplice. Send for Colonel Hutchins. You – Finch – go now!"

Finch stumbled from the room and Campbell turned his glare onto Wheat. "Find him, Sergeant. Find him. He must still be inside the compound. Get as many men as you can and search this post – Now, damn your eyes!"

At the end of the day Campbell listened to Sergeant Wheat's report. They had found the rotten timbers at the corner of the blockhouse and the shackles between the wagon and the north wall. The entire post was searched as was the town to the north. There was no sign of the prisoner. They knew he had somehow gained access to the headquarters while several officers slept on the second floor. The storm masked any sounds he may have made. The jerkin, lance and mace taken from Flying Bear when he was captured were gone. So were several wineskins and the message pouch, the contents of which Campbell did not disclose.

That night, Sergeant Wheat managed to separate himself from the post and visited the Pig and Fowl, an alehouse just beyond the clear zone around the palisade. He found a table where two other soldiers of the 16th Foot were downing their pints. Privates Jameson and Potts moved their chairs to make room for Wheat who set three fresh pints of stout on the table.

"'Ow'd 'e do it, Sergeant?" Potts asked, "The top of that wall in the block'ouse 'as to be a dozen feet 'bove the floor."

"Reckon 'e could jump," Wheat said as he filled his mouth with ale.

"'e 'ad to push up the roof and pull 'emself over the top," Jameson said. "We 'ad a ladder and two men to 'eave and din' get through."

"Reckon 'e could," Wheat said.

"'Ow 'd 'e get over the wall? We 'ad guards at every stair to the fire step," Potts said.

"An' we din' find no ladder," Jameson added.

"Maybe 'e *can* fly an' all," Wheat said as he waived three fingers to the barmaid.

"Fly? Wha' cha mean?" Potts said.

"Maybe," Wheat said, leaning forward and speaking in a hoarse whisper, "'E was named 'Flying Bear' 'cause 'e *can*."

"Can what?" Jameson asked, feeling the benefit of his third pint.

"Fly, you fool. That's 'ow 'e done it. The Dago *can* fly," Wheat said.

CHAPTER 21

As Diego jogged west he began to make out a shape silhouetted by the setting sun. He estimated that he had traveled thirty-five miles since hitting the beach at sunrise. The packed sand along the wave-wash was smooth, better than any road he had ever traveled. Now he slowed to a walk and examined the distant object that arose over what had previously been an unchanging horizon. It was a signal tower!

He dropped to a crouch, crabbed up the side of a dune and plunged into a tangle of grass clumps and scrub brush. The tower supported tall poles of a semaphore, their large, unmoving signal paddles were in the vertical position like a giant with his hands over his head. He could see the operator's covered guard station just above the tops of the waving grass and waited for several minutes as the sun lowered behind the tower. He could see a single man casually walking about the stand. Diego decided that he must not have been seen for if he had, surely someone would have been dispatched to investigate.

He moved further north into a wooded area thick with stunted trees and debris, lacking trails of any kind. The debris and damage created by the storm seemed to have dramatically abated as Diego moved west until there was little evidence of a hurricane along the dunes or among the trees. Every now and then, he could see the rigid signal paddles of the watch tower through breaks in the foliage. After moving north for less than a mile, he stepped out onto another beach to see nothing but water spreading to the north. He could see two small, triangular sails about a mile north of where he stood. Both vessels were sailing east and coming closer to his location, so he shrank back into the brush. He was trapped on a peninsula.

Diego slumped in the shade of a twisted tree and, as he brought the last full wineskin to his lips, watched the sails change color as both boats tacked and began to run away from his position. As he drank, he worked to remember what he had seen weeks ago and what Panis had said when they were scouting Mobile. The town was on the west shore of a wide bay, almost an inland sea. Diego had never been south of the town, but Panis had said that the bay narrowed down to a pass into the Gulf of Mexico. He had said the pass was no more than three miles in width and lay twenty-five miles south of the town. It was flanked by watch towers, one on a barrier island to the west and another on a sandy point to the east. The tower he was watching in the setting sun must be on the east side of the pass to Mobile Bay. If so, he was over ten miles from mainland West Florida.

Diego waited until the sun set. As he watched the bay to his northeast, a small light winked on, perhaps five miles away along the north shore of the peninsula he occupied. It was at a place where the sail boats he saw at sunset seemed to have been headed. He surmised that a fishing camp of some kind must be there, maybe even a village. He waited until the moon rose. It cast so much light that he could discern his own shadow as he crept west to within a hundred yards of the tower.

There was a pier running to the north out from the base of the tower and into the bay. Two boats were moored to the pier, one with a single mast, the other a sea-worthy skiff with a high prow and six rowing stations. The tower was supported by four legs, each formed by three timber piles lashed tightly together into a cluster. The floor of the signal tower, enclosed by a waist-high railing, was about eighteen feet above the ground and connected the corner pile clusters to form a rigid structure. A central mast rose far into the sky through the center of the roof that sheltered the watch station. A ladder from the floor pierced the roof and ended at a platform for the semaphore operator. The mast continued past the platform and terminated thirty feet above the platform with a crow's nest. Stays anchoring the tall mast ran down in all directions to pilings set in the ground.

Diego could see five men in the open tower. Two were constantly scanning the horizon with telescopes. As he watched, one man climbed to the platform just above the roof and hauled up two lanterns that had been lit by one of the men below. One lamp had green tinted glass and the other red. The red lantern was attached to the left signal paddle and the green to the right. The paddles were hoisted up and manipulated for a moment, then positioned far apart, level and still.

One of the men with a telescope moved to train his attention toward the west-northwest. Diego followed the direction of the man's telescope and he could see two twinkling lights, one red and one green, move about in a series of seemingly random positions, then stop. Diego tried to fix the direction to the other signal tower in his mind. He remembered the west entrance to Mobile Bay was a barrier island some three or four miles from the mainland. That far signal tower had to be on the island on the west side of the pass. South of those lights lay the open Gulf of Mexico and three or four miles north of the lights lay the mainland.

Diego withdrew to the east into the brush until he was safely out of sight of the tower. He was trapped. If he managed to steal one of the boats on the pier, what good would it do? He could not easily handle a skiff intended for no fewer than two oarsmen. If he took the little sloop, he might manage to it get underway, but the coast watchers could not miss a sail hoisted practically at their feet, particularly in the bright moonlight. They would signal the other tower, maybe others as well, and a fleet of British boats would converge on him. He decided to go east along the bay-side shoreline toward the light he had seen at sunset.

He crept east along a sandy beach that quickly gave way to a reed-covered muddy shoreline. The going was difficult, as every step that missed a clump of marsh grass allowed him to sink to his knees in foul-smelling muck, forcing him to lay the *magado* across the mud and use both hands to pull himself forward. Mosquitoes circled about his head in a great swarm so he scooped up hands full of the sticky clay and spread it over his neck, face and hands. He abandoned his attempts to walk and began to crawl across the grasses along the edge of the shoreline. He was able to make good progress using this technique. Soon he could see huts and a crude pier jutting out into the bay. A large fire was going in a clearing among the huts and he could see people moving about. He was close enough now to hear talking and laughter but he could not understand what was being said.

The shoreline became sandy again, but Diego did not stand. He crawled along the waterline, keeping in the shadows cast by the pier and several moored boats, hidden from the people gathered about the fire. Another boat was pulled up onto the bank. He crawled up next to the beached boat. It was a large dugout. Wide planks standing on edge had been added along both sides of the dugout to effectively raise the freeboard of the vessel. There were two paddles, some poles and a roll of canvas in the bottom of the boat.

Diego peeked over the boat and under the sagging stringers of the pier, watching the figures about the fire. He could see four men and two women, all facing the fire, laughing and enjoying food and drink. Diego's stomach growled. Since his escape, he had not eaten, except for a few berries. He searched for a guard beyond the glare of the fire, but saw no one. Perhaps there was some food in the nearest hut.

He crawled along the side of the boat until he was behind the hut. Standing, he crept in, *magado* at the ready. The hut consisted of one room and was open at both ends. The floor was covered with sleeping blankets and little else. Two canteens hung from the frame in a corner of the hut. He gently swished the canteens. They were full. Pulling the wooden stoppers, he smelled the contents. It was water laced with rum. He removed the canteens and, finding nothing else, returned to the beached boat.

Diego collected the bow rope which had simply been wrapped around a stump, lifted the bow of the boat and slowly slid it back into the water. He put the canteens and coiled rope into the bow. With an arm over the gunnel, he waded with the boat into deeper water. Moving along the shoreline, he held onto the boat as he sometimes swam, sometimes waded, until he was back on the hard sand beach of the peninsula far west and south of the fishing camps. He clambered into the boat and inspected what else was there. To his disappointment, there was no food. The roll of canvas on the bottom of the boat was attached to two poles in several places. The arrangement appeared to be a crude sail and spar contraption of some type. Laying the *magado* on the bottom between his feet where he could retrieve it quickly, Diego chose one of the paddles and began to make his way west toward the pass to Mobile Bay.

The signal paddles of the tower he had inspected at sunset came into view to his left. Diego maneuvered away from the shoreline, fearing even this small craft could be seen on the moonlit bay waters. The red and green signal lights of the west tower peeked above the horizon and he pointed the bow toward a dark mass north of the lights he believed to be the mainland.

A short following chop slapped at the boat, but the extension of the gunnels effectively prevented any wash from slopping aboard. He worked the paddle easily, with long, deep pulls, hoping that he would cross the mouth of the pass well before sunrise. No longer shielded by their mounting frames, he could see the signal lights of the east tower, now behind him. The lights to the east appeared to be as distant as the lights to the west and he surmised he must be in the middle of the pass.

Wanting to keep well north of the west tower, he increasingly had to adjust his course to the north until he was headed directly north and no longer pointed toward the dark mass of the mainland. He realized that he was being pulled south by a powerful current. The tide must be falling and he was being swept south toward the pass. He pulled hard, but made little headway. He could see the west signal lights drifting closer in spite of his efforts. He abandoned the attempt to reach the mainland and maintained a position in the center of the pass, equidistant from the brace of watch towers. He stretched out in the boat to reduce his silhouette and watched as the bracketing semaphore lights seemed to sweep past along the horizon.

The western pair of lights began to move in a jerky pattern, obviously signaling something. The red light disappeared leaving only the green. Concerned that he may have been sighted, Diego looked toward the eastern signal tower. He watched as the green light of that semaphore winked out leaving only the red. He then examined the northern horizon, expecting to see a fleet of boats in pursuit, but he could see nothing. Then he looked south and saw the sails of a tall ship making straight for him.

It was still hull down, but the sails were well lit by the setting moon. Signal lights flickered from somewhere among the sails. Lying in the bottom of the boat, Diego covered himself with the canvas and waited, hoping that those aboard the ship would not see a small dugout bobbing on the sea. If they did see the boat, they may think it to be a log or other debris. He lay back and looked at the cloudless, star-strewn sky and listened.

After a half hour or so, he began to hear voices and the creak of tackle. Not daring to move, he looked out of the corner of his eye over the gunnel and saw the top sails of the ship as it glided by no more than three hundred yards to the east, so close he could smell the stench of too many men in too small a space. *How could they not see me?* Full moon, clear night and his dugout was passing practically beneath the ship's bow. He held his breath, but there were no shouts of alarm, no change of sail, no skiff was launched, nothing.

Eventually, the sails disappeared toward the north and he was able to sit up without fear of discovery. The moon had finally set and the sky to the east was beginning to show signs of a rising sun. He looked north and saw nothing. No lights, no ship, no land. He checked the wineskins and found them all empty, so he removed the wooden stopper from one of the canteens and drank a few swallows. He reset the stopper and placed both canteens at his feet. The top of the sun was beginning to clear the horizon as he began to paddle toward the northwest. There was a gentle breeze from the east, but it was going to be a hot day.

Diego drained the first canteen before he realized what he was doing. The sun was burning nearly directly overhead. He thought he was still headed northwest, judging by the direction of the wind and waves. If they had shifted without him noticing, he might be going in circles. He was close to exhaustion. It had been two days since he had slept, or eaten – or was it three.

He shifted the roll of canvas around, intending to rig an awning for protection from the relentless glare. He pulled on the poles to discover they were attached to the roll of canvas. He levered them up, shook the canvas free until it formed a V-shaped sail. There was a block fitted with slots in the bottom of the dugout in which the bottom ends of the poles neatly fit. Diego was able to prevent the poles from toppling forward by grasping lines running from the upper end of each pole. The moderate, but steady east wind filled the canvas, pulling the dugout forward until it was moving smoothly toward the west. He could feel the pull of the sail through the lines in his hands.

Noticing a pair of cleats on the outer edge of the splash plank, one to his left and the other to his right, Diego lashed the lines to the corresponding cleats and adjusted the tension so the bow of the dugout pointed as much north of west as the following sea would allow. He removed his leather jerkin and, using the spare paddle, rigged a shade. He lay prone to escape the sun, closed his eyes and fell into a dreamless, exhausted sleep.

☙

Diego stirred and blinked his eyes. It was nearly dark. He sat up, pulling the jerkin aside. The sail he had rigged now cast a shadow across the dugout's stern. He could see the outline of the sun through the canvas. He was still headed west. He examined the horizon to his right, but saw no sign of land. There was nothing to his left but endless water. Sore and stiff, he managed to twist around to look astern. A mast crowded with sails filled the sky.

He quickly undid the lines holding his sail and let it drop into the dugout. He looked back again to see a man standing on the bowsprit of the ship. He heard shouts and saw the man pointing directly at him. The ship did not alter sail, for it was moving at a moderate pace in the mild wind. A skiff was swung out and launched while the ship was underway.

Men lined the rails. Some clambered down ratlines and aboard the boat as soon as it struck the sea. Eight oars were pointed vertically as the coxswain fended the skiff away from the ship's side. There was a shout, oars struck the water and the skiff raced ahead toward Diego.

Diego pulled the wooden stopper from the last full canteen and drained its contents. No need to save any water now. He donned the jerkin, hung his *sunta* from his right arm and draped the leather pouch over his shoulder. He picked up his *magado* and struggled to his feet, rocking uneasily in the dugout. He was not going to be taken prisoner again.

"English?" shouted a man in the bow of the skiff.

"*Español*," Diego said proudly.

The man in the bow turned to someone in the stern of the skiff shouting, "He says he is a Spaniard, Lieutenant," in perfect Spanish.

"Are you a Spanish ship?" Diego asked, not daring to hope.

"*El Sagrado Corazón de Jesús*," the man shouted. "Out of Habana; Commanded by *Capitan Don* Manuel Mongioty."

Overcome by relief, Diego became woozy, sinking to his knees as the skiff banged against the dugout. Barely conscious, he handed his weapons to someone. A half dozen hands pulled him across to the skiff where he collapsed between the rowing benches.

"Pull!" commanded the coxswain.

Diego had the sensation of the skiff surging ahead with every pull of the oars. He looked through half-open eyelids to see yards and billowing sails overhead as the skiff was expertly maneuvered to match the course and speed of the ship. Oars were shipped, hauling blocks made fast and the benches emptied as men scrambled up to the ship. Diego, too exhausted to attempt a climb up to the deck, rode the skiff up to the davit and onto the blocks.

He was pulled from the skiff as it was being lashed to the blocks and escorted to the foot of the starboard ladder to the quarter deck. Directed to sit on a small keg, the leather pouch was taken and he was stripped of his jerkin. A bucket of fresh water was poured over his head and a cup of rum was placed in his hand.

"For a favor," Diego said, "could I have something to eat?"

A wedge of cheese appeared before him. He ate greedily, pausing only to gulp from the cup until his head began to swim. The lieutenant that had commanded the skiff pulled the sealed envelope from the pouch and opened it. Diego had forgotten it was there. The officer disappeared up the ladder with the envelope.

People began coming up from below decks. Women, children and soldiers joined the idle sailors to crowd curiously around Diego. These spectators spoke among themselves in *Isleños* accented Spanish. Stripped of his leather jerkin, Diego was dressed only in a worn cotton shirt and cotton trousers. The *náwoti*, containing a lock of Mézu's hair was clearly visible under the dripping cloth against his chest. His trousers were ragged and torn into ribbons below the knees, his feet bloody. A boy of eleven or so separated from the others to stand in front of Diego.

"Are you a wild man of Louisiana?" he asked.

"No," Diego said. He remembered hearing the stories of the wild men of Louisiana when he was transported in on the *San Juan* four months ago. *Four months!* It seemed as if it had been a lifetime since he had waved to Mézu from the gates of Fort Saint Charles. "I am from New Orleans. Where are you from?"

"I am from Candelaria," the boy said, poking out his chest, "Tenerife."

"Ah," Diego said, "I know the place." This was another shipload of *Isleños* bound for New Orleans. He was returning to Mézu. "What is your name?"

"Salvador Guerra," the boy said. "What is your name?"

Before Diego could answer, the lieutenant stormed down the steps, "You, on your feet," he shouted.

Diego managed to stand on shaking legs. "You two," the lieutenant gestured to a pair of idle sailors, "take this man to the captain's cabin."

The men bracketed Diego and pulled him by his arms through a doorway. They entered a short hallway where a sentry opened another door and Diego was hustled in. He had to stoop as he walked, for the overhead was much too low for him to stand. He had to move about hunched over to keep from hitting his head on the heavy beams supporting the deck above. A chair was positioned before a wide, ornate desk and Diego directed to sit. His head was swimming from the rum.

"May I have some more water?" he asked and was given a cup full of cool water ladled from a keg in the corner. He drank it down at once.

The door behind him banged open again and a naval officer walked past Diego, rounded the desk and sat in a high-backed chair, the glittering ship's wake visible through the windows across the aft of the cabin.

The lieutenant from the skiff circled to Diego's right and two more men came in to Diego's left. One was a priest, a bishop according to his head gear, and the other was a gentleman, a nobleman in fine clothes. He thought he recognized the nobleman from somewhere. Looking out the corner of his eye, Diego examined the stylishly dressed man until it came to him. The man was *Don* Alguazil Cabitos, onetime *Ricohombre* of Santa Cruz de Tenerife. It had been ten years since Diego had last seen him, but it was Cabitos. Diego looked away, waiting for someone to speak.

"How did you come by this?" the Captain said shaking the communiqué he had been given from Diego's pouch.

Diego looked stunned, afraid to speak lest Cabitos recognize him.

"This is Captain *Don* Manuel Mongioty y de Málaga," the lieutenant said, "and I am Lieutenant *Barón* Francisco Medeña y Ulla of His Most Catholic Majesty's ship *El Sagrado Corazón de Jesús*, sometimes called *El Natural*."

"I took a pouch from the General's office in Pensacola, Captain," Diego said, finally finding his voice.

"How is it you were in a British General's office?" Mongioty asked.

"I was captured at Pensacola, sir. I was with Captain *Don* Jacinto Panis, sir. We were sent to reconnoiter Pensacola and Mobile." Diego said. "I escaped during a storm."

"Sent? By whom?"

"Governor Bernardo de Gálvez, Captain."

"Gálvez! What is your name?"

Diego could feel all eyes examining him. "I am called *Hika Nitah*, sir."

"Sounds like a woman's name," Cabitos scoffed. Diego did not turn his head.

"It means 'Flying Bear', sir, in the language of the Choctaw, sir."

"I want this copied immediately, Lieutenant," Mongioty said, waving the envelope. "We will be making contact with the mail packet from New Orleans in the morning. I want you to board the packet. Carry Flying Bear and this message to New Orleans. We will continue down the coast and come up the Mississippi to the city. I know Captain Panis. He is on Gálvez's staff. If this man is speaking the truth, they will know in New Orleans."

"Pardon me for interrupting, Captain," Cabitos said. "Could I and Bishop Benitez transfer to the mail packet as well? We are anxious to reach New Orleans."

"That is not possible, *Don* Alguazil," Mongioty said. "The packet is a swift sailor, but she is small. I fear she may be overcrowded with the addition of only these two men."

Diego tried not to show relief. Diego's long, ragged hair, swollen lips and blistered face had prevented Cabitos from recognizing him, but he did not believe the deception would survive the close quarters of a mail packet.

"How long, Captain," Cabitos continued, "before we arrive at New Orleans?"

"A week, ten days, no more."

"And the mail packet?"

"She will arrive at the city by way of Bayou Saint John within two days, provided we rendezvous in the morning."

"Then I must protest, sir," Cabitos continued. "Bishop Benitez has most urgent business in New Orleans. He is under the instructions of the Dominican Order." He reference to the Dominican Order was meant as a veiled threat. The Dominicans were notorious for their aggressive opposition to heresy.

Mongioty held up his hand, "I will not debate the matter, *Don* Alguazil. The mail packet cannot carry more than two in addition to her crew. We may soon be war with Britain. It is vital to that war effort that this information reaches Gálvez as soon as possible and our disheveled native here," he indicated Diego, "must accompany this message to New Orleans so *Don* Jacinto or Governor Gálvez will be able to verify it."

There was knocking at the door behind Diego. "Sir," a voice said, "The mail packet from New Orleans has been sighted."

"Excellent!" Mongioty exclaimed. He gave the envelope to the lieutenant. "You know what needs to be done, Francisco. Hurry now." He looked past Diego, "Get this man a decent change of clothes, feed him some salted pork and get him on the packet. I want him gone within the hour. Within the hour, you hear? Within the hour."

CHAPTER 22

The mail packet *Alacita* was a sloop; a sliver of hull and a mountain of sails. Should the wind fail, she had four sweep stations staggered so the men operating a pair of sweeps worked from the opposite side. Her draft permitted her to navigate the shallow coastal sound, the narrow pass into Lake Pontchartrain, up Bayou Saint John to the very edge of New Orleans. She had been holding her station on the lee side of a chain of islands called the *Chandeleurs* until the sails of *El Natural* were sighted. Then she raced out into the deeper gulf waters for an exchange of messages, news and orders. She would then return to New Orleans, sometimes the same day, alerting the authorities to prepare for the arrival of a ship within a few weeks. Her normal crew complement was five but New Orleans suffered from a shortage of able men so there was just enough room for the two passengers Captain Mongioty ordered aboard her.

"*Señor Capitan*," the grizzled master of the *Alacita* shouted up from the deck of the sloop as Diego and Medeña climbed down to the sloop's rolling deck, "I will expect my passengers to man the sweeps if needed. No idlers on the *Alacita*."

"The *Alacita* is under your command, *Señor*," Mongioty replied, chuckling to himself at the thought of the *Barón* pulling at a sweep.

When the *Alacita* was out of the lee cast by the massive *El Sagrado Corazón de Jesús*, her master, Domingo Palmas, a civilian mariner under contract to the Spanish colonial government, ordered all canvas aloft as he prepared the sloop to run before the wind. She was spanker-rigged and sported a gaff topsail. With her broad jib set to the port, held out by a slender pole, her mainsail and gaff set to the starboard, she leapt before the wind. A low awning had been rigged amidships where the crew sprawled, napping in the shade until needed.

"My *Alacita* loves to run wing and wing," Palmas bragged, referring to sail arrangement, "but you should see her on a close reach, *Señor*," he was speaking to Medeña, "she cannot be caught." Palmas knew his business. There were no better light air sailors in the world than Spain's coastal packet masters.

They had been underway for about two hours when Palmas announced they would shortly see the point of a marsh island to their port. Palmas had not touched a navigational instrument of any kind since leaving the ship. Diego did not see him refer to a time piece, lift a sextant, nor study the compass mounted forward of the tiller. Diego could see nothing but open water in any direction until Palmas pointed toward the port bow. A line of surf became visible, then, grass beyond the surf, and finally a white sand beach took shape, stretching far to the south. Palmas shouted a series of orders, adjusting their course to east-southeast. Sheets were tightened or slackened to adapt to the new direction until the *Alacita* was running comfortably, still "wing and wing." Diego watched as the sliver of grass-covered dunes disappeared astern. Within ten minutes of changing course, the wide horizon was nothing but open sea again.

Medeña joined the crew under the awning, but Diego paced impatiently across a narrow strip of deck just fore of the binnacle mount. Palmas was at the tiller – the *Alacita* did not have a ship's wheel – watching Diego cross from port to starboard and back again.

"In a hurry to get to New Orleans?" Palmas asked.

Diego stopped, momentarily startled. "Yes," he said. "I have been away from my family too long."

"What is your name?" Palmas responded, "The lieutenant did not say who you are, but you must be important to be rushed along with military dispatches."

"I am Private Diego deMelilla y Tupinar, of the Fixed Infantry Regiment of Louisiana, *Señor*." Diego gave a nod. "I am unimportant." Now that he was away from Cabitos he saw no need to hide his identity. If Medeña had heard the exchange, it did not cause him to stir.

"A soldier," Palmas exclaimed. "The sea is a mystery to you then, is it not? I am Domingo Palmas y '*Yo no sé*' (I do not know). I was an orphan, never knew who my parents were. The nuns named me."

Diego looked back toward the horizon.

"Watch just starboard of the bow," Palmas said, indicating the direction he meant. "You must know what land looks like from the sea. There are no mountains, so what you will first see in that direction will be trees, far away, a gray ribbon low against the wave tops. You must know what to look for if you are to see it. Look for a thin, dark line. Tell me when you see something."

Diego resumed his vigil with renewed interest. He had been scanning the horizon for nearly an hour when he noticed that a tiny sliver along the distant sea did not move as did the wave crests.

"I see something there," he said.

"At last," Palmas said, "I thought you would never see it. Now that you know what to look for you will know what you are seeing. That is a point on the mainland of West Florida. It has tall trees so it can be seen from about eight miles. Now look closer to the bow and soon you will see another bit of land. It is a low and grassy island with stunted trees so we will need to be within five miles to see it. It is an island that marks a wide pass into Lake Borgne."

Soon another sliver grew on the horizon, this one close to the bow and when they glided past the island, Diego noticed a tall pole with a tattered flag at the water's edge.

"Stir yourselves," Palmas growled. The deck hands came out from under the awning and padded to their stations at the sheets. Medeña emerged as well, but did not seem interested in helping with the sails.

"Prepare for a starboard reach," Palmas said.

The sailor on the port side took the jib sheet in hand, squatted low to allow the main boom to pass over his head and waited, looking at Palmas. The man on the starboard side freed the mainsheet from a cleat, held it in his left hand and put his right on the main boom. He too looked at Palmas and waited.

"Helm down," Palmas said as he pushed the tiller to port. The starboard sailor guided the main boom across the deck, looped the mainsheet onto a cleat, and then rushed back to reset the gaff topsail sheet. The jib sheet was trimmed and the *Alacita* listed to port slightly as all sheets were heaved taunt, and raced ahead. Running before the wind did not give the same sensation of speed that Diego felt now.

"Del," Palmas ordered, "Get forward and keep an eye out. We are close to the coast and the locals may send a boat to do mischief." One of the sailors worked his way to the bow.

"Never can tell," Palmas said in response to Medeña's questioning look. "We are going to run through the Rigolets. British West Florida will be on our starboard side and Spanish territory to our port. The *godums* have never tried to interfere, but you never can be certain." Palmas used the soldier's slang for the British; the *"godums."* Some say the slang developed from the habit British sergeants had for yelling "God damn" at their troops as they forced them into ranks. To the Spanish troops it sounded like *"godum."*

"God loves and protects the careful man," Diego said.

"Truly," Palmas said. "In this case, most of West Florida along the Rigolets is swamp and cannot support many settlers. If a move were made against Spanish traffic, Gálvez would send soldiers from New Orleans and clean out everything from Lake Pontchartrain to the Pearl River, so the *godums* leave us be."

Palmas hit the opening to the Rigolets, the pass leading into Lake Pontchartrain, without any adjustments to their course. Trees and swamp slipped along the starboard side for a few minutes before a tree-lined bank appeared on the port. The pass meandered slightly, at one point it narrowed to about a quarter mile, yet the *Alacita* raced on unimpeded and emerged into Lake Pontchartrain at three in the afternoon, about one hour after entering the pass.

"We will make Bayou Saint John before six o'clock, Lieutenant," Palmas said. "We will fly a signal flag announcing we have dispatches aboard. Riders stationed at the mouth of the bayou will bring word of our arrival to the Cabildo. By the time we are mooring, an escort will be waiting."

Six o'clock! Diego's heart raced. *Home to Mézu at last!* Less than one week ago he was without hope, a prisoner in an enemy fortress, now he would hold Mézu in his arms tonight. *El Sagrado Corazón de Jesús* was still well at sea and would make the mouth of the river in two days, reach New Orleans in a week, at best. Diego would collect Mézu and the children, abandon New Orleans, head up river to American territory and be safely hidden by then. There Cabitos and his Dominican Bishop could not touch them.

"Prepare to wear ship," Palmas announced. He pushed the tiller upwind as the crew scrambled to adjust the sails, dodge the main boom and clew up sheets as they shifted from a starboard broad reach to a port beam reach. The *Alacita* seemed to leap ahead on this new heading sending brackish spray across the deck. She rose and fell in rhythm with a swell running east to west.

"Del, signal 'dispatches aboard'," Palmas ordered. Del went forward and lifted a section of the deck just aft of the bowsprit. It was a hatch to a hidden locker. Del knelt to sort through the contents, pulled out a bound roll of cloth, replaced the hatch, stood and, timing the pitch of the ship, made his way to the mast. *Alacita*'s other seaman, Pavo, unlashed the base of the signal line and pulled it away from the mast. He untwisted the pair of lines, slapping them against the mast until it was free of tangles. Del clipped grommets in the roll of cloth to rings on the signal line and nodded to Pavo, who hauled on the signal line so quickly his hands became a blur. The flag unfurled as it ascended to the top of the mast, spread out to the lee side over the billowing sails, to become a long white pennant with a horizontal black stripe along the center.

Diego looked south, but could not see who Palmas could be signaling. He moved forward and looked under the jib, which had blocked his view toward the starboard bow, and he could see a lump on the horizon. It slowly took form until he recognized it as the fort at Bayou Saint John. The evening sun glinted off the crude lighthouse at the mouth of the bayou he remembered from his trip into the lake only three months ago.

A thunderstorm crossed the shoreline, obliterating the fort and lighthouse in a curtain of gray-black rain. Lighting flashed in long, dazzling streaks from the high clouds to the ground on the periphery of the storm. The surface of the lake far ahead of the *Alacita* seemed to leap toward the storm as great gusts of air fed the huge cloud, but Palmas did not appear to be concerned. As they approached Bayou Saint John, the storm retreated to the east leaving behind a glistening fort and rain-soaked trees.

"No need for a teamster today," Palmas said. "With this air, my *Alacita* will sail right to her moorings. Station the sweeps."

Palmas wanted the long sweeps unlimbered and ready for deployment if the wind should fail. He was not going to hire a team to pull the *Alacita* to her moorings, never mind the wind. The teamster's fees had jumped to a "dollar," the Kentuckian teamster's name for the Spanish eight-*reales* coin. For that kind of money, Palmas would make a *Barón* pull on a sweep.

The sweeps lay against the gunnels unused as the little mail packet glided past the fort and maneuvered seven or eight miles of Bayou Saint John to moorings within sight of the city. A mounted cavalryman stood in his stirrups, cupped his hands to his mouth and shouted, "I am *Cabo* Landry, dispatches for the Cabildo to me." The man's Spanish had a slight French accent, a common occurrence for New Orleans.

Palmas jumped onto the pier as the *Alacita* was being moored and trotted up to Landry, "Hello, Thomas," Palmas said. "Still running messages, I see."

Landry looked around to see if anyone were listening, leaned down and whispered, "It is the easiest of duties, Domingo. I stand inspection every morning and idle about until some fat old sea captain decides to come in for a pint."

Palmas laughed, "I bring you a navy lieutenant, a *Barón*, no less, so see to your manners." Palmas gestured with his thumb over his shoulder where Medeña was climbing onto the pier, the document pouch clasped under his arm. "He has papers that he insists must be placed in the hands of Gálvez and no other."

"Then he will have to walk to the Cabildo," Landry said. "I will ride as his guard. And who is that?" Landry pointed at Diego. Dressed in borrowed sailor's slops, face blistered, bare feet, beard and hair a tangled mess, Diego stepped onto the pier behind Medeña carrying only his *magado* and *sunta*.

"That is Private Diego deMelilla of the Louisiana Regiment," Palmas said. "The navy picked him up off of Horn Island adrift in a pirogue."

"DeMelilla?" Landry said. "He was with Panis in West Florida. Killed by the British, they say."

"Well, he is not dead, if that be deMelilla. He may be free of the British now," Palmas said. "But I think Medeña has him under arrest. Looks like he has been wrestling the Devil, does he not?"

Medeña strode up, "Are you the courier?"

"*Cabo* Landry, sir," Landry held his salute, "*Mensajero* for Governor General Gálvez's staff, sir. You have dispatches?" Landry dropped the salute when Medeña failed to acknowledge it.

"Urgent and secret, *Cabo*," Medeña snarled. "Give me your horse."

"Not possible, sir," Landry replied. The *Mensajero* for the General's staff could not be put afoot. Landry pointed to a carriage near a stockpile of goods being loaded onto a lighter. It had a team of horses, a driver and a footman. A gentleman, apparently the owner, was preparing to climb aboard. "Convince that merchant of his duty and follow me," Landry said, adding "sir" after a pause.

"You there," Medeña shouted as he hurried toward the carriage. The merchant looked about, confused. Certainly such a rude statement could not be meant for him. He saw a naval officer was striding directly toward him.

"*Vous parlez de moi, monsieur?*" the man said.

"Yes, I am talking to you," Medeña said in perfect French. "I need your carriage. You can ride with us or walk, I do not care." Medeña climbed up into the carriage and sat facing forward. The owner, visibly miffed, took the rear-facing seat, not wanting to be seated next to the lieutenant.

"Come on, man," Medeña gestured at Diego, "get in, hurry."

Diego climbed aboard and sat next to the owner who pulled a handkerchief from his sleeve and held it to his nose. "*Cochon*," the man muttered.

"To the Cabildo, fool," Medeña shouted to the driver, first in Spanish, then in French. The man, a slave, looked to his owner, who nodded, and applied the whip to the team.

Landry, waiting for the carriage to take the road ahead of him, turned to Palmas and laughed. "The lieutenant is off to a bad start, Domingo," he said.

"How so?" Palmas asked.

"The gentleman he just forced to bring him to the Cabildo is *monsieur* Gilbert Antione de Saint Maxent, Governor General Gálvez's father-in-law."

Diego held the *magado* vertically with both hands; butt on the carriage floor between his feet and the needle-sharp point in the air. Saint-Maxent sat on his left switching his disapproving glare from Medeña to Diego and back again.

"*Merci, monsieur*," Diego said in his heavily accented French, "*pour le voyage*," and gave the dignified gentleman a mocking smile.

Landry galloped passed the carriage as it turned onto *Calle San Pedro*. He arrived at the doors to the Cabildo in time to dismount and inform the guards that a naval officer was coming with dispatches. He stepped down to the edge of the street just as the carriage lumbered around the corner of *Calle Chartres* The Cabildo was a two story, wood frame structure that had been originally built by the French. It was called the Cabildo because that is where the governing body of the colony, the Cabildo, deliberated. The building served as the command headquarters for Gálvez as well as a court room. Timber was the preferred building material for the French in New Orleans, but the Spanish were intent on changing that preference to brick and imported stone.

The carriage rocked to a stop and Landry said, unnecessarily, "This way, Lieutenant." The guards snapped to "present arms" as Medeña pushed through the front doors into the lobby. "Lieutenant *Barón* Francisco Medeña y Ulla of His Most Catholic Majesty's ship *El Sagrado Corazón de Jesús*," he fairly shouted, "with dispatches for the Governor General."

The clerk stood, "Yes, sir, *Barón* Medeña. Please wait here, I will see if the Governor General will see you." The man moved to a large oak door and went in without knocking. He had left the door ajar slightly and Medeña could see another desk and another clerk in what must have been the reception area for the General's office.

Diego had not followed Medeña into the Cabildo immediately. He paused by one of the guards and muttered, "*Hola*, Luis."

The guard blinked and looked at Diego. "DeMelilla?" he said uncertainly, "Diego, is that you? They said you had been killed."

"I have made it back, Luis," he said. "The *godums* shot me and imprisoned me, but they could not keep me."

"A week ago, Captain Panis and T'Chien came back from the Floridas. The whole regiment was told you had been killed," Luis stammered.

"Well here I am, Luis. I have to go in with the lieutenant," Diego held the door open, "I do not know how long they will keep me here, but send word to my wife at Fort Saint Charles. Tell her I am alive. Tell her I will be home tonight," he rushed in behind Medeña before Luis had time to respond.

Diego walked into the main reception area just as Medeña disappeared through a doorway. He made for that door only to meet a clerk coming out.

"Give me your weapons," the clerk said. He took the *magado* and *sunta* from Diego. The clerk looked at Diego as if something dead was on the floor.

"Who are you and how did you get past the guards?"

"I am Private Diego deMelilla of the Fixed Infantry Regiment of Louisiana."

The clerk startled. "I thought you were dead."

"I came here with Lieutenant Medeña."

"Wait here," the clerk said as he walked across the wide room to an iron-barred door. He fumbled for some keys, selected one, unlocked the gate and swung it open. Diego could see it was an armory. The clerk placed the weapons against one wall and returned to the main room, locking the armory behind him.

Diego saw a chair next to the door to the inner office and approached it with the intention of sitting down. The clerk cleared his throat, glared at Diego through his eyebrows and shook his head slowly from side to side. Diego decided he was not going to sit so he walked around the room studying the many paintings on the walls. A map of the Mississippi River held his attention. The vast Louisiana territory was highlighted in green starting at the Mississippi and spreading west, fading into an indistinct swath of color without details of any type. The "Isle of Orleans" was designated by a light blue tint and covered all the land east of the Mississippi River, south of the Iberville River, and west of Lake Pontchartrain. Beyond Lake Pontchartrain and the Iberville River the lands were identified as British Territory.

If I am to take Mézu and the children to American Territory, I need to find out where that is, he thought.

The door to the inner office opened slightly and a civilian Diego did not recognize stuck his head out. "Send for Major Panis!" the man said and the door closed again. The clerk scrambled across the room to still another doorway, and called for *Cabo* Landry.

Landry came into the room, nodded to Diego, and said, "what is it Renaldo?"

"Tell Major Panis to report to the Governor immediately. I think he is at home." Landry left through the same door he had entered.

Diego examined the high window that faced *Calle Chartres*. It was growing dusk. "What day is it?" he asked, suddenly realizing he had lost all tract of time.

"It is the feast day of *Santo Etherio*," Renaldo said. Prompted by Diego's blank response, he added, "The 27th day of July, in the Year of Our Lord 1779."

When was it he had left with Panis? The Second or third of May? It had been only a few months, but to Diego it seemed as if a lifetime had passed.

"What happened to T'Chien?" Diego asked.

"The other man with Panis?" Renaldo said. "He returned with the Major with only minor wounds. He is home."

The door to *Calle Chartres* banged open. Major *Don* Jacinto Panis stormed in followed by an entourage consisting of Lieutenant Leyba and two sergeants.

"Diego!" Panis exclaimed, "We saw you shot at Pensacola! We saw a volley of musket fire cut you down, how is it you are alive?"

"I was struck by only one ball, *Señor* Major," Diego responded, "and that only a glancing blow striking me unconscious."

"I must see Governor Gálvez now," Panis said. "Do not leave. Sergeant Vera," one of the sergeants stepped forward, "This is my aid, Sergeant Vera. Sergeant, bring Private deMelilla to the store room. Have him cleaned up and provide him with a proper uniform, then return here and wait for me. Come, Lieutenant." Panis, Leyba and the other sergeant went into Galvez's outer office. Diego saw the clerk snap to attention as the door was closed.

"Well, come on Private, let us make you presentable." Vera said as he led Diego through a complex of doors into a storage and guard barracks area. There were two women in the barracks, civilian housekeepers. The housekeepers were free women of color, slaves were too valuable to waste on barracks policing. Each appeared to be about fifty or more. "Fill the tub," Vera ordered, "and shave this man."

One of the women went out into a yard where the ovens were, Diego could smell the cooking fire when she opened the door. The other woman brought Diego over to a chair and told him to sit. Her Spanish was so heavily accented he could hardly understand her, but he sat obediently.

"Who is that?" Another sergeant came in through the storage area. He was rotund and moved with a shuffling step. Diego remembered him, Guerido, the supply sergeant.

"Private deMelilla," Vera said, "we need a uniform for him."

"DeMelilla? Was not the man with Panis, the one killed, named deMelilla?"

"I was not killed," Diego said.

"Well, I have his uniform and weapon here. It was sent over from Saint Charles when we learned he was killed," Guerido said. "A good thing, we would not have a uniform that would fit him."

"I was not killed," Diego said again. He was silenced when his *barbera* rubbed soap into his beard with her hands. She began to expertly scrape away his beard, but did not touch his moustache. Privates in the Louisiana Regiment were expected to grow wide moustaches; it was required of Grenadiers.

Guerido disappeared into the storage area and he could be heard barking orders at someone, listing the things he needed and ordering lamps to be lit, for it was growing dark.

"*Levantarse*," *La barbera* said.

Diego stood and the woman directed him out into the oven area. It was in an open courtyard with an awning that covered a brace of brick ovens. Each oven had an attached shelf with cooking surfaces made of cast iron grate. Two pots were on the grates tended by the other housekeeper. His barber pulled him over to an iron tub next to a wall. The ground of the oven area, still wet after the evening shower, had been paved with brick. A small drainage ditch formed of brick, ran through the yard and out through a hole in the stone wall.

"*Desnudar*," the barber said as she began to pull his shirt over his head. Diego stood still for a moment after the barber tossed his shirt to the other woman. He expected them to give him some privacy, instead the barber hissed, "*desnudar*" again and began to unbutton his borrowed sailor's slops. Steaming water was added to the tub while he waited. The women were unconcerned about Diego's nakedness. It was as if he were a piece of equipment that needed cleaning. Wearing only his *náwoti*, he stepped into the tub when directed to do so, and the women left the oven yard. Relieved that the housekeepers were not going to bath him, Diego washed. A stock clerk came out and placed clothes on a chair. "Draw your weapons when you leave," the man said.

❧

Count Bernado de Gálvez y Gallardo, Viscount of Galveston, fifth Spanish Governor of Louisiana and General of His Most Catholic Majesty's army stood at his desk, reading the dispatches Navy Lieutenant *Barón* Medeña had brought in the mail packet. Also in the room were Lieutenant Colonel Esteban Miró, Juan Antonio Gayarré, newly promoted Major Panis, Lieutenant Leyba and various aids.

"Do you confirm it is – what was the name, Medeña?" Gálvez said.

"Flying Bear, General," Medeña replied. Gálvez had come to Louisiana as a Colonel and interim Governor, but on July 19th, a *junta de guerra* had been declared he had been temporarily promoted to General. News of the declaration of war had reached Gálvez that same day, but he decided to keep the news secret from the general population.

"Yes, Flying Bear. Was that your man in the outer office, *Don* Jacinto?"

"Yes, General," Panis replied. "That is the man we saw shot in Pensacola. We thought him dead."

"Some men are not so easily killed," Gálvez said. All in the room knew the history of Gálvez. He had been wounded seriously many times during his military career. Fighting the Apache in New Spain he was wounded several times, once near death. He was wounded again in Algiers, but survived. Gálvez was a professional warrior.

"Are we convinced this document is genuine, not a diversion?" Gálvez asked.

"It cannot be a deception, General," Panis said. "How could the British have anticipated the capture of one of our spies, his escape during a storm and his rescue by *El Natural?*"

"I agree, Major," Gálvez said. "I will translate this dispatch for those here who do not speak English. It is addressed to General John Campbell of Strachur, Superintendent of West Florida from Lord George Germain and George III, King of Britain. Campbell is directed to prepare to move against New Orleans. He is to secure naval forces from Jamaica under the command of Admiral Sir Peter Parker, marshal all available forces in West Florida, recruit native mercenaries and foster slave rebellions. All expenses will be provided by the Lord Commissioners of the Treasury."

"How many could he bring?" Medeña asked, stunned by the translation of the dispatch he had carried.

"Three times what we could gather and support if we wait," Gálvez said. "Any suggestions, gentlemen?"

Panis added up the numbers in his head. Perhaps, the British could muster a force of as much as 10,000 including Natives of East and West Florida, Tory militia, and professional soldiers from several garrisons and supported by sea while New Orleans, forced to wait in defense, could support no more than two thousand. The city, surrounded by swamps, no fresh water, little capacity for the storage of food, without an extensive protective wall, and a week's sailing time from the Gulf of Mexico, would not survive a siege.

Gálvez waited for a moment. None of his staff presented any suggestions. "The answer is obvious, gentleman. When one cannot defend, one must attack! Do not speak of the declaration of war outside of this room. We will move first. We must surprise British forces along the Mississippi River, take Baton Rouge to secure our flank. Then we will pick off the British forts of West and East Florida as one picks melons in a field – one at a time."

CHAPTER 23

Diego dressed and returned to the outer office where Sergeant Vera was waiting. The demeanor of the reception clerk had changed appreciably now that Diego presented himself as a proper soldier in His Most Catholic Majesty's army. He lacked the powdered wig so popular among some army units – the Louisiana Regiment did not require such niceties of the enlisted ranks – but his towering height and broad shoulders made for an impressive sight.

Lieutenant Leyba came out of the General's office. "Private deMelilla, I see that our staff has taken care of you."

"Yes, sir." Diego had snapped to attention. The informal attitude he was permitted to display as a spy was gone. "Sir, if I may ask, sir. Could I send word to my wife and family, sir, that I am alive? They had been told I was killed."

Leyba's face contorted a little. "Word of your safe and healthy return has already been sent to your son and daughter, private."

Diego felt a sensation in his chest as if he were falling. "And my wife, sir?"

"There was an epidemic, private," Leyba lowered his voice slightly. Sergeant Vera, who had been listening to the conversation, signaled the clerk to follow him into another room and left.

"During the first week of July, a yellow fever epidemic descended upon the city," Leyba put a hand on Diego's shoulder. "One hundred and fifty died. Of the two hundred *Isleños* who arrived on the *San Juan*, seventy perished. Maria Artiles left this world on the ninth day of July."

"It cannot be," Diego felt the room spin. "Mézu has never taken sick. You must be mistaken."

"Your children were with her when she succumbed. Major Panis' wife was also in attendance in the hospital," Leyba said. "The major has sent for his wife. We are to wait for her here."

Don Jacinto Panis, a Lieutenant of Infantry, had married Margarethe Wiltz four years after being posted to Louisiana. Margarethe, a beautiful young *Criolla* woman, was a widow and the daughter of a respected planter. She had the reputation of being most generous with her time, particularly when tending to the ill. Her first husband, Joseph Milhet had been one of the leaders of the French colonialist rebellion against Spanish rule in 1768. The rebellion was put down by Governor O'Reilly and Milhert was arrested, tried, and convicted. In 1769, Milhert was executed by a firing squad – commanded by Lieutenant *Don* Jacinto Panis.

Guards opened the great doors onto *Calle Chartres* and admitted a lady of about thirty tended by two maids. She was well proportioned, not thin, and stunningly beautiful. She wore a wide-brimmed hat decorated with a diaphanous veil pulled away from her wide face and piled upon the crown of the hat. Her full lips were set in a tight, somber line below a turned-up nose. Her dark brown eyes glistened in the flickering lamp light.

"*Doña* Margarethe," Leyba said. "Your husband is with the General now. I was instructed to wait here for him."

"Is this Mézu's husband?" Margarethe asked while she looked up at Diego, who was standing at attention.

"*Doña* Margarethe Wiltz," Leyba said, "This man is Private Diego deMelilla, of my company of infantry."

Margarethe extended her hand, palm down. "Please accept my condolences on the loss of your beautiful wife, Private deMelilla. She was helping in the hospital, tending to the ill when she herself took ill."

Diego, shaken and confused, did not take the offered hand. Not knowing what to do, he lowered his head. Margarethe dropped her hand, understanding his grief, compassion showing in her eyes she added, "Mézu was a brave and uncomplaining woman. She was able to bid her children farewell and was given the Last Rites." It was most unusual for a titled lady, such as *Doña* Margarethe, to tend to the sick, even more unusual for that lady to befriend the wife of an enlisted man. But Mézu was herself a titled lady, *Doña* Maria Artiles y Ventomo; perhaps that was the difference.

"*Doña* Margarethe Wiltz," Diego felt his throat tighten, "I thank you for your efforts. Where are my children?"

"Miguel Campo and his wife have accepted your children into their home. They have a homestead in Concepción. They are good people and your children know them."

Diego remembered Miguel Campo and his daughter, Isabella, but he could not remember Miguel's wife's name.

"Yes, I remember them," he said. "They are good people." He glanced up, "Where is Concepción?"

"It is a village on a small bayou about thirty miles downriver from New Orleans. I am certain my husband will provide you leave to go there." Margarethe touched Diego's arm, "But first, Private deMelilla, you must visit the priest at the Cathedral, the keeper of records, there are documents to be completed."

Diego felt numb. How could Mézu be dead, yet, because he had not seen her since – *when was it? April* – it was if she had been dead for months. He groaned. He closed his eyes and tried to bring the memory of her face to his mind, but could not.

The door to the General's reception area opened again and a host of officers spilled out. Panis separated from the group and, reaching for his wife's hand, he said, "I see that you have conveyed our sad intelligence to Private deMelilla."

"I have just now reported the sad news," Margarethe said, pulling Panis to her in a slight embrace. "Pray, do give him leave to see his children."

The *junta de guerra* had enforced several new regulations designed to reduce desertions. Regular soldiers of the Spanish army could not simply walk about the city alone. Private soldiers were required to have written permission, a *permiso*, to be away from their unit. A soldier without a pass was subject to arrest. Neither were soldiers of the regular army permitted to have civilian clothes in their possession, lest a man dress as a civilian and slip away.

"I will do better than simply provide a *permiso*, I will give you the use of my *calesa* (town buggy) and driver. Lieutenant Leyba will expect you to report to him at Fort Saint Charles this Friday," Panis said. "The information you brought from Pensacola will save New Orleans from the British, but you must not speak of it to anyone."

Diego shrugged, "I did not even know what was in the pouch."

"Then it was the hand of God, nothing less," Panis said. *Doña* Margarethe crossed herself and muttered, "Amen."

I would have much rather the hand of God protected my Mézu, Diego thought.

ᜨ

Father Étienne Cordier had been forced into retirement. He was a Jesuit, an order that had been officially disbanded by the Pope in 1773. He had managed to remain as a diocesan priest, but he had not adjusted well to the Spanish Capuchin Bishop of the Diocese of Santiago de Cuba, or the pastor, another Capuchin, Father Diaz, now in charge of Saint Louis Church, or the indict of *Patronato Real*, which gave the King of Spain the power to nominate bishops to Louisiana. The Jesuit order, even though disbanded, was held in suspicion by His Most Catholic Majesty. Because Father Étienne was a Jesuit, elderly and, because he refused to leave New Orleans, he had been assigned the task of keeping the records on all marriages, births and deaths in New Orleans. The records were kept in a store room in the rear of the Church of Saint Louis, next door to the Cabildo. Father Étienne was dutiful in this office.

He was in the records room when a young altar server, one of the orphans he supported to work in the church, came in.

"Father," the young man said. He paused for the priest to recognize him.

"What is it, Jacques?"

"Father, a soldier is here. He says he is here to settle his wife's affairs."

Father Étienne rubbed his eyes. Another widower, or widow, or orphan; the stream was endless. Yellow fever had been rampant, proliferating voraciously among new victims, settlers from the Canary Islands, who had been imported by the shipload. There was a reason an entire class of citizens of New Orleans were recognized as *Criollos* – born in Louisiana. The *Criollo* was not as susceptible to the many diseases that struck New Orleans.

"Ask him to come in, Jacques. Then get to bed."

Jacques evaporated and a soldier folded himself through the small doorway.

"What is your name, my son?" Father Étienne closed the record of births he had been amending and looked up at the huge uniformed man, clearly a private soldier of the Louisiana Regiment.

"Diego deMelilla, *Padre*."

"DeMelilla? The man who was with Major Panis?"

"Yes, *Padre*."

"We thank God for your safe return, Diego." Father Étienne paused. "Jacques said that you are here to settle your wife's affairs."

"Yes, *Padre*."

"What was your wife's name and when did she die?"

"My wife was *Doña* Maria Artiles y Ventomo, *Padre*. She was a native of Santa Cruz de Tenerife," Diego said.

Doña? Father Étienne thought. *This peasant's wife was a titled lady?* He shrugged, having long ago given up on understanding the Spanish.

"Most knew her as Mézu. They tell me she died on the ninth of July. I do not know if that is true, I was not here."

"Mézu!" Father Étienne exclaimed. "I should have known. She was an angel; an angel. She and *Doña* Margarethe did so much." The priest dug through a stack of books and produced one worn ledger. He opened the book, "Ah, here it is. Now I can complete the entry," he began to write. "*Doña* Maria Artiles y Ventomo," he mumbled. "Santa Cruz de Tenerife."

Father Étienne looked up from his notes. "I administered the Last Rites on the ninth of July, and your dear wife departed this world before the eleventh hour. I have something for you." The priest rummaged through some items on his desk and came out with something cupped in his hands. He gave it to Diego. It was several coins wrapped in leather. The leather was Mézu's eye patch.

The realization struck Diego. Mézu was dead. He held the eye patch to his chest, pressing it against his *náwoti* containing a lock of Mézu's hair. He wept great, choking sobs. "*I am doing you no favors, Maria Artiles,*" he had told Mézu the day he married her. The memory of her face flooded back into his mind at last, and he composed himself.

"Where is she buried?"

"You must understand, we had three score die that day alone. In less than a week, nearly two hundred souls departed," Father Étienne seemed embarrassed.

"Where is she buried?" Diego repeated.

"The soldiers dug a trench along the lakeside of the rampart. We wrapped the dead in sheets and buried them all together."

A mass grave! The thought of his wonderful Mézu wrapped in a sheet and tossed into a trench with a hundred other corpses nearly overpowered Diego. Anger welled up. Anger at – then he forced it down, willed himself into composure until the rage ebbed away. Diego turned away from the priest, ducked through the doorway and walked out into the alley between Saint Louis Church and the Cabildo without saying another word, not trusting himself to speak.

He went to the armory and retrieved his *magado* and *sunta*. He signed out a short sword, but told the arms clerk to keep his musket, bayonet and cartridge box. He would return for those later.

᷄

The open carriage Panis had provided to Diego slithered along the road next to the Mississippi River. Wagon ruts and deep grooves cut by heavy ox sleds were filled with muddy water. The ridges between ruts were slick, sending the thin wheels of the little town carriage skidding into one set of ruts or another. Concepción was downriver from New Orleans situated on a small distributary called Bayou Terre Aux Boeufs. The carriage driver, a Spanish veteran who had lost a foot during the campaign in Algiers, had followed Gálvez to New Orleans and had been hired by Panis. He went by the name Zapato.

"They used to call me 'one shoe,'" Zapato had said when he first introduced himself to Diego. "But now they just say 'shoe.'"

Panis, true to his word, had sent Zapato with the carriage to Fort Saint Charles where Diego had spent the night. He had slept in the barracks; the small quarters he had shared with Mézu for one night had new tenants. Some of the men recognized him and congratulated him on his return, for news of his rescue had raced through the city. He had managed to sleep because the men in the barracks had each donated their evening tot of rum to Diego and he had fallen asleep quite drunk. The sloshing carriage ride felt more like a boating expedition.

They reached the place where a stream flowed out of the Mississippi River. A ferry was moored against the bank, but Zapato turned left to follow the bank of the bayou.

"This is Bayou Terre Aux Boeufs," Zapato said. "In two hours we will be at Concepción."

Diego looked across the bayou at some ramshackle buildings along the far bank and recognized the place. It was where his small detail of soldiers had been dispatched to put down a slave rebellion. Images of the fight, the enraged black man he had bayonetted sliding into the water, pulling a comrade down with him, flashed into Diego's mind. He remembered how distraught Mézu was when he returned to the fort, hatless from a near miss and covered in blood – *What was the name of that fort? – Fortaleza Santa Maria.* He realized Zapato had been talking.

"..mostly local contractors. Nice houses, though. And the soil is rich. Push a pole into the ground and it will grow." Zapato droned on, providing details about the country they were passing through. Diego returned to thoughts of Mézu, their children and their home underneath the dog stone above *Pueblo de Cuevas.*

The road they were on now was nothing but an ox sled trail next to a haul path for mules pulling fishing boats to the Mississippi River when wind and currents were unfavorable. They passed farmsteads and moored fishing boats intermingled with long stretches of wilderness. The people they passed would wave to Zapato, call out greetings in French and gawk at the carriage. A carriage on this ox trail was an uncommon sight. A carriage with a single Spanish private as the passenger was a wonderment.

"We are coming into Concepción now," Zapato said, shaking Diego out of his brooding thoughts.

"Where is the home of Miguel Campo?" Zapato asked of a man loading an ox cart with woven baskets of lettuce.

"There," the man said, "see the people gathered next to the trail?" The man's Spanish was pure *Isleños*. They might have been in Agüimes. "The man is Miguel Campo. The woman is his wife, Catalina Bebera. The oldest girl is Isabella Campo and the other two are the deMelilla orphans."

"They are not orphans," Diego said.

"Then it is true," the man said. "You must be Diego, the soldier the *godums* could not kill. So many stories have proven to be false these days, how is a man to know?"

Diego stood, whistled the phrase "I am home" and waved. He watched as Pedro and Maria separated from the Campos and come running toward the carriage. Diego jumped down and rushed toward his children. Pedro reached him first and stopped. Diego hugged him and kissed his cheek. He could see that Pedro was struggling to keep his composure. *How he has matured*, Diego thought, *how hard it must have been for him to watch his mother die*. Maria reached them and jumped up into Diego's arms, knocking his hat askew. He kissed Maria on both cheeks and placed her on his right hip, transferred his hat to Pedro's head and walked along to meet the Campo family. He could hear Zapato bringing the carriage along the road behind him.

"*Hola*, Miguel," Diego said as he held out his hand. Miguel pulled Diego to him and hugged him.

"I am glad to see you alive, my friend," he said.

"*Hola*, Catalina," Diego said after Miguel released him.

Catalina, tears streaming down both cheeks, kissed Diego first on the left cheek, then the right and then the left again. "I prayed for you every day since our Mézu left us."

"*Hola*, Isabella," Diego held out his left hand to touch Isabella's shoulder.

"I am happy to see you well, *Don* Diego," Isabella said with a curtsy. Unlike her mother, who was wearing the traditional *Isleña* skirt, blouse, bodice, scarf and wide brimmed hat, Isabella was wearing clothes more indicative of New Orleans; a blue dress with white horizontal stripes, a hem that reached to the ground, hiding her shoes, and a matching blue bonnet. The dress had long sleeves that ended in a frilly cuff. It was a fine cotton dress and Diego was certain Isabella had worn it just for this occasion. She had grown into a woman in just a few months.

"I thank you for caring for Pedro and Maria," Diego said, addressing them all.

"They were more help than trouble, Diego," Miguel said. "I should be paying Pedro wages. He has had a hand in much of what we have built here." He looked up to see Zapato and the carriage.

"This is my friend, Zapato," Diego said. "He was kind enough to bring me here from New Orleans."

Miguel took the bridle of the horse, "Come, bring your carriage off of the road and get down. Catalina has prepared a meal. Please, Diego, you and Zapato, join us in the house."

"Let us show you the house," Catalina said excitedly. "It has many rooms, and a wooden floor."

"I have never lived in a house with a wooden floor," Diego said. In truth, he had never lived in a house. The home he had shared with Mézu for ten years was more cave than house.

The house was wood frame made of newly milled cypress planking, unlike many of the houses in New Orleans which were made from disassembled barges. It stood on brick piers, about two feet off the ground. A porch about eight feet deep ran across the width of the front of the house. There were two doors and two windows opening onto the porch. There were four rooms in the house situated at the corners so that each room had two exterior walls and a window in each exterior wall. The front rooms each had one door leading outside and two doors leading to adjoining rooms. One rear room had a door that opened onto the rear porch. The two front rooms had a common fire place as did the two rear rooms.

The rear of the house had a porch across its width, a mirror of the front. An oven under an awning was about ten feet beyond the back porch and, fifty yards beyond that, Miguel had begun a barn. A vegetable garden filled the land between the barn and the oven. Miguel had been clearing the land beyond the barn. The trees had been removed and he had begun work on the stumps.

"You have done well in this short time, Miguel," Diego said.

"The land is rich, Diego. We will grow enough to feed ourselves this year and next we will be selling in the market. I think I shall add pigs," Miguel said.

Miguel had made the table and chairs in one of the front rooms from planks recovered from a Kentuckian's river barge. It was filled with food prepared by Catalina and a pitcher of wine. The Campos had been advised that Diego was coming, and they wanted to welcome him properly. Zapato joined them reluctantly. He felt that as a servant, he should not be included, but Catalina was adamant.

After they had eaten, Catalina asked Isabella and the children to come into another room "so the men can talk," but Diego stopped her.

"One moment please, Catalina," he said. "I have to talk to you all. Zapato, I think you need to tend to your horse and prepare to spend the night."

Zapato recognized the need to be elsewhere for a moment. "*Señora* Catalina, thank you for the finest meal I have had in my memory," he said as he went through the back door to where the horse and carriage were tethered.

Diego turned to Miguel. "I am most grateful to you and Catalina. I will not forget how you have cared for my children."

"It was our duty, Diego," Miguel said holding up his hands. "We owe you more than we could ever repay."

"I am afraid I must ask more of you." He turned to Pedro and Maria who stared back wide-eyed, "and more of you two as well. Miguel and Catalina, could you keep my children here for a while longer?"

"Of course, we love them," Catalina said. "Pedro does the work of a man."

"Maria is a big help to me," Isabella said.

"I tell you this in confidence. There is a man, a nobleman, coming to New Orleans. He should arrive within the week."

"Is it Cabitos?" Pedro asked.

"Yes," Diego had forgotten that Pedro had known why they fled Gran Canaria.

"*Don* Alguazil Cabitos y Cabrón, former *Ricohombre* of Santa Cruz de Tenerife has followed us to New Orleans," Diego continued for the benefit of the Campos. "Cabitos hated Mézu for affronts given over a decade ago. We were safe in Gran Canaria until our protector, *Don* Raphael Arinaga died. We came to New Orleans to escape Cabitos. Now he is coming here."

"But mother is dead," Maria whimpered. "He can do her nothing now."

"Yes, but until I can determine what this mad man might do, I need to keep you safely away from New Orleans."

"Of course they can stay," Miguel said. "They can stay as long as it takes."

"I have some money to leave."

"Do not think of it," Miguel interrupted.

"Still, I will feel better if I can leave some money, you may find a need. And I will leave my *magado* and *sunta* here as well." Diego said.

—⁊

The next morning they took breakfast on the back porch. Zapato had spent the night in the carriage. He had rigged a canvas roof and netting to keep the dew off and the mosquitoes out. "The best sleep I have had in years," he said when he came to the breakfast table.

"*Hola!*" called a voice from the front of the house.

"Come to the back," Miguel responded.

Two men appeared around the corner of the house. One was a priest and the other a gentleman.

"*Don* Blas! *Padre* Josef! Welcome!" Miguel said as he waved the men up onto the porch. "Catalina, my love, we have two more for breakfast."

"No, no," *Don* Blas said. "We have had our breakfast. Do not trouble Catalina."

Padre Josef's expression was one of disappointment, perhaps *Don* Blas had spoken too soon.

"We have come to meet the famous Diego deMelilla," *Don* Blas continued looking intently at Diego.

"Here he is," Miguel adopted a formal posture. "Diego deMelilla y Tupinar, may I introduce you to *Don* Blas Ansolo, *alcalde* of Concepción and commander of our militia." Diego nodded and Don Blas acknowledged with "my pleasure."

"And here is *Padre* Josef, our pastor."

"My pleasure, *Padre*." Diego said.

"I have made so bold as to impose on Miguel," Blas said, "because I see a soldier here without a commander. May I see your pass?"

Diego produced the paper from a pocket in his coat. Blas examined it, a scowl working across his face, and returned it to Diego.

"Also, I have to discover for myself if what I have heard is true," Blas said, tilting his head back to look up at Diego.

"And what have you heard, *Don* Blas," Diego asked.

"That you had been shot and left for dead in a British camp. Yet, somehow you escape and carried a message to the city that now has everyone preparing to act," Blas said.

"I was shot and captured. I did escape, but I carried no messages," Diego said.

"The Governor is collecting the army. He is gathering ships. He is preparing to move the army. Soon he will take our protection with him leaving us to fend for ourselves. Should the British declare war and decide to attack New Orleans, it will fall on us. He needs to stay here," Blas was clearly concerned.

"Governor Gálvez is the one who should hear your advice, *Don* Blas," Diego said. "I am merely a private soldier."

"Please, have some breakfast," Catalina interrupted. "I have ham and biscuits."

"I have to make preparations," Blas said. "I must take my leave of you." He turned without another word and disappeared around the corner of the house.

"I think I shall accept your kind offer, *Señora*," *Padre* Josef said. He looked at Diego. "We all thank God that you have been returned to us, Diego. Fear can sometimes overpower decorum. I do hope you can forgive our zealous *alcalde*."

"I have already forgotten him, *Padre*," Diego said.

CHAPTER 24

Diego watched from the raised gun platform of Fort Saint Charles as the sails of *El Sagrado Corazón de Jesús* appeared down river. The ship was over five miles below the city, but he could see the tall topsails over the trees as she ran upriver on a starboard beam reach. She would make her moorings in an hour and a half, for the air was light and the current swift. When her lookout high in the *carajo* sighted the Spanish flag in the *Plaza de Armas*, she would fire a seven gun salute, recognizing they approached a post commanded by a Governor. The guns on the walls of Fort Saint Charles would answer with five, in recognition of the *El Natural*'s captain.

Smoke billowed from the port side of the ship. Another cloud billowed out before the report of the first salute reached them. Diego could hear the four gun captains – Fort Saint Charles had only four guns – calling to their crews and preparing for the order to return the salute. He was standing near the first gun to fire. When it discharged he flinched involuntarily. It was the first cannon fire he had heard since gunnery exercises on the *San Juan*. As soon as the gun fired, the gun captain was shouting to his men;

"Stop the VENT!" A gunner pushed his leather-padded thumb onto the touch hole to prevent air from rushing in and out, causing a smoldering remnant of the canvas powder casing of the previous shot to ignite.

"Search the PIECE!" A pole with twisted wires on one end was inserted into the tube and turned about to search for burning bits of the spent canvas cartridge, and withdrawn. Bang! The second gun fired.

"Sponge the PIECE!" A wet, sheep's skin-covered pole was introduced into the gun to extinguish any burning embers.

"Charge CARTRIDGE!" A canvas bag of black powder was shoved into the cannon. Bang! The third gun fired.

"Ram CARTRIDGE!" A ramrod was used to push the canvas bag down the bore.

"PRIME!" A wire was inserted through the touchhole to pierce the canvas cartridge. Bang! The fourth gun fired.

A quill filled with fine powder was pushed into the touch hole.

"FIRE!" The gunner touched a slow match to the quill, flame spurted up and the gun banged out the fifth and final salute.

Diego realized several formal steps had been skipped, but if this had been a battle, a few more steps might have been set aside.

The ship passed Fort Saint Charles, her rails crowded with people, some waving, as sailors scurried about to shorten sail, haul mooring lines across to the pier, and prepare to discharge a fresh mass of *Isleños* settlers. Diego noticed Josef Herrera, the experienced veteran who had trained the recruits aboard the *San Juan Nepomuceno*, standing on the pier. Herrera's wife, Francesca Olives y Espinosa, was aboard the *El Natural*. Herrera was now a lieutenant. Diego realized that it must have been politics that forced Lieutenant Herrera to board in Tenerife as a civilian recruit. The rise from recruit to sergeant before the voyage was half completed spoke to the man's ability. The rise from sergeant to lieutenant could only mean his political troubles remained in Europe. *Would my troubles have stayed on Tenerife*, Diego thought.

He had caused Mézu to travel here, and now she was dead. He began to wonder if they had not fled, perhaps she would still be alive. No, Cabitos would have had her tortured to death and probably the children as well. Besides, it does no good to think on what might have been. He remembered something his father had said. They had been traveling up a rugged trail that snaked back and forth until they reached a point that seemed to be a dead end.

"We should have taken another way, Father," Diego had said.

Doramas shook his head, "We are here now. It matters not the trails we passed. We decided on a course and we must work to make it succeed, adjusting to what comes."

Mézu was dead. He tried to convince himself it had been her destiny. Now the children must be preserved. The decisions he made now would not change the past, but determine the future. Diego watched the ship being unloaded. So many others had made their decisions; they had cast their lives into a strange place, Louisiana. Nothing they did now could undo that fact.

Four hundred twenty-three settlers had arrived from the Canary Islands aboard the *El Sagrado Corazón de Jesús*, over twice the number who had traveled with Diego and Mézu. Of those passengers, one hundred ten were soldiers, but of that number, only twenty were single men. Ninety new families would be sent to settlement sites not chosen for arability or commercial potential, but for strategic reasons, blocking potential avenues of approach to New Orleans.

Gálvez was mobilizing his forces and the city was alive with activity, and activity was an unusual condition for August. Normally, New Orleans would be hibernating through the heat of the summer. The markets would have opened late and close early. Citizens of means would have vacated the city for the plantations or anywhere away from the oppressive heat and pestilence that accompanied summer. This August, a great army was mobilizing. Ships were armed, militia activated, messages sent to places as far away as Béxar on the San Antonio River where cattle were gathered into herds to be driven to the Mississippi River, food for Gálvez's army.

The Governor had decreed that all new arrivals, virtually all *Isleños*, would form home guards (militia) in their strategically chosen settlements, if they were married soldiers. Single recruits would be transferred to the Fixed Louisiana Regiment, the promise of a house and acreage deferred for the duration of the war. Eighteen recruits would be joining Diego, a widower, as infantrymen in the Louisiana Regiment.

Two gentlemen were the last to come ashore, well behind the throng of milling and confused settlers. Diego could see, even form this distance, Cabitos haughtily directing the sailors carrying baggage to place the several trunks at the end of the pier. The other was the Dominican Bishop. There was no greeting party, no groveling official and no waiting carriage for the men, and they were clearly miffed at the slight.

There was something about Cabitos. The man seemed to move in a shuffling fashion, not a fluid, smooth walk, but a sort of half-step. Syphilis! Cabitos had a halting gait, an apparent inability to lift his heels from the ground, a head-down posture, all indications of syphilis, an affliction not uncommon among the aristocrats. Insanity could also result from the disease. Sane, Cabitos was a vengeful, evil man. Insane, only God knew what he was capable of.

"Form ranks!"

Diego had been idling on the ramparts of Fort Saint Charles during a "private time" set aside after the noon meal. Now his unit was being formed up. All single soldiers of the rampart guards, twenty of them, would be marched to a bivouac Gálvez had established upriver of the city. He was collecting troops from throughout Louisiana for his regiment. Established units from around New Spain and even a few from Europe had contributed troops to the campaign. Over six hundred regular troops, infantry and grenadiers, had been assembled. Several militia units had been called up and were scheduled to combine with Gálvez's army along the way to Baton Rouge.

Diego's contingent, under the command of a grenadier sergeant dispatched to collect Fort Saint Charles' contribution to the expedition, marched along the levee road to collect the eighteen single soldiers that had just arrived on *El Sagrado Corazón de Jesús*. The sergeant had the squad in column, two abreast. Diego's position in the rank was on the left flank of the column and in the center of his file. They were at the position of "carry arms." The soldiers' muskets were against their right sides, held by the right hand around the firelock, right arm straight down, musket pressed against the right trouser leg, the tip of the muzzle even with the top of the hat, and the butt plate about one foot above the ground. Carried in this manner, soldiers could march for extended periods of time, through tight spaces, in crowds or wooded trails without snagging their weapons on brush, limbs or low sills.

The squad snaked along the low levee that served as a loading, unloading and temporary stockpile area for ships and river boats and separated the river from the road. Civilians and slaves moving material between ship and shore were forced to separate, allowing the squad to pass. The army commander who had accompanied the new recruits on the trip from the Canary Islands, by way of Havana, had formed his uniformed men in several ranks beside the levee and was in the process of segregating the single men from the settler families.

"Squad – HALT."

The grenadier sergeant had halted Diego's squad directly in front of an agitated Cabitos and a fuming Bishop.

"To the Left – FACE."

The squad faced left. Diego was standing no more than five paces from Cabitos and looking directly at the man.

"Order – ARMS."

The squad moved their muskets from the "carry arms" position to "order arms." Each soldier used his left hand to guide the weapon down until the butt rested on the ground next to his right foot, held in place by his right hand on the stock.

Diego forced himself to stare past Cabitos, who seemed to take no notice of the soldiers. Cabitos carried a quirt which, not deigning to touch a commoner, he used to stop a passing civilian workman.

"Summon a *fiacre* (a coach for hire), man," Cabitos said in French. "Send it here, for Bishop Benitez."

The man, thinking Cabitos was the Bishop's servant, turned to the bishop, bowed, and said, "Yes, Excellency. Right away, Excellency." The man's French carried a heavy German accent. The majority of the people in New Orleans spoke their French with an accent other than Parisian. The man rushed off, passing his foreman to explain why he was leaving the levee. The foreman glared toward Cabitos and the Bishop, but said nothing. One did not ignore the requests of a bishop in Spanish

Louisiana, particularly if you were directing a labor gang loading munitions onto a river *bateau* to be smuggled north past British-controlled Baton Rouge and Natchez to American rebels.

Cabitos fidgeted as he waited for his carriage. He glanced at the ranks of soldiers on the levee, but showed no reaction. Cabitos did not see individuals – just men – standing before him. He saw a formation of soldiers, not worthy of consideration or recognition. A *fiacre* rumbled into view and stopped between Cabitos and Diego's squad. Cabitos climbed onto the open carriage first, shuffled to a seat not five feet from where Diego stood at attention. The baggage was loaded into the boot, a platform at the rear of the carriage, at the close direction of the bishop.

"To the Cabildo," Cabitos commanded the instant the bishop climbed in.

"One *real*," the driver said and he held out a leathered hand.

Cabitos slapped the hand away with the quirt. "You will be paid when we arrive," he said. He looked to his right to avoid the driver's protest and in doing so his eyes fell on Diego, who continued to look past the carriage and its riders, not meeting Cabitos' eyes. If Cabitos shouted out or made some other overt act of recognition, Diego decided he would draw his short sword and kill the man. He would be instantly caught and imprisoned, eventually convicted and probably put to death, but the children would be safe. Cabitos frowned, but said nothing. The carriage lurched forward, wheels kicking up dust and bits of manure and rumbled along the levee until, clear of the formation of soldiers, it turned down onto the road.

The grenadier sergeant had been waiting for the carriage to depart. "*Atennnn-CIÓN*," the sergeant barked. The squad obeyed.

"To the Right – TURN." The squad faced right and they were now in a column of twos once more. Diego could hear another sergeant commanding troops as another column of twos, the single men from the *El Sagrado Corazón de Jesús*, was marched up alongside Diego's squad. The new columns were halted and the formation became a column of fours with Diego practically in the center.

"Carry – ARMS."

Muskets were shifted into the correct position.

"At the Quick – MARCH"

The formation of soldiers, now a platoon-sized unit, moved out at a brisk walking pace. The grenadier sergeant positioned himself at the right-rear of the formation to direct the platoon. They moved down onto the street and marched upriver. A carriage had pulled to the side of the road and waited as the soldiers marched by. It was the *fiacre* Cabitos had hired. As the formation marched by, Diego could see Cabitos studying the rank nearest the carriage. Evidently he did not realize two new ranks had been added. The man on the column nearest Cabitos was shorter than Diego, most men were, but the man was an *Isleño* from *El Natural* with Diego's general coloring. Cabitos stared at the man as they marched past, shook his head.

After the troops passed, Cabitos shouted, "To the Cabildo, fool." The carriage turned right, crossed the levee road onto *Calle San Pedro*.

ℰ❨

The carriage carrying Cabitos and Bishop Benitez attempted to turn from *Calle San Pedro* onto *Calle Chartres*, but was halted by a brace of guards.

"No civilian traffic here, *señores*," one of the guards said. The man was a *cabo*, a corporal, as evidenced by the single blue epaulet on his left shoulder. He wore a tall beaver-skin hat, wide, black moustache, white coat with blue facings, cuffs and collars, black gaiters, white blouse and trousers; the uniform of a grenadier of the Fixed Louisiana Regiment of Gálvez's army. His musket sported a fixed bayonet of polished steel. The other guard had grasped the halter of the horse to insure the carriage went no further.

"Do you know who we are?" Cabitos raged.

"You are the civilians that will not pass this point," the corporal said.

"I am *Don* Alguazil Cabitos, *Ricohombre* of Santa Cruz de Tenerife," Cabitos said. The part about being *Ricohombre* of Santa Cruz de Tenerife was not true, but he still went by the title. "Bishop Benitez is with me and you will let us pass!"

"We are not in Santa Cruz de Tenerife, and I am not a priest," the corporal turned his head slightly and bellowed, "sergeant-of-the-guard!"

The street in front of the Cabildo was a sea of uniformed men, some coming out of the building, some queued to enter. Six guards tended to the Cabildo doors onto *Calle Chartres*. As each officer came to the door guard, all of the men in the queue were officers, proposing to enter the Cabildo, he told the guard his name, business, and presented his documents before he was allowed into the building. All the while, a steady stream of uniformed couriers rushed in and out of the doors, sometimes jostling the officers in the queue.

A sergeant appeared from the flowing mass of uniforms. Armed with a halberd and two blue epaulets, his hardened face marked the man as a sergeant as well as an experienced soldier.

"What is it Matherne?" the sergeant growled.

"Matherne?" Benitez snarled to Cabitos. "What kind of name is that?"

"Louisiana, Bishop," Cabitos said. "I am told over a third of the soldiers in Gálvez's army were born under a king other than Spain's, and almost all of the militia."

"Are they Catholics?" Benitez was horrified.

"They must say so."

"These *señores* refuse to turn away, Sergeant," Matherne reported. Benitez decided he did detect a slight German accent in the man's Spanish.

"State your business," the sergeant said.

Cabitos repeated, "I am *Don* Alguazil Cabitos, *Ricohombre* of Santa Cruz de Tenerife and with me is Bishop Benitez, a Dominican sent here by Madrid." The words "a Dominican sent here by Madrid" were intended to intimidate the sergeant, but the expression on the man's face did not flinch.

"What is your name, sergeant? Who is your commanding officer?" Benitez interjected, deciding to escalate the intimidation.

"I am Sergeant Domingo Grillo. My superior is Lieutenant Amado of the Governor's headquarters staff and if you do not state your business immediately, I will have you in chains. Now, state your business," Grillo repeated.

Benitez, shocked into silence, looked as if he had been slapped. Cabitos managed to say, "We are here to pay our complements to Governor Gálvez and to inform him of Bishop Benitez's appointment to New Orleans."

"Where are your papers?"

"Our documents are in our baggage. We did not expect to have to produce them to gain an audience," Cabitos explained.

"Return to *Calle San Pedro*, pull to the side so that you do not impede traffic and write whatever message you wish to convey to the Governor, bring it to Corporal Matherne and I will put it in his clerk's hands myself." Grillo said.

"I must protest this treatment," Benitez managed to sputter.

"We are under martial law, your Excellency," Grillo said. "After you bring your message to me, go to *Calle Real*, it is the next street from the river," Grillo gestured toward the west, "turn right on *Real* and go to the back of the church. I will send word to the rectory informing you of the time you will be expected to see Governor Gálvez."

Benitez was still sputtering objections as the soldier holding the horse's reins pulled the animal around and released it, pointing toward *Calle San Pedro*. As they were instructed, Cabitos had the driver curb the carriage and ordered the man to offload one of the chests. Cabitos fished out a writing kit, composed a letter of introduction, including protests over their reception, and, after Benitez added his own notes, instructed the driver to bring the note to the guard.

"Make certain you give it to that German Corporal," Benitez shouted to the driver as the man headed toward *Calle Chartres*.

Cabitos and Benitez stood at the rear of the carriage, neither man willing to repack the trunk and return it to the luggage boot. They had intended to wait for the return of the hapless driver so he could perform such physical labors, but they were forced to remount the carriage to avoid being splashed by mud, manure and horse piss thrown up by passing traffic. The road was congested, particularly where the carriage narrowed the travel lanes. Soldiers, wagons, ox sleds, mounted men, and pedestrians crowded on wooden walkways next to the buildings surged in both directions.

The driver, dodging through the throng, returned. "I gave your note to the corporal," he said.

"Then, load the trunk and bring us to – wherever it was that fool of a sergeant said. You heard him did you not?"

The driver reloaded the trunk, mounted his carriage bench and slapped the reins on the flanks of the horse. They trundled along to the next corner where the driver coaxed the horse right onto the intersecting street. The traffic and noise on *Calle Real* was as brisk as *Calle Chaters*, just reduced in rank. Here the people scurrying about were not officers, but clerks, messengers and servants of every kind. The rear of the Cabildo was as congested, and guarded, as the front. The driver worked the carriage through the throng, walking the horse until halting it at a small cemetery behind the rectory of the Saint Louis Church. Benitez leaped from the carriage and stormed toward the rectory leaving Cabitos to deal with the driver.

"That will be two *reales, señor*," the driver said in English-accented Spanish.

"You said one *real*," Cabitos said, startled by the man's Spanish. Cabitos had assumed the man spoke only French, which is why he had used that language with the driver.

"That was for one destination, *señor*. I have had to carry you to two destinations and delivered a message for you."

"I will not pay it. The *Ricohombre* of Santa Cruz de Tenerife will not be extorted," Cabitos raised his chin until the lesions under his neck showed over his high collar.

"Then I will leave you, *señor*," the driver said as he climbed back into his seat.

"Wait! You must unload our trunks," Cabitos reached for the horse's bridle.

"Those trunks are mine, if you refuse to pay."

"I will call a catchpole!" Cabitos threatened.

"Do so, and you will explain how you refused to pay in advance and refused to pay after the many things I did. Then the *alcalde* can decide."

"I do not have time for this," Cabitos growled. He dug an *ocho reales* silver piece from his pocket, the coin that everyone on this side of the ocean called a "dollar" and tossed it to the driver. "Now get our baggage and bring it to the rectory."

The driver examined the coin.

Noticing the Chinese proof stamp he refrained from testing the coin with his teeth and pocketed it. It required three trips for the man to transfer the luggage to the hallway of the rectory. Benitez had not reappeared, so Cabitos dismissed the driver.

"I owe you change, *señor*," the driver said and he sorted through his pockets until he had collected three shards of silver. One was a "dollar" that had been cut in half and the other two were pie-shaped one-eighths of a "dollar."

"I said two *reales*, two bits. Let it not be said Jeremy Cobbler cheats his fares," the driver said as he proffered the fragments of a coin to Cabitos. The man said "bits" in English, a language unknown to Cabitos.

"What are these?" Cabitos said.

"Six bits, *señor*. Welcome to Louisiana."

⁓

Bishop Benitez stormed up to the door of the rectory and opened it without knocking. A priest coming into the hallway from a side room turned toward Benitez, startled, his arms overflowing with papers and ledgers.

"How may I be of service to your Excellency," the priest stammered as he attempted to adjust to the sudden appearance of a Bishop at the rear entrance of the rectory.

"I am Bishop Benitez, of the Dominican Order, sent here by Madrid to insure the propagation of the Faith in this province."

"Welcome, my Brother in Christ. I am Father Étienne Cordier, keeper of the archives for Saint Louis Church," Father Étienne said, trying to bow without dropping his cargo.

Benitez's eyes narrowed as he examined the habit of Father Étienne. *A former Jesuit*, he thought. *At least he is not a Franciscan.* Benitez considered the Franciscans as being much too lenient in matters of enforcing doctrine. "I and my *compañero* will require rooms for the night as we await an audience with the Governor," he said.

"I am certain our pastor, Father Diaz, can accommodate you, Excellency," Father Étienne said. "We have spare sleeping quarters for those priests forced to travel about the country. Is your companion a priest?"

"No, my companion is *Don* Alguazil Cabitos y Cabrón."

"I think he would find a priest's cell much too uncomfortable, Excellency. May I suggest a public inn is more suited for a titled gentleman? There is a fine one less than a block away on *Calle Borbón*. It may have rooms to let, though with all the activity in the city, it may not."

A priest's cell! The prospect was not to Benitez's liking. "Send word to this inn to prepare to receive me and *Don* Alguazil Cabitos." Benitez ordered.

"I will send our caretaker to your Excellency. He will happily serve as a messenger for you," Father Étienne said. Noticing the baggage being delivered to the hall by the carriage driver, he continued, "Please leave your things here, they will be safe, as you arrange for rooms. If you cannot contract a room, I will have another cot added to our vacant cell and you are welcomed to use it."

"I am expecting a message from Governor Gálvez. It is to be sent here. Notify me the instant it arrives. You will know where I am."

"Of course, Excellency," Father Étienne said, again bowing as low as his burdens would allow.

෬

The platoon-sized formation of soldiers bound for the Louisiana Regimental bivouac continued down the levee road until they reached an area that had been cleared of trees. Several large headquarters-type tents bordered a dirt road. Further along were bivouac areas congested with tents of all types. Each unit had a central cooking fire. Muskets were clustered before tents and a festival of flags, banners and regimental signs identified each group. Beyond the soldier's tents were wagons, mules, storage depots and the crude tents of camp followers. If the Louisiana

Regiment were to consist of three hundred men, it seemed as if a thousand souls would need to be encamped.

Diego realized his contingent of new recruits was approaching the command tent of the Louisiana Regiment.

"Detail – HALT." The contingent of recruits was not a recognized unit, so the sergeant addressed them as a "detail."

"To the Left – FACE." The recruits, having been well drilled during transport, all executed the command crisply.

"Order – ARMS." Muskets were lowered until the butt was grounded next to the right foot of each man.

"*Atennn-CIÓN*."

An officer accompanied by several sergeants came out of the command tent.

"I am Lieutenant Colonel *Don* Esteban Miró," the tall young officer announced. "I am the commander of the Fixed Infantry Regiment of Louisiana. You are to be assigned to a *pelotón* (platoon). A sergeant for each platoon will instruct you further. Regimental Sergeant!"

A sergeant, decorate with a sash as well as epaulets, marched into place between the officer and the formation of recruits, snapped to attention, held his salute and said, "*Señor*."

"Take charge, *Primo*," Colonel Miró said as he returned the salute and disappeared into the tent.

"*Primo*" was army slang for the top ranking sergeant of a regiment. The daily maintenance, training and condition of the enlisted men of the regiment were under his direct charge, subject to the supervision of the regimental officers. Army life was made easiest if none of the officers even knew your name, but the *Primo* considered you a good soldier.

"I am *Primo Sargento* Monzon. The front rank is assigned to Sergeant Macais of the First Platoon. Sergeant, take charge of your men."

A sergeant stepped forward and ordered, "Front rank. To the Right – FACE. Carry – ARMS. At the Quick – MARCH." The front rank of recruits marched off under Sergeant Macais' commands.

Logically, Diego's rank was assigned to the third platoon under the command of Sergeant Ortega, a wiry, hard looking man nearly half the height of the halberd he carried. They were marched to an open area between army tents and supply depots, ordered to stack arms, ground accouterments and queued to draw tents, tools and ground cover.

"Remember the wagon from which you drew this gear," Ortega shouted as the men collected the equipment. "When we strike camp, this is the wagon to which you must bring those things you are not ordered to carry on your backs."

The remainder of the day was consumed with placing tents, and replacing tents when Ortega found some flaw in alignment or ground cover. The sun began to set before Ortega permitted the men to occupy their tents and meet the others in their platoon. Mercifully, it had not rained all day, or the whole exercise would have been performed in a sea of mud. The heat had been relentless, and most soldiers had opted to spread their bedrolls in front of their tents, until the mosquitoes convinced them otherwise.

The large camp fire that centered each platoon encampment served as the gathering place where the new men met the rest. The new men were separated among the squad corporals and the evening mess was called. Soldiers carried their metal plates and cups to draw a ration of boiled potatoes, ham and rice. After eating, the men would draw a tot of rum, be given some personal time, and allowed to rest before the drums tapped out "retire."

Two of the men in third platoon recognized Diego from the *San Juan Nepomuceno* and re-introduced themselves. Josef Suares and Juan Galan had been the only two single recruits on the *San Juan*. They both greeted Diego happily until it began to dawn on them how it was Diego had been assigned to the regiment.

"I fear to think how it is you are here," Galan said. "Have you become a widower?"

"Yes, my friend," Diego said. "You have guessed it. My Mézu died a month ago. My children are with friends. And I am here."

Both men crossed themselves. "It is Louisiana," Suares said. "Many are widowed and orphaned in this place."

"Truly," Galan added. "It was told to me we numbered two hundred two when we set sail from Tenerife. Now, no more than six score survive."

"God knows, this is a strange place," Suares continued. "Rich soil, plentiful water, food just there for the gathering, and pestilence like Egypt of old."

They had drawn their tots of rum now and the soldiers gathered about the fire, using the smoke to keep the mosquitoes at bay. Stories of where each man was from, where he had been and how he had been fool enough to find himself in the army circulated, generating laughter, building camaraderie.

"DeMelilla," Suares called across the fire. Soldiers typically addressed each other by their surname, or enlistment name. *Apodos* – nicknames – would come later, after lengthy service together. "I have heard you sing. Grace us with a *décima*." One of the other men, Pérez *dos*, had a miniature *vihuela*, a stringed instrument he had named "Maria." His full name, José Pérez, did not distinguish him from the other two soldiers named "José Pérez," so he became José Pérez number two – Pérez *dos*. Pérez strummed the appropriate chords for a décima and nodded to Diego, whose beautiful baritone voice could be heard throughout the regimental encampment. From headquarter tents to the camp followers; the gatherings around every campfire grew silent, as his song filled the night.

> *She came as a nightly vision*
> *A spirit to the grotto and me*
> *Beneath the light of the moon*
> *A trembling voice called to me*
>
> *She had come seeking refuge*
> *She had come seeking safety*
> *She found me in the grotto*
> *I could not promise safety*
> *I promised her only love*
> *A tender night in my embrace.*

CHAPTER 25

edio tonto, Diego thought. A soldier's life is nothing but tedium. "What is not boring," Diego's father used to say, "is terrifying." The bivouac area had been transformed into a tent city, acquiring a repetitive daily routine each individual man trudged through on the way to becoming part of an army. Every morning the drums would beat "first call" rousing those off duty from their tents. Men coming in from guard duty or others with special chores would already be moving about, but the rest of the men would crawl out of tents or rise from bedrolls between tents. The cooking fires would be rekindled, a contractor would drop off fire wood, pots would be hung from iron hooks, men would stumble off to the slit trenches, weapons would be checked, and a breakfast of porridge spooned out onto tin plates.

Another roll of the drum, "assembly," a distinctively different beat, and muskets were retrieved from the cone-like stack of arms, cartridge boxes slung on the right hip, haversacks, short swords and bayonets slung on the left , uniforms checked and caps adjusted as the men fell into ranks. Their routine daily uniform, what was called the "*obrero*" consisted of cotton trousers, shirt and a brown cotton frock. The cap was a simple brown cotton stocking cap with a turned-up bill displaying the letters "LA" painted in red.

Then it was drill, lunch, drill, dinner. Bayonet training became a welcomed interruption to drill. Sergeant Ortega had seven-foot poles fitted with a sheepskin-covered block of wood. Soldiers in pairs, later in opposing squads, would square-off using the poles in place of bayoneted muskets. Once the men had learned the fundamentals of bayonet work, these contests became full-speed fights complete with bloodied noses, bruised ribs and humbled pride. Diego established himself as the company champion and was never bested in any competition around the regiment.

Evenings were filled with repair of clothing, cleaning weapons and longing for news from loved ones. Many soldiers had families in Spain, Cuba or South America. Messages from home to these men were rare and unexpected. Some of the soldiers, such as Diego, had families in Louisiana. These men would often receive news of their families from the many civilian contractors that supplied the army. A man driving an ox sled of firewood would pause before a platoon cooking fire and announce he had word from one community or another. Men with families in the named village would reply and the local gossip or obituary would be recited.

The news from Concepción always reported the Campo household to be prospering. Crops were doing well, there had been no fever about and Miguel Campo had even bought another pig. No one, it seems, had attempted to harm Pedro, Maria or anyone else. Still, Diego was troubled. Cabitos could not have forgotten why he was here. If he would simply read the roster of the Louisiana Regiment he would see the name and know where to find Diego. Could it be that Cabitos learned of Mézu's death and returned to Spain? It had been two weeks since the day Diego saw Cabitos and the Bishop disembark from *El Natural*. Had the feud ended? Diego hoped it had, yet knew it had not.

Diego never went anywhere in the camp without his short sword. Even when he went to the latrine, he was armed. The other soldiers in his platoon considered the habit to be odd. What man would buckle on a sword just to visit the slit trench? Soldiers were constantly burdened with weapons and other gear and the chance to go about unencumbered was a great relief for every man except, it seemed, for Diego, who was never unarmed.

"How long do you think they will keep us at this foolishness?" Pedro Gonzales asked Diego one evening as they ate their evening stew.

"Until the Governor says we are to stop," Diego replied.

"Huh. Do you think there will be war soon?"

Diego stopped spooning the stew into his mouth to give the question consideration. "We are already at war, Pook," he said as he resumed eating. "Pook" was Gonzales' *apodo*. "Think of the money it takes to keep so many in the field, Pook. We are at war, do not doubt it. The Governor is just preparing us for what is to come."

"Word is, we are to move out in the morning," Pook said.

"Fresh teams for the wagons, river sloops are anchoring nearby, the officers have all disappeared," Diego observed. "I think you are right."

"I think a rain is coming," Pook said, looking up at a sky speckled with high, small clouds that raced overhead going east to west. "The air smells full of water," Pook said.

"I cannot recall a week without rain since coming here," Diego said. He looked into the sky. The setting sun painted tall, heavy clouds to the east a bright orange, and the wind began to rise. "I have heard this song before," he said.

"¿Qué?" Pook, a *peninsulare* and an ex-convict, shrugged his shoulders when Diego did not reply, deciding he would never understand the big *Isleño*.

Diego looked toward the river where men were hurrying to secure barges and sloops, a line of wagons, field-mounted cannons and caissons cluttered his view of the river. The army was going somewhere. *And when I leave with the army, how will I protect my children? Where is Cabitos?*

"*Don* Alguazil Cabitos y Cabrón, Governor General," the clerk announced as he ushered in a thin, ill-looking man of about fifty into Gálvez's office. Gálvez stood, but remained behind his cluttered desk, gesturing toward a chair.

Please sit, *Don* Alguazil Cabitos," he said. "I must apologize for asking you to delay our meeting, but, as you can see, military matters occupy my time."

"Of course, Governor General," Cabitos replied as he administered some snuff to his nose. "I understand completely. Affairs do seem to suggest war is imminent." Cabitos was lying. He was furious that he had been forced to wait two weeks – two weeks – for an audience with Gálvez. They would hear about this in Madrid.

"How may I be of service to you, *Don* Alguazil Cabitos," Gálvez said.

"I have been – given a mission, a quest, my General," Cabitos began in a slow and fragmented speech. "As a penance, I have – accepted the responsibility for – providing support –to Bishop Benitez, special – envoy of the Dominican Order of the Archdiocese of Madrid as his Excellency – pursues the enemies of Our Holy Mother Church."

Then you both should have stayed in Madrid where her enemies flourish, Gálvez thought, but he said. "And how has the pursuit of these fiends brought you to Louisiana?"

"General causes – and particular reasons, my General. His Majesty has been made aware of – the spiritual condition of His Most Catholic Majesty's most recent – *huérfanos*." Cabitos used the Spanish word for "orphans" instead of subjects, implying the citizens of Louisiana lacked spiritual parents, a slight not lost on the astute and court-wise Gálvez. "Madrid – has deemed it wise to – direct our Majesty's new subjects to the true – Mother Church. The wisdom of this – decision has been – verified by – inquiries we have made while we – awaited an audience. For example, His Excellency has been informed that many of the people in Louisiana refrain from – regular worship. Many who – profess their Catholic Faith – do so – with less than pure – intent. Marriages are often – attended by the children of the – celebrants."

"Where there is a shortage of priests, *señor* Cabitos," Gálvez said, clearly not impressed by the case being presented, "accommodations must be made."

"Indeed, Governor General," Cabitos spread his hands in a gesture of conciliation, "The time has come for us to become more influential. That is His Excellency, Bishop Benitez's intention."

"Why has not the Bishop come in person with this message?"

"He is still visiting the new settlements – Spanish settlements with Spanish – Capuchin priests. The French Capuchins have been – lax."

"That is an old argument, *señor*," Gálvez observed, "settled log ago by my predecessor." The King of Spain, not his cabinet, had personally intervened in this precise argument during the Governorship of *Don* Luis Unzaga y Amezega. The King decided Spain was not to attempt to make Louisiana a Spanish colony. French *alcaldes* and judges were to be appointed. French citizens would be allowed to retain their traditions, customs and their more lenient Capuchin priests. Unzaga had also married Marie Elizabeth de St. Maxent, goddaughter of the first Spanish Governor of Louisiana and sister to Gálvez's wife, a relationship that must have been part of the considerations.

There was a loud knock at the door, interrupting the conversation.

"Come!" Gálvez snapped without breaking his eye contact with Cabitos.

A clerk rushed in. "Major Panis to see you sir, he says it is most urgent."

"Send him in, Renaldo," Gálvez held out his hand indicating that Cabitos could remain.

"Governor," Panis began without acknowledging Cabitos' presence, "I fear that a storm is upon us. On my own initiative, I have informed *Don* Julian Alvarez and he has had our mariners unload the river vessels and tend to their moorings. I have informed Colonel Miró and sent word throughout the city, although the *criollos* have already begun to act."

"Send for Colonel Miró, *Don* Manuel Gonzales, *Don* Juan Antonio Gayarré and *señor* Oliver Pollock," Gálvez said to the clerk. "Tell me when they all can assemble here." The clerk rushed out. Gálvez touched Panis by the elbow when the man made to leave, indicating he was to stay, turned to Cabitos and said, "*Don* Alguazil Cabitos," Gálvez said, "I do beg your pardon, but affairs of state are pressing. Do make another appointment when Bishop Benitez can accompany you, and we can discuss your concerns further, provided we are not at war, that is."

"And, if I may make so bold to inquire, Governor," Cabitos said with a bow, "Are we not at war?"

"No war lasts forever, *señor*. Then we shall resume when peace has been restored. Good day, *Don* Alguazil Cabitos."

"Thank you, and good day, Governor General Gálvez," Cabitos said as he backed toward the door. He nodded toward Panis, mentally making a note that Gálvez had failed to introduce him.

The door to the office closed and Panis, who had watched Cabitos backing out, turned to Gálvez, "Who was that, General?"

"The self-appointed hounds of God have come," Gálvez said. The Dominican Order had been derisively called the "domini canes," Latin for "God's dogs" by some, but quietly.

"Dominicans?"

"Someone claiming to serve the Dominicans. I doubt their credentials. Renaldo!"

The clerk appeared at the door, "Yes, Governor?"

"Come in, close the door."

The clerk did as he was ordered and stood before Gálvez. "Yes, General?"

"Have you sent for the officers?"

"Yes, General."

"Good. Now I want you to send a message to Father Étienne Cordier, the archivist at Saint Louis Church."

"The Jesuit?"

"Yes, the Jesuit," Gálvez said with irritation creeping into his voice. "Is there any other Father Étienne Cordier? Tell him I want to know all he can find about *Don* Alguazil Cabitos y Cabrón and Dominican Bishop Benitez – I do not know the man's *apellido materno*."

The clerk paused.

"Do it now, Relando."

"Yes, Governor General." Renaldo rushed out, closing the door.

"I had thought this whole matter of religious structuring of Louisiana had been settled," Panis said, concerned for he was also married to a *criolla*.

"It has been settled and I will not have the question revisited. This is not England, *Don* Jacinto," Gálvez said. "I am not going to begin imprisoning people because of the language they use during their prayers or burning people at the stake for witchcraft. I have a war to fight and half of my army follows the Capuchin French and half of what remains are Catholic in name only. No one in the army is writing books against the Crown. I doubt if a third can even read. We would be fools to attempt to submit the people of Louisiana to the test."

∽

Diego shouted, attempting to be heard above the howling wind and driving rain, but his words were swept away. Sergeant Ortega had ordered them to stake down wagons on the lee side of the small brick building that served as a powder magazine. The squat building was too small to store all of the powder that had been assembled by Gálvez so the excess ammunition had been secured in wagons sealed in waxed canvas-lined boxes. Tents had been collapsed over equipment then covered with dirt to protect the gear from the relentless, wind-driven rain. Diego watched as several barges broke loose and raced downwind to disappear behind a curtain of gray rain/wind/spray. Some of the buildings in the city had collapsed and were converted into missiles that hurled through the streets, whipping past the sides of the magazine. Most of the regiment had taken shelter in Fort Saint Charles. A few men had been selected to save those provisions which could not be moved for lack of time. These last few found shelter where they could to wait out the storm.

"Tomorrow," Diego had moved close enough to shout into Pook's ear as they huddled under a cannon's muzzle. They had manhandled a carriage-mounted twelve pounder against the wall of the magazine and converted it into a temporary shelter by the addition of some canvas anchored to the ground by stakes. "It will be clear, blue-skied and hot."

"How do you know?" Pook screamed.

"I told you, I have heard this song before."

The winds began to subside around midnight, though few had kept track of the time, and the sun did rise into a blue, cloudless sky, shining down on destruction and confusion. The barges and river schooners that had not been grounded were either sunk or simply gone. Some buildings along the levee road were without roofs or had come apart, but most seemed to have survived.

"Show some order here," Ortega bellowed as he emerged from one of the warehouses. "Uncover that gear," he shouted, pointing to a field of canvas lumps.

Diego gathered a few soldiers and, along with Pook, began to uncover the equipment stores and return them to a semblance of order. As they worked they could hear the steady cadence of the remainder of the regiment coming upriver from Fort Saint Charles. Soon the bivouac area was alive with shouting sergeants and sweating soldiers. Tents were erected, wagons up-righted, muskets stacked, and, with the help of storm debris, cooking fires lit. Before the sun set, the Louisiana Regiment had re-established the camp. Gálvez inspected the army's efforts as the evening light began to fade. When he had arrived at the riverfront he was somber, but after viewing the quick recovery of his army his mood visibly brightened. Every enlisted man was given an extra tot of rum with their evening meal.

The next morning Sergeant Ortega gathered his platoon and had them draw weapons, bedrolls and a day's rations. Gálvez was sending patrols to new settlements around New Orleans to assess storm damage and send barges or schooners that survived the storm to the river docks near the powder magazine. The local militia commanders were to be ordered to the Cabildo for instructions.

As a matter of luck, or maybe design, Ortega's platoon, including Diego, was ordered to Concepción. There were no river schooners or skiffs available, so they had to march the entire way, about twenty miles, passing through a place called Terre Aux Boeufs before arriving at Concepción at about five in the afternoon. The amount of storm damage lessened as they moved east. At Terre Aux Boeufs a few houses were tilted off of their foundations and rows of crops were flattened. At Concepción only two houses had to be levered back onto their foundations, but that work had been completed by the time Diego's platoon arrived.

Sergeant Ortega assigned men to work on damaged barns or cisterns while he sought out *Don* Blas Ansolo to deliver Gálvez's summons.

"Papa!" Maria's little voice came from a cluster of wagons on the road. Diego paused to look for her and whistled the "Here I am" phrase. Pedro's answer came immediately. Maria appeared, running up a small trail from behind the barn, and rushed to Diego who picked her up with kisses and a hug. Pedro and Isabella joined Diego, pulling him away from his work.

"Where are Miguel and Catalina?" Diego asked, concerned that he had not seen them.

"My father is searching for his pigs," Isabella said. "My mother is at home. We saw you pass on the road, so she sent us along to see you." Isabella was wearing a cotton print dress and a white bonnet. It had been less than a year since she was a scared little girl on a great ship. Now she seemed to have grown into a woman, though Diego was certain she was not older than sixteen.

"How did you pass the storm?" Diego asked.

"Nothing much was damaged. No crops were lost. The house danced about, but stayed on the bricks," Pedro said.

"Only the pigs got out," Isabella said. "We did better than most."

Pedro gestured toward the road and Diego turned to see Sergeant Ortega returning from his search for *Don* Blas.

"Finish with the cistern," Ortega said as he approached the working soldiers, "then build camp there." He pointed toward a wide, high open area large enough to camp the twenty men of the platoon.

"Use the barn," one of the settlers said. "I have room for two men in my house," another added.

"Those who find rooms must return here at sunrise," Ortega said. "I will give first call in the morning at first light. Everyman had better be here when the sun breaks the horizon."

Ten of the platoon spread their bed rolls in the barn while the rest found rooms among the settlers. Diego returned to the Campo house, Pedro carrying the musket and Maria his haversack. The walk to the new frame house was less than five minutes. Isabella and Pedro said nothing, Maria talked incessantly. She described the storm in wonderful detail for an eight-year old.

When they arrived at the house, Miguel Campo was just coming in with his two pigs.

"Papa," Isabella exclaimed, "You found them! And look who we have found!"

"How did you manage to finds those pigs, *mi amigo*?" Diego said as he shook Miguel's hand.

"Luck, pure luck," Miguel said. "They had sought refuge in a neighbor's barn. He recognized the animals and held them for me. Catalina!" Miguel called, a hand cupped to his mouth. "Come to the front, see who is here."

Catalina appeared on the porch, wiping her hands on an apron. She also wore a cotton dress and long-billed bonnet of an Acadian, not the shawl and flat-brimmed hat of an *Isleña*.

"I know, my husband," she said. "We saw him march by. Come in, Diego. I have prepared a *caldo*."

"*Caldo*! So soon after a storm?" Diego asked.

"We have fish traps in the bayou," Miguel said. "Storm or not, there are always fish. I do not know how a man could go hungry in such a place."

They were enjoying the wonderful seafood stew by lamplight on the porch when a voice called out from the darkness. "Can a humble priest join you?"

"Come, *Padre*," Miguel called into the darkness beyond the circle of lamplight.

Father Josef came into the light and climbed the steps to where Catalina was already setting a place for him. "Hello, Pedro, Maria," he said, "*Señorita* Isabella, good evening. *Señora* Catalina, my friend, Miguel, you are too kind to an old priest." His eyes met each person as he spoke to them. He sat next to Diego. "Diego deMelilla, I am pleased to see you again, friend."

"Hello, *Padre*," Diego said. "I am relieved to see little harm has come to Concepción. I am glad to see you well."

The priest tasted from the bowl and praised the cook. The *caldo* was quite delicious, the fresh vegetables and firm white bits of fish were well seasoned and in perfect proportions. After they had finished with the usual small talk about the storm, who had to repair their houses, whose barn lost a door, Father Josef looked at Pedro and Maria. "It is not my place to say so, but I think it is time for hard-working youngsters to prepare for bed." Catalina stood, gathered some empty bowls and spoons. "Isabella, please help me prepare a place for *señor* deMelilla in Pedro's room."

"I have a bedroll, Catalina," Diego said. "It will be fine here on the porch."

"Nonsense," Catalina said. "Isabella will see to Maria and I will fix a place for Pedro. You can have the bed. We will leave you men to talk." With that, she and Isabella shepherded Maria and Pedro into the house.

"Do you know a man, a bishop, by the name of Benitez?" Father Josef asked once the children were out of earshot. The question was directed to Diego.

"I have never met the man," Diego said warily. "Not formally." He remembered the name from his rescue by the *El Natural* and he had seen the man in the company of Cabitos in the captain's cabin and again on the banks of the Mississippi River. "A Dominican?"

"Yes, that is his Excellency," Josef said, the tone of his voice was strained.

"What has caused you to mention him to me?"

"He had visited our settlement the day before the storm. He asked many questions."

"What kind of questions?"

"He asked me to name the settlers, which I did easily. He asked if they were faithful Catholics. I said 'most certainly.' Then he asked if any of the people were from Agüimes. I said most here were from Tenerife, like Miguel here, or Las Palmas de Gran Canaria. As I said this, Pedro came to this porch, here," he pointed to the steps leading down to the path to the trail by Bayou Terre Aux Boeufs, "within sight of his Excellency, and whistled for Maria." Father Josef crossed himself, "some are from La Gomera, I said."

"What did he say to that?"

"Nothing. Now these things I say, I say to Miguel." Father Josef turned to Miguel, but put his hand on Diego's arm, stopping him from leaving the table. "Miguel, his Excellency asked if I had ever heard of a man named Diego deMelilla." Father Josef paused, crossed himself again and looked up. "I said, 'no one by that name lives in this settlement.' To this, the Bishop said, 'If you meet Diego deMelilla or his wife, you must send word to me.' I said, "I will tell *señor* deMelilla or his wife, to seek you out, if I should meet them. 'Those were not my words,' his Excellency said. 'You shall send word to me, but do not mention to them my interest in them. Understood?'"

"*Don* Blas Ansolo is to accompany you back to New Orleans," Father Josef said. The sudden change in the conversation startled Diego. "*Don*

335

Blas is telling everyone that Gálvez will never bring the army away from the city now that the storm has wrecked the supply fleet," the priest continued.

Diego's head swam as he attempted to catch up with the priest's train of thought. "If that were so," Diego said, "*Don* Blas Ansolo could stay here and receive messages. I think the General will move north, before the *godums* can bring soldiers down from Canada or across West Florida from Mobile and Pensacola. If war has been declared, New Orleans is surrounded. I think Gálvez will strike first and soon." Diego looked at the priest, fully aware of the risk the man had taken in telling Miguel what he was not to tell Diego. "*Padre*, have you heard of a man named Alguazil Cabitos?"

"I have not."

"Miguel," Diego turned to the man, clearly astonished by what he had been hearing. "If Cabitos comes to Concepción, you must hide my children."

"We will," Miguel was able to say.

❧

Sergeant Ortega, true to his word, formed the platoon as the sun broke the horizon. The settlers had seen to it that none of the men overslept and all were present for the muster. Ortega completed the head count and ensured that each man had his full complement of equipment. Soldiers were notorious for selling bedrolls, canteens, cartridges, spare clothing anything they could. He marched the platoon west along the banks of Bayou Terre Aux Boeufs. They passed *Don* Blas Ansolo as the man boarded a small river sloop. A mule and driver waited at the end of a tow line until the *alcalde* settled into the stern of the sloop. The boat would be towed six miles to the Mississippi River. Then the sloop would sail up the wide river to New Orleans. *Don* Blas would probably arrive ahead of the platoon by a few hours.

Diego waved to his children standing with the Campos on the wide porch of the fine settler's cabin as he marched by, his mind racing. *How can I protect my children?* He asked himself. A soldier is not free to come and go as he pleases. He would not know where to find Cabitos or the Bishop, even if he could steal away from the regiment. What could he do if he managed to find the man? The army was preparing to move and the soldiers would be kept close to the bivouac.

On the other hand, Cabitos or Benitez need only examine the regimental roster to find Diego deMelilla. That would bring them to him, not the children. The clerk keeping the roster would not know of Mézu. As far as the army was concerned, Diego deMelilla was a bachelor.

Who in New Orleans knew about Maria Artiles? The settlers that came with them on the *San Juan* knew Mézu by her *apodo* only. The name "Maria Artiles" would mean nothing to them and, besides, Cabitos would have to interview hundreds of settlers just to find someone from the *San Juan*. The Campos knew where Mézu's children were – and the Jesuit at Saint Louis Church! Somehow, Diego decided as he trudged along toward New Orleans, he was going to have to find a way to save his children from Cabitos.

CHAPTER 26

Bishop Benitez strolled along *Calle Borbón* following an altar boy he had hired. The boy carried a tall pole, one end resting in a holster on the front of his belt and a white banner emblazoned with a red crucifix suspended from the other. Occasionally, the boy had to dip the banner slightly to avoid signs that arched over the wooden walkway. Sometimes they passed a new brick building built in the Spanish style with a balcony that covered the entire sidewalk and the banner had to be lowered until the bottom nearly touched the ground.

His Excellency had loved to walk behind the banner in Madrid. People would bow and cross themselves as he passed. He would bless them with sweeping gestures of his right hand while holding the cross hanging from a chain around his neck with his left. The experience, the joy of the prestige was worth the money his family had paid for the appointment. He remembered his father telling him how revered bishops were during the Habsburg Dynasty. Now the *Borbón* Charles the III held the throne and Spain might as well be France. Even in Madrid, the common people were no longer awestruck by the appearance of a Bishop. Here in Louisiana, pedestrians paid him little heed during his official excursions. It would take some work, but that attitude was going to change.

Thanks to the patronage of *Don* Alguazil Cabitos, Benitez was going to be able to establish a foundation for the faithful in New Orleans. Madrid might be satisfied using the power of the Inquisition to simply censor books or ferret out Jews. He, Benitez, was going to restore the power of the church here in Louisiana. They had made a good start. Cabitos had pursued a heretic Jewess here after her escape from Gran Canaria. She had stolen a valuable gem from Cabitos and then subverted the sacrament of matrimony to avoid punishment. But she would be brought to justice here. Benitez would see to that. When the people of Louisiana see such a villainess tried and convicted under his expert direction, they will give him complete control. With that power, Madrid would be next. No more *Borbón* ecclesiastical lassitude, the Church would rule once more.

"Turn here," Benitez shouted to his standard bearer. "No, left." The boy was hopeless. He had told the fool they were going to the Cabildo and yet the boy turned away from the river at *Calle San Pedro*. Gálvez would have to grant him an audience today. He had discovered the true passenger list for the *San Juan Nepomuceno*, not the altered list in Agüimes, the one that omitted the names of the Jewess and her false husband, but the true passenger list from Seville, the one that listed Diego deMelilla and Maria Artiles. Now it was simply a matter of checking the militia rolls of the new settlements for Diego deMelilla and Maria Artiles. *Don* Alguazil Cabitos was going to be vindicated.

As they approached *Calle Chartres* Benitez noticed river schooners and barges had assembled in ordered rows along the bank of the river. A line of wagons and caissons paired with limbered cannons stretched along the levee road pointed upstream. He could hear the shouts of sergeants and the roll of signal drums as white-uniformed ranks of soldiers collected into columns behind flags and standards. Over at the *Plaza de Armas* blue jacketed New Orleans militia men were being arranged into columns of four. Unlike previous visits to the Cabildo, there were no hurried and stressed clusters of officers or couriers rushing in and out of the front doors. Benitez and his standard bearer were halted by the guards at the door.

"State your business," the guard said as he motioned for Benitez to step to one side.

"Bishop Benitez to see Governor General Gálvez. I am expected." Benitez had made the appointment a week ago.

"One moment, *señor*," the guard said and then signaled for a runner. The runner was sent into the Cabildo with the message that Bishop Benitez had arrived. The man returned in moments. "Post your standard bearer there," the man indicated a place west of the main doors, "and follow me, Excellency," he said.

Benitez followed the runner through the main foyer to an anteroom near the east wall where he was directed to make himself comfortable. "The General will be with you momentarily," the man said as he closed the door.

ᥒ

Renaldo rapped on the door and entered when he heard the General say "Come." He opened the door to see General Gálvez, Secretary of War Andrés de Almonester, Colonel Miró, Major Panis, Manuel Gonzales, Judge Pedro Piernas, and Colonel Martin Navarro gathered about a table. Judge Piernas was to take control of the civil government while Navarro would be the military commander. It was Navarro who had given instructions to the various *alcaldes*, *Don* Blas had been one, about what was to be expected of the militia in the strategic settlements should the British advance through their territory. He noted how pale *Don* Blas Ansolo had become as the details unfolded.

"Bishop Benitez has arrived, General," Renaldo said. "I have him waiting in the east room as you instructed, *señor*."

"Gentlemen," Gálvez said as he rolled up a large map on the table, "you have your orders. We depart in three hours." The officers began filing out of the office, but Gálvez stopped Colonel Miró. "*Don* Esteban, tarry here with me a moment. I want you to hear this report." Gálvez turned to the clerk as the last of the other officers left. "Renaldo, please ask Father Étienne Cordier to come in."

"Yes, General," Renaldo said. He returned with Father Étienne and left them.

"Father Étienne Cordier, I believe you know Colonel *Don* Esteban Rodríguez Miró y Sabater, my second in command."

"Indeed I do, General," Father Étienne said. "And if I may, Colonel, congratulations on your marriage to *Doña* Céleste Eléonore Elisabeth MacCarty of our fair city." *Doña* Céleste MacCarty was an Irish *criolla* from an influential New Orleans family and at least the fifth Louisiana-born woman to marry a high-ranking Spanish officer since Governor Unzaga began the practice.

"Please report to us what you have discovered about Bishop Benitez and his friend *Don* Alguazil Cabitos," Gálvez said as he sat behind the desk, a bemused smile on his lips.

"Bishop Francisco Benitez y Jaén is the fifth son of *Barón* Ricardo Benitez and *Doña* Antonia Jaén. He was born in 1732. The family is *cristiano viejo* with a long history of service to the Habsburg, Charles the Second. The family has fallen out of favor during the *Borbón* reign. The family purchased the title for Francisco when it became obvious he lacked the – uh –temperament to be a soldier. He is a Bishop without a diocese. The Dominican Order has all but expelled him, and he was – encouraged – by the prelate of the order to leave Madrid because of his insistence on reestablishing an Inquisition. He has come to Louisiana under the sponsorship of Cabitos."

Gálvez looked toward Miró for a response.

"Our wives will not be well appraised by such a cleric," Miró said.

"Indeed. Now Father, tell us of Cabitos."

"*Don* Alguazil Cabitos y Cabrón, the first of six children of Duke Cabitos de Santa Cruz and Maria Cabrón, was born in 1729 and inherited the title of *Ricohombre* of Santa Cruz de Tenerife. He was reported to have been betrothed to the only daughter of *Don* Pedro Artiles and Maria Ventomo, a Guanche, in 1763. The daughter, Maria Artiles y Ventomo, born in 1750, broke the betrothal in 1766, alleging Cabitos' involvement in the murder of a Scotsman, George Glas, his wife and young daughter, a child reported to be somewhat – simple."

"Had Cabitos been, as you say, involved?"

"It appears so, General."

"Please, continue."

"Cabitos, when confronted by Maria Artiles about the murders, struck her in the face so savagely she lost an eye. Artiles – by this time she had been orphaned – took her brother with her and fled Tenerife for Gran Canaria where she found refuge with the people of *Pueblo de Cuevas.* There she married a goatherd, Diego deMelilla y Tupinar and, under the protection of the *Regidore* of Gando, Gran Canaria, lived with him until the death of the *Regidore.*"

"Did you say she married Diego deMelilla?"

"Yes, General."

"Is he the same Diego deMelilla, *soldado* of the Louisiana Regiment, who had recently escaped the British?"

"Yes, General."

"Damn! Continue."

"When he learned of the death of the *Regidore* of Gando, Cabitos renewed his pursuit of Maria Artiles. Escaping Cabitos, Diego deMelilla brought Artiles and their two children here on the *San Juan Nepomuceno.* While deMelilla was in West Florida with Major Panis, Maria Artiles, *apodo* Mézu, contracted yellow fever and died."

"So why is Cabitos still here?"

"Since arriving at New Orleans, Cabitos has rarely ventured onto the streets, preferring to remain drunk, keeping to rooms he and the Bishop have taken in a public inn on *Calle Borbón.* He has, from time to time, had a few visitors; women of the street. I do not believe he is aware of Maria Artiles' death, General," Father Étienne said.

"And if he were to be made aware of this fact, Father?"

"Cabitos has frequently expressed a desire for revenge against deMelilla, for a humiliation in a duel."

"A duel? How does the *Ricohombre* of Santa Cruz de Tenerife become involved in a duel with a goatherd?"

"I cannot say, General," Father Étienne shrugged. "The report I have is that Cabitos fled from the field."

"Personal disputes mean nothing to me," Gálvez said. "DeMelilla will be with the army, so we need not worry about Cabitos causing trouble until we return. It is the Bishop that must be dealt with in our absence. If he should rouse fears of religious persecution, our friends will disappear. I will go hear what his Excellency has to say."

"*Don* Esteban, please advise Judge Pedro Piernas of our – Dominican problem," Gálvez said as he walked to the door. "He will have to keep the noble Bishop free of mischief until we return."

⁓

"Muskets, cartridge boxes, haversacks, bedrolls, ground cover, a change of trousers, backpacks, short swords, bayonets, twenty rounds of ammunition, canteen, and two days rations," Ortega rattled off the list of equipment each man was expected to carry. "If you are not carrying it, *muchachos*," he shouted, "you will not have it."

"What about tents?" someone asked.

"No tents, no fat cooking pots," Ortega said. "We are going on a little walk."

"Where?"

"Where the General sends us. Why do you worry so?" Ortega was clearly enjoying himself. "We will sleep on the ground at night and slough through the wilderness during the day. What else does a soldier of Spain need to know?"

The ranks formed up on the levee road. Each man was so burdened with equipment that it appeared as if an army of hunch-backed giants was standing inspection. Diego watched people walking along *Calle Chartres* as he stood at attention awaiting Ortega's examination. He noticed a boy struggling with a white banner decorated with a red cross turn the corner onto *Calle Chartres* and recognized Bishop Benitez striding along behind the standard bearer as if on parade. Fear gnawed at his stomach. He was going to be miles away and there was nothing he could do to protect his children.

He had been able to learn of the conditions in Concepción through one of the washerwomen. She had a sister who was married to a fisherman and lived near the Spanish settlement. Miguel would send word to him from time to time. No one had ever seen Cabitos on Bayou Terre Aux Boeufs and Bishop Benitez had never returned after the one visit weeks before. Diego had begun to hope his children had been sufficiently hidden and would be safe with the Campos.

"By the Left – FACE." The regiment became a column of four.

"Sling – MUSKETS." Each man loosened the sling on his musket and pulled it over his right shoulder. The sling was tucked under a clasp on the cross belts so it was not necessary for a man to hold the musket onto his shoulder.

"At the Quick – MARCH." The army began to move upriver, followed by a train of cannons, caissons and wagons. The road quickly disappeared to be replaced by a faint trail through dense woods, occasionally breaking out onto a road again as they crossed plantations or farms before plunging into wilderness once more. Each night, sick or injured soldiers were placed aboard barges that had followed the army up the Mississippi River or were housed in a plantation's barn. Some days a group of local militia would be added to the march. The army shrank from disease and increased by volunteers as it moved north, as if it had become a living organism.

On the eleventh day Gálvez's army arrived at the Saint Gabriel Church. A wooden stockade had been built about a quarter mile upriver from the church where the faint trace of a waterway separated from the Mississippi River and headed east. During flood conditions, water would flow from the Mississippi eastward to the Amite River. The water way was named the Iberville River or Bayou Manchac, but it was neither a river nor a bayou. Where it met the Mississippi River, the Iberville was no better than a slough. Fort Bute was on the banks of the Mississippi River across the Iberville River from the stockade at Saint Gabriel. Fort Bute was the frontier of British territory.

The wide encircling veranda of the Saint Gabriel Church served as a temporary field office for General Gálvez. It was there he announced to the assembled army that war had been declared between Spain and Britain because of Spain's support for the American rebels.

"We are going to take Fort Bute," Gálvez promised. "And then we are going on to Baton Rouge and take that fort as well." The soldiers grounded all non-combat equipment and prepared for action. Backpacks and bedrolls were piled to the eves all around the veranda of the church.

Diego was dispatched with a score of men under the command of Sergeant Ortega to cross the Iberville, which they were able to do by simply wading through a foot of muddy water, and move several hundred yards north of the fort to watch for reinforcements coming down from Baton Rouge. The German Coast militia, having just recently joined the march, was the freshest body of men in the army. They were selected by Gálvez to make the assault on Fort Bute while the remainder of the army circled around the fort to prevent escape. The British, having decided to concentrate their defense at Baton Rouge when word of the Spanish army reached them, left only a score of men in Fort Bute to offer a token resistance. Sixty German Coast militiamen led by Antonio Saint Maxent the younger, Gálvez's brother-in-law, stormed into the fort, killing one defender, capturing two officers and eighteen men.

Diego saw a half dozen men running along the riverbank just before daylight, but they were gone by the time he and the rest of his squad managed to fight through the brush to the riverbank. They had heard one volley of musketry from the direction of the fort and it was all over. When they returned to Fort Bute, the army was preparing to camp. Scouts had been dispatched to guard against a counter attack, but the British had gone, withdrawn far to the north to their refurbished fort at Baton Rouge.

Gálvez gave the army two days of rest and repair before they pushed upriver. During that time some of the Americans were sent upriver to scout as far north as Natchez. Other scouting parties were sent toward Baton Rouge and east to the ford across the Amite River, still others out onto Lake Maurepas. Gálvez was not going to be surprised by British forces coming down from Canada on the Mississippi, or from East Florida by land or across Lake Maurepas. He had secured Lake Pontchartrain with an American sloop-of-war and Spanish gunboats before beginning the campaign.

It was the middle of September, the height of the hurricane season, so a British fleet invading up the Mississippi River from the Gulf of Mexico was most unlikely, but possible. The thousands of militia men left in the settlements along the approaches from the gulf were there to slow down such an invasion until Gálvez could bring his army back to New Orleans. Gálvez knew Baton Rouge must fall or Britain would take New Orleans and encircle the American rebels.

⁓

Benitez returned from his audience with Gálvez angry and frustrated. He had requested the rosters of the militia units in the *Isla de Orleáns*, which was all of Spanish Louisiana east of the Mississippi River. Gálvez insisted such information was of military significance and, in light of the growing hostilities with Britain, information the Bishop did not need to know.

"I am searching for a sly enemy of the Church," Benitez had said.

"Which enemy is that?"

"A Jewess and thief, General."

"I am going to exercise the army for a few days, Excellency," Gálvez had said. "When I return, we can discuss your request."

Benitez sent a messenger to Cabitos' rooms asking if they could meet in the lobby of the inn *Auberge de la Chemise Blanc*, which also served as an ale house. Cabitos had a room on the corner of *Calle Borbón* and *Calle Santa Anna* with a private entrance off of *Santa Anna*. Benitez had preferred a second story room above the stench of the streets where one could sleep with the windows open.

The messenger returned to report that Cabitos was "indisposed" but would meet the Bishop tomorrow, ten in the morning, at the rectory entrance to Saint Louis Church. Cabitos was frequently "indisposed," but as long as the rent was paid, Benitez tolerated the man's vices, limited as they were to strong drink and pox-riddled women. Benitez had to admit Cabitos was sly if indiscreet. That bit about the Artiles woman being a Jewess was brilliant. Benitez had discovered the truth before they had departed Tenerife. The Artiles family was firmly *cristanos viejos* while the mother had been a Guanche. No Jews, no Moors were known to have even visited, much less inhabited the Canary Islands. The accusation of Jewish blood was enough to stir up cooperation among the clergy in Europe. Even in Protestant England, the charge alone could warrant arrest. But here in Louisiana, no one seemed interested in preserving the faith; even the French priests were content.

Benitez arrived at the rectory entrance as the last peal of ten vibrated from the church bell. Cabitos, of course, was nowhere in sight. The man considered it a sign of weakness to arrive on time. Benitez knew this and was not surprised. He rapped on the rectory door planning to ask for his banner, which he had stored in the rectory, and one of the altar boys to serve as standard bearer. A boy came out with the banner. Evidently someone in the rectory had seen Benitez come to the door.

Benitez walked to the edge of the roadway and waved down the street in the direction of a carriage stand. A driver saw the signal, and, eager for the fare, started up the street to Benitez just as Cabitos stepped to the corner, intercepting the carriage. He climbed on and directed the driver to continue up the street to Benitez.

"Good morning, Excellency!" Cabitos beamed, uncharacteristically cheerful. "Come aboard and we can talk on our way to Concepción."

The standard bearer was directed to the driver's bench where he could display Benitez's banner. Cabitos switched to the rearward facing seat and indicated Benitez sit opposite him. Cabitos turned around and handed the driver several coins. "To Concepción," he said. The driver slapped the reins and the carriage jerked forward. Concepción was a three or four hour ride.

"Why Concepción, *Don* Alguazil," Benitez asked. "I was there some weeks ago and the priest there did not know of a Maria Artiles or a Diego deMelilla."

"I have not been idle, Excellency," Cabitos leaned forward, the smell of rum heavy on his breath. "I have learned that the majority of settlers from the *San Juan Nepomuceno* had been sent to Bayou Terre Aux Boeufs. Concepción is only one of the villages on that bayou."

"I met the local militia commander when I was there last, *alcalde Don* Blas Ansolo," Benitez said. "Gálvez denied me the opportunity to examine the rosters at the Cabildo, but it is certain *Don* Blas has a roster, and he will not keep it from me."

The carriage turned onto the levee road and the driver slapped the horse into a canter. Fort Saint Charles bordered the levee road, forming a choke-point against the river. Benitez saw a pike was set across the road and several soldiers, New Orleans Militiamen by the looks of their blue uniforms, were posted as guards. There had never been guards on the road before.

A soldier with a black epaulet on his left shoulder stepped forward, extended his hand palm outward and shouted *"Arrêt!"*

"What is the meaning of this?" Benitez stood in the rocking carriage and had to catch himself before he fell into the rear-facing seats.

"Français seulement!" the man said.

"Speak to him, *Don* Alguazil," Benitez said. "My French is lacking. To think of it, here in a Spanish colony we, Spanish *Dons*, are being ordered about by a French – whatever he is."

"Why are we being stopped, *Caporal*," Cabitos asked in perfect French without a hint of accent. Better French than the corporal, whose accent was one of a dockside ruffian.

"Show me your travel permits, gentlemen," the corporal held out his hand.

"We need travel permits?"

"Orders of the Governor," the man said. The smug expression on his face revealed how much he enjoyed ordering aristocrats about. "No one is to leave or enter New Orleans without a travel permit. There is a war on, have you not heard."

"We have not heard."

"Now you have been informed. Permits, gentlemen."

"We have no permits. We are only going to Bayou Terre Aux Boeufs."

"You are returning to New Orleans or I will place you both in irons," the corporal almost laughed.

"Where does one obtain a permit?"

"The Cabildo," the corporal pointed toward the building.

"I know where the Cabildo is," Cabitos was beginning to resent the man's attitude.

"See the travel permits clerk there. He will tell you how to obtain a permit to leave the city."

One of the other guards assisted the driver in turning the carriage around and even gave the horse a swat to start it back toward *Plaza de Armas*. He watched the carriage for a few moments then turned to his corporal with a shrug. Both men laughed loud enough for the retreating Benitez to hear.

There was no "travel permits clerk" when Benitez and Cabitos inquired at the front doors of the Cabildo. Both men insisted to be allowed to speak to the Governor. A messenger was sent into the building. When he returned he asked Benitez and Cabitos to follow him, the standard bearer and banner were to remain in the carriage. The man led them into Gálvez's office where they were introduced to Judge Pedro Piernas.

"Gentlemen, sit down," Piernas said. "Renaldo tells me you are distraught about travel restrictions. How may I be of service?"

At last, Benitez thought, a *man who appreciates nobility*.

"We desire to visit Concepción," Cabitos paused. "I am sorry, but I do not know how to address you. Are you a Judge or a General?"

"I am the acting Governor," Piernas said. "You may simply address me as '*Señor*.,"

"*Señor* Piernas," Cabitos resumed, "we wish to visit Concepción and were turned back at the Fort Saint Charles gate."

"Yes, you need a travel permit to leave New Orleans," Piernas said. "War has been declared."

"Where can we obtain such a permit?"

"I issue special permits. Regular vendors and suppliers have already been given their permits."

"We would like to obtain a travel permit, *Señor* Piernas," Cabitos said, his voice dripping with impatience.

"Why do you wish to travel to Concepción, *Don* Alguazil?" Piernas asked quietly, calmly.

"We are searching for a Jewess!" Benitez blurted out, no longer able to restrain his emotions.

"There are many Jews here in New Orleans," Piernas said. The news clearly shocked Benitez. "One need not go to Concepción to find a Jewess."

"You cannot keep us here against our desires!" Benitez was shouting now. "We are Spanish nobles and, war or no, we demand to be allowed to leave the city."

"You are right, Excellency," Piernas said. "I will issue travel permits; one for your Excellency and one for *Don* Alguazil Cabitos. These permits will allow the bearer to book passage on any ship leaving New Orleans."

"We are not interested in leaving the city by ship, we want to travel a few miles by land," Cabitos said, attempting to recover his emotions.

"Land travel out of the city is specifically denied, *Señores*," Piernas said.

Before Benitez could say more, Cabitos caught the Bishop's arm. "We would like two sailing permits, *Señor* Piernas. We may, at some time in the future, desire to leave Louisiana. We would not want to have to impose on you again."

CHAPTER 27

álvez dispatched a swift river schooner, the *Caballo Azul*, from Fort Bute to New Orleans. It carried prisoners of war, the more critically ill soldiers of the expedition, and news of the victory. A flotilla of mail packets and re-supply vessels had been assembled by Gálvez to support his move against Baton Rouge and, if necessary, swiftly move his entire army back to New Orleans on river barges if the British should appear near the city.

A deck hand on the *Caballo Azul* had family in Concepción. He agreed to carry personal messages from the half dozen soldiers of the regiment with family in Terre Aux Boeufs. Diego, the only man among them who could write, thanks to Mézu's tutelage, filled a sheet of paper with words dictated by each man. Diego added his message to Miguel, saying all was well and begging that Miguel reply immediately concerning conditions in Concepción. The single sheet would be delivered to Father Josef at the church. Few of the settlers could read, so it was up to Father Josef to deliver the messages. He would take the dictated replies and return them to the deckhand. The officers of the different militia regiments were able to organize a regular messenger service to their home villages, but soldiers of the Louisiana Regiment who were from places too far away or were single men with limited families, had to do for themselves. Perhaps it was the isolation imposed by the circumstances of a campaign that caused soldiers to develop a comradeship stronger than anything found in civilian life.

They had begun the trudge up the Mississippi River from Fort Bute to Baton Rouge. It was only ten miles to Baton Rouge, but the army had to follow the river and the trip was increased to twenty miles. A flotilla of barges, some towed by men from the bank, followed the army. Gálvez knew the advantage of surprise was gone. The British at Baton Rouge would be prepared and the intelligence Gálvez was receiving was not encouraging. The fort they were moving against was armed with thirteen cannons, four hundred red coats, and one hundred fifty armed settlers. Against this entrenched force Gálvez brought ten cannon, three hundred eighty-four regulars, four hundred armed settlers – some were militiamen, most were not – and a dozen artillerymen. The British were rested and entrenched; the Spanish had been on a foot march for nearly a month, their forces reduced by illness.

"We must move into position and attack without delay," Gálvez had confided to Miró, "or the British will learn of our numbers and come out to overrun us."

❧

He heard her humming. The beautiful, lilting song of her own creation she always purred when she was grinding grain. He could hear the stone rasp in the bowl that had been hollowed out of the rock near their front door. Generations of *Amazigh* had used the rock to grind wheat and other grains until what had been a small depression had been converted into a shallow bowl.

Diego realized he had been staring at the Rock of the Clouds, brightly lit by the setting sun, and turned from it to watch Mézu grinding grain.

"What is it you sing, wife?"

He walked toward her as he spoke. She stopped, placed the grinding stone onto the flour she had been making, and wiped her hands on her apron.

"I have not named it, my husband." She removed her wide-brimmed hat and placed it over the grinding bowl. She wore a tight leather bodice over a cotton blouse. Her wide, colorful skirt touched the ground.

"Where have you been?" he asked. She seemed to be no closer to him than when he had begun walking. He stumbled, looking down for an instant to regain his feet. He looked up again and Mézu was now wearing a glittering green gown. Her hair was hidden by a lacy veil supported by a silver comb. He could see her grey eyes as they seemed to fill with moisture. The ugly scar and sunken hollow of her left eye were gone, her face unblemished. Diego wanted to ask how could it be, how could her injury have been healed.

"Where are the children?" he heard himself say.

"They are with Catalina, of course."

"Does Catalina live in Agüimes?" The town was far down the valley from their home above *Pueblo de Cuevas* and he wondered why the children would be there.

"Catalina Bebera, Miguel Campo's wife. Do not worry, they are safe. It is you, my husband, who must take care."

He was closer to her now. *How young she looked!* Her grey, sparkling eyes and flawless face were framed by the veil, the swirling patterns in the Tenerife lace contrasting with her smooth cheeks. He reached to touch her, but she was just beyond his outstretched fingers.

"What cares do I have, Mézu?"

Someone behind him was calling his name. "DeMelilla!" the voice was almost shouting. He turned to see who it was that called and the day faded instantly into darkness.

⟋⟍

The soldier who had been assigned to camp watch, a night duty every *soldado* had to fill on a rotating basis, was standing at Diego's feet. The man had waded between the sleeping forms of the exhausted men of the regiment until he had found Diego.

"DeMelilla!" He gave Diego a gentle kick on the foot. "DeMelilla. Sergeant Ortega wants you now."

"What time is it?" Diego asked as he struggled to his feet.

"It is about an hour before first call."

Diego pulled on his boots. He wore no socks. Stockings were for officers, not the ranks. He had slept in his shirt and trousers, so he slipped on his uniform coat and reached for his gaiters.

"Gear up later," the man said. "Sergeant Ortega wants to see you now."

"Where is Zurita?" Zurita was the corporal commanding Diego's file and should be advised of Diego's absence.

"Already with Ortega," the soldier said. Diego could not remember the man's name. "Come, follow me," the soldier said.

They found Ortega, Zurita and three other file leaders standing around a cooking fire. Eleven other men, all private soldiers, huddled in the background.

"Nice of you to join us deMelilla," Ortega snarled. "Stand over there and listen."

Diego moved to the cluster of soldiers He saw Plata and gave him a questioning gesture. Plata shrugged his shoulders.

The cluster of corporals around the fire broke apart, returning to their sleeping men to announce first call.

Ortega approached the dozen soldiers, gesturing for them to gather around him.

"After first call," he said, "I want you men to collect your gear and meet me at that barge." He pointed toward a dark lump silhouetted against the river. "Do not fall in with the regiment. Any questions."

"What happens," one of the men said. Diego recognized the voice. It was Pook.

"We have a special job for you," Ortega said. Behind him, the camp was stirring with first call. Some men were ambling toward the slit trenches while others collected their gear.

"Tend to yourselves and meet me at the barge before assembly," Ortega said.

The men had dressed for the march as they met Sergeant Ortega at the river bank. He had them load their backpacks and bedrolls onto barges to be towed by militiamen, following the army toward Baton Rouge. "You will not need them," he said. "Bring your arms, two days rations, full canteens, full cartridge boxes and follow me."

Ortega directed them east and well away from the column of troops, wagons and cannons. He ordered them to form into a single rank under the canopy of a large oak tree. A man in a blue uniform, not unlike a New Orleans militiaman, was leaning against the tree, waiting. The coat had gold epaulets, one on each shoulder, identifying the man as a captain.

Ortega inspected his men. Satisfied that they were properly equipped, he centered himself on the rank, came to attention, faced about and held a salute. "Here are some of my best men, Captain," he said to the man who was puffing on a clay pipe. The captain straightened, removed the pipe with his left hand, lowering it next to his trousers and returned Ortega's salute. "Thank you, sergeant," the man said. "You may return to your duties." Ortega dropped his salute and marched away toward the regiment, the sounds of the assembly drums rolling above the murmur of an army preparing to move.

The officer looked at the soldiers, who were locked at attention. He cleared his throat and said, "My name is Captain Barrett of the American Continental Army. You men have been assigned to me to scout east toward the Amite River." Barrett was a small, thin man with dark, searching eyes. The blue-coated uniform hung on him as if it had been sized for another man. Diego recognized him as one of the men who had been accompanying Oliver Pollack.

"You," he pointed to Diego, "what is your name?" Barrett's Spanish was excellent, only slightly accented.

"DeMelilla, sir."

"Good. I was told you have some wilderness experience. Choose two men and move northeast now. We will follow." Barrett indicated the direction of travel with a gesture, pointing with his arm, his flattened hand, thumb up.

Diego selected "Pook" Gonzales and "Plata" Perez, and moved them east a few steps. Plata earned that *apodo* because his hair was pure white with an almost silver sheen. "Pook, walk parallel to me but to my left at least twenty yards. Watch to your left and ahead. Signal me if you see anything. Plata, you do the same to my right. Stay as far from me as you can and still see me. No talking, hand signals only, any questions?" Pook and Plata shook their heads. They had watched others depart on scouting patrols, but this was their first. They did not know enough to formulate a question.

The patrol moved out through heavy brush and into a thickly wooded area. Barrett nodded approvingly as Diego deployed the point men then directed the remaining soldiers to fan out just as Diego's men had. Barrett carried a small compass which he would consult from time to time and occasionally adjusted Diego's line of travel using hand signals.

They crossed a small, sluggish bayou and almost immediately began to climb a steep slope. At the crest of the slope, they broke out onto a well-traveled road running southeast and northwest. A farm house and cleared field bordered the road opposite the bluff they had just ascended. Diego sent Pook left to a turn in the road and instructed him to hide where he could see well up the road and signal if he should see anything coming in their direction. He sent Plata down the road, southeast, with the same instructions.

Barrett came up to Diego, panting heavily from his climb up the slope. "This road runs to Baton Rouge," he said. "Let us examine the house. Watch the windows." He began to walk toward the house. Diego pulled one of the soldiers to him, "Come with me," he said and gestured to two others, "You two, go around the far side of the house until you can see the back porch. Get to a corner and stay away from the windows."

Diego moved to the left rear corner of the house, glanced around the corner across the porch. One of the men he had sent around the right of the house peeked around the right rear corner of the house. They heard nothing.

"Look toward the tree line," Diego said. "Yell if you see anything coming out of the trees." He stepped up onto the porch from the side, ducked under a shuttered window and stood next to the door. The shutter had a firing loophole. Using hand signals, he directed one of the men on the opposite corner of the house to watch the tree line, and the other to join him on the porch next to the back door.

He heard Barrett calling out something from the front of the house. Then Barrett changed to Spanish. "We are going in," he yelled.

Diego pulled up on the door latch, pushed the door open, and rushed in, bayonetted musket at the ready. A pistol was pointed at him and he swatted it away with his musket. He was in the act of reposting with a bayonet lunge when a woman's voice behind him called out, "No!" The pistol discharged into the ceiling and Diego stopped his thrust with the tip of his razor sharp bayonet at the throat of the *pistolero*, or in this case, *pistolera*.

The woman was blond. She had a round, pretty face, blue eyes wide with terror and a smoking pistol still gripped in her trembling hands. Diego pulled his bayonet from her throat. How he had managed to stop his reflexive thrust, he could not say. He took a deep breath of relief, reached out to remove the pistol from the woman's quivering grip, and tossed it on the bed. The woman gave a small cry and retreated to a corner of the room where she cowered behind a blanket she had pulled from the bed. A small boy, no more than five, jumped from an armoire and rushed to the woman who accepted him with open arms.

"Open the shutters," Diego said to the other soldier who had followed him into the room.

Light filled the room as the shutters were pushed open. The woman was crying and mumbling something in a language Diego had never heard. He looked around for the woman who had cried "No," but there was no one. Barrett and the men with him were stomping through other rooms in the house until they finally arrived where Diego waited.

"What was that shot?" Barrett asked.

Diego pointed at the pistol on the bed. "She was trying to protect herself," he said.

"Anyone hit?"

Diego shook his head slowly from side to side.

Barrett spoke to the woman who looked back with a blank stare and said, "*Deutsch.*"

"Ah!" Barrett looked at Diego, "*Ella es Alemana.*" He began to speak to the woman in German, the guttural sounds making no sense to Diego.

When they reached a pause in the conversation Diego asked, "What did she say?"

"She begs us not to harm the boy. She fears we will – abuse her."

"We are not Englishmen," Diego said.

Barrett laughed. "I will tell her to follow you to the front porch. She is to wait there with the boy until we withdraw. I must emphasize to you, she is to suffer no indignities, deMelilla."

Feeling a little insulted by Barrett's last remark, Diego removed the bayonet from his musket, sheathed it, adjusted the sling on the stock and slung the firearm. He then gestured for the woman to accompany him saying, "*Por favor*" repeatedly.

"Say '*bitte,*'" Barrett said. "When you go onto the porch, have her and the boy sit on the bench and wait for me."

"*Bitte,*" Diego said, gesturing again. The woman struggled to her feet clinging to the small boy and still shaking with fear. Without touching her, Diego directed her toward the front of the house and out onto the porch. He could hear Barrett ordering the men at the rear of the house to go to the tree line and search for any signs of recent movement.

Diego pointed to the bench and said, "*Bitte.*"

The woman sat, clutching the boy tightly. Images of Mézu holding her sleeping little brother, Ignacio, that day a decade ago, raced through his mind. It was the day he had first spoken with *Doña* Maria Artiles y Ventomo. She and Ignacio were huddled together, alone, afraid and desperate, under the crude shelter at the *santuario* of the Most Blessed Virgin of the Clouds, a place that was now a world away, a time that was gone forever.

"*Mierda,*" Diego said.

"*Was?*" the woman said.

Diego shrugged his shoulders and watched as Nedo, one of the soldiers Barrett had set as watch at the front of the house walked over to the porch.

"I see you have found something nice," Nedo said without taking his eyes off of the woman, who began to tremble anew.

"She is not to be touched. Captain's orders," Diego said.

"Looking is not touching," Nedo said.

"Get back to watching for *godums*, fool."

"You talk as if you were an officer."

"Go see what has Plata excited," Diego said, pointing toward the southeast where Plata had stepped out onto the road and was waving agitatedly.

"Do as deMelilla says. Go see what the man has to report." Both men were startled by the appearance of Barrett behind Diego.

Without saying another word, Nedo trotted down the road, bayoneted musket at port arms. Barrett watched Nedo for a moment, then turned to the woman and began to converse with her in German. Diego descended the porch steps and went to the corner of the house where he could see Plata as Nedo reached him. He could see Pook watching up the road to the northwest and beyond the field behind the house where several white uniforms were moving among the trees.

Nedo and Plata had separated and disappeared into the brush beside the road. Diego watched as two men rounded the bend in the road and then stopped suddenly, reacting to something beside the trail. The men raised their hands as Plata and Nedo emerged from opposite sides of the road. Diego had been half listening to the woman and Barrett talking behind him. The tone of her voice suddenly changed and the guttural foreign words came more rapidly. The drama taking place on the road had created a change in the woman.

"Must be her menfolk, Captain," Diego said without turning around.

"Her husband and brother," Barrett said. "She fears for them."

"Plata will not harm them, Captain, if they do not resist," Diego said. "As for Nedo, he thinks like an Englishman."

Plata and Nedo disarmed the men and started them toward the house, Plata followed with the captured arms and Nedo took Plata's post to watch down the road. Diego looked back toward Pook's location and saw him watching up the road. He looked to the northeast; the soldiers who had been searching the tree line were coming back to the house.

Plata brought the prisoners to the porch and laid their weapons, two old fowling pieces, on the planking. He had opened the priming pans of the guns and emptied them of powder. The older of the two men said something to the woman who replied, *"Nein, Bin ich nicht."* This seemed to calm the captives.

Barrett silenced them with a word. "DeMelilla, take the woman, the boy and that young man there," he pointed at the younger of the two captives, "back into the house. I want to talk to the father without interference from them." Barrett pointed toward Diego and said something in German.

The three followed Diego into the house where he directed them to a room with a table and several chairs and indicated they should sit. The small boy sat on the woman's lap, the young man turned a chair away from the table. Before he could sit, Diego gestured him to turn the chair back toward the table. After the man sat down, Diego made him move the chair closer to the wide, heavy table until his stomach touched the edge of the table, rendering him incapable of suddenly leaping out of the chair. When they began to talk, Diego hissed them into silence and touched a finger to his lips. They waited in silence until Barrett came into the room after several minutes.

"Our friend says there are Redcoats up the road to the northwest. He says there are five of them in a blockhouse. They have a cannon aimed up the center of the road, loaded with grape, I should think." Barrett said. "What do you advise we should do?"

Startled that an officer would ask his advice Diego managed to say, "Stay out of the road, Captain."

"Yes, clearly," Barrett said. "But how do we take the place? Let us go have a look."

"What about these folks, Captain? We need all of us if we are to try the blockhouse."

"I agree, deMelilla," Barrett said. "We will leave them here, with their weapons. We will not be back this way unless we fail at Baton Rouge. I will tell the old man we are going to leave him in peace and he need not fear us."

Barrett walked out of the room. Diego looked back at the woman and touched a hand to his hat, nodded to the glaring young man and walked out of the house.

Nedo was called in from his post, and the other soldiers assembled, except for Pook, who maintained his post at the bend in the road.

"DeMelilla," Barrett said as the men prepared to move north, "I will take the men north through the trees and out of sight of the road. I want you to take one man and scout along the edge of the road until you can see the blockhouse. The old man said it was only a half mile up the road. See what you can make of it. Then find us in the trees to tell us what you have seen."

Diego took Pook with him and Barrett moved the rest of the men north into the tree line. After Barrett and the remaining men of the patrol faded into the trees, Diego huddled with Pook.

"We will move along the up-hill side of the road. Keep back in the brush until you can barely see the road. Move slowly and tuck your hat in your sling," Diego said. He showed Pook how to loosen the musket sling until the tricorn fit snugly between the leather loops. They moved slowly at a crouch through tall dead grass. The wind was brisk, causing the grass to sway, making it more difficult for a less than alert observer to see them move. After a half-mile or less of painfully slow movement, Diego saw a wood-tiled roof and the top edge of a brick wall. He stopped Pook.

"I think I see the blockhouse," he whispered. "Stay here."

Diego removed his cartridge box and haversack, lay down his musket and crawled toward the blockhouse. There was no ditch or other depression to help his concealment, but he reached a point where he could see the blockhouse well without being discovered. The blockhouse was square, made of clay bricks, and a wood-shingled roof. Diego could see only two walls of the building. Each of the walls he could see had one shuttered window with firing loopholes. The blockhouse sat in a curve in the road so one window was facing east down the road and the other faced north across the road toward open farmland.

There were two uniformed men, Redcoats, lounging next to the northern wall. One was on a bench smoking a pipe and the other standing and gesturing wildly as he talked to the seated soldier. Two muskets were leaning against the wall. Beyond the soldiers, Diego could see a horse, saddled and tethered to a post. A tree line came up to the road about a hundred yards west of the blockhouse. Diego withdrew, listening for shouts of alarm, but all he heard was the babbling tale that was being poured out to the seated Redcoat. He crawled back to Pook and directed him to move north, away from the road. They crept north several hundred yards from the road before Diego stood, donned his accoutrements and hat.

"Let us find Barrett," he said and both men trotted north into the woods that bordered the farmlands. Barrett and the ten soldiers were easily located. Their white uniforms moving in a dark forest quickly caught the eye.

"It seems to be some sort of guard post," Diego reported, "meant to stop and inspect road traffic. I think the men outside of the blockhouse were accustomed to seeing people approach up the road. They seemed to not be very alert to movement elsewhere."

Barrett thought for a moment. "How many men?"

"We saw two. The block house may have held more, but not many. It is a small place," Diego said as Pook nodded next to him.

Barrett was quiet. When it seemed he was not going to say anything Diego added, "A tree line comes from the north to the edge of the road just west of the house. If we move quietly, we can be in position to rush the house from no more than a hundred yards away. The door must be on the west side. I could see the east and north walls. The south wall faces the edge of a bluff."

"Do you think you can lead us to the tree line?"

"Yes, Captain."

"Then we will go in file. When you think we can, deMelilla, signal me and we will rush the west wall in line. Make for the door and do not allow anyone to mount the horse. Fixed bayonets only. Do not load." Barrett did not want an accidental discharge to prematurely reveal their presence.

Diego found the tree line and discovered a worn path following the western side of tall brush mixed in with the trees, concealing their movement right up to the road. Diego led the file, halting them at the edge of the road. Barrett walked up to Diego and peeked through the tall weeds to see the two men Diego had reported still engaged in an animated discussion. The door was on the west wall, facing them, and it was open.

Barrett moved back until he was centered on the file of Spaniards. He pulled a brace of pistols from under his coat and whispered to the men as they leaned in to hear him.

"We will march out onto the road as if on parade," he said. "When I order 'line – left' you will face left and come to 'charge – bayonet,' give a shout and rush the *godums*. DeMelilla, I want you to secure that horse. I will be the first through the door."

"Then the sot tries me, so 'e did," the standing Redcoat was saying, "'n you knows me, Pete. I says 'one more word, 'n I'll...'"

"Jake! Look! What in bloody 'ell," Pete said as he pointed toward a dozen white-coated men march out across the road. "'oo's that lot?"

The men stopped, faced toward the Redcoats and with a yell rushed toward them, bayonets leveled. Pete, eyes riveted on the charging Spaniards, reached for his musket, but only managed to knock both weapons to the ground. They held their hands up as the screaming men stopped, holding cold steel inches from their chests. There were some shouts from within the blockhouse, then silence.

"Don't move, Pete, my boy," Jack whispered through clenched teeth.

"I ain't even thinking on it, Jacko," Pete said.

The three British soldiers in the block house were marched out to stand alongside Pete and Jack, the sergeant glaring at the two who were supposed to be on guard. An officer in a French-looking uniform followed the Spaniards.

"My name is Captain Barrett of the American Continental Army," the officer said in perfect English. "You are prisoners of General Gálvez of the Spanish army. You will not be harmed."

The captured weapons were collected, the pitiful little three pound gun was spiked, and Barrett led the men southwest until they rejoined the regiment preparing to camp for the day. The prisoners were interrogated for what little information they might have and sent to a barge for the trip to New Orleans. Diego and the rest of the expedition were released to Sergeant Ortega and the entire camp was filled with enhanced tales while they prepared for tomorrow's attack on Baton Rouge.

CHAPTER 28

Benitez sat in the back of the carriage and watched as excited citizens rushed around the vehicle. The driver had pulled to the side of the levee road when the mob had overtaken them. The people were rushing toward the *Plaza de Armas*, still called the *Place d'Armes* by most citizens, to hear the latest news of the war with Britain. A river schooner was seen descending the Mississippi River flying the white pennant with a black stripe.

A week ago the victory at Fort Bute, a nearly bloodless affair, had mollified fears among some of the populace of an imminent British attack on the city.

"Bring me to the *Plaza de Armas*," Benitez ordered. The driver paused until an opening in the rush of buggies and pedestrians allowed the carriage to proceed. The congestion around the open parade ground of the *Plaza de Armas* forced Benitez to climb down and join the throng pressing toward a raised wooden platform near the levee road. A grey-haired baritone, hired by a local entrepreneur to herald a brevet version of the latest reports from Gálvez's army, stood on the platform.

"Baton Rouge falls!" The man's deep voice carried across the murmuring crowd, "Three complete dispatches," he waved a fistful of handbills over his head, "for the cost of one *picayune*." The boy at the foot of the platform was handing out papers and collecting coins at such a pace Benitez was certain the lad had no idea of which papers were purchased and which were simply whisked away. "Natchez taken!" the man boomed. "British settlers paroled to their homes!"

Benitez waded to the young pamphleteer and pushed a copper coin in the boy's hand. He clutched the three dispatches to his chest and worked his way back toward the river in time to see the schooner's lines being looped around the pilings of a pier. The river was low and the deck of the river schooner was below the level of the dock. A gangway appeared at the edge of the dock and two Spanish soldiers, bayonet-tipped muskets at the ready, climbed onto the dock gesturing people away. Shouts and the sound of a sergeant calling a cadence came from the direction of Fort Saint Charles. A guard of a dozen soldiers marched onto the pier, forcing the crowd back. When a sufficient space had been created on the dock, the sergeant in command of the guard nodded to the two soldiers from the schooner.

"Ready!" one of the soldiers called down to the unseen deck of the schooner. Disheveled red-coated men began to appear at the top of the gangplank and were herded into the center of the guard. In ten minutes over three hundred British prisoners of war had been collected on the dock. Satisfied that he had retrieved all of the enlisted prisoners from the schooner, the sergeant of the guard marched the glum cluster of men back toward Fort Saint Charles. Some of the citizens followed the departing POWs while others tried to gain firsthand news from the ship's company.

A man sat on a piling and read the handbills aloud to a cluster of dock workers. "It says here over twenty of the British were killed," the man exclaimed, punching the newsprint in excitement. "General Gálvez artfully demonstrated his militia just out of range of British guns," the man was paraphrasing. The paper was printed in French and the stevedores were Spanish. "During the night of the 20th of September, the army had constructed artillery emplacements on a small rise overlooking the fort while the defenders were distracted by the militia. Once the guns were in place, screening brush was removed and the guns began to hammer the walls of the fort. Answering shots were ineffective. When the wall fell, the Louisiana Regiment of Infantry formed into a line of battle before the mouths of the still-smoking guns." The man looked up to ensure everyone in his audience was paying attention. He raised a fist and shouted, "But before an attack could be commanded, the fort surrendered." The clump of listeners cheered and the reader pumped his fist in the air.

Benitez read through the leaflets. The first was old news about the victory at Fort Bute. The second reported a daring attack on a barge in the narrow pass from Lake Pontchartrain into Lake Maurepas by a dozen Acadian sailors under the command of Lieutenant Vizenre Rillieux. The Acadians had leapt down onto the barge one early morning, trapping four dozen British soldiers below decks. A British surrender was negotiated and the triumphant militiamen poled the barge onto the lake where they were loaded onto a Spanish schooner. The prisoners, captured without a single casualty, were transported to New Orleans by way of Bayou Saint John. The supplier contracted to provide food for prisoners was becoming a wealthy man.

The third leaflet described the fall of Baton Rouge. Benitez, who struggled with French, was absorbed in the details of the handbill and did not notice a sergeant climb up from the schooner and stride off toward Fort Saint Charles.

"Sergeant deMelilla!" one of the soldiers shouted.

Benitez's head shot up. He saw a sergeant stop and turn as one of the soldiers from the schooner trotted up to him, said something, and returned to the gangway. *Sergeant!* Benitez thought. *It must be someone with the same name. The man they sought had been a mere goat herder in Gran Canaria less than a year ago.* He knew he could never follow the sergeant, even though he was without his standard bearer. Carriages attracted attention and even if bishops could walk around unnoticed, he was not about to traipse through the filthy streets of the city, the very reason he had hired this carriage for the day. He beckoned over the guard who he had seen talking to the sergeant.

"Yes, your grace?" the soldier said.

"Excellency," Benitez corrected.

"Yes, Excellency?" the soldier repeated, now at attention.

"Who is that sergeant?" Benitez asked as he pointed toward Fort Saint Charles and the departing Diego.

"That is Sergeant deMelilla, Excellency," the man said.

"How well do you know him?"

"We were *compañeros* until he was promoted to sergeant after the fall of Baton Rouge."

"I did not think married men served in the ranks of the regiment."

"He is *viudo*, Excellency."

Benitez crossed himself. *A widower!* "I shall pray for his poor wife's soul."

Benitez returned to the carriage and clambered aboard. "Saint Louis Church!" he barked to the driver. They wheeled away from the levee road, manure and mud flying from the wheels. Benitez glanced back to see a stunned soldier standing on the dock, watching them speed down *Calle Santa Anna*.

Benitez understood everything. They had not been able to find Maria Artiles among the settlers because she had died! They could not find deMelilla because he had been campaigning with the army of Gálvez, but he had to be certain before he told Cabitos. If Maria Artiles had died in New Orleans, her death would be recorded in the Church archives.

Benitez found Father Étienne Cordier in a small alcove performing his daily office of contemplation and reading prayers from a worn Latin breviary, the words droning out in a soft chant.

"I am told you are the archivist," he said, startling Father Étienne. Interruption of a priest during his daily office was beyond rude, even for a bishop.

"Yes, Excellency," Father Étienne answered as he tried to regain his composure.

"I wish to examine the death records for this year."

Father Étienne closed the book, slipped it into a pocket, removed his stole, struggled to his feet and mumbled, "This way, Excellency."

Benitez followed the priest to a small room containing a chair and a desk stacked high with ledgers. The books covered the period from January 1763 to August 1779.

"I have not cataloged September as there are three days remaining," Father Étienne explained. "I make notes during the month and verify as much information on the deceased as I can before committing to the ledger. Sometimes, I have to go back several months to a year to correct or clarify an incomplete posting. What month are you interested in?"

Benitez thought for several moments, mentally calculating the time. "I will start with May."

Father Étienne pulled a ledger from under several others. "May, 1779, Excellency."

Benitez opened the ledger and was dismayed to see that it was not indexed and in French. A list of names ran down the left edge of each page. Under the heading *"de Famille"* was a column of surnames, some easily recognized, some obscure. The following columns listed *"de Christian,"* *"Surnom"* and *"de Jeune Fille."* None of the columns were in alphabetical order.

"How am I to find an individual in this?" Some of the spaces were left blank. A few only listed a *surnom*.

"What is a 'surnom?'" Benitez snapped.

"It means *apodo*, Excellency. Some of the poor souls were known only by their nicknames."

"Why are the names not in order?"

"I record the deaths as they occur, Excellency. People do not die in alphabetical order. I am writing an alphabetized index for each ledger. I am up to 1769."

"I am only interested in May to September of this year. How many names am I going to have to shift through?"

Father Étienne rubbed his mouth with one hand. "Five hundred seventy three, I think," he said. "I may be off a few, but that should be close to it."

"Over five hundred! Have we been at war all year?"

"No, Excellency. Yellow fever."

"Here is June, July and August," Father Étienne said, touching each volume in turn.

"Perhaps you remembered recording someone. It would save me much time."

Father Étienne said nothing.

"Artiles. Maria Artiles. Do you remember anyone of that name?"

"Excellency, there were so many. How could I possibly remember one person?"

"I am not going to huddle here like some penitent, ruining my eyesight searching the ledgers. Father, I want you to read through these ledgers until you find the name Maria Artiles y Ventomo. When you find the name, send for me at once."

"And if the name is not in the ledgers?" Father Étienne asked.

"Send word to me that you could not find the name listed."

"Please, Excellency, write the name down for me. I am forgetful."

Benitez pulled several drawers out until he found a writing kit. He used quill and ink to write "Maria Artiles y Ventomo" on the back of one of the ledgers.

"I will search when I can, Excellency. I have my regular duties."

"I will speak to Father Diaz. He will allow you the time."

"Yes, Excellency."

Father Étienne stepped aside so Benitez could leave the room.

"Get to work," Benitez snapped, pushing the May ledger into Father Étienne's hands. The priest bowed, waiting for Benitez to leave.

"Get to work now, immediately!"

"Yes, Excellency."

Father Étienne shuffled to the desk, sat and gingerly opened the May ledger to the first page. He adjusted the book to catch the light from the oil lamp and, running his finger along the paper he said, "Badeau, no Christian name listed," he glanced up at Benitez before continuing. "*surnom* 'T'Pouce', no mother's name listed. Date of death 1 May, 1779."

"Good God, Father. It will take you a year at that pace, man," Benitez could not believe how dense the man was. *A Jesuit indeed!* "Just read the family names until you find Artiles."

Benitez took the ledger from Father Étienne. "I have changed my mind, give me the ledgers, I will bring them to my room and do a proper job."

"These cannot be removed from the archives room, Excellency."

"Nonsense," Benitez stacked the ledgers for the other three months onto May and stormed out of the building. Father Étienne followed the bishop to his carriage, protesting the removal of the ledgers. Benitez placed the books on the floor of the carriage and pushed Father Étienne back. "To the *Auberge de la Chemise Blanc*," Benitez shouted.

Farther Étienne watched the carriage trundle away. *How am I to get word to Diego deMelilla?* He thought.

☙

Diego sought out the commander at Fort Saint Charles intending to sign over the prisoners of war he had transported down the Mississippi from Baton Rouge. He found the post commander, Captain du Foreste, agitated.

"Sergeant, I have fifty men under my command," du Foreste complained. "Last week, the General sent me twenty prisoners and now you bring me three hundred sixty-five. Captain Rillieux landed sixty prisoners and the American, Captain William Pickles, has seized the schooner *West Florida* and is sending me prisoners as if he were delivering potatoes."

There would be over five hundred and fifty prisoners of war in New Orleans before the end of October. Concerns on how and where to keep so many may have been why Gálvez ordered all British militia and armed settlers paroled to their homes as soon as they surrendered.

"When will Leyba return?" du Foreste asked.

"He has been promoted to captain, sir," Diego said. "He has been ordered to garrison Saint Louis with eighty men. I have been sent here to deliver these prisoners and bring dispatches to *Don* Pedro Piernas. I think, sir, we are to begin preparations for an assault on the fort at Mobile."

Diego reached into the heavy leather document pouch slung across his shoulder. It was nearly identical to the one he had taken from the headquarters at Pensacola. He pulled out an order of transfer for the prisoners. "Please, sir, sign here." He indicated a blank area just over the words "*aceptado*."

Du Foreste signed, muttering, "How I am to deal with so many –."

Diego walked from the captain's meager office under the fire step of the east wall of Fort Saint Charles and walked through the crowded courtyard. He glanced at the doorway of the small apartment where he had last seen Mézu and felt his stomach sink. Once he had delivered the dispatches, he would see if he could get a pass for a few days to visit Pedro and Maria. As he walked through the gate he met Pook coming the other way.

"Our sick and wounded have been moved from the schooner to the hospital," Pook said.

Diego could see four wagons roll up to the hospital, which was less than a hundred yards from the gates of Fort Saint Charles.

"Thank you, Pook. We will collect the rest of our detail and march to the Cabildo. We are soldiers of Spain and we will report in a military manner."

"Yes, Sergeant," Pook said, a sarcastic emphasis on the word "sergeant."

"You are right, Pook," Diego laughed. "I have not been a sergeant for a fortnight and I sound just like old Ortega."

"I did not know you had such high ranking friends in the church, sergeant," Pook said.

Diego stopped. "What are you talking about?"

"A bishop saw me talking to you at the dock. He asked if you were Sergeant deMelilla."

"What did you tell him?"

"I just said that you had been promoted, nothing else."

"Did he ask about my children?"

"No. He just said he would pray for your wife's soul."

They had reached the dock where the other transport guards from the Baton Rouge campaign were lounging about.

"Fall in on me!" Diego shouted. It angered him to see men lounging about. "Smartly now, the city of New Orleans is watching. Show them how the conquerors of Baton Rouge return home."

The dozen men of the guard detail formed a line on the dock facing deMelilla. He inspected the men, directing one to button his coat, another to adjust his cartridge box. When he was satisfied he stepped back.

"*Atenn–CIÓN*."

Twelve soldiers snapped to attention.

"To the Left–FACE."

The line of men became a column.

"Column of twos to the Right–MARCH."

Each second man in the column stepped to his right and then moved up until two columns of six men each had been formed.

"Carry–ARMS."

Each man lifted his musket a foot clear of the ground, wrapped his right hand around the trigger guard and held the weapon tight against his side.

"At the Quick–MARCH."

The men moved out at the pace of a brisk walk. Diego took a deep breath and ordered, "At the double-MARCH."

They began to jog, muskets held vertically against their sides. Diego trotted next to the formation, grunting a cadence. He directed them down the center of the street, horse drawn wagons and pedestrians parting before them. He halted them before the doors of the Cabildo. He placed Pook in charge of the formation and instructed him to have the men rest in place. He entered the doors of the Cabildo unchallenged by the guards. He heard people gathering around the squad asking the men who they were and where they had been. He heard the pride in Pook's voice when he said, "We are home from the Battle of Baton Rouge."

"I am Sergeant deMelilla with dispatches from General Gálvez," Diego said as the clerk at the reception desk rose to greet him.

"One moment, sergeant," the clerk said. He rose and opened the door to the General's outer office. Diego could see another clerk seated at a desk next to the entrance to the General's inner sanctum. The door closed, leaving Diego alone. He remembered the clerk from his first visit a month ago. He marveled how improved the reception was for a crisply uniformed sergeant than for a disheveled private dressed in sailor's slops. The clerk retuned.

"*Don* Piernas will see you now," the clerk said as he stepped aside to allow Diego to pass. The clerk guarding the inner office jumped to his feet and hurried to open the door. He held it open and Diego could see a man sitting at a wide desk. He had never met Piernas, but assumed this must be the acting Governor. He removed the pouch from his shoulder, placed it under his left arm and assumed the position of "attention."

"Sergeant Diego deMelilla, sir, with dispatches from General Gálvez." Diego saluted and offered the pouch across the desk with his left hand, fixing his stare on a spot on the wall just over *Don* Piernas' shoulder.

Piernas took the pouch. "Thank you, sergeant. I am informed that you arrived with over three hundred prisoners of war."

"Yes, sir."

"Have accommodations been arranged for your men?"

"No, sir. We have two day's rations and little else. Our bedrolls and other equipment are in Baton Rouge. "

"I will issue orders for you and – How many?"

"I have twelve men with me, sir."

"Twelve men to guard over three hundred fifty?"

"The schooner had a crew of twenty, sir."

"Humph! You will be assigned to one of the barracks barges docked on the river. My clerk will bring your orders to you in the outer office."

"Yes, sir, thank you, sir."

Diego paused.

"Is there anything else, sergeant?"

"Yes, sir. We are temporarily without an officer, sir. I was wondering, sir, if the men could be given passes, sir. When General Gálvez returns, we will all be busy preparing for the attack on Mobile."

"You know about those plans, sergeant?"

"No, sir. Just seemed to be the next step, sir."

"Talk to my clerk, sergeant. He will prepare three day passes for your men."

"Thank you, sir."

Diego saluted, faced about and marched out of the office. The clerk closed the door and sat at the desk.

"Twelve passes good until the thirtieth of September," the clerk said as he pulled a sheaf onto his desk."

"Thirteen," Diego corrected. "I need a pass as well. And while you are at it, I will need a travel permit for Terre Aux Boeufs."

"I did not hear *Don* Piernas say anything about a travel permit."

"I have family in Concepción. What good will a pass be to me without a travel permit?"

The clerk shrugged and began writing. "You will be assigned to the barracks barge moored at Fort Saint Charles. It flies a blue pennant. The commander of the barge is Ensign Piernas. He has been in the army for two weeks, but do not take advantage of him." The clerk poked a thumb toward the closed door behind him, "Papa."

Diego returned to the street in front of the Cabildo to find his men surrounded by enthusiastic citizens. Most of the questions his men had been fielding were in French, a language all but three of the men understood. The young ladies in particular seemed to hang on every word the handsome Pook Gonzales had to say.

"Fall in!" Diego shouted in his best sergeant's voice. The men scrambled to form a line and the citizens scattered, the ladies squealing in fright. He waited until his men were positioned at attention.

"By the Right – FACE."

The line became a column facing *Calle Santa Anna*.

"Shoulder – ARMS."

Each man placed his musket on his left shoulder, the butt in the cup of his left hand and each weapon slanted at the same angle. Each man carried all that he owned, back packs, bedrolls, canteens, bulging haversacks, cartridge box, short swords, knives, bayonets and muskets.

"Forward – MARCH."

Because Diego had not prefaced his order with "At the Quick" the men moved out at the slower "lock-step" pace usually reserved for maneuvering a full infantry regiment. Each soldier's pace was measured so that every man stepped into the foot print of the man in front. The line of men seemed to rock slightly with each step, like a long, narrow ship. With Diego's deep baritone voice calling the cadence, the squad seemed to move as if it were a single, powerful entity.

The man hawking handbills pointed at the squad as they passed him. "There!" He shouted, "There are the victors now!" The crowd parted to allow for the passage of Diego and his squad. The people, particularly the Acadians in the crowd, had suffered at the hands of the British. The French had been embarrassed by the loss of the Seven Years War, but the Acadians, who were present in significant numbers, had been exiled, robbed and humiliated. Now the people cheered a small line of white-uniformed Spanish soldiers as if these men alone had visited vengeance on the hated British.

Diego halted his men at the foot of a gangway attached to a barge with a single blue pennant nailed to its stump of a mast. He had the men wait as he ascended the gangway, found Ensign Piernas, who seemed no older than Diego's son, and delivered his billeting orders.

"Your men will store their muskets in the armory," the Ensign said. He pointed to a wooden locker fastened to the bulkhead of the sleeping quarters. "You have your choice of bunks. Your men are the only ones billeted here tonight."

"They have passes, sir." Diego showed the papers to the Ensign.

"Then they will store their muskets and short swords before they depart this barge. I doubt if they will go any farther than the *Cuatro Jinetes* across the street."

"I have a travel permit, sir," Diego said. "I will be in Concepción, sir."

"Fine, fine," the Ensign said as he waved a hand. "You may keep your short sword."

Diego returned to his men, instructed them to store their arms in the locker and then return to him. The men did as they were instructed and when they re-formed on the street, Diego notified them of their passes, accepted their cheers, and distributed the papers.

"Lose these passes or get too drunk to walk or get into a fight where blood is spilled and you will bunk in the jail until I fetch you out," he warned. Five minutes later, Diego stood alone on the bank of the river. It was about noon. He could make Concepción before dark.

༄

Benitez struggled up the stairs to his room with the stack of ledgers. He has stopped at Cabitos' room, but no one was there. Benitez reflected on the peculiarities of Cabitos. The man was a drunkard and a whoremonger. He would spend days in his room inebriated and hostile to any interruption. Sometimes he would send everyone away and lock himself in his room for days, the windows shuttered despite the sweltering heat, then emerge, calling for rum and a whore. But the man paid the bills. If, with Cabitos' backing, Benitez could establish himself as the Inquisitional authority in Louisiana, the bishop would become powerful – and rich.

Benitez stacked the ledgers on the desk next to his bed and opened the window, letting light from the setting sun stream in. He opened the first ledger and began to skim down the column labeled *"de Famille."* Badeau was the first listing, then Jumonville. *What kind of name is that?* he thought. He shrugged his shoulders and continued down the list. When he completed May, he looked at the other three ledgers and decided he would take supper before attempting the rest. Eight of the entries in May listed only the *apodo* of the deceased. If Artiles had died and was listed by her nickname only, he would never find her. He did not know what Maria Artiles was called by her friends.

When Benitez returned to his room, fortified by a fine meal of smoked ham, potatoes and several large cups of rum, it was dark. He had to light the oil lamp on the desk, a task he accomplished after several attempts to strike a spark with the fire kit. He adjusted the flame, opened the window wider until the night breeze blew the thin, ragged excuse of a curtain into the room. It was almost cool. The breeze was from the east and carried little of the stench of the city street below.

The June ledger contained half again as many entries as May. The yellow fever had not yet come, but the summer pestilence of the crowded city consisted of many maladies that shortened lives. An hour later, he set the June ledger aside. Names filled his head. So many strange, foreign names; He did not think it possible such a city could be governed. He opened the July ledger and began to trace his finger down the list. He passed it up, caught himself, and returned to the name "Artiles." There it was! Artiles – Maria – Mézu – Ventomo – 9 July 1779 – yellow fever.

"I have found you!" Benitez shouted. Tomorrow he will inform Cabitos. Now he knew everything. DeMelilla was a sergeant in the Fixed Infantry Regiment of Louisiana and Maria Artiles was dead. Now he could be free of the relentless search for a fugitive and get to the real purpose of his coming to New Orleans.

He changed out of his robe and slipped on a nightshirt. The window, far above the street below, provided such a pleasant breeze he left it opened wide, climbed into bed – no need for prayers, no one was watching – and lay still for a moment rejoicing in his discovery.

CHAPTER 29

B enitez struggled to pull the bed cover over him. It had been a mild night when he lay down, but now it was quite cold. He drifted off again only to wake to a freezing room. He slipped out of bed, pulling the covers from the bed, draped them over his shoulders, stumbled to the open window and closed it without latching the catch. He had never been warned of the possibilities of such a fall in temperature. The moonlight streamed in casting enough light in the room to make out the desk, piled with ledgers, the chair and the bed. His breath frosted. He could not remember ever having been this cold, even in that awful winter he had spent high in the Pyrenees at a crumbing mountain-top retreat called *Estopiñán del Castillo.*

He went to the desk and examined the lamp, which he had turned down when he retired, relieved to see it was still burning faintly, a small, yellow tongue of flame holding to one corner of the wick. He carefully turned the knob to lengthen the charred braid. The flame filled the lamp and lightened the room. It was still incredibly cold. He lifted the lamp, intending to leave and find a warmer room. Perhaps the oven in the court-yard was burning in preparation for breakfast. He turned to go when he was immobilized. There was someone in the room, a shadowy figure next to the door to the hall.

"Who are you? What are you doing here?" Benitez demanded. He shifted the lamp to his left hand and dug under his pillow with his right. He fumbled about before he pulled out a dagger and pointed it menac-ingly at the shadow. He quickly realized that the dagger was still in a scabbard, so he tried to shake the leather case off of the blade.

"I am Bishop Benitez," he shouted. The scabbard clung tenaciously to the dagger. "You must leave now!" He put the scabbarded blade under his left armpit, squeezed it between his arm and body, and pulled the dagger free. He pointed the naked blade at the figure. "You are mistaken if you think you can rob a bishop!"

He circled to his right hoping to get to the window, open it and call for help. The figure moved to block the path to the window, coming out of the dark corner and into the light from the window. Benitez could see the figure now. It was a woman.

She was young, perhaps seventeen or so. She wore a green gown that seemed to shimmer in the moonlight. The high silver tiara in her hair supported a lacy veil. Her eyes were bright, gray, but in a color that sparkled in the reflected moonlight.

"You have found me, priest," she said in perfect Latin.

How can this be? Benitez thought. Latin was the language of the Church. Only priests studied Latin, and even then only those priests with ambitions for higher office. Benitez had forced himself to learn the language that cold winter north of Aragón. Women, particularly young women, were eager to learn French, the language of courtiers, not Latin.

"It is you who have come into my chamber," he replied in Latin.

"You have sought me out intending to do me harm, you and Cabitos." Her pronunciation of "Cabitos" conveyed pure contempt.

"Leave now," Benitez was shivering with cold and fear. "I will call for help." He took a deep breath, but when he attempted to yell, he produced a feeble whimper. "This is a dream," he stuttered, "I am asleep and this is a dream."

"You do not dream, priest," the woman said. "You have found me. Do your worst to me."

Benitez blinked, the cold was beginning to cause his eyelashes to stick. He rushed at the woman holding the dagger outstretched, only to become entangled in the curtains. He slashed back and forth blindly, striking nothing. He looked about, confused and terrified. The woman was now seated at the desk, a hand on the open ledger.

"You are Artiles!" Benitez pointed with the dagger. "You are not dead after all."

"Death is not what you suppose, foolish priest."

"I am a bishop!"

"You are a fallen priest, conniving, greedy and foolish. What awaits you, I cannot describe."

Benitez distorted his face with a snarl. "You have faked your death. This I can see. You bribed that Jesuit to forge the ledger."

The woman laughed quietly. The left side of her face began to glow, brightening until Benitez had to turn away. "I can tell you this," she said, her voice seeming to come from within Benitez's head. "If you are still in this city when the sun sets on this day, you will never see it rise again."

He rushed at her, the bright light and fear obscuring his vision. The tip of his dagger stabbed into the soft plaster of the wall behind the desk. The woman was gone. Benitez bolted for the door, threw it open and ran into the hall. Suddenly he realized how warm it was in the hall. Gasping for air, he listened intently. There were voices drifting up the stairway from the inn's common room. The staff was preparing for the morning. He re-entered his room, dagger at the ready and crossed to the window and pulled it open. He could hear a buggy pass on the street below, the driver slapping the reins against the horse's flanks. The cold was fading from the room as the warm night air drifted in. He had not been dreaming.

Benitez placed the lamp on the desk and pulled his sea chest into the center of the room. He put on his finest clothes and his great robe. He selected several other garments from the chest, tossed them onto the bed, pulled the corners of the sheet up and tied it into a bundle. He opened the desk drawer and pulled out several papers, sifted through them one at a time, examining each in the lamplight before discarding them. He found the paper he wanted and stuffed it into his purse. He looked around the room one more time before he rushed through the door and down the stairs.

He shouldered his way past the servants who were preparing the common room for breakfast and found the door to Cabitos' room. He pounded on the door until someone in a neighboring room growled for silence. No one answered the door and Benitez grabbed a servant by the arm.

"Where is your master?" He said in his poor French.

The servant just pointed toward the courtyard.

Benitez went into the courtyard and found one of the owners of the inn. He took the man by the elbow. "Where is *Don* Alguazil Cabitos?" he said, a hint of desperation creeping into his voice.

"Was he not in his room, Excellency?"

"No. I would not be asking you if he were."

"Then I do not know, Excellency. I am told there are some establishments on Levee Street he has been known to frequent. Perhaps you should look there."

"Never mind. How would I find a listing of ships departing New Orleans?"

"The Cabildo keeps a schedule, Excellency. Few ships leave the city in September, but it is nearly October and there maybe a few willing to risk a late season storm."

Benitez returned to his room, hefted the bundle onto his back and ran down to the street. When he could not find a carriage for hire, he bustled along *Calle Borbón* toward the Cabildo, the rising sun lighting the faces of the buildings to his right. He had to stop twice to catch his breath, sweat pouring down his face. He reached the Cabildo and was stopped by the guards at the door.

"There is no one in this early, Excellency," one of the guards said.

"I must find out which ships leave today," Benitez said.

"Go to the alley," the guard pointed toward the alley between the Cabildo and the Saint Louis Church. "They post a list of vessels in port there. If a ship is scheduled to depart today, it will be posted there."

Without a word of thanks to the guard, Benitez went to the alley and found the list posted to a door, just as the guard had described. There were only two departures scheduled. One was for the twenty-ninth of September and the other for the First of October. He had to think, *what day was it?* He was certain today was Wednesday, the twenty-ninth of September. *What if the ship sailed at first light?*

The ship scheduled to depart today was the *Santa Maria de las Montañas*.

Benitez hefted his bundle and rushed to the levee.

Although it was first light, sweaty men labored along the river front. Benitez found a *jefe* scribbling on a small chalkboard.

"Where is the *Santa Maria de las Montañas?*" his voice shaking with fear that he may have missed her sailing.

"She lies there," the man said, pointing to a ship not a hundred paces away. Sailors were uncoiling her mooring lines from the pilings.

"Wait! *Oíga!*" Benitez shouted as he ran forward. The sailors paused and he scrambled aboard over the gunnel only to fall, sprawling on the deck.

"We would have waited for your Excellency, had we but known," a short, round man said as he looked down at Benitez.

"I require passage on this ship. I have a permit." He began to dig in his purse.

"You do not need a permit, Excellency," the man said. "This ship is bound for a colony of Spain. I am Agustín Monterojo, Captain of the *Santa Maria de las Montañas.*"

"I am Bishop Francisco Benitez y Jaén. I can pay for my passage."

Monterojo nodded then shouted, "CAST OFF ALL FORE LINES – PLAY-UP STERN LINES!" without looking away from Benitez, who started at the command.

"Then welcome aboard, Excellency. I will have your bundle brought below. We will fashion a place for you. TEND PORT SHEETS, SPANKER AND MAIN! " The captain waved a black sailor over. "Look to his Excellency," he said as he climbed to the quarterdeck. "CAST OFF ALL LINES. UP HELM." The *Santa Maria de las Montañas* was underway.

A stevedore and foreman watched the ship slip downriver, its masts outlined against the rising sun.

"The bishop was in a great hurry," the stevedore said.

"Well, he made his ship," the foreman began to write on his slate.

"Where is that ship bound to put his Excellency in such a state?"

"I cannot think why the man was in such a hurry. That ship is bound for *Las Islas Malvinas*."

"Where is that?"

"Pray to God you never find out," the foreman said before growling the stevedore back to work.

ℰↃ

Cabitos staggered to a doorway to an alehouse on Levee Street, the rim of the sun just beginning to appear across the river. He had forgotten the name of the place, but he began to remember how he had arrived. It was the girl in white. He had been seeing her, here and there, for the last week or more. The first time he saw her, she was standing at a street corner. The light from a corner alehouse cast a yellow hue on her dress and face. She was a small girl, wearing a full-length white dress. Her black hair streamed down over her shoulders, dripping water.

As he approached the corner, she ducked away. He reached the place she had been standing. A puddle of water covered the banquette where she had been. Cabitos looked down the side street only to see several sailors staggering toward him. The girl was nowhere in sight. Since that time, she began to appear with increasing frequency. Two nights ago, he saw her standing in the doorway of his room as he came up the hall. She retreated into the room and Cabitos, certain he had trapped her at last, rushed to the door only to find his room empty. The windows were latched, nothing under the bed, no one in the armoire.

Then last night, when he hurried to the corner where the girl in white appeared and, for the first time, she did not vanish. He turned the corner to see her retreating along a row of bawdy houses fronting Levee Street. He followed her until she entered an alehouse. Cabitos followed to find several soldiers joking loudly and drinking heavily.

He grabbed one by the arm. "Did you see a girl come in here? She was dressed in white and soaking wet."

The soldier looked around, his eyes bleary. "Nothing in here but soldiers, *amigo*."

Cabitos pushed the man aside and walked around the one room alehouse.

"If it is a girl you want, *amigo*," the soldier slurred. "Try the *Cuatro Jinetes* next door. We went there first, but were faced with a hard choice." The soldier paused, grinning.

"What choice was that," Cabitos asked.

"Sobriety and a *puta*, or drunken celibacy. I think we have chosen wisely. We will stay drunk all night and not be asking the surgeon for mercury."

"Why not choose a drunken night with a woman?"

"On a soldier's pay?" The man laughed so hard his friends, who had not even heard the conversation, laughed as well.

Cabitos grunted, pushed through the soldiers and placed a silver coin on the table. "Rum" was all he said.

Now he stood in the glare of the rising sun, alone in the doorway. The soldiers had gone, he knew not when or where. He saw a man with a bundle on his back running along the levee. A ship was casting off, and the man was shouting for the sailors to wait. He thought he recognized the man when he tumbled over the gunnel of the ship. *Was it Benitez?* He thought. Then he shook his head. Benitez would not walk fifty paces in a city full of carriages, much less run with a bundle on his back, and to leap aboard a ship as it left the dock was beyond possibilities.

"Time to return to *Auberge de la Chemise Blanc*," Cabitos said to no one. It struck him suddenly. He had been pursuing, searching for a girl in a white dress and he had taken a room in the Hotel of the White Blouse. He wondered if there was some connection. He waved at a *fiacre* as it passed, causing the driver to pull up sharply on the reins and doff his hat.

"Where are you bound, *monsieur?*"

"*Auberge de la Chemise Blanc*," he said and climbed into the carriage.

He walked into the common room of the inn to find it overflowing with breakfasters. The owner, happily busy, asked Cabitos what he would like for breakfast.

"Nothing for me." His stomach had not recovered. "Why the great crowd?" The city, though busy, was not crowded since Gálvez had moved the army to attack Baton Rouge. No doubt that would change. Gálvez was expected back soon and more troops would be arriving from Cuba to prepare for the next attack.

"Gálvez is due back today. He has called a conference of all the militia commanders," the proud owner said. "Most come here because we have the best breakfast ham in the city."

Cabitos was unimpressed and he turned to go to his room.

"A moment, señor," the owner said. "Your friend, the bishop, was looking for you urgently this morning. Did he found you?"

"Bishop Benitez was about this early?"

"He accosted me in the courtyard at about sunrise. He was searching for you, señor."

Cabitos passed his room and climbed the stairs to find the door to Benitez's room slightly open. He entered to find an overturned sea chest, some clothes scattered about and the armoire open. The room had the look of having been burglarized. The lantern, still burning, was on the floor. Reflexively, Cabitos picked it up and put it on the table. He noticed the stack of ledgers. The book on the top of the stack was labeled *Libro de los muertos, Agosto 1779.* There was a ledger open on the desk. Cabitos glanced at the listing and the name "Artiles" captured his attention. He read aloud, "Artiles – Maria – Mézu – Ventomo – 9 July 1779 – yellow fever."

The emotion he felt surprised him. He was saddened. Maria Artiles was dead, had been dead for months. Instead of feeling joy or satisfaction, Cabitos was disappointed. He could never visit a proper revenge on Maria. He had imagined, planned and plotted for years the brutality of his revenge for the humiliation he had suffered, and she had escaped his vengeance. He sat in the chair, cursed and then wept. After all he had endured because of her, she had escaped. A new idea began to form in his mind. She left a husband behind, and children. The husband was dangerous and needed to be dispatched quickly, safely, but the children – revenge may yet be possible.

He had been asking all of the wrong questions. He had been looking for Maria and her husband. He needed to search for a widower and two children who had lost their mother. He quietly stood, left the room and went down to the common breakfast. Benitez had mentioned most of the settlers from the *San Juan* had been sent to the same place? He finally remembered.

"*Señores!*"

The room, which had been churning with conversation, grew quiet. "Is there anyone here from Concepción?"

A timid-looking man raised his hand. "I am, señor," he said.

Cabitos rushed over to him. "I am *Don* Alguazil Cabitos y Cabrón, *Ricohombre* of Santa Cruz de Tenerife," he said, offering his hand. The man was silent. "And you, my friend?"

The man cleared his throat, "I am *Don* Blas Ansolo, *alcalde* of Concepción and Colonel of the Militia."

"Yes, Colonel, my friend," Cabitos snatched a passing servant, "Bring my friend a cup of rum from my personal store."

"Now Colonel Ansolo, *Don* Blas," Cabitos managed to sit at the same table with Blas by edging another man from his chair, a planter by his dress. "Pardon me, *señor*," Cabitos said to the disposed man. "Important matters of state, you understand. Another rum for my friend here." The servant had returned with the cup for Blas and now hurried off again for another to placate the planter.

"Tell me, *Don* Blas," Cabitos leaned in as if desiring to confer in secret. "Do you know a man by the name of Diego deMelilla?"

"I do," Blas said. "I have met the man at the home of one of my militiamen."

"Which militiaman, may I ask?"

"Miguel Campo. He is a private in my command."

"How does this Campo know deMelilla?"

"They shipped here together. They are good friends. Campo even cares for deMelilla's children. DeMelilla's wife died this summer."

"What is your measure of the man?"

"Campo is a good man, steady, clear headed. He never reported to drill drunk."

"I meant deMelilla. What do you think of deMelilla?"

"I have only met the man once. Why do you ask?"

"I think he may have married to a kinswoman of mine. When do you plan to return to Concepción?"

"I am ordered to the Cabildo today to receive instructions. Then I shall return to Concepción"

"I am in New Orleans seeking a tract of land suitable for tobacco or even sugar cane. You seem to be a man with knowledge of the land, and I would be grateful for advice. Could I accompany you to Concepción? We may have some business to discuss."

"That would be fine, *Don* Alguazil. When I am finished at the Cabildo, I will return here."

"Perfect. Call for me at my room. I will have a carriage ready for us both."

CHAPTER 30

The guards at the pike across the levee road next to Fort Saint Charles recognized *Don* Blas and addressed him as "Colonel Ansolo," a title the man preferred. Though a militia officer, it was customary to be addressed by one's military rank during a time of war. Many of the people in Concepción continued to address him as *"alcalde"*, a practice he was quick to correct.

"Colonel Ansolo," the guard did not inspect *Don* Blas' orders, "who is the gentleman accompanying you?"

"This is *Don* Alguazil Cabitos, *Ricohombre* of Santa Cruz de Tenerife. He is accompanying me to Concepción on business."

The guard nodded and waved them through. He did not ask for papers from Cabitos. Restrictions on travel had been relaxed after the successful attack on Baton Rouge. All of the Mississippi Valley had fallen into Spanish control and the anxiety of the people of New Orleans had been reduced. The British were not going to be able to send a force down the river and cut New Orleans off from the rest of Spanish Louisiana. Soon, Gálvez would return with his victorious army.

The carriage driver had to slow the horse to a walk soon after passing the guard station because of a large produce wagon lumbering down the narrow muddy trail. It had been a long day at the market and the driver was not inclined to hurry. Everything had sold well, there were so many more buyers in the market now that summer was over, and what little had been left would go to his pigs, so the satisfied driver dozed as the horse plodded down the road.

"Tell that fool to give us the road," Cabitos snarled.

"I know the man, *Don* Alguazil," Blas said. "He is called Susorro. I forget his Christian name. He is old, toothless and exempted from my militia." Blas stood in the carriage seat and shouted. "Give us the road Susorro!"

Susorro jerked awake and looked around, searching for the origin of the voice that woke him. Finally, he stood and twisted around. "Oh! *Alcalde Don* Blas. I did not see you there."

"How could you have seen anything? You were asleep!"

"*Sí, Don* Blas. It has been a long day."

"Give us the road. I am on the King's business."

"*Sí, Sí,* I can pull to the side here." Susorro worked the reins until the heavy draught animal pulled the wagon so close to the edge of the road the wheels sank in the soft shoulder.

"See, *Don* Alguazil," Blas said as they passed the wagon, "The wagon was full of produce this morning and now this farmer is returning to his place with silver in his purse. The soils are rich here, my friend. All crops flourish. I will show you several promising sites for your consideration."

The carriage tossed up mud onto the wagon's seat as it careened past. Susorro flicked a few bits of sod from his trousers and urged the horse back onto the road. He hawked deep in his throat and spat into the ruts left by Blas' carriage. *"Culo,"* he said contemptuously as he pulled a brown jug from under the seat. He passed a forefinger through the loop in the neck, pulled the wooden stopper, balanced the jug on the crook of his elbow and rocked the opening to his lips. After a long pull on the jug, he replaced the stopper and swung it into place under the seat.

❧

Diego was nearly a quarter of a mile from the Campo farm when he whistled his greeting. He was rewarded by an answering whistle from Pedro. The shrill, sliding tones translated into "I hear you, father!" Diego turned the slight bend in the road along Bayou Terre Aux Boeufs and could see his children and the Campos clustered where the path from their fine house met the edge of the road. Maria and Pedro began to run toward him, arms outstretched, faces beaming. He went to one knee to catch them. Maria leapt into his arms, wrapped her legs around his hip and clung to him. Pedro, who would be eleven years old in December, greeted his father with a warm embrace and one kiss on the cheek, as any man would greet his father.

Miguel and Catalina waited by the trail to their house, giving the children time with their father. Isabella stood shyly on the opposite side of the trail from her parents as if she expected to be overlooked, which was not possible for she was nearing her sixteenth birthday and maturing rapidly. Her figure was beginning to fill, converting the simple white cotton dress she wore into a stunning shape.

"Diego, why is it you are here?" Miguel asked. "We were told the army was not expected back for several days."

"I was sent ahead escorting prisoners."

"And promoted I see," Miguel indicated the blue epaulets Diego wore on his shoulders.

"Proof that the army does not know what it is about," Diego laughed. "As soon as we captured Baton Rouge, I was given a sash by the General's aid. 'You are temporarily given the rank of sergeant,' he said. 'Conduct yourself well and we will make the promotion permanent.' Now here I am – a goat herder from *Pueblo de Cuevas* made sergeant in the service of His Most Catholic Majesty. Is not the world mad?"

"Welcome to our house, *Don* Diego," Isabella said with a curtsy. As the daughter of Diego's close friends, she should have used the more familiar *Señor* Diego. A stranger would have said *Señor* deMelilla, but, ever since the mysterious disappearance of *Barón* del la Paz from the *San Juan Nepomuceno* Isabella had insisted upon addressing Diego as "*Don* Diego.*"

"Thank you, *Señorita* Isabella," Diego said, answering her curtsy with a bow.

"Come to the back," Miguel said. "We have a supper spread on the porch. It will be no trouble to set another place. Tell me, my friend, how long can you stay with us?"

"I can stay two nights, and then I must report to Fort Saint Charles. We are going to attempt to take the fort at Mobile before spring, I think."

"That must be so," Miguel added. "It seems that every day brings a new regiment to New Orleans."

The family gathered on the back porch to enjoy the evening meal and each other's company. Maria and Pedro sat on the porch, their legs swinging above a vegetable garden Catalina had planted right up to the edge of the porch. Miguel pointed out his fine pig sty and the now completed barn. Beyond the barn, a field was being cleared for next year's crop. "I will plant maize," Miguel said. "It is a crop that can feed men, beasts or fowl equally."

"*Don* Diego, I will go prepare a bed for you in the room where Pedro stays," Isabella said. She wanted to participate in the conversations, but she feared her emotions would betray her desires, so she sought something to do.

Pedro slept in a room where Catalina kept her fabrics and spinning wheel. Miguel had constructed the wheel for her so she would not have to spin thread from a bobbin. She would make spools of thread to sell or barter with other families. Pedro's bed was a moss-stuffed sack pushed against one wall. Miguel had prepared a bed frame, but had not woven the rope within the sides. Isabella moved the frame to the window to catch the fading light and began to run lengths of rope through holes in the sides of the frame. She had removed her bonnet and sat on the open window frame as she worked at the rope. Her vantage point offered a clear view of the road along the bayou and she often glanced up to enjoy the colors created by the setting sun.

A carriage came down the road from the direction of the Mississippi River. The driver must have been in a hurry, for he was keeping the horse at a canter. Isabella recognized the man riding in the forward-facing seat as *alcalde Don* Blas. There was another man in the carriage riding in the rearward facing seat. *Don* Blas said something and gestured toward Isabella. The man in the other seat turned to look. His eyes looked directly at Isabella. His narrow face and sneering expression made her shiver. She could not explain it, but the man looked – evil. The carriage continued down the road and out of Isabella's sight. She followed the carriage until it passed from view and, shaken with a dread she could not explain, continued to fix the bed.

♻

"*Don* Alguazil, you mentioned deMelilla." Blas said. He was a talkative man and they had ridden in silence for a half-hour after passing the produce wagon. "I believe he was the soldier who had escaped from the British in Pensacola."

"Yes, I had heard that. It was that report that sparked my curiosity," Cabitos lied. "I remembered a daughter of one of my vintners in Santa Cruz had married a deMelilla and I wondered if he was the same man. Did you know the name of deMeilla's late wife?"

"I confess, I do not," Blas said.

"Well, I will ask if I chance to meet deMelilla when he returns with the army," Cabitos said. "Just to be polite, you understand. I think her name was Maria, her father was an Artiles. In truth, I hardly knew the daughter."

Blas swept his arms in a wide gesture. "See how rich the land is hereabouts. Never a shortage of water, either."

Cabitos seemed not to hear. "You say deMelilla's children stay with one of your people in Concepción?"

"Yes, Miguel Campo."

"You must point out Campo's place to me, if we pass it. If he is the same deMelilla, I would want to visit the children as well. The vintner was a good friend, you see."

They came to a turn in the road and Blas pointed to a house set back about a hundred feet from the bayou. "There is Campo's place now."

Cabitos had to twist in his seat to see the house. It was a small house, wood-framed and typical of the contracted settler's houses that were sprinkled along the bayou. There was a new barn and a pig sty. A woman was sitting at a window facing the road. She wore a white dress without a bonnet. Her eyes followed the carriage, her hands, which had been working on something, were motionless. Cabitos began to wonder if the woman was real or was she a vision, the specter who had haunted him since coming to New Orleans. He watched until the window and its occupant passed from his view.

"Who was sitting in the window?" Cabitos asked after they had passed the Campo farm.

"I did not notice a woman, *Don* Alguazil," Blas replied. "I was admiring the progress Miguel has made on clearing the field. I think he will be ready for the spring."

Cabitos sat in silence until Blas suddenly said, "Here is the place I wanted you to see, *Don* Alguazil. It is not cleared, but you will see how perfect the soil is." Blas pointed to a farm just a little further down the road. "That is my place. We can take supper there. Please, be my guest for the night."

Cabitos nodded. "Do me a favor, please."

"Certainly, anything."

"Send for Miguel Campo. Have him join us. Tell him it is a militia matter; do not mention me or my interest in the land. The peasants have become so bold of late, more so here, where Gálvez coddles all, even foreigners. Campo may gossip and the owners, hearing such stories, may increase the price knowing I am a titled gentleman."

"As you wish," Blas said with a shrug. "Come to my house, please. I will send one of my men for Miguel. I will have the man say it is militia business."

Cabitos could hardly contain his anticipation of vengeance. When Blas' man escorts Miguel from the Campo home, the children would be there with only the Campo woman to protect them. Cabitos would slip away to the Campo house, kill the deMelilla boy and steal the girl. When deMelilla returned with the army, Cabitos would send a message to deMelilla that he had the girl and lure the man into a trap. He watched as Blas sent a house slave up the road on foot with instructions to call Miguel down to meet with him.

"I am going to inspect the land you showed me while we wait for Campo," Cabitos said.

"It is growing dark, and I think a rain is coming," Blas replied. "We can inspect the land in the morning. Besides, the carriage has gone. You would have to walk."

"It is nothing. I want to see the land alone."

"Take this lamp, at least," Blas said as he plucked a hanging oil lamp from a hook by the door and offered it to Cabitos. The lamp was lit, but the wick was turned down until it barely flickered.

Cabitos accepted the lamp and twisted a lever, raising the wick until it burned brightly. "I will return in only a few moments." He touched the rapier at his side. "What is there to harm me?" It was the same rapier he had been forced to buy back from that Artiles witch, an act calculated to increase his humiliation.

More of his plan began to form in Cabitos' mind as he left Blas' house. After disposing of the Campo woman and the boy, he would carry the girl deep into the wooded land beyond the farm and deal with her as he had intended for her mother. And then he would kill her, hide the body, return to Blas and report an encounter with run-away slaves. That would explain any blood he may have on him and the mutilated bodies he intended to leave in the Campo house.

Then he would return to New Orleans, find that fool Benitez and wait for Gálvez's army to arrive. Benitez would summon deMelilla on the pretext of having information on his daughter. Cabitos would surprise and kill deMelilla and report, with Benitez's confirmation, the man had attacked the Bishop. It would all be too easy.

Cabitos walked along the road holding the lamp until he found a trail leading into the wooded land bordering the road. He entered the trail, following its twists and turns until he found an oak tree with great branches swooping down over the trail. He hung the lamp on one of the branches and returned to the road. Looking back from the road, the lamp moved and winked through the leaves giving the impression of someone moving in the woods. He drew his rapier and continued up the road toward the Campo house. He knew he would encounter Blas' man returning with Miguel Campo. He planned to duck into the brush and hide well away from the road when he saw the light from the lamp the servant was carrying. After they had passed him, he would return to the road and go to the Campo house.

A light appeared on the road. Cabitos scurried into the brush, found a large tree and stood next to the trunk. As the light approached on the road, he moved to keep the wide trunk between himself and the men on the road. He could hear Blas' servant talking to Campo. "The Colonel only told me he wanted to see you, *Señor* Campo. He –." The rest of the conversation was obscured by a gust of wind. *Rain will be good*, Cabitos thought. It would be easier to hide the girl's body with rain to wash away any signs his movements might leave. Cabitos returned to the road, glanced back toward the Blas house and, seeing only a bobbing light, began to jog up toward the Campo house and vengeance.

∼

Diego, his children and the Campo family gathered on the wide front veranda of the house where they were enjoying the cool night air. The smell of the coming rain was sweet and refreshing. The wind generated by the storm was blowing from the north, so the south-facing front of the house would be protected from wind-driven water. A candle in a glass-encased keep swung from the porch rafter. Maria was seated on Diego's lap as he recounted his adventure on the high road to Baton Rouge and the capture of the Redcoats. Pedro and Miguel asked several questions, prying away details of the action.

"Father," Pedro asked, "why did the British not fire on you when you formed on the road? Why did they not rush into their blockhouse? They would have been safe there."

"They were surprised. They had done nothing for months at the block-house except stop travelers, look for contraband and wait for their relief. Tedium and boredom are a soldier's chief enemies. They should have exercised everyday on what was to be done if the unexpected occurred. They were poorly led."

"We know what to do if there is danger," Maria said. Her serious expression emphasized how much she resembled her mother. The sparkling grey eyes, the way she formed her lips when she was in thought, she was a replica of Maria Artiles. "We have a place in the woods where we can hide if there is danger."

"She has heard too many stories of slave revolts," Catalina explained. "There is no danger now. There are settlers all along the bayou and we watch out for one another. *Señor* Susorro has three strong sons and *Don* Tavián is a good man," she said, naming their neighbors along the bayou whose homes were no more than a quarter-mile away, one west, one east.

"Look who is coming," Miguel said as a man carrying a lamp turned onto the path to his house. "I think that is *Don* Blas' man, José." Blas was one of the few along Bayou Terre Aux Boeufs rich enough to own slaves. Most of the settlers were poor subsistence farmers. Owning slaves was far beyond their capabilities. Many shunned the practice as evil, as did Diego, because of a history of the practice being visited on their ancestors.

"*Señor* Campo," José said when he reached the foot of the steps onto the porch. "Colonel Ansolo has sent for you *Señor*. Military matters, *Señor*."

"Do you remember our *alcalde*, Diego?" Miguel said. "*Don* Blas Ansolo, you met him here some months ago."

"Ah, yes. The shy one who feared Gálvez was going to leave Concepción to the British."

"That is he. He is the colonel of the militia and, to his mind, a rival to Gálvez. José here is his house servant and José's wife, Rosa, rules them all. Is that not so, José?"

"Please come with me, *Señor*."

"Will you come with us, Diego? It would do the Colonel a service to meet someone who is actually a soldier."

"Please, let me go as well," Pedro pleaded. "I want to hear about Baton Rouge."

"Go," Catalina said. "We have women's work to do here. Just do not be long."

Diego rose, lifting Maria as he did so and placed her on the chair. "If it seems that *Don* Blas will delay Miguel's return, I and Pedro will come back alone. We will not be long." He kissed Maria, nodded to Catalina and bowed to Isabella before descending to the path.

"If *Don* Blas were to tell me all he knows of military matters," Miguel said, "we will be home in the time it takes to walk there and return."

Miguel kissed his wife and daughter before he joined José on the path. The wind gave a fresh gust. "I think we will return wet," Miguel said as they followed José onto the road.

"Men," Catalina said, "always about when the wise would stay at home. They will be soaked by the time they are back. We had better build up the fire and stack more wood in the bin. They will be all night drying out. Come, ladies, we have chores to do." She herded Maria and Isabella into the house.

༄

Cabitos pulled the collar to his coat up to ward off the large droplets of rain that were beginning to fall. The darkness that surrounded the road was not complete. Despite the rain, enough light from a full moon filtered down through breaks in the clouds to allow him to see the road. He had passed several houses, most had light showing through a window. He finally reached the path to the Campo house. He heard a noise on the road ahead and hid in a cluster of bushes.

The produce wagon they had passed on the way to Concepción appeared on the road. The driver halted his rig, wrapped the reins around the brake post and climbed down. Cabitos laughed to himself. What a fool the old man was if he thought that broken-down plow horse would move had not the reins been kept tight.

"Miguel," the old man called toward the house. "Miguel, I have your share of the market."

"Good evening, *Señor* Susorro," the Campo woman had appeared on the porch. "Miguel is down by *Don* Blas' house. He will be back in a moment. Come, sit on the porch and I shall get you something to eat and drink."

"Thank you, *Señora* Catalina," Susorro said. He climbed the stairs, "just a cup of rum, please. I must pay you and then be gone." He spoke to someone inside the house Cabitos could not see, "Good evening *Señorita* Isabella."

If the old fool stays too long, I will have to kill him first, before I deal with the woman, Cabitos thought. He moved to a new position nearer the rear of the house. He could not hear the people on the porch. *I will give him five minutes to be gone,* Cabitos decided. *If he does not leave by then, there will be one more body.*

"Fetch *Señor* Susorro a cup of rum, Isabella," Catalina said.

Isabella brought the rum to the front porch. Susorro had just finished counting a handful of coins, which he gave to Catalina. Miguel had sent some cabbages to market with Susorro for sale on consignment. They had made almost a dollar.

"*Don* Blas passed me on my way home," Susorro said. "All full of himself, he was. Blas had some kind of nobleman in the carriage with him, an arrogant ass. They were in a big hurry, nearly forced me into the ditch."

"What would a nobleman be doing with our *alcalde?*" Catalina asked.

"Only God knows," Susorro shrugged. "He called the man '*Don* Alguazil.'"

Maria, who had been standing next to Isabella at the door gasped, than began to cry.

"What is the matter, child?" Catalina asked, but Maria just cried.

"I do not know what that is all about," she said to Susorro. "Thank you, and good night. I need to deal with little Maria."

Susorro bowed and said good night. "Tell Miguel I will see him tomorrow," he said as he returned to his wagon. He shouted to his horse, gave the reins a slap and continued down the road. The rain was falling again.

CHAPTER 31

"Maria," Catalina spoke softly, kneeling so her eyes were even with the eight-year old. "Please tell us. What is the matter, child?"

Maria forced herself to stop crying. Choking back great sobs, she said. "The man who hurt momma, the bad man who made us leave our home was named 'Alguazil.'" Then she fell to crying anew.

"Can it be the same man?" Catalina asked, looking at a stunned Isabella.

"I saw the man who was riding with *Don* Blas when I was at the window." Isabella shuddered. "He was dressed as a nobleman. Mézu told me once they were forced to come to New Orleans by a man who had been the *Ricohombre* of Santa Cruz de Tenerife. A man named 'Cabitos.' The man I saw in the carriage with *Don* Blas – frightened me."

"What shall we do? Miguel and Diego must be warned."

"Susorro is home. We can run there and send one of his sons to find father and *Don* Diego."

Catalina pulled a blanket from a chair and wrapped it around herself and Maria and went to the front door.

"Wait," Isabella said. "Let me look first to see if it is safe to leave. I will get the *magado*. It is the only weapon we have." Isabella picked up a candle, lit it from the oil lamp by the door, and hurried to the back of the house.

Cabitos had moved away from the road along the bayou. He stood against a large tree where he could see both the front and the rear of the Campo house. The old produce farmer had finally left, driving his lumbering wagon along the road past Cabitos' hiding place. He watched as a light moved from a window in the front of the house and appeared in the rear. A woman stepped out onto the back porch. She was wearing a white dress without a bonnet. Apparently oblivious to the rain, the woman descended from the porch and walked purposefully to the barn. She rounded the barn and disappeared from view. Cabitos pushed from the tree and, holding his rapier wide, ran across the open area between the house and the pig sty to the place behind the barn where the woman disappeared.

Trees overhung the side of the barn, blocking the scant light from the clouded night sky. Cabitos listened, holding his breath. Rain, water dripping from leaves, wind and occasionally distant thunder were all he could hear. He had seen her go behind the barn and the rear of the barn seemed to be blocked with debris or brush. He took a few steps and stopped again, listening. Breathing, he heard someone breathing, but he could not ascertain where the sound came from. The woman must have found a hiding spot and was waiting until Cabitos left.

He shouted suddenly and swung the rapier into the dark bushes beneath the tree, but discovered nothing. Then he heard a giggle, a little girl's giggle. He whirled around to see the woman standing in the barnyard taunting him. Water cascaded down her long hair and simple white dress. Her face was in darkness, but he could see her teeth as she smiled. Cabitos roared in frustration, pointed his rapier at the figure and ran toward the barnyard only to trip over a root and fall to his knees. He pushed himself up from the mud and regained his feet in time to see the woman run toward the front garden along the side of the house. Enraged, he ran after her.

⁊

Isabella went into the room where Pedro kept his few possessions and placed the candle down on the floor. She stood and moved toward the clutter of weaving material against the wall. Her dress brushed the candle and put it out. The room went dark except for the faint light coming in from the window. She began to feel around under Pedro's bedding near the window when a flicker of lightning lit the barnyard. She saw a man, the same lean, evil-looking man who had been with Blas, cross the yard near the pig sty and go behind the barn, his sword flashing in the faint light.

Isabella hurried back into the front room where her mother and Maria were waiting by the door. "Go now," she hissed urgently. "I saw a man run behind the barn. Go now, before he comes to the house. I will get the *magado.*" Catalina opened the door and, carrying Maria, rushed out into the rain. They would be to Susorro's house in a few minutes.

Isabella returned to search for the *magado.* She fumbled around with her hands while watching the barn, counting aloud, trying to gauge the time it would take her mother and Maria to reach the neighbor's house. She felt the smooth, sound shaft and pulled the weapon free and stood, gripping the shaft as she had seen Pedro demonstrate. The gleaming, needle-sharp blade that tipped the *magado* transmitted a feeling of power down the worn, polished shaft through her hands and into her body, turning her fear almost into exhilaration.

She saw the man come out from behind the barn, his teeth bared, gleaming. He paused to look about and ran toward the side of the house, the side away from Susorro's place. *Mother and Maria must be at Susorro's by now*, Isabella thought. She moved to another room, intending to watch the man through another window, when she heard someone jump onto the front porch and walk toward the door. Isabella retreated into a back room and huddled in a corner, *magado* at the ready, fear beginning to rise within her. She heard the latch on the door as the man pulled it up and opened the door. Rain began to beat against the window as a gust of wind swirled down from the fading storm.

The man was moving cautiously in the house now. He crossed from one front room to another, his boots thudding firmly on the wooden floor. The intruder stopped, only the intermittent droplets of water falling from his clothes broke the silence. He was waiting, listening.

Isabella decided she would not be trapped in a corner. She opened the window and went through it onto the back porch. She heard the man run through the house, reacting to the sound of the window being opened. She felt the blood pulsing in her throat as she braced herself against the wall of the house, the tip of the *magado* leveled at the open window as she listened to the man pound into the room she had just abandoned. A head appeared through the open window. He looked to the right, saw nothing and turned his head to his left toward Isabella. She stabbed at the head as a flash of lightning washed the porch, house, wall and the evil face of Cabitos with a blinding silver hue. Isabella felt the point of the weapon pierce flesh and strike bone. She withdrew the weapon, jumped down from the porch and ran toward the front of the house.

Cabitos screamed and pulled his head back into the house. The pain was searing. He clamped his hand over his left eye. He felt blood ooze between his fingers. Someone, a woman, laughed behind him. He swung his rapier around the room, striking nothing but walls and a spinning wheel. Tears filled his right eye, but he managed to glimpse a figure in white move across the doorway. He stormed out of the room, slashing and stabbing as he went. He stumbled from room to room, trying to find the source of the laughter. He heard more than one woman laughing now. One said "Are you hurt?" followed by more laughter.

As she ran along the side of the house, Isabella could hear Cabitos stomping though the rooms, screaming, cursing and colliding with the walls and doorframes as he went. She ran to the front of the house where the trail ran from the porch to the road. She could see the front of Susorro's house now and was relieved when the distant door opened to pour light across two figures huddled in a blanket. *Momma and Maria are safe*, she thought. Soon her father and *Don* Diego would be here.

The door to the porch near where she had paused was thrown open. Cabitos ran out, swinging his sword wildly. He shouted in the direction of the bayou, "Who are you? I will cut you into scraps for the pigs." Still holding his left eye, he jumped down into the garden not ten feet from Isabella. He twisted his head and saw her in the shadow of the porch.

"You! I have you now." Cabitos stabbed the rapier at Isabella, but she moved to her right and the blade harmlessly hissed passed her left shoulder. Cabitos tried to swing the sword across Isabella's neck, but he had stabbed between the house and the porch's supporting column so the blade struck the wooden post. The steel blade gouged a scar into the soft cypress wood of the porch column. Cabitos stepped back as he withdrew the blade, exposing his arm.

Isabella lunged forward, extended the lance-like weapon and pushed the point of the *magado* into Cabitos' sword arm at the inside of his elbow. He screamed again and retreated to the path, his right arm hanging at his side. He whirled around as if something or someone were behind him. His sword arm would not lift, so he shifted the rapier to his left and turned back to face Isabella. She made another lunge at him, but he easily slapped the bloody *magado* point aside and spun around again as if to confront another foe.

Cabitos shouted, *"Silencio, espíritus,"* and fled down the path toward the road. Isabella followed, yelling unintelligible sounds and thrusting the *magado* at Cabitos' retreating back. It began to rain harder. The sound of the wind in the trees, darkness and blinding sheets of pouring rain isolated, concentrated Isabella's vision until the world became a small circle through which the path, not she, seemed to flow, and before her was

Cabitos, running, swinging his rapier blindly behind him, attempting to fend her away, but she was beyond relenting.

⁓

Diego walked beside Pedro, enjoying his son's company. They had worked together daily at their home on Gran Canaria and were with each other every day of the long voyage, but since arriving in Louisiana they had been separated. Diego had not even had the opportunity to console his children after the death of Mézu. Pedro and Maria had faced that tragedy without any family to help them with their grief, yet they seemed to have adjusted, with the help of the Campos. Diego and Pedro trailed slightly behind Miguel and the slave, José as they made their way along the road toward *Don* Blas' farm in the sporadic rain.

"I have never heard of a place where it rained more," Diego said.

"Our neighbor, *Don* Tavián, has lived here for over ten years," Pedro said. "He tells us that this is normal, but October will see an end to it."

Pedro said 'our neighbor.' Diego thought. *He considers the Campo house as his home, and why should he not?*

They came to the path to the Blas house and José motioned for all to precede him up the dozen steps to the front porch. The house was larger than the settler's cabins which were constructed under a contract by the Spanish government. It had eight wide rooms on the first floor and large floor-to-ceiling windows for each room as well as a wide front door. The small procession made considerable noise coming up the steps and a black woman opened the door to meet them before José could step across the porch.

"Rosa," José said, "Tell Colonel Ansolo *Señor* Campo is here."

Rosa rolled her eyes when José said "Colonel Ansolo."

"Tell them to wait here," Rosa said, even though they were all crowded on the porch behind José and could hear every word. She closed the door.

Miguel looked at Diego and shrugged. Gentlemen would have been invited in. Clearly, Rosa considered them to be common people and she expected them to remain on the porch. Blas opened the door and stepped out onto the porch.

"Campo," Blas said, smiling as if his appearance was a surprise. "I am glad José found you." He glanced over toward Pedro and Diego and, seeing the blue epaulets remarked, "A sergeant. Congratulations on your promotion deMelilla. I am glad you came as well. I did not know the army was back in New Orleans."

"The army has not yet returned, Colonel," Diego said. "I was sent ahead, escorting prisoners."

"Well and good. José, go find our guest from New Orleans. He is inspecting the land just up from us." Blas said. "Tell him the *Isleño* he had asked about is here."

"He is looking at the land in the dark?" José said.

"Do not question me. He had a lamp with him. Now go."

"Yes, Colonel," José said. Holding the oil lamp high, he went down the steps to the path. He reached the bottom of the steps, turned around and pointed toward the west. "I think I can see his light."

"Someone was asking about me, Colonel?"

Blas looked at Miguel, not certain how much he should reveal. "Yes, a man from Tenerife. He said he may have been a kinsman of you late wife."

"Does this man have a name, Colonel?"

"Yes, Sergeant, he has a name," Blas replied, irritated at being questioned by an enlisted man. "His name is *Don* Alguazil Cabitos. Do you know him?"

Diego's left hand shot to the hilt of his short sword before he could check himself. Blas saw the reaction, a quizzical expression on his face.

"I see José returning," Blas said, not knowing how to interpret Diego's reaction.

"Colonel," José called from the road. "I found a lamp hanging from a tree. I cannot find *Señor* Cabitos."

"Pedro, stay with *Señor* Miguel," Diego said. He bounded down the steps two at a time and ran toward the road.

"I have not dismissed you, Sergeant," Blas yelled. He would have said more, but Diego was out of earshot and he realized that he had no authority over the sergeant.

"What is the matter?" Miguel yelled, but Diego was already on the road and racing up toward Campo's house. He turned to Blas. "I think we should follow him, Colonel."

Blas was stunned. "Uh, yes. This is most curious. José, saddle my horse."

Miguel looked at Blas. "Your horse, sir?"

"I am not about to go stomping around in the rain and the dark on foot, man. You and the boy can follow the sergeant if you want. I will catch up with you when I can." He took a deep breath and yelled, "José! Where is my horse?"

Miguel and Pedro ran down the steps and into the dark as Diego had, without the aid of a lamp. Pedro managed to whistle, "We follow."

Diego had no problems following the well-worn road along the banks of the Bayou. The road, called a *cordelle* for the long tow cables used to pull vessels along the narrow waterway, was wide. The rutted, muddy surface of the center of the track made the going easier along the edge nearest the bayou. Diego was forced to slow his pace. He heard Pedro whistle and answered with the tone, "I hear you."

He had nearly reached the Campo house when his attention was drawn by voices and lights from the porch of another house. Several people were gathering on the porch and he recognized Maria and Catalina in the group.

"Catalina," he called from the road. "What is happening?"

"Diego!" Catalina instinctively pulled Maria closer to her as she called back. "A man, a stranger was lurking about our barn. Isabella is still at our house."

Diego ran further up the road toward the Campo house when he saw a shadow cross the road toward the bayou, disappear down the bank, closely followed by a figure in white. He ran to edge of the road where he saw the figure descend the bank and found a woman in a white dress stabbing something down into the bayou. He tried to go to her, but slipped into a sitting position and slid down behind her. She pulled back on the shaft she was plunging down into the swirling water and Diego recognized the brass cap, it was his *magado*, the one he had left in Pedro's care. He grabbed it. The woman turned to see what was impeding the weapon.

"Isabella!" Diego said. It was Isabella he had seen cross the road. She had been stabbing down into the bayou with Diego's *magado*.

The rage in her eyes immediately fell away. "*Don* Diego," she dropped the weapon and threw her arms around Diego's neck. "Thank God, you are here." She began to weep uncontrollably. Diego looked over Isabella's shoulder to see the body of Cabitos drift slowly out into the bayou. The corpse's face had been stabbed repeatedly, one eye was missing and the other remained open, but sightless as the body slipped under the water.

Diego supported Isabella against him with one hand and, using the *magado* as a staff, managed to carry her up the steep bank to the road. The people that had gathered at Susorro's house were stumbling toward them along the road.

"Listen to me," Diego whispered in her ear, "Stop crying and listen. I must tell you something important."

Isabella stopped sobbing. She choked from the effort, but she remained against Diego, clinging to his neck so his lips were next her ear. "What do you want to tell me, *Don* Diego?" she said.

"You must not say you stabbed Cabitos. No one can know. When you are asked what happened, you must say a madman chased you through your house and onto the road. He ran away when you heard others. You do not know where he went."

"Why should I say that?"

"Do it. No one must know what really happened, not even your mother. Later, I will explain why."

Miguel and Pedro were the first to reach Diego and Isabella. Diego placed the still weeping Isabella in her father's arms.

"She has not been harmed," Diego said. "She said a man had chased her, but now he has run away." He stepped aside after giving Isabella to Miguel, then backed away, tugging Pedro by the elbow as he did so. They moved free of the crowd that was forming around Isabella and her father.

Diego handed Pedro the *magado*. "Put this back where it belongs. Tell no one it has been here. Absolutely no one, understand?"

"Yes, father." Pedro took the weapon and went into the house. Diego watched the excited crowd. Catalina had arrived, loudly thanking God her daughter had not been harmed. None noticed Pedro go, nor when he returned.

Diego heard Isabella say, "A man, a madman, chased me through the house and out into the road. I first saw him by the barn and warned my mother and little Maria. They ran to *Señor* Susorro's house. I was trapped in the house and had to climb out of a window. He chased me into the road, but ran away when he saw so many people at *Señor* Susorro's house." She was looking at him while she repeated the story. Diego nodded.

Miguel carried Isabella into the house with Catalina following closely, pulling Maria and Pedro inside behind her. Diego stopped the others at the porch. "She has not been hurt. Please let her mother tend to her," he told them. "Go to your homes, with our thanks for your concern. We will be able to tell you more in the morning."

Blas rode up to the porch as Diego was attempting to disburse the crowd. He did not dismount, but pointed to Diego. "What has happened?"

Susorro, who was next to Diego on the porch said, "*Don* Blas, a madman invaded Miguel Campo's home. His wife was forced to flee to my house. His daughter, Isabella, was chased out onto the road. The man ran away when he saw us coming to help Isabella."

Forgetting he had addressed Diego, Blas turned to Susorro. "What? Was she hurt?"

"No, *Alcalde*. None have been hurt."

"Have you seen *Don* Alguazil, the man who accompanied me from New Orleans today?"

"No, *Alcalde*," Susorro said.

"Let us hope he has not encountered this same madman, Colonel Blas," Diego said.

Blas began to speak, but changed his mind, racked the reins of his horse around and rode home, José jogging behind the horse. Susorro and his sons stepped down from Miguel's porch and were joined by others as neighbors gathered around a lamp in the yard below the porch. The rain had stopped. Everyone was filled with curiosity and excitement. They repeated the story of a raging madman to each newcomer to the gathering. The tale of a wild lunatic was readily accepted and repeated.

Diego separated himself from the group and returned to the road. The rain had finished and the skies were beginning to clear, allowing light from the moon and stars to expose details hidden by the storm. Diego could see the footprints left by Cabitos as he fled across the road and the tiny barefoot prints of Isabella as she pursued. It would be light soon.

He saw a glint of steel in the mud. He stooped and pried a rapier from a wheel rut. It was the same sword he had taken from Cabitos eleven years ago after their duel in the *cuatro maderas*; the one Mézu had sold to *Don* Raphael Arinaga for one hundred *escudos*. Diego looked about. Everyone was gathered around the lamp gossiping, none were watching him. He held the rapier by the hilt and threw it far into the bayou.

ా

Isabella sat in a chair on the front porch wrapped in a blanket in the cool morning air. Catalina and Maria were in the garden near the road weeding, taking advantage of the rain-soaked soil. The sounds of hammering came from the rear of the house. The storm had wrenched the barn door free and Miguel and Pedro were mending it. Diego stepped out onto the porch dressed in his uniform. It had taken all night to clean and dry the white coat and trousers. He would be leaving soon to return to Fort Saint Charles. He stepped close to Isabella.

"Most people in this world are good, kind and can be trusted. But some are malicious and a few are truly evil," Diego said. His voice was soft so only Isabella could hear him.

"If a man is alert, prepared to fight, the malicious can be deterred, forced to seek mischief elsewhere. But evil men must be driven away or eliminate. That is simple enough if the evil one is a commoner. When the evil man is rich and powerful he cannot be driven away. He can twist the law to suit his purposes, corrupt the forces of justice into his weapon and inflict suffering with impunity. Cabitos was such a man. He had family, associates, and powerful friends, who would have distorted the truth to do you harm. None must ever know the truth."

"And *Barón* del la Paz," Isabella whispered. "Must he remain our secret as well?"

"There was no other way."

"Do you need to leave today?"

"Yes, I will call my children to me and say goodbye in a moment."

"During the long voyage from Tenerife, Mézu taught me to read and write," Isabella said, smiling up at Diego. Her large, brown eyes swam with moisture. Her red/brown hair tumbled across her shoulders, glistening in the cool morning light.

"She taught me to read and write as well," Diego laughed. The memory of patient Mézu tutoring her husband in their stone house swept over him.

"*Don* Diego, will you write to me?"

"Yes, *señorita* Isabella, I will write to you."

Diego whistled for his children. It was time to go.

CHAPTER 32

iego reported to Ensign Piernas at the barracks barge near Fort Saint Charles as darkness fell on the last day of September. The trip upriver to New Orleans might have been uneventful had it not been for the local militiamen. Word had traveled fast and mounted men scoured the road looking for the lunatic. Diego was stopped and required to show his pass. He had to explain his reason for being on the road and recite the pass documents as he indicated the individual words to the patrol leader, for the man could not read.

"Take care, sergeant," one of the riders had advised. "They tell me the madman has injured a score of people, mostly children."

"None have been killed," another added, with apparent disappointment.

"I am confident you will deal with such a man adequately," Diego said as he returned his pass to a pocket. *I pity a stranger caught about without papers this night*, he added in thought.

The militia patrol thundered off, hooves spewing mud and manure, leaving Diego to continue upriver to Fort Saint Charles where he had to retrieve his pass once more and show it to the guards at the pike.

He pocketed the pass and walked a few paces to the gangplank leading up to the barracks barge. It had been only two nights since he had left his men at the barge, but it seemed as if it had been months. He nodded to the guard at the foot of the gangplank and stopped at the top to salute the officer of the day, Ensign Piernas. *Surely, he is no older than my Pedro*, Diego thought.

"Your men returned this morning about sunrise," Ensign Piernas said as he relieved Diego of his pass document. "I think they were quite drunk. Most of them managed to make the evening mess, which you have missed."

"Where am I to bunk, sir?

"The sergeant's berth is just inside the door to the barracks hold. It is only an area cordoned off with canvas hangings, so you can keep an eye on your men," the ensign said, indicating a door to Diego's left. "They are in the first dozen bunks to the left. The rest of the hold is occupied by the Fixed Regiment of Habana, about fifty men – two sergeants." He fumbled through some papers in a leather case, found a folded document and presented it to Diego. "Here are your orders, sergeant. You and your men are to report to the Cabildo at first light tomorrow."

Diego accepted the papers, saluted the child-officer and ducked into the barracks hold. An oil lamp hung from a beam between two rows of cots. There were six dozen cots in the hold. The first dozen on the left side of the aisle were occupied by Diego's detachment. The men were sprawled in a variety of positions. Most were sleeping. Some had not even removed their uniforms. Coats, some torn, others bloodied, hung from hooks against the bulkhead. Four men sat on the floor between bunks playing cards. The men who were awake looked at Diego questioningly. They were a pathetic sight and looked in a sickly state.

The other soldiers in the hold were grenadiers of the Habana Regiment. Each grenadier's uniform coat, clean and neatly brushed, hung behind the man's bunk. Some were sharpening blades, some were cleaning muskets and those not employed were sleeping. Diego's meager squad looked like beggars pulled in from the street by comparison. Diego felt his anger rise.

"Pook!" he snarled.

Pook, who had been playing cards, stood when Diego called his name and stumbled toward Diego.

"Good evening, Sergeant," he said, his breath reeking of rum.

Diego lowered his voice so the grenadiers could not hear. "Where is your pride, Pook? Look at you. Look at the men. The squad looks like gutter trash."

"Been at the Four Horsemen," Pook said, his face wrinkled in confusion. "Been on leave, Sergeant."

"Pook, how could you let the men turn in without cleaning up?"

"I am not an officer. I am not a sergeant," Pook said. He threw his head back in a gesture meant to be prideful. "I am not even a corporal."

Diego choked back a rebuff. It was his fault. He had been so anxious to be off to see his children he had failed to designate a soldier responsible for the men in his absence. He could have easily placed Pook, who was a dependable man, in charge of the squad in barracks. It could not be changed now, but he had learned a lesson. Diego went to those men who were sleeping and roused them. He broke up the card game. He ordered the men to clean their uniform coats, inspect their packs and bedrolls, rinse and refill their canteens, clean muskets and sharpen edged weapons.

"Tomorrow, we report to the Cabildo," Diego said. "We will be given new assignments." Diego felt the condescending stares of the grenadiers on his back while his men attempted to regain some semblance of military order.

☙

The next morning Diego had his men up before first call. By the time the grenadiers were being served breakfast, Diego's men had finished eating and were gearing up for the short march to the Cabildo. Their uniforms had been brushed, but many still showed wear and stains from the month-long campaign against Baton Rouge. Diego had the men fall in for inspection before setting out for the Cabildo. Each man was burdened with gear and weapons, nearly a hundred pounds of baggage for each man. Diego could feel the eyes of the grenadiers on him as he checked his men and their equipment. Satisfied, he returned to the center position, came to attention, faced about and held a salute. Ensign Piernas, who had been temporarily distracted, turned to faced Diego, and accepted the salute, indicating temporary command of the men. Normally, an officer would inspect the men before releasing them to a sergeant, but Ensign Piernas simply counted the number being released from his barracks.

Diego could see the grenadiers of the Habana Regiment. Their uniforms were spotless, their tall bearskin hats made them appear gigantic. Wide black moustaches converted each face into a fierce glare. But Diego recognized something unexpected in their expressions. Admiration for his ragged squad of veterans filled each face. The men of the Habana Regiment had never faced battle and their respect for Diego's men was palpable.

"Take command of this unit, Sergeant," he said, his voice cracking slightly. "You are to report to the Cabildo."

"Yes, *Señor*," Diego replied. He saluted again, indicating acceptance of command.

Diego faced the squad.

"By the Left – FACE."

"Carry – ARMS."

"At the Quick – MARCH."

The men sensed the admiration of the watching grenadiers and, filling with pride, they stepped off perfectly in step. Diego began a cadence then shifted to a marching song. He would sing a verse and the squad would repeat a standard refrain. Diego chose a melancholy tune.

"My *Novia* waved goodbye," Diego's fine baritone voice carried across the river road.

"We are the warriors of Spain," answered the marching column.

"Tears fell down from her eyes."

"We are the warriors of Spain."

"But José was standing close."

"We are the warriors of Spain."

"And wiped her tears away."

"We are the warriors of Spain."

The traffic along the road parted to let the column through, some applauded and shouted congratulations. Gálvez's army was expected to arrive by barge today and curious citizens were beginning to gather at the river landing across from *Plaza de Armas*. The pamphlet barker was announcing the fact that General Gálvez had arrived before dawn on a river schooner and the bulk of the army would arrive this day. Diego reported to the Cabildo and was directed to bring his men to the bivouac area on the road to the powder magazine and prepare the site to receive the Fixed Infantry Regiment of Louisiana.

The tents and other camp gear of the combined forces had been stockpiled in a warehouse when the army departed for Baton Rouge. Diego marched his squad to the warehouse, located the property of the Louisiana Regiment and began the process of bringing the equipment to the bivouac area. The Regimental tents were bound into tight bundles and stacked against a wall of the warehouse. Each bundle contained the canvas, ground cloths, poles, ropes and stakes needed to erect one of the seven-foot by seven-foot bell-ended four-man tents.

Two men were required to carry a single tent bundle to the bivouac area where Diego directed them to be placed, still tightly bound, into platoon-sized clusters. Each cluster formed a cul-de-sac branching off from the regimental assembly area, five tents on the left, five on the right, and two across the back. The two tents at the end of the cul-de-sac were reserved for non-commissioned officers. Diego had his men place camp-fire hardware in the center of each cul-de-sac so the arriving squads could build their own cooking fires. When the job was done, he marched the squad back to Fort Saint Charles, saw to it that they were fed and provided some private time.

Diego used the time to clean and sharpen his short sword. As he ground a smooth stone against the razor-sharp blade, he saw a messenger hurried through the gates and into Captain du Foreste's office, the post commander. Moments later, du Foreste's clerk, a fat, insolent man, made his way across the courtyard to Diego and presented a message.

"You are to attend to this *inmediatamente*, Sergeant," the man said and then retreated into du Foreste's office without waiting for a reply.

The message read: "Bring the prisoner escort squad to the Fort Charles Landing." It was signed, illegibly, by a clerk who had added "for Colonel Martin Navarro."

"Time to move," Diego said as he sheathed the short sword. "Pook, gather up our people."

A crowd had been gathering at the landing across from Fort Saint Charles all afternoon. Diego formed up the squad and moved them to the foot of the pier where the fleet of barges and schooners carrying the army was scheduled to land. Ensign Piernas appeared escorting a regimental bandsman carrying the banner of the *El Regimiento Fijo de Infanteria de la Luisiana*.

"Good, Sergeant deMelilla. Stand here with your squad and this standard. Those of the Fixed Infantry Regiment of Louisiana who come ashore have been instructed to muster on this banner," the ensign said and disappeared into the crowd.

The signal tower across the river had been active earlier in the day as the news of the progress of the returning victorious army filtered downriver. It was nearly four in the afternoon before the first barge was sighted and a cheer spontaneously rose from the crowd. The first barge was followed by a small fleet of barges and river schooners. Landing at several locations along the pier or simply grounding on the muddy bank, the flotilla began to disgorge a convoluted mixture of soldiers, militiamen, sailors and civilians.

"Show the standard," Diego snapped to the bandsman who lofted the base of the staff to his chest and canted it outward so the ragged red cross of *Borgoña* emblazoned on a white field could be easily seen. Diego watched as small unit leaders recognized the banner and segregated squads or platoons under their command from the throng to join him. There seemed to be half as many rallying to the banner as there had been when the Louisiana Regiment set out for Fort Bute just a few months before. None of the soldiers moving toward Diego were officers, but he recognized Sergeant Ortega moving a platoon of infantry toward him.

Ortega halted the group of men and walked over to Diego. "Good afternoon, Diego," Ortega said. "I am *Sargento Primo* of the Regiment. I will have the regiment fall in on this banner." Ortega centered himself on the banner and shouted, "Fixed Infantry Regiment of Louisiana – Prepare to form ranks on me by name." Ortega opened a ledger and read.

"First Company – Sergeant deMelilla." Diego moved to the position reserved for the commander of the first company and waited for the remainder of the first company to be called.

Ortega named Sergeant Jennessey as the Second Company sergeant. Then Ortega read the names of the men assigned to the first company and those assigned to the second. When the process was completed one hundred forty-one men were standing at attention before the regimental banner. Three names elicited no response and one soldier who was not on the roster was placed in the second company. The Fixed Regiment of Louisiana Infantry in New Orleans had been reduced to the size of an under-strength company. The First Company was unofficially named the Tiger Company and the Second Company was nick-named the Leopard Company.

Diego and Jennessey met with Ortega as the regiment was being billeted in a warehouse-turned-barracks. The neat rows of tents set out earlier by Diego's men were to be assigned to others.

"Where is the rest of the regiment?" Jennessey asked.

"Sickness and the march to Baton Rouge had reduced the ranks considerably," Ortega replied, "But, in truth, most were assigned to duties elsewhere. Baton Rouge and Natchez had to be garrisoned and the General sent Captain Leyba and eighty men to occupy Saint Louis and God only knows where else. Those who mustered this evening are all that is left."

"And with an army of seven-score men we are expected to take Mobile?" Jennessey said.

"Reinforcements have been coming in for weeks," Diego said. "I have seen grenadiers from Habana and I am told of others."

"Let us hope so," Ortega said. "Gálvez intends to take Mobile before the summer is here. He will attempt it with whatever force he can muster, so let us pray he can find many."

Diego spent the next two weeks scavenging equipment, uniforms, and recruits for the Regiment. In addition to his regular duties as a company sergeant, Ortega had appointed him the regimental instructor in bayonet training, an assignment Diego enjoyed. Soon other units that were being encamped in New Orleans solicited Ortega to allow Diego to provide bayonet demonstrations to their men.

Diego was in the *Plaza de Armas* and had just completed one such bayonet instruction to men of the Regiment of Prince when a messenger sought him out.

"Are you Sergeant Diego deMelilla, First Company, Fixed Infantry Regiment of Louisiana?" the man said, though Diego was certain the man knew who he was.

"I am," Diego said.

"This is for you, sergeant."

Diego accepted the sealed paper from the man and watched him leave, weaving his way through the cluster of soldiers, on his way back to the Cabildo. Diego looked at the seal. It was the official seal of the Governor of Louisiana. The only words on the outside of the folded paper were "Deliver to Diego deMelilla y Tupinar, Sergeant, First Company, Fixed Infantry Regiment of Louisiana." These were not military orders. Diego shrugged and broke the seal to read:

"Sergeant Diego deMelilla y Tupinar:

By order of General Governor Bernado Gálvez you are ordered to appear and present testimony before a court of inquiry at the office of Governor General Bernardo Gálvez at nine o'clock on the morning of 23 November 1779."

It was signed *"Gálvez."*

Diego turned the paper over several times searching for any other words, but that was all there was. He was to report to the Cabildo tomorrow morning at nine.

✑

Diego had spent much of the night preparing his uniform for his appearance before the court of inquiry. The weather was cool and he would have welcomed a woolen uniform, but he did not have one. His coat was white cotton lined and faced with *Borbón* blue that had faded into a soft sky blue. Epaulets of blue cotton, matching his coat's facing, decorated both shoulders as an indication of his rank. He wore his blue trousers and shirt and white over-the-knee gaiters, which covered all but the tips of his ragged shoes. His red-cockaded tricorn needed replacement, so he selected his barracks cap which was a white, conical cotton cap, lined in blue with a blue tassel. He had no brass plate for the front of the cap. The peak flopped over until the tassel hung at this left ear. The choice of cover did not matter, for he doubted he would be under arms when he gave his testimony. A soldier, indoors but unarmed, was expected to remove his hat, so he planned to have the soft cap tucked into his belt.

Diego armed himself with his short sword only, certain the Cabildo's clerk would relieve him of it before he entered the General's office. He hung a haversack across his left hip, hiding the sword. He decided against adding a canteen. His musket and ceremonial halberd would stay in the company armory.

"Well, Pook," he asked once he was finished dressing, "I am off for the Cabildo. Try to keep Ensign Piernas out of trouble." The young Piernas had been assigned to the first company as third in command and was officer-of-the-day.

"I will see he takes his milk," Pook said, impressed at how formidable and competent the tall, rugged *Isleño* appeared. The rank of sergeant seemed to have been created for the man.

Diego strode out of the warehouse-barracks onto the wood-planked walkway along the edge of the roadside ditch. He would cover the short distance to the Cabildo and wait with the guards at the front door until the Saint Louis Church bell began to strike nine. Only then would he enter the outer office and present his summons.

Soldiers nodded respectfully to Diego as he strode along the wooden walkway. Ladies placed their fans over their lips and smiled with their eyes as he passed. More than one shopkeeper called out *"Bonjour, Sergent."* These cheerful pedestrians along his route lifted his spirits and pushed down lingering feelings of trepidation. *What was this all about?*

The guards at the great doors of the Cabildo recognized Diego from his several demonstrations of bayonet proficiency.

"Sergeant deMelilla," the corporal of the guard said as he greeted Diego at the foot of the Cabildo steps. "What brings you to my humble watch?"

"Cabo Gusman," Diego suddenly remembered the corporal's name. "I am to appear before the Governor General at nine." Gusman was an *Isleños* from Tenerife.

Gusman, clearly flattered that the famous deMelilla remembered his name, called to a clerk who was seated at a desk next to the entrance, "What time do you have?"

The clerk consulted a large clock at his feet. "It lacks nine by a quarter."

"And who is scheduled for nine?"

"DeMelilla, for the Governor General."

"What is the subject of the audience?" Diego asked.

Gusman looked at him is surprise, "You do not know?"

Diego shook his head slowly from side to side.

"Well, answer the sergeant, man," Gusman said, angry that the clerk had returned to scribbling in a ledger.

"It does not say, Corporal Gusman."

Gusman shrugged, "I do not know what it means, but a Colonel I did not recognized went in at eight, if that is any help."

"It does not, but thank you."

Both men waited for the church bell to strike the hour.

The hour of nine began to strike. Corporal Gusman ceremoniously opened the Cabildo's massive front door as Diego reached into his coat pocket and retrieved the folded summons. He crossed the threshold on the third strike and Gusman closed the doors behind him, muffling the church bells as Diego walked up to the reception clerk. Two guards were posted at the doors to the General's office, something that Diego had not observed during his previous visits to the Cabildo "Sergeant deMelilla reporting as ordered," he said and he gave the clerk the summons.

The clerk, Diego thought his name was Renaldo, accepted the document and waved one of the guards to him. Without opening the paper, Renaldo waved one of the guards over and gave him the summons. "Bring this in to the court," he said and the guard disappeared into the General's outer office.

"We have been expecting you, Sergeant. Please remove your sword." Renaldo made a show of inspecting Diego for other weapons and, seeing none, continued. "I will place your sword in the armory until you are dismissed. The court is being conducted by Colonel Esteban Miró. Do you know the Colonel by sight?"

Diego nodded.

"Good. Place yourself before the Colonel, report to him and say nothing to anyone without the Colonel's permission. Is that clear?"

Again Diego nodded.

"The other members of the court are *Don* Pedro Piernas and Colonel Martin Navarro of the New Orleans militia."

The guard returned, held the door open, but gestured for Diego to stop. "This way, sir," the guard said to someone within the office.

Don Blas Ansolo, *alcalde* of Concepción appeared at the door. Dressed in his colonel of militia uniform, he was pale, clearly shaken and on the verge of tears as he brushed by Diego and scurried out of the Cabildo.

"The Colonel has forgotten to retrieve his sword and pistol," Renaldo said to no one in particular.

"He will likely send for it when he recovers his wits," the guard said. "This way, Sergeant."

Diego tucked his cap into the top of his trousers and marched into the room. The outer office had been converted into a courtroom of sorts. Three officers sat at a long desk, two recording clerks huddled at a table to his left and a priest, the one who kept the death records, sat alone on a bench under a window. The door closed behind Diego as he marched to a front and center position before Colonel Miró, the center officer. Diego halted, came to attention and held his salute.

"Sergeant Diego deMelilla, reporting as ordered, Colonel," he said, He fixed his eyes on a spot on the wall just above Miró's head. He could hear the noise of traffic drifting through the window behind the priest.

"Stand at ease, Sergeant," Miró said as he returned the salute. "My name is Colonel Esteban Miró. The officer to my left is Colonel Martin Navarro and the gentleman to my right is *Don* Pedro Piernas." Miró gestured toward the window, "Father Étienne Cordier will administer the oath and conversations will be recorded by these clerks. Do you have any questions?"

"No, Colonel."

Father Étienne walked over to where Diego stood.

"Do you swear before Almighty God and upon peril of your immortal soul that you will answer truthfully to the questions presented to you by this court?"

"I so swear," Diego said without hesitation.

Father Étienne returned to his seat under the window.

"Have you been advised of the reason we have called you here?" Colonel Miró asked.

"No, Colonel."

"State you full name, rank and position for the record, please."

"Diego deMelilla y Tupinar, Company Sergeant, First Company, Fixed Infantry Regiment of Louisiana, Colonel."

"When and where were you born, Sergeant?"

"15 July, 1748, at *Pueblo de Cuevas*, Gran Canaria, Colonel."

"May I, Colonel?" Father Étienne interrupted. Colonel Miró nodded his consent.

"Tell me, Sergeant. We are all aware of your father's history, the famous warrior, Doramas. But the name 'Tupinar' brings to mind the notorious *alzardo* (rebellious one) of Gran Canaria. Is there a relationship to that man?"

"He was my grandfather, *Padre*."

"Oh, indeed," the priest said. "Thank you, Colonel."

Diego had the distinct impression that the panel of officers were interrogating from a script and they knew the answer to every question asked so far, except the one the priest interjected.

"When and where did you enter into the service of the King?" Miró continued.

"8 December 1778 at Gando, Gran Canaria, Colonel." *He had been in the army for a few days short of one year,* he thought. *It seems to have been a lifetime.*

"Before entering the service, what did you do?"

"I herded goats and farmed the land under *El Roque Nublo*, Colonel."

"Marital status?"

"I am a widower, Colonel."

"What was the name of your late wife?"

"*Doña* Maria Artiles y Ventomo, Colonel."

"When did your wife die?"

It had only been five months since Mézu died, but over seven months since he last held her in his arms. He had been absent when she died, gone when she had been buried in an unmarked, mass grave. He yearned to hold her again, but struggled to remember her face. On what calendar does a man log such an illusionary grief?

"9 July 1779, Colonel," Diego said, feeling his throat tighten.

"It is reported, Sergeant," Miró said, "*Doña* Maria Artiles was betrothed to another when you married."

"Her family had contracted a marriage, but there were no vows of betrothal before God, Colonel."

"How is it then, Sergeant? How does it chance that a common man, born of Guanche parents, marry an Artiles?"

How could such a thing happen? How could he explain Mézu's flight from the murderous, but highborn, Alguazil Cabitos? How could he describe that night Mézu came to his bed under *El Piedra de Perro*? Years later, Mézu had confided to Diego. She believed that night was to have been the last she would live in freedom. She had believed Cabitos would catch her, if not in the morning then the next and have her taken back to Tenerife. Cabitos would have forced her into a convent or worse.

"I do not know, Colonel."

"Who was the man *Doña* Maria Artiles had been contracted to marry?"

"Alguazil Cabitos, Colonel."

"Would that be *Ricohombre* Alguazil Cabitos y Cabrón of Santa Cruz de Tenerife?"

"Yes, Colonel." Diego wondered why they were asking such questions. He was certain they knew the answers.

"Have you ever met, or had words with *Don* Alguazil Cabitos?"

"Yes, Colonel."

"When was the last time you spoke with *Don* Alguazil Cabitos?"

At last, Diego thought, *this is about Cabitos.* He paused for a moment. "I confronted Cabitos in a trial at arms over ten years ago. I have not had words with the man since he fled the *cuatro maderas* in disgrace."

"You say a 'trial at arms.' It was a duel, was it not?"

"Duels are against the law, Colonel; Particularly, a duel between a nobleman and a goatherd."

"Trials by combat are a thing of the past, Sergeant."

Diego shrugged.

"You must speak your answers, Sergeant. The clerk cannot record a gesture."

"It is what happened, Colonel. The trial was sanctioned by the *Regidore* of Gando."

"What was the dispute?"

"Cabitos accused my wife of theft, Colonel. It was a lie."

"Is it not so, Sergeant, this same *Don* Alguazil Cabitos and his confessor, Bishop Benitez, were passengers on the Spanish warship *El Sagrado Corazón de Jesús* when you were pulled from the sea after your escape from Pensacola?"

Diego remained silent, the question was obviously rhetorical.

"Why did Cabitos not confront you then?"

"I gave the Captain my Choctaw name, Colonel."

"What is your Choctaw name?"

"*Hika Nitah*, Colonel. It means Flying Bear." Diego waited for someone to comment about sounding like a girl's name, but no one did.

"Why did you give your Choctaw name?"

"I did not want Cabitos to recognize me, Colonel."

"Why?"

"I joined the army to move my family away from Cabitos. The *Regidore* of Gando had died and Cabitos, seeking revenge, sent men to take *Doña* Maria. I thought we had escaped to New Orleans, Colonel, but Cabitos had followed us. I wanted to warn my wife, gather my children and escape once more, Colonel."

"Did Cabitos recognize you?"

"I do not believe he did, Colonel. I came ashore with the mail packet. Cabitos and Bishop Benitez continued on the ship and landed a week or so later. By that time, I had learned of my wife's death. She is now beyond any danger."

"Have you had any contact with *Don* Alguazil Cabitos or Bishop Benitez here, in New Orleans?"

"No, Colonel."

"Do you know *Don* Blas Ansolo?"

"The *alcalde* of Concepción? Yes, I know the man, Colonel."

"The former *alcalde*, *Don* Blas Ansolo tells us that *Don* Alguazil Cabitos was in Concepción on the 29th of September, the same time you were in Concepción visiting the Campo family."

"I did not know Cabitos was in Concepción until *Don* Blas mentioned it at his house. I have never spoken with Cabitos or encountered him here in New Orleans."

"And in Concepción?"

"I have never spoken with or encountered Cabitos in Concepción."

"What of Bishop Benitez?"

"I have never spoken with or encountered Bishop Benitez anywhere."

"What did you do when *Don* Blas let it slip that Cabitos was in Concepción?"

"I ran back to the Campo house, Colonel. I feared for my children, but when I arrived, my children were safe at a neighbor's house. The people of the village had been alarmed by reports of a madman prowling about, but none was found."

Colonel Miró leaned back in his chair. "Any questions of this witness, gentlemen?"

Judge Piernas cleared his throat. "Sergeant, would it interest you to learn Bishop Benitez had boarded a ship bound for the Malvinas Islands less than a day before your encounter with Cabitos in Concepción?"

"I never encountered Cabitos in Concepción, *Señor.*"

"Yes, of course. But why would Bishop Benitez leave for the Malvinas Islands in such haste?"

"I do not know, *Señor.* I have never heard of the Malvinas Islands until today."

"The inn keeper tells us the Bishop seemed terrified. Would you know anything about that?"

"No, *Señor.* Perhaps you could ask Cabitos."

Judge Piernas leaned toward Diego, his eyes intent upon Diego's face. "*Don* Alguazil Cabitos has not been seen since September in Concepción. We thought, perhaps, you could tell us where he might be."

"I cannot, *Señor.*"

Miró waited for a few moments, and when no one else sought to be recognized he said, "Come to attention, Sergeant." Diego resumed the position of attention, fixing his stare on a spot on the wall.

Miró addressed the recording clerks. "This concludes our investigation into the disappearance of Alguazil Cabitos y Cabrón of Santa Cruz de Tenerife. This court has interviewed over twenty witnesses, including several settlers from Concepción. It is the finding of this court that Alguazil Cabitos voluntarily departed this colony, as did Bishop Benitez."

The members of the court stood, and, with the exception of Colonel Miró, exited into the main lobby. The clerks collapsed their portable writing tables and scurried out of the room, followed by Father Étienne.

Diego had not been dismissed, so he remained locked at attention facing Colonel Miró across the table. The door to the outer office closed leaving them alone. Miró pulled out a clay pipe and walked around the desk as he fed tobacco into the white bowl from a small pouch. Diego continued to stare at a spot on the wall.

Miró inverted the pipe over the chimney of an oil lamp and gave it a few puffs until the tobacco caught. He sat on the edge of the desk, drawing gently on the pipe.

"General Gálvez has assigned a new commander to first company, Captain Josef Herrera. I think you know him, Sergeant."

"I shipped over with a Josef Herrera. He was promoted to corporal while we were at sea, Colonel."

"It is the same man. Ever wonder how such a man could be promoted to Captain so quickly?"

"He is an experienced soldier, Colonel."

"Truly, but there are many experienced soldiers in the Fixed Infantry Regiment of Louisiana. He asked for you as his company sergeant, did you know that?"

"No, *Señor*."

"I will tell you something about your captain, Sergeant. Herrera was sent for by Governor Gálvez over a year ago. It seems that a politically protected enemy of our Governor's family and our *Borbón* King was coming to Louisiana to do an unknown mischief, perhaps conspire with the British, who knows. Captain Herrera was placed aboard the *San Juan Nepomuceno* by friends of the Gálvez family. He had been assigned to watch this enemy carefully, closely, during the voyage to New Orleans. We did not know what we could do to counteract the mischief this man planned and we could not confront him without proof, so Herrera was just to watch. Herrera fulfilled his mission, Sergeant. He watched this man night and day. Do you know who this enemy of our Most Catholic Majesty was?"

Diego shook his head, "No, Colonel."

"It was *Barón* del la Paz, Sergeant. The *Barón*'s life mission was to thwart Governor Gálvez, even if it came to treason against Spain. But then *Barón* del la Paz disappeared, fell overboard some said. All of the Gálvez family and the Crown rejoiced in that particular mishap." Miró paused and looked intently at Diego before he continued. "We think you may have done away with Cabitos as well. How, we cannot tell. We interviewed a score of people and it does not seem possible."

"I did not kill Cabitos, Colonel."

"So it seems." Miró placed the pipe on the desk. "After Herrera made his report, you were ordered to accompany Panis into West Florida. We needed time to decide what to do with you. Regrettably, in your absence, your lovely wife succumbed to yellow fever. She had been helping in the hospital, but you know that. *Doña* Margarethe was boundless in her praise of *Doña* Maria's dedication, courage and kindness. May I offer you my condolences and those of the Governor for your loss. Father Étienne has offered several masses for her soul."

"Thank you, Colonel."

"Stand easy, for the love of God." Diego relaxed from attention. Miró stood and continued to look at Diego intently, seemingly in appraisal. "You have been appointed sergeant of the First Company because Governor General Gálvez believes it is wiser to have you in the service of Spain than hanging from a scaffold."

Miró waited, expecting Diego to say something. When Diego remained silent, Miró sighed and said, "That is all, Sergeant. You are dismissed."

Diego saluted and marched out into the lobby. Renaldo closed the door behind him and returned Diego's sword.

"Is the paymaster about?" Diego asked.

Renaldo gestured toward a door near the entrance, "The pay clerk is in there."

Army regulations allowed a soldier to authorize members of his family to draw from his pay. Only a member of the soldier's family could draw a portion of the man's pay, otherwise the unscrupulous could extend a soldier credit against his pay, keeping him in unending debt. Private soldiers made so little they rarely assigned away a portion of their pay, but Diego was a sergeant.

"I wish to assign twenty-four *reals* of my monthly pay to Isabella Campo. She will appear here to collect it." Diego explained to a bored clerk.

"You can only assign pay to your mother, your wife or your woman," the clerk said. "Which is she?"

"My woman," Diego said. He would have to explain the arrangement when he next wrote to Isabella. The Campos had practically adopted

Pedro and Maria, so Diego was determined to provide as much support as he could.

After he had finished the paperwork required for the allotment, Diego went into the street. Corporal Gusman was still on guard duty.

"Done for today, Sergeant deMelilla?" he asked.

"No," Diego replied. "The real work has only begun." He headed toward the barracks that housed the Fixed Infantry Regiment of Louisiana. Gálvez was marshaling his forces for the effort to take Mobile from the British and Diego would be busy.

Historical Note:

This story began with the discovery of the murder of George Glas, his wife and young daughter. George Glas is best known for his translation of Juan de Abreu Galindo's *The History of the Discovery and Conquest of the Canary Islands*. This translation was printed in 1764. Glas was briefly imprisoned in Santa Cruz de Tenerife in 1765. He was released in October of 1765 and, accompanied by his wife and daughter, set sail for England on the British ship *Earl of Sandwich*. It was reported that on 30 November, 1765 "Spanish and Portuguese" members of the crew mutinied, killed the Captain, George Glas and threw Mrs. Glas and her daughter into the sea. The perpetrators were said to have been executed in Dublin. History does not explain how an English ship was crewed by Spaniards and Portuguese.

The Spanish war ships, *San Juan Nepomuceno* and *El Sagrado Corazón de Jesús* were only two of the eight ships that participated in a migration effort that transported settlers from the Canary Islands to Louisiana during the years 1778 to 1783. The Canary Islands, conquered by Spain in a protracted and sporadic campaign that lasted from 1402 to 1492, were inhabited by people of an unknown origin. Contemporary paintings depict a people who have a striking resemblance to the Celts of Ireland and Scotland. Modern theory proposes that Goths, Vandals and Berbers formed the nucleus of the fifteenth Century *Isleños*. Spain heavily recruited men from the Canary Islands for her army and navy for their physical size (the typical *Isleño* was tall by European standards) and their fierce abilities.

The crushing poverty of the common people of the seven islands increased the success of recruiting efforts. By the time our story begins, 1765, *Isleños* have been scattered across New Spain. One notable settlement effort occurred in 1735. Fifteen families and a few single men were sent to San Antonio, Texas. The decedents of this early migration still populate the southwest region of Texas.

Many characters Diego encounters on the *San Juan*, such as Captain Morera and the "experienced soldier" Josef Herrera actually lived but are presented in fictionalized historical roles. Many of the names were drawn from the passenger manifests of the *San Juan Nepomuceno* and the *El Sagrado Corazón de Jesús*, and are presented in fictional roles. If the reader is surprised at a few non-Spanish sounding names, be reminded that passenger rolls and contemporary reports were the source of most of the surnames appearing in this fiction.

The conditions of daily life in New Orleans presented are as historically accurate as the poor records of the period allow. The great fire of 1788 leveled much of the city, destroying the wooden buildings. The Spanish rebuilt most of the city in brick using the typical Spanish architecture of the 18th Century. This reconstruction has given a distinctive Hispanic ambiance to what is known today as the "French Quarter."

Don Jacinto Panis was an officer in the Spanish army who, fluent in English, conducted intelligence gathering missions into the British-held territories known as East and West Florida. His most documented mission occurred well before Spain allied with the American rebels, but other missions were conducted after hostilities were imminent and were, naturally, secret. Plans of the British invasion of New Orleans were actually intercepted by agents of Gálvez, perhaps Panis himself. Gálvez used this intelligence to launch his preemptory attacks resulting in the expulsion of the British from the Mississippi Valley and Florida. After the American War of Independence, Panis became a judge in Spanish New Orleans. He did marry the *Criolla* Lady, Margarethe Wiltz, the widow of Joseph Milhet, a man executed for treason in 1769. Panis was the officer who commanded the firing squad that executed Milhet.

Spain's attitude in accepting the former French colony of Louisiana and the Isle of Orleans was one of minimum interference. No attempt was made to supplant the French language, indeed, most of the Spanish officers developed fluency in that language. Spanish Governors Ungaza, Gálvez, and Miró married Louisiana women. The Spaniards designated a person born in Louisiana, regardless of parentage, a *Criollo*; *Criolla* if female. Ungaza and Gálvez married sisters, daughters of the rich and influential Gilbert Antoine de Saint Maxent.

Local customs were allowed to continue, *Criollo* officials retained their offices and even the religious leadership continued with only minimal disruptions. Imposition of the more austere Spanish version of Catholicism was attempted several times with little success. The most notable attempt, and probably the last, occurred during the Governorship of *Don* Esteban Miró. The Bishop who was attempting to force the change was awakened in the middle of the night by soldiers sent by the Governor. He was placed aboard a ship before dawn and returned to Spain.

Only two of the many successful military campaigns led by Gálvez are mentioned in our story. Later victories by the Spanish over British interests in Florida and the Mississippi Valley were pivotal in the eventual American victory and the establishment of the United States. General Gálvez rode beside General Washington in the American victory parade. Subsequent conflicts, the push of Manifest Destiny and the propaganda campaign known as the "Black Legend" has obscured Spain's vital role in the establishment of the United States of America.

England in particular, propagated stories of Spanish atrocities in an effort to widen the divide between Protestant Western Europe and Catholic Spain. Stories of torture and religious persecution by the Spanish were exaggerated, embellished or created from whole cloth. The Spanish were particularly characterized as blood thirsty, cruel and heartless during the rule of Henry VIII, a king who perpetrated outrages far beyond those his propagandists attributed to the Spanish. The Black Legend developed a life of its own during the American period of "Manifest Destiny" as proponents of the expansion of the United States sought to justify military action against the only remaining European influence in the Western Hemisphere, Spain. Because of these influences, American history books and historians, fail to properly report Spain's contribution to the creation of the United States.

The deMelilla Chronicles are a series of novels intended to uncover the deep, but often hidden, influence of Spain in general and the *Isleños* in particular on Louisiana customs and genealogy.

39579670R00256

Made in the USA
Charleston, SC
11 March 2015